CHILDREN
OF THE
FIFTH SUN

T0159855

OTHER BOOKS BY GARETH WORTHINGTON

The Children of the Fifth Sun Trilogy
Children of the Fifth Sun: Echelon (Book 2)
Children of the Fifth Sun: Rubicon (Book 3)

FORTHCOMING FROM GARETH WORTHINGTON

A Time for Monsters (2021)

BOOKS BY STU JONES AND GARETH WORTHINGTON

It Takes Death To Reach A Star Duology
It Takes Death To Reach A Star (Book 1)
In The Shadow Of A Valiant Moon (Book 2)

AWARDS

Children of the Fifth Sun
2019 Eric Hoffer Award Honorable Mention Science Fiction
2019 Eric Hoffer Award Grand Prize Shortlist
2019 Eric Hoffer Award First Horizon Finalist
2018 London Book Festival Winner Science Fiction
2018 Killer Nashville Silver Falchion Finalist Science Fiction

Children of the Fifth Sun: Echelon
2018 Hollywood Book Festival Winner Science Fiction

It Takes Death to Reach a Star
2019 IPPY Bronze Award Science Fiction
2019 Feathered Quill Gold Award Winner Science Fiction
2018 Cygnus Award First Place Ribbon Dystopian Science Fiction
2018 Dragon Award Nominee Best Science Fiction Novel
2018 New York Book Festival Winner Science Fiction
2018 Readers' Favorite Honorable Mention Science Fiction

CHILDREN
OF THE
FIFTH SUN

GARETH WORTHINGTON

Children of the Fifth Sun

Cover Design by John Byrne

ISBN: 978-1-944109-40-0

VESUVIAN BOOKS

Published by Vesuvian Books
www.vesuvianbooks.com

Printed in the United States of America

10 9 8 7 6 5 4 3 2 1

To Italia Gandolfo, Renee C. Fountain, Liana Gardner for supporting me as an author and bringing this book to life;

To Jonas Saul, Allison Hegan and Harriet Evans for editing;

To John Byrne for visualizing the cover;

To Marie D. Jones, Peter Burdon, Doreen Anders, Beatrice Pujol, Bonnie Molloy, Sam Walford, Kelly Hambly, Stu Jones, and Dominica Büchi-Worthington for your help along the way;

My sincerest thanks
~ Gareth Worthington

THE FIFTH SUN

While this is a work of fiction, many of the places described are real and the theories and mythologies based in solid research.

According to some South American cultures, there were four worlds, or suns, before our present universe. Each world was destroyed by a catastrophe; giving rise to a new world. The fifth sun—our sun—is coming to its end.

PROLOGUE

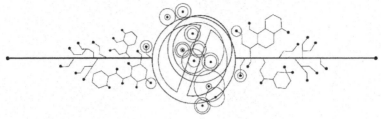

Location: Unknown

Benjamin stared at it. It didn't stare back. He then looked at the reinforced glass between them. Benjamin's piercing blue eyes appeared gray in the smoked transparent shield he had created.

Was this the only way?

Too late to worry about it now. Everything was already in motion. He blinked and once again gazed into the dark, frigid water.

It was gone.

His heart faltered. *Damn, where is it?* Benjamin placed both hands on the cold glass wall and peered inside.

Seconds passed. Minutes. It felt like years.

A violent *crack* tore through the room as the thing propelled itself against the invisible barrier. Benjamin reeled backward, and fell to the floor. His head smashed onto the tiles, spilling blood like an explosive fan of crimson paint. He propped himself up on his elbows. Could it get through? No. The glass was intact. The strange creature slowly glided back and forth in the murk, before disappearing out of sight.

Benjamin slumped back on the floor and felt the back of his head. Warm blood trickled through his leathery fingers, matting the silver hair to his scalp. Sickness roiled in his stomach. He turned to the side and heaved a thick, off-white liquid onto the tiles. He wiped the vomit from his beard as the blackness closed in.

In the darkness, voices called out to him. But their words were muffled. Benjamin couldn't understand them. They didn't make sense. Only one thing made sense to him.

This was going to end badly.

CHAPTER ONE

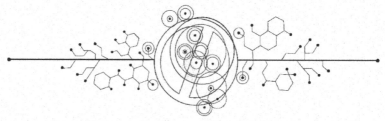

Location: Somewhere on the Amazon, South America

Kelly Graham hung suspended in the cloudy, pink water, gently kicking his feet. His left hand and arm were wrapped in a thin yellowish rope that ascended from the dark water below and through the ceiling of scattered light and rippling currents above his head. In his right hand, he held an underwater camera. It was large and cumbersome, but he'd had it for years and wouldn't use anything else—didn't trust anything else.

He pointed it at the white, ghost-like forms gliding around in the distance. They gracefully sliced through the liquid, dancing with each other. He waited patiently and kept very still.

A ghost came closer, intrigued by this hairless ape hanging from his underwater branch. It hovered there, its head cocked to one side as it looked at him. Its eyes were wise and knowing yet playful. It opened its long beak as if it wanted to communicate, to bestow some mystical knowledge.

Click. Kelly gently squeezed the button and captured the almost human curiosity on the animal's face. *Click.* Another precious second in time preserved on film. The river dolphin lost interest and turned away, flicking its tail once before disappearing into the fuchsia haze.

Kelly exhaled, spilling thousands of bubbles out through his mouth. Had he been holding his breath for that long? He couldn't have been. He looked up and admired the bright, shimmering sun through the rose-colored liquid. Kelly released his tangled hold on the rope, kicked once, and floated upward. As his face broke the surface, he was greeted by the contrasting warm air. With closed eyes, he let the sun begin to dry the skin on his face.

"Where the fuck have you been?" A short, tubby Hispanic man in his mid-twenties glared at Kelly from a little wooden boat, his hand outstretched for his friend to grab. Chris was dressed in blue cargo pants and a grubby, gray t-shirt that may once have been white; his tanned Latin skin juxtaposed by peroxide blonde, crew-cut hair.

2

"Taking pictures, esé, where'd ya think?" Kelly grinned and grasped his friend's wrist, making an enjoyable slapping sound as his wet hand made contact.

"Could have fooled me. I didn't see any bubbles for like fifteen minutes. I swear, thought you'd been swept away by an undercurrent." Chris's voice strained at the end of his sentence as he heaved Kelly's muscular frame from the water.

"That was the point of our makeshift anchor though, right?" Kelly nodded at the buoy bobbing on the water's surface. "Was a great idea to use that lump of metal and a bit of old rope. I think I'm a genius." Kelly lay panting in the bow of the boat, propped up on his elbows.

"Yeah, but remember there's no *genius* without *us*, oh great and wise one." Chris swept Kelly's arms from underneath him and sent him sprawling backward.

Kelly quickly leapt to his feet and grabbed his rotund friend by the shorts, lifting him into the air, his biceps straining under the weight.

"Ah, wedgie! Stop it." Chris wailed, clawing at his shorts as they disappeared between his buttocks.

"For God's sake, can you boys not act like children for more than five minutes?"

The tall, blonde woman stood in a meaningful pose on her little boat, closed fists resting on her hips, her long hair blowing gently to one side in the breeze. With her gray-green tank top, half-thigh camouflage shorts, and military-issue jungle boots, Kelly thought she looked like she had bought her outfit from an Adventurers-R-Us catalogue. The boat stuttered through the water, powered by a loud chugging outboard motor.

"Well, as I live and breathe." Kelly smirked. "Been a while, but I see time hasn't changed anything. You BBC wildlife types are still *way* too uptight. I could sort that out for you if you like?" Kelly grinned and winked at his long-time rival. His one open, dirty-blue eye flashed in the sunlight.

"I see National Geographic is still in the business of hiring Neanderthals. Have you gone round to a relative of yours and snapped some cave paintings with your ancient camera?" Her hands were cupped together to form a megaphone, ensuring that Kelly would hear the entirety of her clever remark as she drifted downriver.

"Was that Vicky?" Chris asked.

"Yeah, been a while since we saw her, huh?"

3

"Like five years."

"Exactly. She still wants me, but we're just passing ships on the Amazon." He laughed and shrugged his shoulders. "Come on, Paco, let's go."

"Still?" grumbled Chris. He stumbled to the back of their small boat and pulled at the starter cord of the outboard motor. The engine spluttered into life. The little craft chugged along, leaving a pinkish wake behind it. Chris sat by the outboard, directing them on their meandering path while Kelly remained up front, keeping watch for various obstacles—the odd large river animal or fallen tree.

With his black short-leg wetsuit pulled down to his waist, Kelly plonked down into the lotus position on the bow and grabbed an old guitar that was sitting in the boat. It was a light brown, almost leathery color and badly beaten. He strummed it a few times, twisting the machine heads until satisfied with the tuning. He swept his wet, wavy, chin-length chestnut-brown hair back onto the top of his head so he could see the strings, but it fell back about his unshaven face as soon as he tilted his head forward. He strummed the guitar softly, singing quietly.

He stopped singing and looked around him, making an arc with his eyes from one riverbank, to the sky, the other bank, and then at the river. It was beautiful. He loved the Amazon—peaceful, old, wise, and dangerous.

Chris looked at his companion. Obviously "Adonis" was admiring his reflection or something. Even at thirty-five years old, Kelly could be so bloody vain. "Okay, Narcissus, we're almost at camp; best stop looking at yourself. We're going to pull in over there." Chris's pointed to a nearby shallow close to the starboard riverbank. He swung the rudder to the left, allowing the boat to glide closer to the bank. He cut the motor and stood, eyeing up the moving land beside him.

Kelly put down his guitar and rose to his feet. Grabbing a thin brown rope beside him, he leapt from the boat onto the soft mud, rolled, and then stood. Bending his knees and bracing like a human anchor, he held onto the rope. The boat stopped suddenly, swinging into the riverbank. It threw Chris forward, causing him to slam his palms into the deck.

"Thanks, asshole!"

"No problem, esé."

"Kelly Graham?" The voice was deep and gravelly, like it belonged to a lifetime smoker.

Kelly dropped the rope and slowly turned his head, squinting as the sun

4

glared behind the huge frame of his questioner. "Well, that depends there, André, doesn't it?"

The huge Shadow Man offered him a blank stare.

Chris sighed, looking on from the boat. "He means André as in *the Giant.*"

"You must be Christopher D'Souza."

"No one has called me Christopher in a long time."

"Forget that, Chris. I still can't believe he didn't watch wrestling as a kid. Look at the size of him." Kelly stood straighter, his forearm resting against his sweaty forehead in an attempt to shield his eyes from the sun. He had a wry grin on his face.

"Are you Kelly Graham or not?"

"Look, pal, if you have to ask me who I am, then quite obviously you are not someone who appreciates my work. Ergo, you're someone of authority who reckons I don't have a permit, blah, blah, blah. Either way, you're annoying me. I'm tired, wet, hungry, and quite honestly I need to take a shit. So, it's been a blast, but you can leave a message with my secretary there on my boat." Kelly gestured to Chris before giving a sarcastic salute to the Shadow Man and marching off in no particular direction.

"That's gotta be him."

Kelly felt a sharp pain in his neck and frantically clasped a hand to it. Everything around him went dark as he tumbled to his knees. *The bastard darted me. Of all the fucking nerve. Fuck it's dark ...*

Location: Los Angeles, California, USA

"Hmm, are you seein' this?" Jerry was an inch from his screen, and the luminous image bounced off his glasses. He had one hand clasped to his clammy forehead, and the other pressed a cellphone to his left ear.

"Yes, I'm seeing it. It's gotta be wrong. I mean, someone would have noticed it before, right?" The voice on the other end of the line was calm, nonchalant.

"How the frig should I know? But I mean, think about it, the power of the Internet now, it's more than any supercomputer. I mean, we're talking about linking up satellite systems from nations all over the world and pooling data from hundreds of databases. Shit, isn't that what we set out to do?" Jerry was excitable. His voice trembled.

"Dude, it's *Google Earth*—a public project. We set out to let people say, 'Ooh, there's my house!'"

"Well, we found something else. What do you think we do with it? Do we tell someone? The government?"

"What, like ring up the president and say, 'Hi, erm, so like it's Jerry from *Google*. Yeah, hi, long time no speak, I know. So, dude, you gotta see what we found on *Google Earth* today?'"

"Why do you always do voices and characters, man? For Christ's sake, let's just figure this out."

"Look, dumbass, use your head. If we've seen it, it means someone else has, too. Like you said, it's a public project—right?"

"Yeah, I guess you're right."

Click.

"David? Hello? David?"

CHAPTER TWO

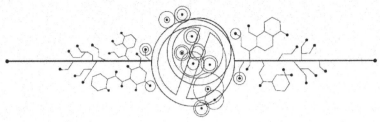

Location: Unknown

Kelly could hear her moaning in pain. He had to find her, but he couldn't see. There was no light. Only her voice—whimpering, sobbing. Kelly flailed in the dark, frantically clutching at the damp air. It was so cold and the stench … he could smell sulfur.

A light in the distance, a muted speck, flickered like a flame in a light breeze. And her voice—it was louder now. He was getting closer. Kelly's feet picked up pace into a brisk walk. Then he jogged. The sound of his panting echoed around in the dark. He broke into a full-blown sprint. She was sobbing so loud; she was in so much pain.

"I'm coming!" Kelly called into the darkness. "Where are you?" His voice cracked as he tried to catch his breath. Swollen, his voice box filled his throat. He opened his mouth, but no more words would come.

Running.

Running.

Kelly stopped, his heart pounded in his chest—a hammer against his ribcage. He stared through the pitch down a dimly lit staircase at her tiny body. She was lying crumpled on the oak floorboards. Her crimped black hair was tousled around her head and the burgundy dress she wore was pulled awkwardly above her waist. One pantyhose-covered leg was twisted over the other. He stumbled frantically down the stairs, tripping over his own feet and grasping at the banister for support. Kelly dropped heavily to the floor, smashing his knees into the hard wood. Tears filled his eyes, and his hands trembled. He touched her hair softly, sliding it across her face.

Her broken frame jolted upright, forcing a warped gray face with hollow black sockets inches from Kelly's eyes. "Leave me be!"

Kelly jerked awake, driving his head into the metal frame of the bunk bed. His vision was sharp, his senses alert. His eyes darted around before falling on the familiar face of a friend.

"Same dream?" Chris was sitting on his haunches with his back to a white wall, forearms resting on his knees, and his head hung low. He raised his eyes to meet Kelly's.

"Yeah."

"Figured."

"Ah, you're awake." The booming voice of the Shadow Man blasted across the room.

Kelly squinted in pain as the shockwave of sound sliced into his brain. "Damn, I thought it was the sun in my eyes, but you are actually a huge fucker, aren't ya?"

The Shadow Man stood almost seven feet tall, with shoulders that appeared six feet wide. A crisp gray suit clung to his bulk and looked almost ridiculous on his monstrous body. He was African American, and his large, bald head shone in the artificial light. He grinned, revealing two rows of pearly white teeth and a small gap between his incisors.

"Well shit, aren't you a regular Einstein? Are we sure this is the only fool we can get?" He directed the question over his right shoulder to the hazy figure behind him.

"Well, that's kind of the point. We need a fool." Her voice was soft and alluring. *Definitely not to be trusted*, thought Kelly. "And considering you've lost most of your men down there, Mr. Tremaine, we don't have much choice now, do we?"

"Okay, Okay. Just stop there, lady and big bald … thing … Tell me what the fuck is going on. Or I walk." Kelly rubbed his temples in an attempt to ease his aching head.

"And just where would you go, Mr. Graham?" the mystery woman asked. "Your talents underwater are the reason you're here, but I doubt even you could swim back to land." Kelly looked around the room, searching for a window to the outside world. His gaze fell upon a small porthole just next to his bunk. He ran to it and pressed his nose against the glass, peering outward. All he could see was water—a lot of water. A large lake perhaps? No, he was rocking from side to side and could see no land at all. He was at sea.

"What the fuck? Where are we?" Kelly spun on his heels and glared at his subjugators.

"It doesn't matter where we are. You have a job to do. And we are willing to pay you to do it."

"And that's why you drugged me?" Kelly's voice carried more than a little indignity.

"We don't have time to waste on this. We needed to get you here first. We could convince you once you were here … with substantial compensation."

The woman slid into the room, gliding effortlessly toward Kelly. Her slender frame was shrouded in a long, gray, wrap-around dress, and a patent leather belt cinched her midriff. Kelly looked into her emerald-green eyes, the focal point of her oval, doll-like face. Jet black, shoulder-length hair contrasted with her porcelain skin. She reminded Kelly of *her*.

"So," the woman began, eyeing Kelly, "what would your price be to help us, hmmm?"

"Look, lady—"

"Freya Nilsson," she interrupted.

"Whatever. Even if I wanted to do whatever it is you want me to do, you couldn't afford me. So why don't you just put me back where you found me, huh?" Kelly marched over to Chris and plonked on the floor like a defiant child.

Chris shifted his head toward his friend. "Mature. Oh, and by the way, I wouldn't mess with these guys. While you were having your beauty sleep, I had a little conversation with our new friends. Turns out, they're with the CIA or something."

Kelly's eyes widened. Chris nodded.

"I assure you, Mr. Graham, we have deep pockets. You will be well-compensated." Ms. Nilsson took a single step toward him.

Kelly studied her. "I'm sure you do."

"I'm sure if you offer him a warm cave and a shiny new clubbing implement, he'll be as giddy as a schoolgirl." Victoria stood in the doorway, leaning against the bulkhead.

"Oh great, it's a fucking party. What are you doing here?" Kelly rolled his eyes, elbowed his friend in the shoulder, and then motioned toward the doorframe.

Chris choked back a laugh. "It's your girlfriend. She's probably here because she wants you."

"Hello to you, too, Chris."

"Hi, Victoria. Long time no see. What's it been, twenty-four hours?"

The Shadow Man tapped at his oversized military watch. "Look, I hate to break up your little reunion, but we got a thing to do here, and we're on a bit of a time schedule, ya know."

"Indeed. Mr. Graham, I must insist." Ms. Nilsson's icy stare cut through Kelly, causing his skin to horripilate.

Kelly glanced at Chris and then Victoria. "Okay, first things first. I don't need your money. I'll hear your request, then decide if I wanna do it. If I do, I will. If I don't, I leave. Deal?"

"Deal. Follow me. I'll explain in the briefing room." Ms. Nilsson turned on a dime and tramped out of the room.

Kelly stood and minced after Ms. Nilsson, swinging his hips mockingly. "I guess we follow her," he called over his shoulder.

Victoria and Chris exchanged a glance and smirked before following suit, marching out the room.

The group meandered through the narrow white corridors, ducking overhead pipes, stepping over the lips of bulkheads, all the while trying to keep pace with Ms. Nilsson. The maze of passageways was incomprehensible and never-ending. Each hallway looked just like the last.

Eventually, Kelly stepped through a doorway and into a large room. Ms. Nilsson was already sitting herself at the head of a large, rectangular table. The group conformed, each taking a place, waiting expectantly.

Finally Ms. Nilsson spoke. "We need you to collect something for us."

"Okay, what?" Kelly asked. "And from where?"

"From a thousand feet below us," she replied.

"A thousand feet? That's it? You drug me and drag me halfway round the world to dive a thousand feet?" Kelly began to rise from his chair.

"Technically, we don't know where we are, so we can't really say it's halfway round the world," Chris whispered.

Kelly glared at him.

The military woman offered an emotionless smile. "We need you to free dive a thousand feet."

"Free dive a thousand feet?" Kelly sat again. "You're fucking crazy. Okay, I get why you called on me now—I hold the free dive record—I get it. But I've only gone eight hundred fifty feet, and that was no limits apnea; I had a guide rope, weighted sled, fins, and an inflatable." Kelly shook his head and gesticulated frantically.

"I have a more practical question." Victoria raised her slight hand. Her delicate English accent and reserved politeness commanded attention. "Why free dive? Why can't we use tanks?"

"A sensible question." Ms. Nilsson pointed a remote control at the opposite wall and pressed a button. An overhead projector suspended from the ceiling whirred into life, flooding the white wall with a bright blue light. Another press of a button, and a new image flicked onto the wall. "Okay, here we are." She wielded a laser pointer like a long-distance marker pen to fleetingly circle in red the simulated image of a large ship. "There's the sea floor and structures below us. We need to retrieve something, but every time we send divers down, their equipment malfunctions, and we lose them ..." Her voice trailed off.

"By *lose*, you mean they died—right?" Chris asked.

"Yes," the Shadow Man replied.

Victoria furrowed her brow. "Why? What happened to their equipment?"

"We don't know," Ms. Nilsson replied. "The divers who came back ... their equipment was corroded. The cylinders were destroyed."

"And you can't send an ROV?" Chris was frowning, clearly trying to get his head around the situation.

"No, the terrain down there makes it difficult to pilot any kind of remote submersible."

"Can I see a cylinder? A corroded one, I mean," Victoria asked.

"Of course." Ms. Nilsson flicked a glance at the Shadow Man, who immediately left the room.

A few seconds later, he returned carrying a large, plastic crate full of diving gear. He slammed the heavy cage down on the table. The three friends sifted through the equipment, picking up individual pieces, examining each, and then moving to the next. A few confused glances were shot across the table.

"This is very peculiar," Victoria whispered.

11

"You're not fucking kidding." Kelly exhaled through his nostrils. "There's no burn edge and nothing to indicate acidic corrosion. And it's not the seals. Something has literally eaten through the cylinder."

"Okay, no, we're not going." Chris stood up. "We have no idea what we're collecting or what happened to this equipment—*or your divers.*"

"I'll do it," Kelly said.

Chris spun around and stared at his companion. "Are you nuts? Look at this stuff."

"I assume the divers died from drowning, not anything else?" Kelly asked.

"As far as we know," Ms. Nilsson replied.

"Fine. Let's just do this so I can get the hell out of here." Kelly pushed away from the table with his palms.

"That's the spirit, Mr. Graham. We're on a schedule anyway. Let's go." Ms. Nilsson stood, ready to leave.

Chris leaned into his friend. "What are you doing?"

Kelly looked into his friend's eyes, a playful glint in his own. "I wanna know what's down there. What the hell did that kind of damage? You get me?"

Chris paused, studying his comrade. "You'll need a buddy. I'll go with you."

"No!" Kelly shook his head. "No, I'll be fine."

"Don't be an idiot. Diving 101—you need a buddy." Chris's arms were folded across his chest, a schoolteacher scowl on his face.

"Yes, he does. And that's why she's here." Ms. Nilsson nodded toward Victoria.

"What?" Kelly demanded. "No, I'm fine."

"What's the matter, Kelly Graham? Scared I'll dive deeper than you?" Victoria taunted him from across the table.

"In fact, Miss McKenzie, that's exactly why you are here—to double our chances." With that, Ms. Nilsson left the room.

"You heard the woman. Let's go." Victoria winked at Kelly and sauntered out of the room. He quickly followed, mumbling something about dive records and the female lung capacity.

"Are they always like this?" the Shadow Man asked.

Chris sighed. "Well, they were friends a long time ago. And they were like this then. It's like they're still in high school."

Location: Los Angeles, California, USA

It was open, only slightly but open nonetheless. Jerry pushed at it tentatively. The hinges groaned as the door slid slowly backward. He peered inside—no lights. He stepped cautiously into the dim hallway of the apartment.

"David?"

Light flickered from the living room at the end of the hall. Jerry shuffled slowly down the passageway. He paused next to the kitchen door and pushed it open—empty. He continued, eventually stepping into the open-plan living room. It was dark except for the muted flat screen TV flickering images of some music video.

Jerry picked up the remote control, switched off the television, and looked around the dark room. The brown leather couch looked like it had recently been sat on. A human impression was still carved into the seat. He stepped over to the wall and flicked on the main light. The brightness hurt his eyes as the unshaded light bulb hanging from the center of the ceiling burst into life. He blinked, adjusting to the new environment.

There was nothing suspicious or out of place.

He looked to the spiral staircase leading to the upper level of the duplex. Taking a deep breath, he strode toward it and grabbed the hand railing. Slowly, he ascended, each step heavier than the last. He circled upward to reach the opening to the bedroom. As his vision crested the floor's horizon, his eyes fell upon David slumped face down over the bed. His body was sprawled out, arms and legs outstretched, his head turned to the left with eyes open, staring off into nowhere. The white sheets were stained red.

Jerry could see a single gaping wound in the back of David's head; a bloody mix of plasma and brain tissue glinted inside the small hole.

Jerry's stomach convulsed; the need to vomit was overwhelming. He stepped slowly to the corpse of his friend.

"Fuck." He clasped a hand to his mouth, afraid of who may have heard him. Jerry swallowed hard and leaned to feel his friend's neck.

The cell phone exploded into life, vibrating in his jeans. Jerry leapt back squealing and grabbed at the object shuddering on his left leg. His heart raced, thumping through his chest. He pulled the iPhone from his pocket and looked at the screen: *Caller out of area.*

"H ... hello?"

"Listen to me carefully, Mr. Caulfield. You have a few minutes at best. Go to the bedroom window and leave via the fire escape."

"Who is this? What do you ...?"

"I suggest you do what I say. Your friend's killer is probably still in the building."

The front door creaked open. Jerry muffled a squeak from his lips and started to the window, the cell phone still clamped to his left ear.

"When you get to the bottom of the ladder, there will be a black sedan with the keys in the ignition. The satellite navigation has been pre-programmed. Just follow the instructions."

Click.

Jerry looked at his phone. The call had been ended. He paused and peered out the window and over the rusty metal framework of the fire escape into the wet street below. There was the sedan, just as the caller had indicated. Jerry clambered through the window frame onto the metal stairs and started downward but froze as the clanging of his feet against the metalwork echoed all around him. He looked up through the grated platforms at the open bedroom window. *Shit. Probably should have closed that. Fuck it. Keep moving.*

Moving more stealthily, he tip-toed down the rest of the ladder until he reached the bottom platform. It must have been twenty feet to the street below. Should he unlock the last ladder to get down? No. That would make too much noise. Jerry climbed clumsily over the slippery railing and slid down the other side until he was hanging by only his hands from the platform, dangling above the street below. It didn't look that far. His fingers slipped. Jerry fell to the concrete below, twisting his left ankle awkwardly as he crashed into the pavement. He cried out in pain, clutching at his leg, and rolled about the pavement on his back.

Two yellow beams of light pierced the dark street, drowning Jerry's face. He covered his eyes with one free hand. The cones of light shook as the car's engine growled into life. Jerry froze. He couldn't move. He knew he should, but his body wasn't listening to his brain. He looked up at the black sedan waiting for him. It was too far away. His attention snapped back to the other car as its screeching tires propelled it toward him. Jerry closed his eyes and covered his head, as if that would protect him from a ton of metal crushing his frail human skull. The roaring of the engine grew louder as the car accelerated. Jerry squeezed his eyes closed and prayed.

The car gunned past his head and off into the night. Silence. Jerry opened his eyes. He was alive. He pried himself from the floor and limped over to the sedan, his heart still racing. He grabbed the door handle, opened the car, and jumped inside—safe, at least for now. He twisted the key in the ignition, firing up the engine. The satellite navigation screen flickered on.

"Drive 400 yards, then turn left." The mechanical woman's voice was somehow reassuring.

Jerry sucked in a deep breath and held it for a few seconds before letting go—expelling his fear. He released the handbrake and pressed the accelerator. The car slid calmly forward and picked up speed. He was on his way.

The starless night sky was covered in thick, invisible clouds that poured cold rain on to the city streets. The glass-like needles of water shattered across the car, obscuring the windshield for a second, before the wiper swept them away, and the cycle started over.

The sedan weaved through the streets as Jerry numbly followed the mechanical woman's voice. He wasn't concentrating on the road. He was thinking of David. *What the hell had happened? And who was the guy on the phone? What the hell was going on?*

"You have arrived at your destination."

Jerry glared at the sat nav screen and pressed hard on the brakes. Where was he? Peering out through the gaps in the rain as the windshield wipers shuffled backward and forward, he could see a large sign: *Zen Lounge.*

"Why the fuck would someone bring me here?"

Once again, Jerry's iPhone chimed, as if on cue. He picked it up, slid his index finger across the onscreen bar to unlock it, and held to his ear.

"Go inside now and head to the bar. Order a drink and stay there. I will call you in ten minutes."

Click.

Jerry stared at his phone, and then out at the club. He looked at his watch: *7:08 pm.* He sighed, opened the car door, and stepped out into the rain. His ankle burned. Jerry winced. Covering his head with his sport jacket, he limped across the road and into the club. A large man dressed in a dark gray suit was standing in the doorway. He eyed Jerry closely.

"I'm meeting a friend inside," he lied.

The doorman opened the door with a nod.

Jerry shook off the rain and re-adjusted his jacket onto his shoulders. His slim-fitting blue jeans and brown brogues were sodden and considerably darker in color than they were supposed to be when dry. A crowd of giggling girls to his left stopped their clucking and turned to him, a look of disgust on their faces. Used to this kind of treatment, and with bigger things on his mind, Jerry smiled weakly and carried on into the club.

The room was lit with a dim red hue, barely illuminating the various Buddha-esque statues dotted around the edges of the space. Large plasma screens adorned the walls, flashing images of people dancing. The dance floor was virtually empty, though it was relatively early. Jerry walked across to the bar, a large structure that had been fashioned to resemble a Chinese building; it was square, allowing access from all sides, and had a sloping roof. Red circular stools were placed all around.

Jerry sat on the nearest stool.

"What can I get you?" The barman rested both hands on the bar and offered a practiced grin that barely hid his disdain for working yet another nightshift.

"I'm sorry?" Jerry asked.

"Yeah, music's a bit loud. What can I get you?"

"Oh, I'm waiting for a friend."

"Well, it's a two-drink minimum tonight, pal, so why don't you order for you and your friend?"

"Right, sure, two beers, then."

"Sure, what would you—"

"Anything! Anything, it doesn't matter."

The barman raised his eyes to heaven and turned away briefly before reappearing with two bottles of beer. "That'll be fifteen bucks."

"Okay, thanks." Jerry rummaged in his jeans and pulled out a twenty-dollar bill. "Keep the change, okay."

Jerry sat nervously, eyeing the smattering of people in the room. There were two middle-aged women in the corner, their handbags on the floor, gossiping while necking large glasses of champagne, and a strange little man standing on his own near the toilet doorway, nursing a glass of draught beer. It could be anyone. Any person in that room could have called him. *Which one was it? What did they want?* He picked up one of the beers and took a long swig.

16

CHAPTER THREE

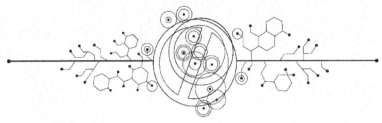

Location: Unknown

Kelly sat on the deck. The ship looked smaller from up here. It was definitely military. Turrets with huge elongated gun barrels were strewn down either flank. A command center protruded into the blue sky some three hundred feet from him. This thing had to be as big as a frigate. Still, it was empty. A ship this large and no crew? It just didn't feel right.

He glanced over his right shoulder. Chris was busy checking the free dive equipment, hopping from one place to the next like a small bird bouncing from spot to spot while looking for a meal that might crawl out of the earth. Chris was always like that—a little worrywart forever checking the equipment, double-checking it, and then triple-checking, just in case he'd missed something.

Kelly sighed and jumped to his feet. A dark blue wetsuit clung to his muscular body. He reached back, trying to grasp the long cord attached to the rear zip without success. He turned in a circle to his left and then right. "Goddamn amateur wetsuits. I want mine."

"Our new friends said we didn't have time to pick your stuff up." Victoria slid up behind Kelly. "I did tell them you were a big baby and only like your own equipment. Want a hand there?"

He didn't even turn around. "If I need your help, it won't be to zip me up."

"Very funny, Kelly. I think it's more fun to watch you spin like a dog trying to catch his own tail."

"Just zip me up."

The zip jolted awkwardly upward in short bursts, straining to pull the neoprene fabric together across his broad back.

"You know," she said, while tugging on the zip cord, "it's been five years. You could have called." She finished closing the zip.

"Well, so could you. Anyway, a lot happened. You know how it is."

Kelly glanced at Victoria; for a brief moment, their gazes met.

He was a big flirt, but she knew it was just that: flirting. He didn't mean it. He was too in love with himself as always.

"By the way," he called, walking backward, "you look hot in a wetsuit ..." His voice trailed off as he spun mid-stride and kept on toward Chris.

Just when she thought she had him figured out, he reeled her back in. He was a cheeky bugger but an irresistible one. She started after him.

Chris was tending to the equipment. He surveyed each piece closely. This was going to be a deep free dive and a very dangerous one. The lift bag had to function properly. He'd seen one malfunction before at five hundred twenty-five feet. The diver had panicked and exhausted the oxygen supply in his lungs. Chris had been his buddy and offered the spare regulator, the octopus, but the diver refused—determined to make it back to the surface unaided. They had swum steadily toward the surface, a broken mosaic of blue fractured by sunlight. A hundred feet, fifty, twenty, and then suddenly, the diver stopped kicking and began to sink. His eyes were wide open, but he was limp. Chris grabbed him by the arms and dragged him to the surface. Once he was above water, Chris spat out his regulator and screamed for help. The boat crew came *en masse* and lifted the diver effortlessly from the water. Chris just floated there, exhausted. In the hospital, the doctors told Chris that the diver had suffered from deep water blackout—a rapid drop in the partial pressure of oxygen in the lungs on ascent, resulting in cerebral hypoxia. In other words, lack of oxygen to the brain. Chris had tried his best, but the diver died.

"How we doing there, esé?" Kelly waltzed up behind his friend and slapped him on his bare back.

"Ah, shit. You asshole. Just for that I should mess with your equipment."

Kelly grinned. "Yeah, but you won't."

"I know. Anyway, it should be me buddying up with you down there. I don't like this one bit. Instead, I got to trust the Queen of England over there is willing to get her manicure dirty in order to help you out." Chris randomly picked up face masks and put them down with purpose.

"Okay, easy there. You heard the talking China doll—use of equipment down there is a no-no. Victoria can free dive, and you can't. Anyway, I'm not willing to risk your life on this."

"Just yours."

Kelly looked sternly into Chris's eyes. "Yep."

Ms. Nilsson and the Shadow Man walked out onto the deck and marched toward Kelly and Chris. She had changed into an all-black wetsuit, cut off at the thighs and upper arms. Her hair was pulled into a tight ponytail behind her head. He was still in a suit but carried a large black cube-shaped, metallic case with substantial clasp locks on one side.

"Okay, I'm liking your new look there, Ms. ... Nil ... poi ...?"

"Nilsson. It's Norwegian."

"Yeah, that's what I said. But you, André, I know it's December and not so warm out here, but you could have changed." Kelly stood on tip toes in an attempt to puff up to the same size as the Shadow Man. It was no use.

"They didn't have a wetsuit in extra, extra, extra, extra, extra large," the Shadow Man replied, his face deadpan.

"Well, bugger me. The walking freezer does have a sense of humor." Kelly laughed and then turned his focus back to the equipment. "Where in the world are we, anyway?"

"You're on a need-to-know basis, Mr. Graham. Just be happy you are doing your country a service." Ms. Nilsson glided over to Kelly and sat on her haunches next to him. Her face was close to his. "And I am personally, eternally grateful." Her lips came close to his stubble-covered cheek.

Chris burst out laughing. "Jeez, are you barking up the wrong tree, lady. Just let us do our job."

Kelly, Victoria, and Chris climbed down into a life boat on the port side of the ship. The Shadow Man remained on the deck and used the winch to lower them to the water below.

It was calm, no breeze at all. The life boat bobbed on the water as the three friends fixed and fiddled with equipment. Chris grabbed at the weighted guide rope that swung above his head, suspended from an arm attached to the main ship. The rope was only an inch thick, but it was clearly strong. He waved to the Shadow Man up on deck to release the winch lock. The rope lowered toward him. It had a large rubber weight attached to the end. Just above that was the sled. It resembled a large ring with spokes pointing inward that attached to a tube that had the rope running through it. Chris grabbed the ring and used it to swing the rope toward him. Holding onto the sled, he released the lock and allowed the weighted rope to drop into the water beside him, plummeting into the depths. The rope whizzed past his head, whirring as the weight pulled it deeper into the water—three hundred feet, five hundred feet, seven hundred feet, eight hundred feet. The rope went slack. Chris waved again and the Shadow Man locked the winch.

"How much weight do you want on the ring?"

Kelly looked up from sliding his feet inside the monofin—a large blue, flipper-like appendage that fixed his feet together, making him look like a merman. "Best make it a few hundred pounds, enough to pull us both down quickly."

"Right." Chris pulled the ring into the life boat and rested it on the deck, before clipping strings of rubber weights to the inner spokes. "Why are we using rubber again? I gotta clip a whole bunch of these things to get the total weight."

"Cause our new friends told us their divers' equipment came back corroded, so I'm just avoiding using metal as best as possible. Anyway, pass me the inflatable."

Chris handed Kelly the lift bag, a long yellow piece of material that looked like an unraveled parachute with black straps. Kelly climbed into the harness and clipped the contraption together across his chest. The canary colored parachute rested on his shoulders like an untied scarf.

"Need a push, you big girl?" mocked Victoria.

"You just can't wait to get wet and slippery with me," Kelly replied.

Kelly put his right arm across his chest, his left over his face, and leaned backward. His back slapped the water as if it were solid. The ocean water was cold as it seeped between the wetsuit neoprene and his skin. Kelly shuddered.

"Okay, I'm going to need to get warmed up here before I attempt anything." He buried his face in the water and opened his eyes. It wasn't murky, but the sunlight only penetrated a few feet down; he still couldn't see his quarry—not that he could see a thousand feet down anyway.

It was calm here—peaceful, like a whole other universe. Sound didn't really exist except for the beating of his own heart, which he could feel slowing. Everything appeared as if it were in slow motion, like time had no hold here. He wondered if he just kept his head down, whether everyone else would go away. Maybe he could float away. A fish swam in a zig-zag fashion in the distance. He couldn't see what species it was, but he wanted to be that fish—free, with only a three-second memory span. He smiled. Fish don't really have a three-second memory, but the sentiment was what mattered.

His underwater sanctuary was violated by the crashing of Victoria's body into the water next to him. Kelly lifted his head from beneath the water and gave her an annoyed look.

"Watch it, sweet cheeks."

"Sorry. Okay, let me get warmed up."

Kelly and Victoria pulled the hoods of their wetsuits over their heads and tucked in their hair until only their faces could be seen. Then, like a synchronized swimming team, they repeatedly duck-dived down several feet before coming to the surface and resting in the fetal position.

"Okay, we're both going to go down together, but Victoria, you remember to drop off at about a couple hundred feet—okay? You can support me on the way back up." For the first time ever, Kelly sounded serious.

"I understand."

"Right, so I'll go as deep as I can and grab … whatever it is down there. It's small enough to carry—right?"

"Right," called Ms. Nilsson from the boat above him.

"Okay, Chris. Mask."

On cue, a diving mask flew over the rim of the life boat and plopped into the water next to Kelly. A second appeared as if from nowhere and hit Victoria in the head.

"Sorry!" called Chris from the safety of the boat. Kelly snickered.

The two washed their goggles in the ocean water and then spat on the inside, spreading the viscous fluid around with their index fingers before repeating the washing cycle. They pulled the mask straps over the backs of their heads and placed the masks on their faces; the rubber seal cut into their cheeks.

Chris leaned over the side of the boat and looked for his friend. Kelly was treading water. He gave the okay sign: an index finger and thumb touching to form a circle. Chris grabbed the ring structure and heaved it to the side of the life boat.

"It's locked. I could only get three hundred pounds on there. I hope it's enough. When you're ready, just release the lock. And don't forget to use the brake. And…"

"Stop fussing and pass me the sled, Paco."

Chris gave the sled one last heave and pushed it over the side, narrowly missing Kelly's head. It crashed into the water, pulling the rope above it tight. The winch above strained under the weight.

"Heads or tails?" Kelly asked.

"I think heads. I don't like tails," Victoria replied. She faked a shudder.

"Heads it is. Okay, grab the sled."

Victoria swam up to the sled and held on to the opposite side of the ring with both hands. "Okay, ready?"

Kelly nodded. He started taking deep breaths, slowly inhaling and exhaling. Inhaling and exhaling. He suddenly stopped and just opened and closed his mouth, like a fish out of water. It looked almost painful.

Ms. Nilsson yelled from above, "What the hell is he doing?"

"Preparing," Chris replied. "It's a diving technique."

Kelly nodded at Victoria and released the brake. The pair was pulled violently underwater. There was a deafening sound as the ocean crashed in above them, sealing the rift they left behind. The sound of the sled speeding toward the ocean floor along the length of the guide rope pierced Kelly's ears with its loud, constant drone. His feet strapped into the monofin pointed toward the surface, flapped behind him like a flag in the wind. He could feel the weight of the water increasing, crushing his lungs, his organs. *Jesus, it's been a while since I've done this.* The pressure built up in his ears. Kelly swallowed hard to equalize the pressure. It worked.

The water was becoming darker. How long had he been going? It seemed like hours. He looked across at Victoria. She was still with him. He hadn't even reached two hundred feet. Kelly focused his thoughts on his heartbeat.

Thump, thump. Thump, thump.

C'mon, slower.

Thump, thump. Thump ... thump.

That was better.

He closed his eyes and thought of her and her voice—calming, soothing, calling him deeper and deeper. Kelly was warm; the blood in his veins seemed to slow and meander around his body. Deeper still.

Suddenly, he jerked forward. Kelly opened his eyes and swiveled his head around. Victoria had let go. He must have passed two hundred feet. Without her drag, he was accelerating now—faster toward the bottom.

Kelly squinted, trying to see through the rushing water. It had to be soon. He could feel the oxygen reserves in his lungs start to deplete and the carbon dioxide build up in his blood stream, slowly poisoning him. What the fuck was he doing here? The ocean continued to rush past his head. He'd blocked out the sound of the sled and was concentrating on his own reflexes. Keeping his heart rate low. He squinted again. A ridge, some rocks. The excitement of seeing his quarry stole the last molecule of oxygen in his lungs. His chest convulsed. The uncontrollable urge to breathe took over his every fiber. His lungs were on fire. If he just opened his mouth, it would be over. The water would quench the flames.

Kelly hit the bottom. He lost his grip on the sled and rolled off onto his back, but the weight belt held him to the sea floor. He looked around at his upside down world. It was virtually pitch black. Where was it? What was it? How the fuck was he supposed to see it? His chest hurt. He screwed his eyes up. *Calm yourself, Kelly*, he thought. *Find it.*

He opened his eyes and flipped onto his stomach. He was on some kind of underwater atoll. The faint outline of peaks and troughs was everywhere—an underwater mountain system. Where the fuck in the world had they dragged him?

There was no way he was going to find anything down here. He had to go back. He kicked with both legs like a dolphin, propelling himself forward. Then he caught something in his peripheral vision. It was silvery, round, and jelly-like. He glided toward it. It was leaking some kind of liquid. Inside its translucent form, he could see … light, a bluish-green light. Was it alive? Was it a medusa of some kind? No, he'd seen thousands; it wasn't a medusa. He coughed. Tiny bubbles escaped his mouth. Shit, his heart cramped. *Fuck it.* He grabbed the gelatinous orb in one arm and pulled the cord attached to his gear with the other. A mass of foam surrounded him as the inflatable burst into life. The yellow scarf lifted from his chest and formed two balloons above his shoulders. Kelly pulled at his weight belt. It fell from his waist and sank to the atolls below. Now, he was rushing to the surface. Kelly tried to let a constant stream of used breath escape through his lips as he ascended, but there was hardly anything to release.

The light above him suddenly darkened. Kelly looked up to see the outline of the winch. It was in the water and plummeting toward him. He flicked his monofin desperately to maneuver out of the way. The winch slid silently past him into the darkness, a trail of bubbles behind it. Where the fuck was Victoria? What the hell was going on? The inflatable pulled him upward still. But the light was dimming. It was cold, very cold. Kelly closed his eyes.

Darkness. Peace.

Water rushed into his lungs. *I'm coming home*, he thought.

Location: Los Angeles, California, USA

Jerry sat nervously on his stool. He occasionally swigged from his now warm beer, but very little liquid actually entered his mouth. The club was beginning to fill; packs of testosterone-fueled men in their mid-twenties prowled the room with little on their minds other than the scantily clad, and clearly none-too-bright, platinum-blonde females huddled together like bleating sheep being stalked. Still, they all somehow made him feel safe. Protected in the crowd. It had been an hour. Jerry had stared at his phone, watching the minutes on the clock screensaver pass by. Why hadn't the man called? What did the man want? To kill him? No, why bring him here? It didn't make sense. Jerry fiddled with his watch again. 8:03 pm. Maybe he should leave? And go where? He shook his head. No, he was safe in here. Jerry shifted on his seat as people shoved and pushed past each other to get to the bar. He squirmed, feeling claustrophobic.

"Jerry."

He froze. His heart leapt into his throat. The voice was behind him—close behind him. It was deep and gruff. He couldn't move, paralyzed by fear. Shit. He slowly turned his head to face the man.

"Jerry, you look like shit, man." It was Craig—a short, skinny man with a pot belly, spectacles thicker than milk bottle bottoms, and a mustard-colored, plaid sports jacket—his work cubicle neighbor.

"You scared the crap out of me, Craig. What the hell are you doing here?"

"It's ladies' night in here. Perfect prey, know what I'm saying?" The greasy little man wiped his pathetic comb-over across his head in an overly confident sweeping motion. Jerry could feel the bile rise in his throat. It was annoying guys like this who gave techies a bad name and was probably why Jerry couldn't find a girlfriend.

"I'm kinda busy here, Craig. I'll see you at work."

"You don't look busy to me, Jerry. Unless you are waiting for a lady friend—hmmm?" Craig made some kind of vulgar motion with his hips.

"No, no lady friend. I'm just preoccupied."

"Well, I just figured, 'cause that lady over there just asked me to give you this." The greasy, little man handed him a small white envelope sealed with a wax heart.

Jerry sprang from his seat, snatching the envelope, his worried stare darting about the room. "Which woman?"

Craig waved toward the door. "That one ... oh well, she was there a minute ago. But, to be honest, she wasn't a looker. Maybe she saw you and didn't want to come over, huh? Left you a note, hey?"

"Craig! Just fuck off, will you!"

"Woah, jeez. Who rattled your cage?"

"Look, I'm just a bit stressed. I'll see you around, okay?" Jerry patted his neighbor on the shoulder and limped off into the crowd toward the bathrooms, clasping the envelope to his chest.

The door opened without as much as a creak. No one inside. The bathroom was almost as fancy as the bar itself, with toilet stall doors fashioned to look like paper-thin Chinese walls. *Not very safe*, thought Jerry as he quickly made his way inside a stall and closed the door behind him. He sat on the toilet and exhaled, his heart thumping in his chest. He looked at the letter and slowly started picking at the wax heart. A waft of perfume filled his nostrils as the envelope popped open. Inside was a small USB key, millimeters thin, and a white piece of paper. Jerry eyed the key. Too small to have much memory capacity. No, it was a web uplink key, something to direct him somewhere else. *Shit, more cat and mouse stuff.*

He held the paper up to read the tiny scrawl: *answer your phone.* Answer his phone? Jerry's phone sprang into life, once again sending him into near cardiac arrest. "Hello?"

"You have the key?"

"Y ... yes."

"Good. There is an Internet café about six blocks down the road; head south. Go inside and wait for further instructions. Do not leave the café under any circumstances. It may be a few hours."

"Why, what do you people want? Wha—"

Click. The phone went dead.

Jerry sighed. He put the key in his pocket and headed back out into the main room. It was heaving with people, each one squashed against the next. He repeatedly apologized as he pushed through and past groups of men and women, feeling their keys and phone edges prodding into him. Each time he tried to squeeze through, he received a look of disgust. He didn't care. He wasn't in the mood. He wondered if they were really guests or actors paid to make all of this look real—spies watching his every move. When he peered out the front door, it was a relief to see that at least the rain had stopped. He sucked in a deep breath, nodded to the doorman to open up, and stepped outside.

CHAPTER FOUR

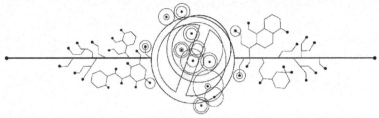

Location: Somewhere over the Pacific Ocean

The whir of the massive rotors droned through the hull of the immense Chinook. Victoria had been in a few of these choppers in her time but had not seen one like this before. Usually, they were slow and sluggish—not something in which she would have chosen to be rescued. This one was different somehow—larger and faster. She'd asked the pilot what model it was and if it was capable of getting them the hell out of there.

"This is a MH-47G," the pilot had replied, "upgraded with the latest digital Common Avionics Architecture System. And, well, the rest is classified, ma'am. We'll get you home."

But they weren't going home, she'd thought.

Victoria leaned back on her seat, a red piece of material stretched over metal framework, and fiddled with the silver crucifix that rested on her chest. Behind her, a lattice-work of red cloth was suspended from a metallic pole that ran the length of the cargo hold. It formed a poor back support. She peered out through one of the small porthole windows and admired the calm, black-purple water. A light breeze rippled the moonlit surface. The chopper was screaming along at an extraordinary pace, very close to the water's surface.

She turned her attention back to her traveling companions. The Shadow Man and Ms. Nilsson were sitting side by side, almost bolt upright, hands in their laps, with their eyes closed. It was as if they slept but could at any moment regain consciousness and perfect agility should the need arise. Chris was on his haunches, his back against the cushioned lining of the interior. Victoria followed Chris's gaze to the large Kelly-shaped lump underneath an army-issue blanket. He was squeezing his eyes tightly together as if in pain and making the occasional grunt.

"He's having a nightmare." Chris spoke quietly, his gaze never leaving Kelly. "He has them a lot."

"Is it the same dream each time?" Victoria asked.

"No, but usually the same theme."

"You know what it's about? Perhaps losing his hair or getting a really big spot?"

"No, it's about his wife and daughter."

Victoria's attention was more focused now. "I didn't know he's married."

Chris sighed. "He was married before we met you."

Victoria furrowed her brow.

Chris turned to face her and took a deep breath. "About seven years ago, Kelly was in South Africa to take pictures of sharks, near Seal Island in False Bay, south-east of Cape Town. He was part of a scientific exploration team. It was a year-long project, and the company was paying him a lot to do the underwater photography. Freediving photography, you know? He didn't want to go for that long, but the pay would have set his family up for a good few years. Izel, his wife, had supported him and said he should go; it was only a year and would have been worth it. Carmen, his daughter, was only three, so it was better to be away at that time than when she would be older and would remember."

Victoria stared and nodded slowly, unable to think what she really wanted to say.

"About nine months into the trip, he got a phone call. Izel had slit her wrists and had been found dead in their family home in California. Kelly dropped everything and got the next flight home. When he got to San Francisco airport, the police collected him and took him to the station."

Victoria's gaze fell on Kelly's frame. He was still twitching and grunting. "Oh, my … Why? Why did she do that? Was she that lonely?"

Chris coughed lightly and rubbed his face. He sighed again and started speaking slowly, his eyes fixed on the cabin floor. "About three months after Kelly had left for South Africa, Carmen had an accident. She had fallen down the stairs. She was so little, and her neck wasn't strong enough. She died instantly." Chris's eyes filled with tears. "Izel was distraught. She didn't know how to tell Kelly and wouldn't let anyone else tell him. She became increasingly depressed. Until one day …"

Victoria couldn't look away from Kelly. "And you've been looking after him ever since? Watching his back, as it were?"

"Actually, it's the other way around. Kelly was determined to look after me. I guess 'cause I was her little brother. And I had no family."

Victoria cast a pained look over to Chris, who was hunched over like a small boy, afraid and alone in a playground of older children. "You never said you had a sister."

He ran his forearm across his nose and sniffed hard. "Well, you met us about a year after she died. We didn't like to talk of her much back then. Anyway, it's been him and me ever since. But it changed him. Silly bastard doesn't have any fear any more. Says if it's his time to go, then it's time, and he'll just see them again all the sooner. To be honest, I know he doesn't believe in all that. I think he just says it to make me feel better."

Kelly awoke with a start, his body viciously jerking. His eyes were wide as they searched the dark cabin.

"Decided to join us, did you?" Chris forced a laugh from his throat.

"Yeah." Kelly paused, placed both hands on his face and wiped the sweat off, pulling at his skin. "Can't let you have all the fun, now can I? Where the fuck are we? Last thing I remember, I was ascending, but I couldn't find Victoria, and the crane, the crane came past my head, and then I blacked out."

Victoria sniffed and dabbed her eyes. "We're not sure ourselves. It all happened very quickly. There were a lot of flashes above the surface. I couldn't hear anything, but it looked like chaos. The next thing I knew, Tremaine was in the water with me, dragging me by the arm. When I broke the surface, everything was going crazy. There were explosions and gunfire; it was hectic. Tremaine yanked me to this helicopter and threw me inside. Chris was screaming and fighting to get into the water to find you, but Ms. Nilsson had already gone in and was pulling you out. She's stronger than she looks. I thought she might have broken a nail." Victoria glanced over to the still sleeping woman.

Kelly rubbed his head, still feeling a little groggy. "Okay, but you still don't know what happened?"

Victoria shook her head. "No, Ms. Nilsson said we'd drifted into someone else's territory. Pissed someone off, so we had to get the hell out of there."

"Now, we've been flying for hours. I wonder where we are going." Chris's voice trailed off.

Kelly stood and stumbled across to the window next to Victoria, placing a hand each side of the porthole. He could only see a black sky and black water—no stars, nothing. Clouds must have been covering the moon. Kelly

29

scanned what he thought was the horizon, a faint, barely discernible horizontal line halfway through his line of sight. In the far distance, he could see an even darker shape dotted with yellow and blue pinpricks, something long, something huge—a ship. "I think we're heading to that; it must be an aircraft carrier or something. It's the only thing out there." He twisted his body back around and plonked down wearily next to Victoria.

"It's to refuel. We're heading back to land. It will be a short stopover. No need to leave the chopper." Ms. Nilsson's voice was quiet but purposeful, delivering only the most important information—no more, no less. Her eyes looked bright and alert as if she had never been asleep.

The three friends sat silently, too tired to speak any more. A light spattering of raindrops against the hull and windows filled the stillness. The night sky appeared to draw darker as a massive cloud of fog enveloped the helicopter. It was going to be a rough landing.

His stomach lurched in his abdomen, abruptly startling Kelly awake. Where were they? He could hear the constant whirring sound, droning through his skull. The chopper. They were still in the chopper. It dropped ten feet in a sudden jerking movement—they were descending.

Kelly threw a glance over to Victoria; she was curled up in a ball with her head in Chris's lap. Chris sat upright, head tilted backward, mouth open, snoring. Kelly continued surveying the cabin until his eyes fell upon Ms. Nilsson and the Shadow Man, who were very much awake and still dressed immaculately, their hands resting in their laps.

"Where the fuck are we?"

"At our destination," the Shadow Man replied.

"Destination? What destination?"

"You and your friends were tired, so we let you sleep through refueling on the carrier. We are back over land. The General would like to speak with you." Ms. Nilsson's voice was again without emotion.

"General? What general? Look, I've had about enough of you people and your secrecy."

"Jesus, what's all the fuss about?" Chris yawned and stretched. "Are we there yet?"

Ms. Nilsson nodded. "Yes."

"There yet? Where yet? You know where we are going?" Kelly threw an irritated glare at Chris.

"Chill, esé." Chris patted his friend on the shoulder. "They said they were taking us to a safe place following the attack."

"Attack?" Now Kelly was good and pissed.

"Yeah, while you were playing mermaids down there with Victoria, we got attacked by some kind of special ops guys in black wetsuits. Came outta nowhere. Our new friends here say we drifted into someone else's territory. Before I knew it, André over there had grabbed me and stuffed Victoria into this chopper. Ms. Nilsson had gone in for you. All happened very quickly."

Kelly frowned, unconvinced. "And you guys just had the ability to get us out of there? Sure thing. And I suppose you got what you wanted?" He directed his question to Ms. Nilsson, who still sat serenely.

"We did," she cooed, pointing at the metal box sitting at Tremaine's feet.

"Right, then no need for—"

The chopper landed with a jarring thud, waking Victoria. Before she could speak the side doors were flung open, clunking to a hard stop. Several men in flight suits and pilots' helmets that obscured their faces scrambled inside, grabbed the three friends and dragged them from their seats through the opening into the cold night air.

Kelly stumbled, his legs still a little rubbery. "Jesus, you guys don't think much about manners or being a good host, huh?"

"Welcome to Paradise Ranch," bellowed Tremaine, his voice almost drowned out by the noise of the Chinook rotors.

"We at some kind of resort? Are you shitting me?" Kelly's eyes rolled around in his head.

"Just follow us, please." Ms. Nilsson marched on ahead.

The landscape was bleak and monochromatic. The moon shone overhead, a bright white eye judging the three friends and their hosts as they trudged toward a small gray building.

Chris searched the horizon for some clue as to their whereabouts—a landmark, a tree, anything that might help with orientation—but he didn't recognize anything. He glanced at Victoria, who was walking head down, pulling at her crucifix again, and lost in thought. Kelly was a few paces behind, still unable to pick up his feet properly.

The troop approached the gray building. There were no windows, no signs, no markings, just a heavy, metallic door. Ms. Nilsson strode toward it. Chris watched her touch a panel and type something quickly. The door clunked open, and a guard appeared. Ms. Nilsson showed her ID and nodded to the group. He couldn't hear what she was saying, but clearly she was talking about them. The guard looked over her shoulder and then nodded.

Kelly and the group were frog-marched through the narrow door. The three friends glanced around. The inside of the building was even bleaker than the landscape outside—no wall markings, no windows, nothing except an elevator.

Kelly fidgeted on the spot, uncomfortable in the cramped space. "You still haven't told us who this general is and why he wants to see us."

"General Lloyd heads up this facility. And given the current circumstances, he felt it was safer for you here." Ms. Nilsson spoke without even looking at Kelly.

The elevator door slid open and the group sauntered in. It was equally as bleak as the building and somewhat cramped. They stood inside, uncomfortably close to one another with shoulders pressed together. The lift dropped, whooshing as they descended. It seemed to take forever to stop, but soon enough the door glided open again. Ms. Nilsson strode out and without stopping marched down the only corridor that led off into the darkness. Kelly and Chris shrugged and started after her, Victoria in tow.

The slender woman weaved left and right through the maze of corridors. Kelly followed her lead, all the while musing on the military's preoccupation with rabbit warren-like structures. He glanced over his shoulder. His best friend was muttering, trying to memorize the course they were taking, probably to later have an escape route. Victoria was staring at the floor and following the herd, holding her crucifix between her finger and thumb.

Kelly shook his head and turned his attention back to Ms. Nilsson. She had now stopped at large double doors. Ms. Nilsson showed her ID to the guard, who stepped aside and triggered the door mechanism. The huge doors slid silently apart, allowing the group to meander in.

Inside, the room stretched far beyond them. Everything appeared hermetically sealed—no joints between stark white walls or between wall and ceiling, as if it were meant to be air- or water-tight. At one end of the room, a huge wall stood with a single, black, glass plate set into the right-hand side about five feet above the floor. At the other end, a collection of desks was bolted to the ground with various monitors and notebooks strewn all over them.

Standing at one of the desks was a tall, broad man in a crisp, dark military suit. The thick, blue material looked heavy and regal. His black boots were adorned with glass-like toe caps, clearly the result of many hours of polishing and smoothing with a hot spoon—the proper military way to shine boots. The medals on his uniform appeared to vibrate in the hum of the fluorescent light, a mosaic homage commemorating a lifetime commitment to the U.S. forces and a testament to the blood he had shed in the name of freedom and the American way. Kelly looked the man in the face. He was leathery and craggy with crew-cut silver hair and a beard adorning his square head.

"This is General Benjamin Lloyd," announced Ms. Nilsson.

"Is this the bit where I'm impressed?" quipped Kelly.

The General eyed him. "In fact, Mr. Graham, it is." He walked toward the group and then directly through them, silently commanding them to move aside but strangely slowed to rest a hand on Ms. Nilsson's shoulder before continuing to storm to the opposite wall. The General pressed his open palm against the black glass panel for a few seconds, then pulled it away. A fluorescent white imprint of his hand remained on the screen—every fingerprint, every whorl, every line in perfect detail. A metallic voice sounded overhead.

"Verifying identity."

Kelly looked back at the black monitor. Small, red circles had appeared at different points on the handprint of light, marking key identifying areas—a scar, a whorl with six grooves, the length of the index finger.

"Identity found. General Lloyd, awaiting voice command."

"Lloyd. Benjamin. Access code: FEMA, dash, 751, slash omega. Password: Viracocha." The General spoke loudly, enunciating every syllable.

"Access code and password confirmed."

There was a dull clunking sound as a lock released. The huge white wall in front of them parted, forming into sliding doors that glided effortlessly and without a sound. Behind the separating wall stood an enormous aquarium. The water was black—cold. At least, Kelly assumed it was cold. It looked it—uninviting, empty, soulless, and nothing like the ocean he loved so much.

Something jerked inside the tank. A brief second of movement, a white flash, and then it was gone. Kelly, Chris, and Victoria ran over and rested their palms on the glass. Their eyes were wide, flicking from place to place, trying to penetrate the darkness.

It slapped its body violently against the glass, its webbed hands landing in almost the same position as Kelly's. The group reeled backward, tripping over their own feet.

"This, ladies and gentlemen, is *Ambystoma Sapiens*."

Kelly stepped closer again. "That's quite a mouthful to say."

"Indeed," the General agreed. "We just call it K'in. It's Mayan for—"

"Sun, yes, I know," finished Kelly without looking away.

The creature was the size of a large Nile crocodile. Its trunk was cylindrical, uniformly thick, and segmented with regularly spaced furrows. Its whole body was covered by a thin layer of translucent, white-pink skin. Internal organs shone through its abdomen—the intestine and a beating purple mass that must have been its heart. It had a short, laterally flattened tail surrounded by a thin fin. Its arms, if that was what they were, only had three digits, while the feet only had two toes. Its pear-shaped head ended abruptly with a short, flattened snout. The mouth was small with tiny teeth that formed a sort of sieve. It had nostrils near the end of the snout, though they were so small they could well be vestigial. Six external stalks, each almost three feet in length, lined with bright red filaments protruded flamboyantly from the back of its head—three from the left side and three from the right like the feathers on the headdress of a Vegas showgirl. Curiously, the creature appeared to have eyes, but they were regressed and covered by the same thin skin as the rest of the head and body. It was blind.

They stared at it.

It appeared to stare back.

"What is it?" Victoria asked, her voice cracking. "It looks like a giant axolotl."

"Is it, you know, an alien?" Chris asked.

"No, no, this came from here—from Earth." Kelly sounded so sure. He studied it as if trying to dredge up an ancient memory of somewhere he'd seen it before.

"Mr. Graham is quite right." The voice came from behind them.

A tall, thin man walked toward them through the only door in or out of the room. He wore brown slacks and white boat shoes. His white blazer was buttoned over an open-necked, light blue shirt. He was in his early fifties, but still had piercing blue eyes that contrasted against his dark leathery skin.

"I'm Professor Alexander."

The General marched over to the professor and put one hand on his shoulder. "Professor Alexander is our resident expert and really the driving force behind our understanding of K'in. He'll let you know what's going on."

"Indeed, please follow me." The professor turned around and headed back out through the door. Kelly, Victoria, and Chris looked at each other and then at Tremaine and Ms. Nilsson.

Ms. Nilsson nodded toward the door. "Go on."

The three friends shuffled out of the room, each one glancing backward more than once to chance another fleeting look at K'in. It was still there, gliding gracefully in the water near the glass—its blind gaze firmly fixed in their direction.

CHAPTER FIVE

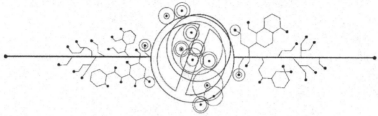

Location: Secret base, somewhere in the Nevada desert, USA

They entered a small, white room. No windows. No other doors. Only a plain oval glass table placed in the center and six see-through chairs made of some kind of plastic. They assembled along the edge of the table while Professor Alexander sat at the head. He rested one leg on the knee of the other, his hands in his lap. Calm. Serene.

"What do you know about evolution?" the professor asked. The question didn't seem to be aimed at any one particular person. They looked blankly at each other.

"Perhaps that was too broad. Let me be more specific. What do you know about human evolution?"

Kelly sat upright in his chair and coughed nervously. "We descended from apes."

"Well, that is very broad and not wholly accurate but close enough. Yes, we descended from ape-like ancestors. However, if you go back far enough, we have ancestors that are common to both us and frogs or crocodiles. According to the fossil record, life began in the oceans and moved on to land. Therefore, our ancestors also originated in the oceans. Understand?"

Kelly and Chris nodded.

The professor stood and tapped twice on the table. The glass came alive, transforming into a transparent working computer surface. It glowed with a faint, blue haze. A series of folder-shaped icons littered the table surface. Professor Alexander placed a finger on the image of a folder and dragged it toward his end of the table. He tapped it twice. The folder opened and spilled its contents around the glass table-screen. His eyes scanned the images and then selected the one he wanted. He grabbed the outer edges of the picture and pulled his fingers in two different directions—the image expanded, almost to the full size of the table. It was the representation of an evolutionary tree, a cascade of electric blue lines leading to a species name. Each line worked backward, connecting to another line at a certain point in history.

The professor flicked his finger along the tree, moving it forward and then backward. "Ah, there it is." He tapped on a species name: *Orcinus orca*. The killer whale. "Did you know orcas and, in fact, all whales are closely related to cows? It's true. If you look at the bone structure,"—he tapped again, bringing up a virtual skeleton of a killer whale— "you can see remnant bones in their fins and a pelvic structure from when they had legs."

Chris wrinkled his nose. "Legs?"

"Yes, legs," repeated the professor. "You see, following the great evolutionary feat of moving from the ocean to land, it seems some of our mammalian cousins went back to the ocean—for some reason unbeknownst to us. We have fossil records showing the regression of land-adapted appendages to sea-faring ones. Interestingly, though, they kept the need to breathe the atmosphere and thus all have lungs. Now," the professor's voice became more excited, "it seems at one point, an ancestor or ancestors of the human race lived very near water. And it had to be deep enough to allow diving."

"Why?" Chris asked.

"The mammalian dive reflex." Kelly spoke softly, unaware he'd vocalized his inner thoughts.

"Quite right again, Mr. Graham, the mammalian dive reflex. I thought you might understand, being a diver." The professor turned his attention to Victoria and Chris. "There are several peculiarities of human physiology. One is that we are one of the few species of ape or monkey that have downward-facing nostrils. If you look at chimpanzees or gorillas, they do not. Another related animal that has downward-facing nostrils is the proboscis monkey—and that species spends a lot of its time in water. That particular nose shape is to prevent water entering the lungs. Now, perhaps more persuasive evidence is the mammalian dive reflex, as Mr. Graham pointed out. When a human's face is placed into cold water for longer than a few seconds, there is a drop in heart pulse rate; the blood vessels contract; the blood is directed away from the limbs. It protects the heart, lungs and brain. In addition, the spleen contracts, releasing red blood cells carrying oxygen; and finally, blood fills the vessels in the lungs. Without this adaptation, the human lung would shrink and probably wrap into its own walls at depths greater than one hundred feet. This reflex can be seen in newborn human babies."

The group looked intently at the professor, absorbing his every word—

mentally filing each and every fact.

"Shall I continue?" he asked.

They nodded.

"Okay. So where was I? Oh, yes, the mammalian dive reflex. All this evidence suggests our ancestors lived very close to water and even developed adaptations that would have meant a substantial amount of time in water—deep water. But we know there were several species like our ancestors that existed at around the same time. So what if one or more of them moved completely back into the water? What if their adaptations took them back into the sea? In this environment, evolution quickened and much more so than on land. In the oceans, gravity is less impeding, and nutrients, essential chemicals, and such are all around—an endless supply of water and oxygen, the two things needed for life."

"So what are you saying? That thing in there is a splice off from one of our direct ancestors? Something that evolved under our noses, alongside us?" Victoria sat back in her chair, her arms crossed defiantly.

"Oh no, Ms. McKenzie. K'in is much more than that. I have only told you half the story."

Victoria glanced at Chris and then Kelly. They were fixated on the professor. "Half the story?"

"Okay, I'm going to skip ahead a few millennia now." The professor closed the evolutionary tree and moved it away from him. His eyes scanned the table as he searched for a new folder. "Ah, there it is." He leaned over the table, stretching as far as his body would allow, and touched two fingertips to a folder marked, *Deluge*. He tapped on it twice, and again, a series of documents and images spilled out. He moved each one around, maneuvering them by sliding his fingers across the surface of the glass. He tapped an image of a wall; it was covered with strange inscriptions.

"In almost every ancient culture on this planet, there is the story of a massive flood. Something so huge that it completely destroyed the majority of life on the planet. The Christians will tell you God sent the flood. Of course, they will also tell you an eighty-year-old man built an ark on his own and traveled around the world collecting two of every animal." He chuckled, but saw Victoria was scowling. "Anyway, the flood story exists in other cultures, and in many of the stories, they speak of a man or men that came after the flood, bringing with them knowledge and skills. Legends from Peru to Sumeria and ancient Egypt to India recount the arrival of god-like beings after the great flood—Osiris and Thoth in Egypt, Vishnu in India, Enki and Oannes in Sumeria and Babylonia, Quetzalcoatl and Viracocha in the Americas. Often, these gods, or men, were closely linked with the sea. In Sumeria, these men were depicted as fish-men or serpents of some kind." He tapped an image on the table. It expanded to show the stone carving of a man with a braided beard. He wore a fish head as a hat; its piscine body draped like a cape on his back. Below the waist, the figure wore a garment formed almost entirely of fish scales. In his hand, he carried an unidentifiable, round object.

"This is an Assyrian carving." He pointed at the image. "In ancient Sumeria, there was a legend of a being called Oannes. Stories from this region describe, at length, a being that came from the water and brought reason and culture to the peoples. This being would return to the water at night, because he was amphibious."

The professor had already pulled up several more documents and was flicking them around the table monitor for the group to inspect. Each was in a foreign and ancient language; all they could do was nod.

"Of course, then you have the Americas. The Aztecs, Mayans, and Incas. In the pre-Inca and Inca mythology in the Andes region of South America, they spoke of a god called Viracocha, which roughly translates to 'foam of the sea.' Viracocha was one of the most important deities in the Inca pantheon. He was the creator of all things—the universe, sun, moon, stars, time, and civilization itself. Viracocha was worshipped as god of the sun and of storms. He was said to have appeared after a great flood."

The professor flicked his fingers, and an image on the table spun 180 degrees to face the group. It was a drawing of something that looked like a man. It had a trapezoid-shaped head with thick lines radiating from it. Black eyes stared out. Its body was square with two arms and two legs. The whole image was a pale yellow color.

"This is how the Incas represented Viracocha. It has long been believed he was represented as wearing the sun for a crown, with thunderbolts in his hands, and tears descending from his eyes as rain. Descriptions of him usually include him being a pale-skinned man with a beard. Look closer at the image. What do you see?"

"It looks like that thing in your tank." Kelly's voice trailed off.

"Indeed, Mr. Graham. That sun-crown looks more like the gills on our guest, doesn't it? And the black eyes or perhaps no eyes … And look at the arms and legs—they don't have the same number of digits as you or I, do they?"

Again, they nodded.

"Moreover, if you consider the Ancient Mayan myths, they speak of the deity named Quetzalcoatl, which translates to 'plumed serpent.'"

"I know these stories." Chris tapped on the table. "My grandfather was from Cuzco; he used to tell them when I was a child. These gods were always described as pale-skinned men with beards, not big gills on their heads."

"You are right in one respect, Mr. D'Souza. However, the stories have been tainted by the conquistadors who ravaged those lands. Indeed, an early description of Quetzalcoatl, written in the original Nahuatl, describes the attire of Quetzalcoatl as a green mask, red lips, yellow face, and a beard of feathers. Unfortunately, the meaning of the word 'beard' was abused by Spanish colonizers." The professor paused for effect. "Furthermore, not one cultural representation of Viracocha or Quetzalcoatl in paintings, sculptures, or the like shows them bearded in any sense the Spanish colonizers described."

Chris stared wide-mouthed at the man who was rewriting his heritage. "Huh?"

The professor continued. "So, when you take all of these facts into consideration, don't you think these descriptions from all over the world accurately reflect K'in? Pale skin, plumed, amphibious. You see, we don't think K'in is just an evolutionary curiosity. We think his kind brought civilization and advanced thinking to the human race. Having split off from one of our ancestors and returned to the nurturing ocean, his species may have evolved much faster than ours. Thus, it is reasonable to assume their civilization and social structure would also have evolved faster. The theories of a pan-continental civilization older than our own have existed for a long time, but it was always assumed it was a human civilization. Only through modern technology have we been able to connect the dots."

Victoria glowered again. "And when was all of this supposed to have happened?"

"Well, that depends entirely on your point of view and interpretation of the evidence at hand. Conventional thinking says many of the advanced buildings and communication systems in both the Americas and the Middle East, such as the pyramids, are a mere three to four thousand years old. However, the stories and legends from these regions describe the coming of the 'teaching men' in the very distant past—much more than four thousand years."

Victoria scoffed.

The professor eyed her. "I could bore you with a variety of strange facts and figures about the antiquity of the great pyramids in Egypt or various structures in Latin America, but that would take many, many hours. If you like, you can browse my extensive research, Ms. McKenzie. However, let's continue. Whatever caused the cataclysmic flood, about which every civilization on Earth has written, must have forced K'in's species to abandon the water and rise to the surface. In any case, it is common knowledge many of the human civilizations around the world started building huge, technically complicated monuments and had the ability to calculate complex equations after the flood; these people were essentially farmers, and then, in a relative blink of historical time, became the best engineers the world has ever known." The professor sat down—pleased with himself, with his evidence, and his complete and infallible story of events.

"That all seems a bit circumstantial to me. Evolution at the best of times seems circumstantial to me, but you are proposing one of our 'ancestors' returned to the ocean, developed faster than us, and then decided to come up to say hello and teach us all how to live." Victoria was red-faced and appeared flustered.

Kelly glanced at Chris and then Victoria. He eyed the woman, studying her every facial movement. She was rubbing her crucifix between her thumb and forefinger again.

"I can imagine as a Christian you would find this perplexing, Ms. McKenzie." The professor's voice was calm and flat. A poor attempt to placate Victoria.

"First of all, I'm a Catholic. And you're damn right this upsets me. Another scientist making huge leaps from bones to fact. I tolerate it most of the time, but—"

Kelly interrupted her. "Okay, for argument's sake, let's say you are right. If these guys were so advanced, where are they now? Where are the great underwater cities of the world? Why don't we see these guys? Huh? If he's so smart, how come he ended up in your pond?"

"Mr. Graham, as always, you ask the most complex questions. Questions I, too, asked myself. We cannot assume to know all of the answers, but if you think about it logically, why would an aquatic lifeform utilize or have the need for dwellings made from stone and such? Hmm? You are thinking in terms of the need for shelter from the terrestrial environment, Mr. Graham. You have to think more like a ... fish!" He smiled. "And as for why they are not around, again, it's a good question. One we are unsure how to answer. What we do know is the human species lost its civilized ways and plunged into darkness both socially and technologically for a long period of time. In many of the ancient stories, there was an uprising; the humans with their newfound knowledge felt they knew better. The civilization-bearers were forced back to the sea or killed. Then, it would seem, without them, we lost our way."

"We wiped them out? Then how the hell did you get your hands on fish face in there?"

"And you still haven't answered my question," Victoria said. "This is all circumstantial—pieces of stories that have been translated and retranslated." Victoria rose to her feet, her face contorted and indignant.

"You could say the same thing about the Bible, Ms. McKenzie," the professor replied, one eyebrow raised higher than the other. Victoria sat down. "Genetic testing of K'in has pinpointed when in history his kind and ours would have split off from one another. He may look different, but genetically, he is not that dissimilar to us. And as for your questions, Mr. Graham, this is where my story ends for now and General Lloyd's starts."

The professor swiveled his chair and gestured to the General, who entered the room and paced a little, eyeing his audience. He was deciding whether to tell them or not. He opened his mouth to speak, but an officer briskly entered the room and whispered in the General's ear.

Kelly piped up. "Okay, regardless of all this crap—why us? Why tell us? And what has this got to do with what you asked us to collect down there—"

"Aaaannnd," added Chris, "for that matter, what the hell happened on the boat, who was—"

"I think this is enough for now," objected the General.

"Yes, Benjamin, I agree. It is late. Perhaps we should let our guests rest." The professor had already pushed his chair back and was starting toward the door.

"A good idea. Mr. Tremaine, show our guests to their accommodation." The General left.

CHAPTER SIX

Location: Secret base, somewhere in the Nevada desert, USA

The door was blocked by a large man whose silhouette was blurred. It was dark, but the sky was strange and dreary with fast-moving, white clouds racing from left to right.

Kelly approached the man but still could not focus properly on him. The huge individual with a featureless face held up one hand, protesting against Kelly's request to move through the door. Kelly paid no heed and, with surprisingly little effort, was able to move the man out of the way with a simple push.

The door knob was ice cold as Kelly clasped his warm hand around it and turned. There was a faint clunking sound as the mechanism shifted, allowing the door to be opened. He gave a short but purposeful shove. The door swung slowly open, revealing a small, dark room. In the dimness, he could see shapes—people. They were huddled around a table, a dim candle burning in the middle.

One of the shapes moved—slowly at first but then jerked from one location to another like a stuttering paused image on an old VHS cassette. Caught unaware, the human-shadow was now upon Kelly, centimeters from his face. Izel.

Her face was gray; her black and hollow eyes gazed into Kelly's. She shook her head slowly and stretched out one arm, palm first, in protest, just as the doorman had done. The door slammed in Kelly's face, waking him.

He sat in the dark for a few seconds, listening to his own heartbeat. *Izel. Shit.* Kelly looked at his best friend asleep on the adjacent bunk. They had to get out of this. Kelly had to get them out. The floor was cold as he slipped out from under the covers. He shivered. Picking up his jeans, he slid them on before wrestling with a t-shirt. Finally, he pulled on his boots and crept out the door.

Chris turned over, watched his friend leave and sighed heavily.

Kelly wandered down the corridor, aware the guards were paying him no attention, until the door to the lab stood in front of him, a single guard in the way.

"It's okay," the professor said behind Kelly. "Let him through." He had on the same clothes from earlier. "Can't sleep?"

"No." Kelly shook his head.

"Come inside. I have a little work to do anyway."

The men stepped inside. The professor walked over to the white wall, manipulated the control panel, and whispered a few words. The doors once again slid back, revealing the aquarium. He turned on his heel and gave a weak smile to Kelly before strolling over to a desk.

Kelly cautiously approached the tank. His brawny shape was silhouetted against the huge glass barricade. The room was dimly lit by the faint yellow glow of a few wall-embedded halogen lights. A low hum rumbled in the background. A motor? A pump of some kind? Kelly wasn't sure. Whatever it was, it was soothing. Gentle vibrations from the source of the noise rose through his feet, massaging him. What the hell had happened? What had he got himself into? And Chris—he was meant to look after Chris.

Kelly peered into the dark water of the massive aquarium. Deep in the cold liquid, he watched K'in swirling, circling, and gliding. What the hell was that thing? He had to admit, he'd never seen anything like it. His thoughts turned to Izel. She would have loved this. She loved all living things. Didn't even kill spiders. She would have found fish-face fascinating. A feeble smile broke across his lips but faded almost instantaneously.

He put his hand up to the glass and pressed his palm against it. The creature swam up, slowly but confidently. It reached out one arm and mirrored Kelly's gesture, pressing its own hand against the glass. Kelly didn't move. He wasn't scared, but he was a little dizzy. Lightheaded. Confused. He peeled his fingers away slowly, staring at the creature. It gently swayed its head from side to side and then slipped back into the dark liquid.

"Relaxing, isn't it?" Professor Alexander stood next to Kelly in the golden haze, his hands resting together behind his back. "I can imagine you have had a long couple of days, Mr. Graham." He paused, considering Kelly.

"You know, I come here a lot myself, when I can't sleep. I feel serene when I'm with him."

"Him?" Kelly asked.

"Yes, well, according to anatomy, K'in is a him." The professor chuckled.

"Interesting … what else do you know about Moby Dick in there?"

"You'd be surprised. We've had sixty-five years to study—we know a lot. For instance, you can see his eyes are regressed; while they do retain some sensitivity to light, our experiments revealed the skin is also sensitive to light. This photosensitivity is due to the pigment melanopsin inside specialized cells called melanophores."

"So he sees through his skin?" Kelly was a little repulsed.

"No, no, we think it's a combination of sensory input—the ability to take in his entire environment through a myriad of senses. Take his head for example; it carries sensitive chemo-, mechano-, and electroreceptors. K'in is capable of sensing very low concentrations of organic compounds in the water through the red plumage that sprouts from the back of his head." The professor was more excited now. "The sensory epithelia—sorry—skin of the inner ear is very interesting; it enables K'in to receive sound waves in the water and vibrations from the ground. In addition, if you look carefully, you can see a line running the length of his body. It's called the lateral line. It's a specialized organ that supplements inner ear sensitivity by registering low-frequency nearby water displacements. Also, also …" The professor flapped his arms, waving them about like a schoolgirl recounting a concert she'd been to. "Also, K'in has the ability to register weak electric fields—like a shark! It's amazing."

"Clearly," Kelly said, smirking.

"But that's not the most exciting part." The professor hushed his voice and beckoned Kelly closer. "The most amazing thing is K'in is adaptable. He retains his neotenous state."

"Ne-ot-what? English, Doc."

"Neotenous, think of it as an adult retaining childlike properties in a suspended state of development. It's what makes Chihuahuas and other similar creatures look cute: big eyes, small head, big ears. Anyway, in the case of K'in, it means he can adapt."

"What do you mean, adapt?"

"Adapt! K'in has rudimentary lungs, but when exposed to air for more than a few hours, these lungs begin to mature and allow him to breathe on land. And his eyes … if he's exposed to strong UV light for an extended period, his eyes begin to mature, allowing binocular vision. It is truly astounding."

Kelly stood silently for a while, thinking, absorbing. "Okay, well, I'm no scientist, but our fishy friend here doesn't appear to be able to speak, so how do you reckon he communicated to a bunch of tribal South Americans all those millennia ago?"

"You would have made quite a scientist, Mr. Graham! Well, you have to imagine him as an empty vessel. We cloned him but have no idea how to communicate with him, so he has not had any education from us. And without it from his peers, he relies on instinct. Don't get me wrong, his innate puzzle-solving skills are amazing. We've set various tests, and he passed them extraordinarily quickly."

"So your answer is: you don't know—right?"

"Essentially, no, we don't know. That's why we needed the object you retrieved; we think it might hold the key. In fact, our preliminary analysis has revealed some interesting things about the object already. Would you like to see?"

Kelly laughed. "Well, perhaps it'll bore me to sleep."

The professor spun around and almost skipped over to a nearby desk and monitor. Kelly duly followed. The excited scientist tapped rapidly on the keyboard, rifling through various password encryptions and security codes. As he slowed, Kelly managed to catch a glimpse of various folders that appeared on the black screen: I, II, III. A final folder was labelled differently, but the professor sailed past it.

"So, as you can see here, we have an image of the object you recovered. Now, as I mentioned previously, many of the images from ancient cultures that we believe to represent K'in also have him holding a strange object in his hand. No one has ever been able to identify what it is. Do you remember I mentioned in Egypt some of their ancient gods, such as Thoth, are described in the same fashion as Viracocha and Quetzalcoatl of the Americas? Well, the Egyptians describe the book of Thoth, which possessed great knowledge. We think the object might be linked to this somehow."

"Okay." Kelly nodded. He was more interested than he had thought he would be. It was probably her fault. She had rubbed off on him. Izel would have loved this.

"From our initial scans and chemical analysis, we can see this is some kind of self-contained neural network—highly structured and very complex. In fact, we have yet to find a way to access or read it."

"Hmmm, stuck again. So not that helpful after all, huh?"

"Well, we have only had it a few hours, Mr. Graham; even scientists need time. But I can tell you what happened to the diving equipment."

This grabbed Kelly's attention. "Oh?"

"Yes. Tell me, Mr. Graham, what are most diving tanks made of?"

"That's easy: chrome–moly alloy."

"Correct, a chrome and molybdenum alloy. Most molybdenum compounds have low solubility in water, but the molybdate ion is soluble. Recent theories suggest the release of oxygen by early life was important in converting molybdenum from minerals into a soluble form in the early oceans, where it was used as a catalyst by single-celled organisms. Molybdenum-containing enzymes became the most important catalysts used by some bacteria to break atmospheric molecular nitrogen into atoms, allowing nitrogen fixation. This in turn allowed biologically driven nitrogen fertilization of our oceans and later the development of more complex organisms."

"Jesus, Doc, give me a break. I got like half of that."

"Basically, there was a strong link between early life and molybdenum. Today, we know of at least fifty molybdenum-containing enzymes in bacteria and animals. Indeed, molybdenum is a required element for life in higher organisms."

"Right, okay. Makes a bit more sense. But what's your point, Doc?"

"Well, the object was leaking, correct? Our analysis has shown a massive concentration of enzymes and chemical compounds that would have basically sucked all of the molybdenum from the equipment. It was like the liquid was engineered to do this. Molybdenum may have been very abundant at that time."

"Well, shit, Doc. That'll do it. But I guess until you figure out the password on the blob thing, we are still no closer to knowing if your little historical journey with the fish-man has any credibility."

"We have a massive amount of evidence, Mr. Graham." He clicked the folder closed. "It would take more than a few hours to be able to properly brief you on all of it."

"I take your point, Doc. But since we're here, what's in these files …

like this one?" Kelly smudged his finger on the screen over the icon of a folder: *fusion.*

"That's classified, Mr. Graham."

"Ah, of course. You guys should really label your folders better. Even I can figure out our fishy friend isn't the first clone."

The professor squirmed in discomfort. "That's true. K'in isn't the first clone. He's the fifth. The four before him were ... used for experiments."

"Which would then lead us on to the 'fusion' folder. Military application, I'm assuming?"

The professor's eyes widened and his voice cracked as he began his vehement denial. "Those are archived files. Those kinds of experiments were stopped a long time ago. General Lloyd and I saw to that. Anyway, the experiments didn't work."

"I'm sure, Doc. Anyway, ain't none of my business. I'll be heading to bed now."

"Good night then, Mr. Graham."

"Good night. See ya later, Moby," Kelly called over his shoulder as he sauntered out of the room.

The professor stared at his monitor. *Analysis complete* blinked on the screen. He double-clicked on the window and scanned the results. He sighed and immediately picked up the phone on the desk next to him. It didn't even ring. "Yes, it's confirmed. Yes, I am sure. I understand. We move to the final phase."

Chris lay on his bed, staring at the ceiling, arms behind his head, one leg resting on the other. What a day. It was crazy. And the creature—could he be the source of his grandfather's myth? All myths had some truth to them, a shred of fact that was built upon, changed and embellished. Perhaps. Izel would have loved this; she wouldn't be lying here waiting. She'd be in there, trying to talk to him through Morse code, or sign language, or interpretive dance. He laughed. Yeah, this little journey was wasted on him.

The door swung open, and Kelly marched in. He strode to his metal-framed bed on the opposite wall from Chris and plonked down heavily onto the mattress, the coiled springs groaning and protesting under the weight. Kelly studied the room. It was as expected—bare, white-walled, no windows.

The U.S. military sure knew how to make someone feel at home. After a few minutes, he felt Chris's gaze boring into the side of his head.

"You wanna kiss me or something?"

"You wish, ya big girl! I was thinking, is all. About this whole situation, about K'in, and my grandfather's stories, and us as humans. It's fascinating, don't you think?"

"Fascinating? I guess. Although the nerd with the perma-tan got all giddy in there spouting this, that, and the other."

"Anything interesting?"

"Not really. Some guff about Moby Dick in there being able to adapt and sense lots of things like chemicals and electrical fields, you know, things we can't. Bit like a shark, I guess. But I did find out what happened to the equipment. Turns out that thing we recovered from the sea floor was leaking some pretty powerful shit—enzymes that like moly-alloys."

"Hell, that'd do it." Chris sat up, swung his legs over the edge of the mattress, and faced his friend. A serious pose. "You know, Izel would have loved this stuff."

"Yeah." Kelly sighed. "I had the same thought myself." He looked solemn. Tired.

"I bet she'd even have named it by now."

"Oh, like Snuggles or Fido?"

Chris laughed. "No. C'mon, she had a thing for the old world and languages, remember? She particularly liked Quechua, the language of old Peru."

"Yeah, I know; just trying to avoid making these connections, you know? It's like someone reached into her head and pulled out all the things she loved and then laid them in front of me."

"Yeah, well, I think she'd have called it—"

"Him, apparently."

"Oh, well, called him 'Huahuqui.'"

"Huh?"

"Wow-kay. I think that's how you say it. It means 'supernatural guardian or brother.'"

Kelly admired his friend. He was so much like her. Ever happy, positive, inquisitive. Never letting the situation get her down ... until. He heaved another sigh. She obviously couldn't deal with losing Carmen. Some things you just can't force a smile through. His thoughts were interrupted by a light, hollow knocking on the metallic door to the small quarters. Ms. Nilsson stood there, her slender body barely filling half of the archway.

Chris rolled his eyes to heaven and swung back into a lying position. "Here we go."

"Excuse me?" She threw a scathing glare in Chris's direction.

"He just wonders what you are doing here so late, Ms. Nilsson."

"Freya."

"So …?"

"I'm checking how you are after your accident at sea. Have you had another check up with our site doctor? We have the best physicians here at Paradise Ranch."

"Paradise Ranch?" Chris looked down his torso, awkwardly pushing his neck forward to see the woman. "You know, this place still sounds like a massage parlor with a happy ending."

The men chuckled.

"Indeed. Although, I imagine you would best know it as Area 51."

The men stopped laughing.

CHAPTER SEVEN

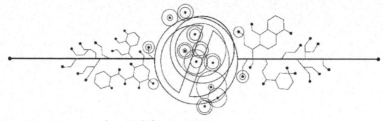

Location: Los Angeles, California, USA

Jerry sat in the Internet café. He'd been there all night and all morning with no word. He was tired and groggy but could not leave—dared not leave. He sipped on his fifth coffee, struggling to stay awake.

There must have been thirty people in the room, all sitting at their desks, yet he felt very alone. The shuffling bodies and smell of coffee were no longer comforting. He listened to a conversation beside him—some guy Skyping with his girlfriend in another country. Driveling on about how much he missed her. Jerry thought of David. God, no one had told David's girlfriend. Did she even know? Had she been round to the apartment? *Jesus.* A man became aware of Jerry staring and tried to hide down behind the small dividing screen. Jerry blushed and turned back to his own desk. In fact, he was feeling a little hot like his skin was burning. *Must be the adrenaline or the lack of sleep.* He pulled off his jacket so the sleeves ended up inside out and shrugged it off over the back of his chair. *That's a little better.*

He wiped the sweat from his brow and stared at the screen in front of him. The *Google* homepage stared back. He thought about how all of this had started with this bloody map project. And David. Poor David. He pulled the USB key from his jacket pocket. Such a small thing—what was it for? What would it show him?

His phone rang. It didn't shock him anymore. He was numb. He fumbled around in his other pocket, struggling to pull the phone out. It popped free. Caller unknown. Jerry knew exactly who it was, or at least, he knew it was the same person who had been calling all night. He slid his finger across the unlock bar.

"Hello."

"Put the key into the computer."

Jerry tried to comply, but was strangely weak.

"Have you done it?"

"Sorry, I'm trying. I just feel a little … dizzy." The room became a little out of focus, and Jerry could feel his stomach begin to knot up.

"You need to concentrate and follow my instructions, I'm sure the people following you will not wait forever for you to leave the café. Eventually, they will come in for you, crowded or not."

"And then what? How will you get me out of here?"

"We will get you out, but first, you need to finish the job. Put the key into the computer."

Jerry complied. Blinking through the sweat running down his face into his eyes, he slid the key into the USB port in the side of the monitor. A small dialogue box appeared on the screen: *enter password*. "Okay, it's asking for a password." Jerry's breathing was labored.

"Okay, it's a 256-bit encryption key. Not hard to crack, but we need you to type it in quickly. So type the following: 721B, E92F, 71D2, FB13, C266, C970, 5E76, D6B5, 8D17, 737F, 4524, 038C, 6E22, 7A2D9A."

Jerry duly typed the numbers but his insides were on fire. The bile rose into his mouth.

"Have you completed it?"

"I'm sorry, I feel so hot and dizzy. What were the last digits?"

"How hot and dizzy?"

"Actually, very."

"When was the last time you came into physical contact with another person?" The voice was cold and hard.

Jerry strained to think. He was sweating profusely. Warm liquid trickled from his nose and down his lip before splashing on the keyboard. Blood. Jerry panicked and wiped his sleeve across his face and then on the keyboard. "Shit."

"What is it?"

"Blood! I'm bleeding from the nose. What's wrong with me?" His voice was hushed but strained.

"It sounds like you've been injected with a form of viral hemorrhagic fever."

"What!"

"Think of it as a weaponized Ebola virus. When did you last come into physical contact with another human?"

"The club, I guess the club. It was crammed in there. What will happen to me?"

"How long ago?"

"I don't know, a few hours? *What will happen to me?*"

"I won't lie to you. You'll die, and you don't have much time."

Jerry whimpered. "Can you help me?"

"Perhaps, Jerry, but I need you to finish the job. Then we can try and help you."

Jerry coughed, spraying blood across the screen and into the face of the young, blonde woman opposite him. She shrieked and reeled backward, falling from her chair, clutching her face. The entire café was suddenly deathly silent. Everyone stared at Jerry, who sat motionless, blood running down his face, the fever overwhelming him.

In slow motion, Jerry saw a nearby man lunge for him, screaming something about a gun. He collided with Jerry, dragging him to the floor. The sound of crying erupted in the room as the punters attempted to stampede out of the tiny establishment.

Jerry clawed at the nearby chair, exhausted and coughing thick red blood over his own face and that of the would-be hero. He desperately looked for his cell phone. Where was it? The man, now smattered with Jerry's blood, panicked. Pushing Jerry off, he scrambled to his feet and fled for the exit.

He was alone now. The sound of the café alarm rang in his ears, but the place was devoid of people. Jerry stood swaying to and fro, trying to blink away his blurry vision—without much success. He caught sight of his phone under a desk and unsteadily bent down to pick it up. Resting on one knee, he put the cell to his face, smearing blood across its screen. "H ... hello?"

"Have you finished entering the key, Jerry?"

"No, no, no. I am bleeding—I'm dying. Everyone ... is gone. I can't ..."

"You must complete the code, Jerry."

"I didn't ... put ... in ... the last set of digits." His breathing was becoming more labored.

"7 ... A ... 2 ... D ... 9 ... A. Have you done it?"

Jerry stared at the keyboard and slowly typed in the command. Each press of a key was heavy and misguided.

"Okay ... done."

53

"Hit return, Jerry."

"O … K." The return key depressed with a clunk. Jerry wearily watched the computer screen rush into life, window after window spewing onto the screen. He could catch glimpses of information, schematics and photos flashing within each box before being covered by a hundred more windows. Whatever he had done, it was spreading—like a virus. Every computer next to him burst into life, projecting the same imagery.

"Thank you, Jerry."

"Okay … please … hel—"

Click.

Jerry listened to the rapidly repeating tone signifying the call had been ended. He stood rocking backward and forward. Crimson tears streamed from his eyes, and his ears filled with the sound of the alarm and approaching police cars, muffled through rushing blood. But it did not matter. No one could help him now.

Location: Paradise Ranch, Nevada, USA

It was nine in the morning, and the room was already full. The others had gathered around the table and were intently listening to the professor, rambling on as always. Freya eyed the group. Chris was a funny, little, Hispanic man, she thought, like some kind of over-fed, chubby lapdog following his master around. What the hell was he wearing? Khaki shorts, jungle boots, and some sort of loud Hawaiian shirt—ugh. Then there was the stuffy British woman, or rather English woman. The snotty bitch had corrected this oh-so-offensive faux pas—Britain was three countries, and she was "distinctly English, not Scottish, Welsh or Irish." Who cared? Stupid little island. Anyway, for all her airs and graces, she still didn't seem to be impressing Kelly. He wasn't falling for it. He was a man's man. He needed a strong woman, not a prissy, whining, little girl. And did she only have one outfit—Jungle Jane? It looked exactly the same as the one she'd been wearing the entire trip. And why was she so twitchy, sitting there shifting in her seat?

Freya turned her attention to Kelly. She stared at him, analyzing his muscular build. He was wearing a relaxed, white t-shirt that just stretched at his biceps and chest, blue jeans, and work boots. He didn't need anything else. His wavy dark hair was brushed backward but fell about his face; it was more like a neat mane than hair, she thought. A pointed grin spread over Freya's lips.

She slid silently behind the chairs and table, gliding effortlessly until reaching the spare seat next to Kelly. Gracefully and in one motion, Freya slithered onto the plastic chair and crossed her willowy legs. The lace top of her silky black stockings peeped from beneath the thigh-length slit in her gray pencil skirt. She didn't look at him but could feel his eyes briefly scan her.

Kelly sighed. Jesus, this girl was not at all subtle. Sure, she was beautiful. She even resembled Izel a little, but that was where the similarity ended. She had no class and no style, though she thought she had both. Shit, he'd stopped listening. What was the General saying?

"The circumstances are such that you are better off here for now, and indeed, it is logical at this juncture we explain a little further the ... political situation you now find yourself in." The General was rambling slightly and darting glances at the professor.

"You have done enough explaining, I think!" Victoria jumped up from her chair. "You are planning something awful with this thing." She glanced at the butt of the gun that was poking from beneath the Shadow Man's jacket, the safety strap of the holster clearly not fastened. In a split second, she made up her mind.

Victoria grabbed the gun from the Shadow Man's holster, then rolled her body off his chest. He tried to grab her, but was much too slow to catch her wiry person. She fell into the corridor and sprinted toward the aquarium room, brandishing the Magnum in one hand.

"No! Victoria!" Kelly leapt across the glass table, feet first, and sprinted out into the hallway. He tumbled into the wall but bounced off it and kept his stride, continuing to chase her down.

The group scrambled to their feet and followed suit, each one filing through the door as fast as they could. Even Ms. Nilsson tottered down the corridor as fast as her high heels and restrictive skirt would allow.

The doors were already open, allowing Victoria to crash into the room. She stopped dead in front of the aquarium and stared furiously into the cold, dark water. The lights were still dim, and she couldn't see it. Where was it?

Slowly, K'in glided up to his window to the dry world. He hovered in front of the glass as if waiting for Victoria to speak. His blind gaze was fixed on her. Victoria lifted the heavy gun in both hands. It was difficult to keep the barrel straight. Her hands were shaking—not with fear but with rage. This abomination had to die. Tears streamed down her cheeks. The gun's hammer eased backward as she squeezed the trigger.

Kelly exploded into the room behind her, followed by the rest of the group and several more armed guards. "Victoria, don't be stupid!"

"I'm not being stupid! This, this thing—it's not right. God would not have favored this thing over us. He loves us. It's not what they say; they are just creating some kind of underwater army. It's all about warfare, as always." She didn't look at Kelly, her words reverberating against the glass tank.

"I wouldn't do that if I were you, Ms. McKenzie." The General stepped calmly next to Victoria, though not in between her and the tank.

"Watch me. You Americans are gung-ho with no regard for life. Traipsing around the world and imposing your ways on everyone! Now this! Blasphemy! Defacing our history, our souls with stories of another species greater than us … creating a false chronology to fit your needs!" She shook with fury and indignation.

"Ms. McKenzie, what do you think the Catholic Church did for centuries? Destroying the peoples of South America? Absorbing pagan—"

"Shut up, Doc. Are you fucking kidding me?" Kelly glared at the professor before turning to his friend. "Victoria, don't do it. Who knows if these guys are right? Huh? Not me. Not you. Hell, it's a theory. And do you think if you take out fish-face they won't make another? This isn't going to achieve anything."

Victoria paused; her pained expression eased as if his words had managed to penetrate her cloak of anger. "But … it's not right. If he is what they say, my life, my whole life, my family's life was a lie."

She raised the gun again, aimed, then pulled the trigger.

CHAPTER EIGHT

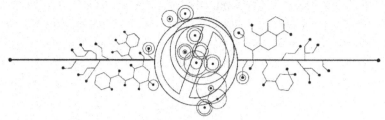

Location: Paradise Ranch, Nevada, USA

Everything shook as a violent sound wave ripped through the room, followed by chunks of exploding brickwork. The desks shuddered, spilling computer screens and stationery to the floor. A single fissure tore a serrated line vertically through the aquarium glass, spraying water into the room from the corners of the jagged fracture.

Victoria fell backward, flailing for something to grab. She had squeezed the trigger of the Magnum, releasing a single shot into the air. It ricocheted off the ceiling and pinged around the laboratory several times. Victoria slammed into the floor, elbows first in an attempt to cushion the fall but screamed in pain as her arm bones splintered.

A guard careened into the room, dodging falling pieces of debris, ducking and diving his way to the General who was stumbling toward the communications system next to the door.

"Sir, we're under attack! They've sent in a Special Forces team. Satellite imagery has identified several attack subs off the western seaboard. We received an encoded message to return the object and the creature."

The General yelled his orders. "Get the emergency transportation ready—I want K'in out of here, now!"

"Yes, sir." The soldier's voice was drowned out as another explosion cleaved the room in two.

Mortar and glass blasted from the aquarium, carried on a swell of salt water. It rushed over the debris and people in a destructive wave, washing everything toward the opposite end of the laboratory. K'in spilled out over the broken window pane and flopped onto the tiled floor. His body twitched as his bare skin was enveloped by the barren atmosphere. Harsh air filled his neotenous lungs, scorching the alveoli with oxygen, making K'in gasp.

"Oh God, K'in!" The professor slipped and slid, trying to reach him. "Mr. Graham, help me!"

Kelly was drenched. His white t-shirt was now see-through and stained pink with diluted blood. He clutched Chris's limp body to his chest, rocking him back and forth like a small child.

Chris looked up at his friend, his brother, his protector. "Shit. And I bet you thought she couldn't shoot." He gargled a bloody chuckle, then winced in pain as crimson liquid oozed from a round hole in his shirt pocket.

Kelly stifled the lump in his throat. "Yeah, who'd have thought?"

"Mr. Graham, please! We have to move K'in!" The professor had managed to crawl over the slippery tiles to K'in's wilted form. He was uselessly tugging at the white, mucus-covered limbs in an attempt to move the creature.

"Fuck your fish, Doc!" he screamed in the professor's direction. "Chris. Chris, you little shit, don't you fucking give up on me."

"Kelly, you can't protect me forever. I was never your responsibility." He breathed deeply, grimacing in anguish. "I'm finished here, esé ... time to see Izel again."

"Fuck you."

"Fuck you right back."

They stared at each other, a forced smirk on both their faces.

"Now, go get that fish and these people out of here. You know it's what Izel would have done."

Kelly shook his head. "Help the military?"

"Help someone who's helpless."

Kelly raised his head to see the professor, and now the General, hoisting K'in into the air. Several guards were rushing around, splashing through the water. Mr. Tremaine, his dark suit wet and clinging to his massive body, had picked up an unconscious Victoria and slung her over one shoulder. Ms. Nilsson, now shoeless, was furiously shouting orders into a cell phone. Kelly turned his gaze back to Chris. He was gone.

He stared blankly at Chris's still warm corpse. His heart slowed. The din around him melted into white noise. The water appeared to ripple in slow motion around Chris's limbs. Kelly closed his eyes and immersed himself in the darkness behind tear-filled eyelids. Chris was gone.

"Mr. Graham! This place is coming down—we have to move now!"

The world spun. Kelly's stomach was in knots as he tried to focus on the General. He clambered to his feet, leaving Chris in a cold mix of water and blood, and stumbled toward the open door. Debris flew across the room, missing Kelly's head by millimeters, but he paid no attention. Without blinking, he staggered onward and out through the door into the corridor.

"Move it!" The General had slung K'in over his shoulder and bolted past Kelly down the corridor. "Freya, move him!"

Freya placed a hand gently on Kelly's shoulder. "C'mon. We have to go, Kelly." It was the first time she had used his first name. Her voice was soft and gentle.

He focused on her weak smile, a vain effort at encouragement. She pointed down the corridor toward the rapidly disappearing forms of the General and K'in. Kelly nodded blankly and followed after them.

The complex shook under the repeated explosions. Smoke and dust filled the narrow corridors, obscuring all sense of direction. The General led the way through the maze, weaving left and right. There was no logic to his movements just a strong sense of instinct like a rat in a labyrinth. They followed him as best they could, their eyes stinging with particles of soot and stone, straining for a glimpse of his boots beneath the haze. He stopped abruptly, causing them to bunch up behind him. The General stepped slowly backward toward Mr. Tremaine before signaling him to press against the corridor wall.

The General unholstered his Beretta with his left hand, being careful not to let K'in slip from his right shoulder. He pointed the firearm toward the floor in front of him and walked slowly to the right corner of the T-junction. He edged forward to glimpse down the right hand passageway. There was something in the smoke—a figure, dressed in black, his head covered in a balaclava. Tremaine tapped the General on the shoulder and communicated through his eyes: what was it? The General shook his head and pointed toward the left corridor, indicating to move quietly down the stairs. The Shadow Man turned to the rest of the group and gestured for them to follow him.

They descended a seemingly endless, circular stairway. The motion made Kelly feel dizzy, and he was about to vomit when the General stopped suddenly. They had reached the bottom. Benjamin ran to the huge door in front of him and typed a code into an embedded panel. A familiar, metallic sound, reverberated around Kelly as the door slid open. Benjamin beckoned them inside. "Move, now."

Kelly stepped in and was immediately awed by the vehicle before him. He gawked at the massive, semi-articulated truck sitting brusquely in the middle of the room. The cab and the trailer gleamed with metallic black paint. A distinctive, shark-nosed chrome grill protruded from the front of the truck above a deep chrome front bumper that protected Harley-Davidson-like headlights. Two huge fuel tanks and two massive chrome stacks with aggressive bologna cut tips were set at the back of the truck, making it appear sleek. The wheels were equally huge, almost two feet across and forged from machined aluminum. The trailer, an elliptical tube sporting six huge wheels placed at the rear, must have been twenty feet long.

"Mr. Graham, help me get him in the trailer."

Kelly's focus was drawn from the machine as the General ran past, K'in flouncing around on his back. He paused for a few seconds, as if the instruction hadn't penetrated his skull.

"Now, Mr. Graham!"

Kelly jolted into action and sprinted after the General. He clambered up the chrome ladder onto the top of the trailer. He found a circular manhole in the top and a full QWERTY keypad embedded in its surface.

"Type 6782, lowercase *a*, uppercase Z, 4, ampersand, 9, and punch enter," called the General.

Kelly tapped in the code. The lid popped open as if it were under pressure. By this time, the General had effortlessly scaled the ladder and was at Kelly's side. The General pulled back the lid until it clanged against the hull of the trailer. Kelly peered inside. A faint, blue haze emanated from within, obscuring the true color of the interior. The floor of the trailer, molded seamlessly into the walls, had two levels—one a few feet higher than the other and bridged by another molded slope.

K'in slipped off the General's back through the manhole and plopped into the water below. The creature looked up through the opening, his neotenous eyes already beginning to change—to develop. They bored into Kelly's eyes, sending a shiver through his whole body. Transfixed, Kelly wanted to look away, but he couldn't.

"Careful with him!" The professor waved his arms in desperation.

"Stop whining and get in the goddamn truck! Mr. Graham, close that lid. Tremaine, start the truck."

"Yes, sir!" The Shadow Man slung the driver's side door open and leapt into the cabin. He stepped into the sleeper section and threw Victoria onto the pull down bed before climbing back into the perforated leather driver's seat. A bizarre instrument cluster of hooded gauges with turned aluminum faces in argent-colored housing stared back at him.

"Can you drive this thing?" Ms. Nilsson had climbed into the passenger seat beside him.

"If it's got wheels, I can drive it—just need to find the fucking key."

"It's voice activated!" bellowed the General from halfway down the trailer ladder. "Truck, initiate! Authorization: FEMA, dash, 751, slash omega. Password: Viracocha!" The truck growled into life, shaking the cabin and trailer. "Let's move! Get the professor in the truck!"

Ms. Nilsson leaned out of the cabin. The Professor grabbed at her sleeve and hoisted himself up inside, stepping behind her seat and into the sleeper section with the unconscious Victoria.

"Go, Mr. Graham!" the General ordered.

Kelly stepped onto the external stair and grabbed Ms. Nilsson's arm. His entire weight suddenly pulled at her jacket as he screamed and fell to the floor. Warm blood spattered Ms. Nilsson's face.

The General leapt on to Kelly's crumpled body, making a human shield, pulled out his Beretta and fired blindly. Ms. Nilsson and Tremaine leaned out of the truck and sprayed the garage stairwell with bullets. The ammunition tore through the black clothing of the gunman, puncturing his chest and limbs. The sheer force of the onslaught kept the man in mid-air until the ceasefire allowed his broken body to tumble down the spiral staircase.

"He won't be alone—move it!" The General clambered to his feet. Blood pooled around Kelly's shoulder and torso.

"Freya, triage, now!"

"Yes, sir!"

The General hoisted Kelly's limp body from the floor and into Ms. Nilsson's waiting arms. She strained under his weight. Kelly groaned in protest. With the General's help, she quickly dragged Kelly into the sleeper section and laid him awkwardly on the bed beside Victoria.

"Go, go, go!" The General slammed the passenger door behind him.

The truck screeched into first gear as the Shadow Man pumped the clutch and shifted the stick. The truck kangarooed forward, throwing everyone against the walls and ceiling. K'in sloshed around inside the trailer.

"Tremaine, make this fucking thing move!"

"Yes, sir! Move, you piece of shit!" Tremaine slammed his foot on the accelerator, powering the massive machine onward. It picked up speed, its weight adding to the momentum. Second, third, fourth. The Shadow Man shifted up the gears, revving the engine toward its breaking point before making the change.

The truck gunned through a small opening at the end of the underground garage and into a long, dark tunnel with roughly hewn rock walls. There was barely enough room for the vehicle to fit. Tremaine feared the wing mirrors would be torn off by a protruding stone, and the small hanging light bulbs that were every three hundred feet would smash into the windshield. He twitched and ducked every time something whipped by his side window. *Christ, when does this tunnel end?* Were they behind him? Had they made it into the tunnel? He didn't think so, but it was hard to see.

"Keep going, Tremaine," the General ordered. "The tunnel blast doors will shut when we pass through, and those bastards won't be getting out any time soon." The General hung in the doorway to the sleeper section, rocking from side to side. "Just keep going. When we get through, you'll come out onto a dirt road. Follow it to the highway, then make for Vegas."

"Yes, sir." Tremaine fixed his eyes on the dark tunnel, focusing on each dim light bulb as it sailed slowly toward him and then shot past at the last second.

Kelly groaned, squirming on the floor. Blood was streaming from his open shoulder. Ms. Nilsson tried to hold him still and examine his gunshot wound.

"Kelly!" she yelled. "You need to stay still. I think the bullet is still lodged, and I need to retrieve it and cauterize the wound. If I don't do this, you'll die from blood loss. Do you understand me?"

Her voice was stern and commanding. He stopped squirming and nodded.

"Is he going to be all right?" the professor asked.

"I don't know. He's losing a lot of blood. I'll see what I can do, but he needs a hospital—as does she." Ms. Nilsson nodded toward the slumped body of Victoria. "I think she smashed her elbows hard. There might be bone damage. Nothing I can do for that."

"Morphine?"

"Maybe, but I need that to remove his bullet. I doubt there will be enough for both."

"Give it to her." Kelly coughed and winced as he tried to prop himself up. His face was pale and sweaty. "Give it to her. She'll need it. Just dig this thing outta my shoulder and I'll be fine."

"I don't think …" started Freya.

"He's right. Do it. Triage, Freya. He'll pass out, but he'll be fine." The General's tone was soft.

"You don't know that."

"One way to find out, Freya." Kelly forced a weak smile. "Let's do this."

"Okay." Freya nodded. She opened the cabinet above his head. The internal fluorescent light flickered on as the doors parted. She scanned the contents. Various first aid items lined the inside—gauze, tape, syringes, needles. There it was—morphine. She grabbed the vial of clear liquid, a syringe, and a needle. Having ripped off the sterile wrapping, she attached the needle to the syringe, pierced the aluminum lid of the vial, and then turned the precariously formed vial–syringe construction upside down. Freya pulled the plunger, sucking liquid into the syringe. The vial gurgled empty. She threw it to one side and pressed the plunger of the syringe gently, forcing liquid into the needle. She grabbed Victoria's arm, pierced her clammy skin, and pressed the clear liquid into her flesh.

Victoria groaned but didn't wake.

"Done. Now you."

"Okay, let's get this over with."

Freya tugged at Kelly's leather belt.

Kelly coughed a laugh. "Thinking of distracting me?"

"No." Freya continued to remove his belt while answering.

"You're going to need something to bite down on." She tugged hard, releasing the belt from under him, and placed it in Kelly's mouth. "Bite. Hard."

Freya pushed a pair of steel tweezers into the open wound. Kelly let out a muffled scream and then lost consciousness.

CHAPTER NINE

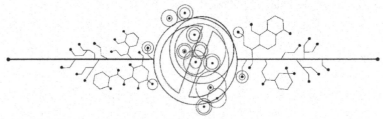

Location: Escape truck, Nevada Desert, USA

Dark, cold, afraid. Raw emotion and adrenaline coursed through Kelly, keeping him alert. He couldn't say he was straining to see or hear, but it didn't feel like his eyes or ears were functioning. It was like his environment was trying to speak with him, pouring information through his pores into his being.

He sensed others around him, moving slowly. Strange noises came from the flapping holes in their faces, and the constant babel gave him a headache.

The dim, blue haze barely lit the smooth walls. Water sloshed around his head, swirling, forming miniature eddies and whirlpools. Kelly lifted his head from the water and looked down at the blue-black surface, a rippling mirror. K'in's reflection stared back at him.

Kelly woke with a start as the truck lurched, swerving around an animal in the road.

"Sorry!" called Tremaine.

"You okay?" Ms. Nilsson sat next to Kelly, one hand on his bandaged shoulder.

Kelly groaned, straining to lift himself onto his elbows without success. "What happened?"

"You passed out as I was removing the bullet," recalled Ms. Nilsson. "It's been an hour, but we are not far from Las Vegas. You have been twitching and making strange noises in your sleep. Were you dreaming?"

"I guess so, but …"

"Not a normal dream for you?" Victoria's voice was calm and quiet, though a little slurred under the influence of the morphine. She was propped up against a wall and still sitting on the bed. Both arms were crossed and held close to her chest as if she lay in a coffin. A single sling supported both her broken elbows. She looked pale and clammy.

"No, not really." Kelly looked confused and stared off into the distance.

Freya looked at him and, for the first time, saw real emotion in his face. No quick quip or sarcastic comment—just the pain of losing someone so close. A pain she knew well and had her own way of hiding. She thought about touching his face in reassurance but shook her head. Focus. Being soft was not going to help here.

"Where's the General?" Kelly asked. "I have to speak with him."

"Up front with Tremaine," Freya replied.

Tremaine's eyes were fixed on the road as he gripped the steering wheel, his knuckles pale. Miles and miles of desert lay before him with little civilization nearby. The roar of the engine and the giant tires tearing up the dirt track were muted by the thick walls and glass of the cabin. It made Kelly feel safer.

The General was in the passenger seat, silent, staring out of the window, lost in thought. He didn't even notice Kelly had entered the cabin from the rear and stood behind him, both hands on the back of the seat—partly for a menacing effect and partly because he was too weak to stand on his own.

"My best friend just died in there, so I think you ought to do some fucking explaining, don't you? Who the fuck would attack Area 51 and risk a war with the U.S. Government?"

There was a lasting silence. An eternity with only the drone of the road. But Kelly didn't push the General. He knew the answer was coming.

Without turning from the window, the General said, "In 1946, Chinese explorers found a frozen corpse in the northern part of the Asian continent. Our intelligence at the time told us it was not human but humanoid. The People's Republic of China wasn't founded until 1949. Prior to that, it was a country ravaged by a century of foreign invasion and civil wars. So it was easy to go in and take what we wanted."

"You just waltzed into China and took it?"

"We were the most powerful nation in the world, Mr. Graham. We thought we could do whatever we wanted. Anyway, the Chinese had already thawed it out by the time we got there. After we acquired it, our operatives constructed a thermal insulating device to try and keep it cool. We put it in an aircraft and transported it back to the U.S. On the way back, we had a technical problem with the aircraft, and it went down in a backwater town."

"Wait. Backwater town? Are you talking about Roswell? You gotta be shittin' me. This just gets better and better." Kelly laughed out loud.

"Yes, Mr. Graham. The debris and the supposed alien body found at Roswell was from that transport."

"And rather than scare the human population with the knowledge of an earthly creature more advanced than we are, you fueled alien stories." Kelly already knew the story before it was told.

"Indeed, Mr. Graham. Think about it. What would be scarier to the people of that time: something home-grown that could hurt them or something from millions of miles away that probably wouldn't come here again? Plus, aliens are less believable. Urban myth was easier to deal with. We did what was needed. Given our little piece of *extraction* from China, it wasn't wise to tell the truth."

The General paused, sorting out the facts in his head. He wanted to be sure he told the story accurately and in order.

"We had been studying the creature's anatomy, biochemistry, etcetera. However, a frozen corpse is still a frozen corpse. We needed a live specimen, and this wasn't possible until recently. Modern technology has afforded us the possibility through cloning. K'in is a clone of the original body found by the Chinese."

"Okay, but it's sixty-five years later. Why the hell would the Chinese Government wait until now to attack you?" Kelly asked.

"I'll get to that. When we realized the creature was from Earth and not an alien, it scared everyone. We were a paranoid nation anyway, but the thought that the specimen or another like it would fall into international hands worried us. As a result of this, and the existing political issues of the time, President Truman signed the National Security Act of 1947. He reorganized military forces by merging the Department of War and the Department of the Navy into the National Military Establishment and created the U.S. Air Force. The act also created the CIA and the National Security Council, and our *organization*. We have been working for the last sixty-five years on finding out everything we can about K'in." The General took a deep breath.

"Wait, and just who are you?"

"This is not a Hollywood movie, Mr. Graham. Having a name would simply make us traceable. After President Truman, we were black boxed. No one knew we existed. Our research at Area 51 was hidden even from the normal military personnel on the base. Now, shall I continue? Three weeks ago, we heard from our intelligence operatives in China that we had not recovered everything from them in 1946. It turned out there was also an object in the ice with the body. The Chinese have been studying it for years. This was considered a threat to national security. We couldn't tell the Chinese we knew they had it, or they would know what happened in 1946. So, we planned another *extraction*."

"That's what we were doing out there? You were stealing the object, the thing they had?"

"Not quite. We had already extracted it. The ship you were on was theirs. They were transporting the object. A Special Forces crew had gone in and … *dispatched* everyone on board. We were meant to rig it to look like an accident at sea. However, during the incursion, we lost the package overboard. We tried retrieving it but, as a result, lost many good men. That's when your services were acquired."

"Are you fucking insane? You're telling me I just helped the CIA, or NSA or whatever, steal something really fucking important from the goddamn Chinese? That's why they attacked us? That's why Chris is dead? You fuck!"

"There was a time, Mr. Graham, when I would have defended my country's actions. But I'm a tired, old man. I carry dozens of medals on my chest, honoring me for my bravery, but they just serve as reminders of how I helped one huge, greedy nation destroy much smaller, weaker ones—all in the name of the American dream." He sighed. "I feared going into China this time to get the object. If the professor was right, China was in possession of an incredibly powerful *thing*. But equally, I couldn't bear my own government having it either. We had to find a way to end the stalemate."

"You and the professor, working together on this one? Seems unlikely."

"Oh no, it is quite likely. The professor and I had worked together for many years and watched as our government played God and meddled with life. When you're young, you follow orders—do as you're told. It's what you're trained to do. But when you reach our level, you are the one giving the orders and taking the responsibility. It's a different ballgame. The professor and I decided we would just even the score if necessary." The General turned back to the window and stared outward.

"What did you do?" Kelly asked.

"We gave the information to the people," the professor said. He was standing in the sleeper doorway, looking at the floor. Kelly had no idea how long he'd been there.

"What do you mean, you gave the information to the people?"

"Humans are arrogant. We believe we are the superior organisms on this planet. We believe this so much that we are arrogant enough to state God, if he exists, made us in his own image, because of course, what other image would he have? We corrected this arrogance a few hours ago." The professor had now fixed his gaze on the General.

"Stop being fucking cryptic! What did you assholes do?"

"If the object turned out to be what we thought it was, then neither government should have sole possession of it. Instead, it was time for humans to take a step into enlightenment. So, we fed satellite information of our incursion in the South China Sea to a couple of average computer programmers—men whose jobs were to deal with global mapping projects. A couple of innocuous but educated men who would be intrigued enough to investigate a little further without dismissing it. Once this had been done, we were to provide the same men with all of our information on K'in and his species—secret files." The professor paused.

"Why didn't you just do it yourselves? Why involve random people?"

"Because they are harder to track. Our enemies will have files on all of our operatives and watch our movements much more closely. Using civilians, particularly ones who don't know what they are doing, is more covert. Plus, if they are captured, they cannot be tortured for any more information—they have none. What's more, we didn't want our own government knowing what we were doing."

"But this civilian anonymity didn't go to plan, did it?" Kelly asked.

"No, it didn't go according to plan, did it, Benjamin?" continued the professor. "The Chinese must have found out the men had the visuals of the incursion. One of the men was killed in his home. The other died in an Internet café in Los Angeles. It seems the Chinese exposed the latter to a weaponized hemorrhagic fever virus—similar to Ebola. But he still managed to upload the files we gave him to the Internet, using a computer virus to spread the data through every multimedia channel and social network on the web. Now everyone knows."

Kelly's eyes widened. His heart raced as his mind sifting rapidly through this new information. "Do you realize what you have done?"

"Of course," the professor replied.

"You dicks. Yo, André, turn on the radio!" yelled Kelly.

"What?" Tremaine looked confused and irritated that he had to take his eyes from the road. "We are coming up to Vegas."

"For fuck sake, I'll do it!" Kelly leaned between the seats and flicked on the radio.

> *"The situation appears to be the same in almost every major city across the state. Groups of religious vigilantes are destroying universities, educational centers, and government buildings. Hundreds of angry mobs are tearing through the city, trying to purify their land.*
>
> *"Our top story again: secret government files have been leaked onto the Internet, apparently proving the existence of another life form on Earth that not only is more intelligent than us but may have even given us the intelligence we now have. At this point, the U.S. Government, NATO, and the Vatican have declined to comment other than to say they are reviewing the evidence."*

Kelly flicked the station.

> *"In other news, a hospital in downtown L.A. is struggling to contain a mysterious illness sweeping through the area. People are flooding into emergency rooms with blood pouring from their nose and eyes."*

Kelly switched off the radio. "You stupid, old, dumbass, short-sighted, fuckwits!" His anger boiled over. "What did you expect, huh? You've just undone two thousand years of fucking human history! You've simultaneously pissed off every religious nut as well as every gun-wielding, conspiracy-theory junkie and UFO, anal-probe-obsessed idiots on the planet. Not to mention, some kind of flesh-eating virus has been let loose. I mean, if they wanted to stop the release of information, why not shoot him?"

"Yes, they could have shot him. They shot his friend. But I think the

Chinese are beyond covert ops now, don't you? They just attacked us on our own soil. Releasing a virus is just another attack. They don't care about stopping the info now. They care about obtaining K'in, the power, and destroying the only nation that stands in their way." The General spoke in a flat tone. "As for K'in and the information we released, it's about time humanity was enlightened. Coincidentally, the timing of everything is quite serendipitous. It's 2012." The professor looked smugly at Kelly.

"Are you talking about end of the world stuff? You fucking nut job!" Kelly was shaking with rage.

"Actually, that's a misconception. The Mayan 2012 prediction is not one of Armageddon but the ending of one era and the birth of a new one. According to the Mayans, there have been five periods, or suns, in history. Right now, we are in the fifth sun, which is predicted to end in this year. And the children of the fifth sun will be no more."

"You're both fucking crazy! This doesn't make any sense! Why bother getting fish-face out of the lab? Why not let him die in the blast?"

"K'in may be our only salvation. Our plan was to return him to a place where belief in his kind still exists, where they would treat him like a god and once again learn from him. With the rest of the world at war, destroying each other, K'in would be able to lift our race into the light. We hadn't planned on the chaos until we had moved K'in and the object." The professor spoke evenly.

"There is no way our government is party to this—you two have to be operating off the grid!" Freya was standing behind the professor. She had been listening the whole time, silently observing.

"That is true," the General replied. "Our operation was so black-boxed that over the last sixty-five years we have become separated from the normal military hierarchy. We have seen too much. We had to take matters into our own hands.

"General... Benjamin," Freya said. "I *trusted* you. You told us we were protecting America from the Chinese." The words from her mouth were barely audible as the General's treachery sank deep into her heart.

"No wonder you didn't give a shit about showing us everything! You were going to expose it to the world anyway."

"Well, only once we confirmed what the object was and what it does. It is very import—" The professor was cut off mid-sentence.

"I couldn't give a tiny rat's ass! So now what, geniuses? Huh? Where the fuck do we go now? Is that fucking illness to do with you, too?"

"The Chinese have been experimenting with weaponized Ebola-type viruses for a while. We didn't think they would use them, but it seems our incursion has triggered a war. It's gloves off for them. As for us, we were to rendezvous with a chopper on the way to Vegas and get airlifted right off the dirt road, but they're late, and we have moved closer to the city than I wanted—"

The air around the group suddenly rose in temperature by ten degrees—the atmosphere became thick and hot. The General's eyes widened as his instinct warned him of the impending danger, but his lips were too slow to make a sound in time.

The missile slammed into the side of the truck, exploding into a million fragments. A mixture of molten metal, scorching air, and unbridled energy distorted the left side of the cabin, ripping through the driver's door. Tremaine screamed as shards of glass and slivers of metal sliced through his face and body. The cabin was pushed across the dirt track, lifted as if it were weightless. The group was tossed to the right side toward the sleeper section as the truck crashed onto its side and skidded through the dust. Then, silence.

CHAPTER TEN

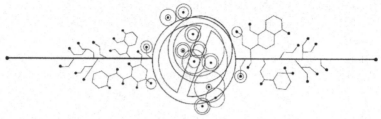

Location: Truck wreckage, Nevada Desert, USA

Freya picked herself up from the ground. Every muscle in her body ached, and her head was ringing. The burning truck lay twenty feet from her, but the heat was still searing. She held her forearm to her head to shield her blackened face from the scorching flames. What had happened? Where was the rest of the team? Her clothes were torn and burnt but intact for the most part.

Her vision blurred through a mixture of concussion, smoke, and tears as she feebly scanned the horizon. Freya's gaze fell on the broken frame of the General. Limping over to him, she dropped to her knees and grabbed him by his disheveled tunic. He groaned as she pulled him from a face-down position to face-up, his head lolling around like a newborn child's. He didn't look as strong or intimidating now. He looked old, tired—worn out.

"Benjamin ..."

The General pried his eyes open. "Freya, K'in—what happened to K'in?"

Freya scanned the horizon again. "I don't know. I can't see him or the others."

"Freya, you have to finish this." He coughed. "We have to end the cycle."

"And do what, Benjamin? What am I supposed to do?" She welled up, her voice cracking. "I'm not saving Americans from the Chinese anymore."

"No, you are saving the human race from itself. The world will tear itself apart. Nations will fight amongst themselves. The virus will kill many. You have to hide K'in." He wheezed painfully. "Take this." The General reached inside a pocket and pulled out a crumpled piece of paper. "Take K'in to these coordinates. These are not on any file or computer system. Only the professor and I know the location. You must hide K'in there. You

72

will be safe, too."

"But I don't even know where K'in is!"

"The Ch … Chinese have him." The professor's voice was weak.

Freya turned her head to see him lying flopped in Tremaine's arms. The Shadow Man stood tall and strong against a backdrop of fire and molten metal, his face streaked with blood and ash. But his eyes were steeled and bright.

"I saw them take him and Kelly."

"And the object?" the General asked, his voice weak.

"Gone. I had the object with me. It was smashed—destroyed. But that doesn't mean …" The professor hacked and rasped.

"Kelly—"

Freya was interrupted by the deafening sound of a landing helicopter. The rotors tore through the smoke-laden air, causing swirls of gray cinders to dance around the burning truck. The Chinook landed with an unceremonious thud. Tremaine squinted to protect his eyes from the flying grit. Freya's hair blew wildly about her face.

A pilot jumped down from the cockpit and ran toward the group. "I'm Captain Wiezorek," he shouted over the din. "We couldn't get here sooner."

Freya looked at the General for approval of this newcomer. He nodded weakly.

"An unidentified chopper just screamed outta here, probably quite a few miles away by now, but can't have gone far. It was only a short range chopper."

"Thank you, Captain. Freya, go—finish it." The General raised a charred arm and pointed at the attack helicopter.

Still on her knees, Freya looked at the General, then back at the helicopter, and then at Tremaine.

"Victoria?" she asked, hopefully.

The Shadow Man shook his head.

"Leave us here, me and Benjamin. We'll just slow you down." The professor tried to climb down out of Tremaine's arms.

"I will stay here with them and radio for backup. You get in the chopper. A unit is inside. They can support you. If you want to follow that chopper, you are going to have to do it now." The pilot hovered over the General, unsure if he was to stay or leave.

Freya glanced once more at the General. "Okay, c'mon." She sprang to her feet, a new sense of purpose and direction coursing through her body. "Tremaine, you're with me. Let's get that fucking chopper."

The Shadow Man's eyes widened in surprise. It was the first time he had ever heard her curse.

"Benjamin, I'll come back for you. I promise." Freya placed a hand on his shoulder.

The General nodded weakly and waved his blackened hand toward the helicopter, urging her on.

Freya and Tremaine stormed toward the Chinook and climbed into the cargo hold through the side door. A team of at least ten soldiers sat in two lines either side of the hold area, staring at them. Each was dressed in black camouflage gear and sported integrated ballistic communications headgear. Most carried an M4A1 assault rifle or HK MP5 submachine gun.

"Okay, boys. Let's do this." Freya sat down next to one of the soldiers and strapped in. "Tremaine, tell the pilot that we got a chopper to catch."

Tremaine nodded and disappeared into the cockpit.

The Chinook rose from the dirt road, whisking dust, ash, and grit into the air. Freya stared through the side door, watching the General and professor slowly get smaller and smaller. A soldier slid the door shut. They were on their way.

The desert sands slipped by. Endless golden dunes rippled and waved like an eerie ocean beneath them. Random bushes dotted the land but seemed to join together to form one long green streak as the Chinook gunned along. The sun was dipping down over the horizon, a blaze of orange and red bleeding outward into the fading blue sky like a paint drop on a watercolor canvas.

The noise of the rotors had become more of a hum now and was almost comforting to Freya. Staring out the window, it was difficult to concentrate on the job at hand. Too much was running through her head.

She had been thirteen when her parents died. Her godfather had taken her in. It was probably inevitable that she'd gone into the military, given his position. Benjamin had loved her, encouraged her, and kept her close. When she was fifteen, she'd been mugged by two older boys. They'd taken her purse and pushed her to the ground, scraping her knees. Tear-filled, she'd told

Benjamin all about it as he dabbed iodine onto her wounds. That evening, he showed her how to break someone's little finger and punch them in the solar plexus—an incapacitating move. She loved it. From that point on, no one touched her again.

Even through military school, when she'd been somewhat bullied by the male recruits, Benjamin had watched out for her—told her she shouldn't stop being a woman just to fit in or lie low. Her strong personality would be an asset and get her noticed—get her ahead. Yes, Benjamin had never steered her wrong—until now. General Benjamin Lloyd. Why had he lied? Why had he kept things from her all this time? It had been eighteen years of lies. How had she been so blind? She shook her head. What difference did it make now? Everything was in chaos. Right now she had to save Kelly and K'in. That was her mission. *Focus. Stay focused.*

"Where are we going?" Tremaine's question disrupted Freya's train of thought. He sat opposite her amongst two SEALs who were busying themselves with firearm maintenance.

"Hawthorne base, Nevada," Freya replied.

Tremaine frowned. "But infrared said their chopper went out to sea—why are we not going to San Diego naval base?"

"Their short-range chopper was headed to something out there—a ship or submarine. Since we are not picking up any ships, we have to assume it's a stealth sub."

He shook his head. That didn't make sense. "Hawthorne is in the middle of the desert—why are we wasting time going there?"

"We can't mount a rescue mission from this chopper, Tremaine. And what we need isn't in San Diego."

"But it's in the desert?"

"Exactly."

The Chinook banked hard left and swooped downward before coming to a near-dead stop just above a concrete landing pad.

"We're here," Freya said.

Freya and Tremaine heaved back the side door and jumped down onto the tarmac. The soldiers followed suit, spreading out into formation to provide a protective perimeter. As one unit, they moved slowly toward the bunker ahead of them. Each soldier watched his line and the soldier's line next to him.

Tremaine swiveled his head back and forth, wondering if a missile would scream out of nowhere and hit him—again.

"Hawthorne makes and tests munitions. I don't get it," he protested.

She turned on her heel to face him. "Hawthorne does test munitions. You are correct. But it also is a place that develops and tests the most advanced stealth attack submarines in the world."

"What? How? In the desert?"

"You don't have clearance to know about this place but, given the situation we are in, protocol is hardly what we are concerned with right now."

She turned back and kept on walking, talking the whole time. Tremaine followed, listening intently. The soldiers continued their vigil.

"The continental shelf from the west coast of the U.S. disappears under California; it's like the state is floating on water. This shelf extends backward and meets a series of large tunnels and channels. Nearby Walker Lake helps to maintain the water table here, too. Hawthorne was built right over the top of a large cavern that is a focal point of many of these tunnels. We've been using this to develop advanced submarine technology for a long time and as a means of hiding our research. It's a perfect way to conceal a sub—underground."

"Okay." Tremaine raised his eyebrows. After the last few days, he could believe most things.

"The tunnels reach from here to Monterey. We have a small attack sub, hard to pick up on sonar, which can reach up to forty knots. At that speed, we can make the west coast in about four hours. If my hunch is right, their sub will be hanging around in Monterey bay where it's very deep."

Tremaine just nodded again as they entered a small door in the side of a lonely, red stone building.

"Going down?" Freya chuckled at her own joke as she punched a code into the elevator keypad beside the sliding doors.

The Shadow Man's stomach lurched as the lift plummeted downward. It halted with a jolt. The elevator doors glided open to reveal the inside of a cavern. Freya gazed around the massive fissure, absorbing every inch of its unexpected beauty. A fluorescent, violet light illuminated the walls and bathed the stalactite-covered ceiling in a peaceful lavender wash. A single row of chocolate brown stalagmites protruded from a massive lake. The black water was lit up and appeared to dance and sparkle with amethyst-colored fire. At the far end was a large platform and a variety of cranes and lifting devices that should have been incredibly ugly against the awe-inspiring backdrop, but in the haze of the light, it looked as much a part of the scenery as the ancient rock.

Radiating around the walls were several pitch black holes. A few were only a few feet wide. Others were more than twenty. Each was too dark to peer into but was eerily inviting—*an ancient labyrinth*, thought Freya. A trap laid down millions of years ago.

Her gaze fell on Tremaine. He was not admiring the natural beauty of the cave but, instead, was fixated on the long, metallic structure that sat in the water next to the platform.

Tremaine stared at the submarine. From bow dome to propeller, it must have been nearly four hundred feet long. The prop was shielded by a large duct. The sail was huge, crowded with a variety of tall masts. Just before the aft rudder, a smaller, torpedo-shaped mini-submarine without a mast, sat perched on the hull of the main vessel.

"That's the advanced SEAL delivery system, or ASDS. We could use dry deck shelters, but we find this more convenient." A large Navy SEAL, clean shaven and crew cut, stood next to Tremaine, pleased as punch and beaming with pride as he described the vessel.

Tremaine nodded. "It's impressive."

"Yeah, and that's the pump-jet propulsor for quieter operations." He pointed at the covered propeller. "This thing here is the best of the best—based on the Virginia Class attack sub. She's got all the bells and whistles. She can launch Tomahawk land-attack missiles from twelve vertical launch system tubes and Mark 48 advanced capability torpedoes from four twenty-one-inch torpedo tubes."

Tremaine nodded again in approval.

"She's designed to conduct covert, long-term surveillance of land areas, littoral waters, or other sea forces. She's also capable of anti-submarine and anti-ship warfare, Special Forces delivery and support, and mine delivery and minefield mapping. With enhanced communications connectivity, she's able to pick up signals our satellites can't. She's even got a pair of extendable, photonic masts outside the pressure hull. Each one contains several high-resolution cameras with light-intensification and infrared sensors, an infrared laser rangefinder, and an integrated Electronic Support Measure array. But the best bit is this one can reach forty knots. Ooh-wee, is she fast!"

Freya tensed her jaw. "See, this is gonna find those bastards and kick their ass."

"Okay, but if we have this, what do the Chinese have?" As always, Tremaine wanted to size up his enemy.

"We don't know. But we do know they have been pouring money into their fleet in recent years. And they have some stealthy subs. Six years ago, in 2006, a Chinese sub surfaced within torpedo range of the aircraft carrier, Kitty Hawk, near the Japanese island of Okinawa—scared the crap out of us. That's why we built this one. Gotta stay one step ahead!" The SEAL laughed and marched toward the sail and sub's porthole entrance.

"Great." Tremaine huffed and started after the marine. Freya followed suit.

The group climbed down the ladder into the submarine. The corridors were narrow, barely enough room to allow one crew member to pass the other. They hastened their pace, heading directly for the command and control room.

"Here we go," the SEAL said. "As you can see, the layout on this girl is a little different than what you may be used to. No periscope, just photonics. Which means there is no periscope platform. The photonics array is there on your left with sonar and ship control. On your right is ESM, combat control, special ops and radio."

"Great, where's the CO?" Freya asked. "We need to brief and get moving."

"We don't have a CO for her yet; we are still finalizing this sub. The XO is here, and we have a skeleton crew at this time." The SEAL was matter-of-fact, unfazed by the lack of personnel.

"Fine, then get me the XO."

"Yes ma'am. He's probably in his berth at the moment. I'll find him."

"Thank you." Freya nodded and watched the soldier march off down the corridor.

"Do you think we can do this? Pull this off, I mean," Tremaine asked.

"God only knows, Tremaine. God only knows."

Freya turned away and busied herself by examining the sonar array. The harsh LCD light cast unhappy shadows across her face as she frowned, wrinkling her normally porcelain skin. Jesus, she hoped they were doing the right thing. She was sure they would all die trying this, but what the hell.

Everyone was going to die, anyway.

"It's a towed array."

"Huh?" Startled, she looked up from the screen to see a tall, good-looking, if not a little young, officer.

"A towed array," he repeated. "It's to eliminate the blind spot in our sonar at the stern of the vessel. The stern and dorsal side are always problematic in submarine warfare. They're every sub's weak spot."

"Oh, right. Are you the XO?"

"Yes, ma'am."

Freya studied him—smooth face, no crow's feet, and a cheeky sparkle in his hazel eyes. Standing incredibly straight, he must have been over six feet tall and was impressively broad, but still looked so young. "Do you mind me asking how old you are?"

"Ma'am, in this division of our forces, it's not an issue of age but of aptitude, skill, and sometimes just a hint of James Kirk." He grinned using only the right side of his mouth.

"You trying to tell me you are into green women?"

"No, ma'am. But you can tell me if you spot a mermaid out there."

She smiled. She liked him. "Okay, have you been briefed of the situation so far?"

"Yes ma'am. One Kelly Graham—male, mid-thirties—and one government experiment—biological entity—have been abducted by the Chinese. Most likely location is a submarine sitting somewhere in Monterey Bay. Our mission is one of extraction."

"Well, that's the long and the short of it, but—"

"Ma'am, I hold advanced degrees in strategic warfare and sub-marine battle tactics, not to mention, I always won at Risk as a kid." He grinned again. "I have a plan, Ms. Nilsson. Just hear me out."

"It'd better be good."

"Well, it's dangerous and has approximately a twenty-percent chance of success, but given our current situation, it's the best we have."

"Twenty percent doesn't sound great. What's the plan?"

"We have two main challenges in this situation: one is boarding a submerged submarine, which is very difficult, and the second is finding the hostages and getting them out to safety without getting ourselves killed in the process."

"You make it sound so easy. So, I repeat, how do you suggest we do this?"

"Right." The XO walked across to the navigation table and tapped a few keys. Within a few moments, the geographical map had been replaced with the schematic of a submarine.

"We think they will be using a variant of the Shang class submarine. Last intelligence reports indicated alterations such as retractable diving planes and a modified hull for greater acoustic stealth. So, challenge one: entering the submarine. We're going to have to sink her. If we can manage that, we will need to gain entry through their lockout trunk." He ran his finger across the bright screen, indicating the entry point, not far behind the main mast.

"The lockout trunk is a fairly new concept and allows subs to deploy divers while submerged. After the incident with the Russian Kursk, we acquired the Norwegian technology to open up escape hatches of sunken subs."

"You won't be able to pressurize the escape hatch though. Surely, it will flood the entire vessel?"

"Affirmative."

"But Kelly might drown." Freya took a step backward, shocked at her own outburst of emotion and concern for Kelly.

"This is a possibility, Ms. Nilsson. However, I am informed that the creature is amphibious and capable of surviving underwater. Given the briefing, it seems that survival of the creature is the primary objective. Taking out the sub and flooding it has the greatest chance of eliminating our enemies while preserving our target."

"You're willing to kill Kelly to do this?" She shook her head and stared at the XO.

"Ma'am, Mr. Graham can be considered expendable—collateral damage, if you will—in this situation. Strategy in warfare needs to consider acceptable losses. More importantly, the fact that we are even engaging the Chinese at this time is only because we have received direct orders from General Lloyd to support you as necessary. As soon as the President or Congress finds out about this, the operation will be shut down. Getting in and out with the creature quickly is priority one."

Freya looked to Tremaine, searching his eyes for a sign he agreed with her and not the XO, but she found nothing.

"The XO is right, and you know it," Tremaine said. "We cannot let personal feelings cloud our judgment here. Our primary objective is to get K'in back. Anything else is, well, a bonus."

"I guess." She didn't like the fact Tremaine had latched on to *personal feelings*. Better not to argue further.

"Right. Ms. Nilsson, once we've extracted the creature, we are going to need to get it away from the area as fast as possible. We will need to get it to the surface for an aerial pick up."

"And how will you do that?"

"You let the SEAL team worry about that. For now, we need to track the sub. We currently have the element of surprise and we don't want to lose it. Once we exit the main tunnel into Monterey Bay, we will be able to begin tracking. This will be difficult since Monterey has much marine life and busy surface activity. For now, I suggest that you get prepared. You will accompany the SEAL team in the ASDS, which has the mechanical arm to open the hatch of the enemy sub. You will evacuate to the surface and meet the chopper, which will be dispatched from San Diego upon departure of the ASDS. In the meantime, the SEAL team will open the Chinese sub. A team will go in, retrieve the creature, and rendezvous with you at the surface."

"And Kelly?" She pushed the point one last time.

"If Mr. Graham is able to be rescued, we will do so. But I am making no promises." The cheeky look in his eyes was gone. He appeared much older and wiser now.

"Okay." Freya nodded and made her way out of the control room.

"Mr. Tremaine, I want you to consider staying aboard with us for the time being. After this is over, we will need to ensure contact with Ms. Nilsson, and you both will understand your protocols. You will be able to authenticate genuine communication and response, even in the event of capture."

"Makes sense to me. How long will it take to find them?"

"It could be minutes, hours, or days. It's hard to tell. But what I am guessing is they are not expecting company. Our submarine fleet is deployed around the world on various operations—Monterey Bay is not exactly high on the list of military significance. Or at least, no one else knows it is. With any luck, they are making a bit more noise down there than they should be. We will drop into a search pattern once we exit the tunnel into the bay."

CHAPTER ELEVEN

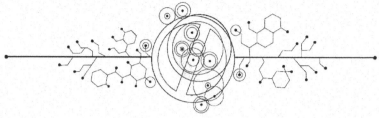

Location: Unknown

It was dark—a strange dark—like looking through fog at night. The fog can't really be seen or touched but seems to hinder vision anyway. Kelly's eyes stung, and there was a constant pressure on them. Where was he?

His leg twitched. He was upright but not touching the floor—not touching anything. He flailed an arm, but it dragged as if he were moving in slow motion. Was he drugged? He exhaled. Bubbles spilled through the regulator strapped to his face. A long hose protruded from the front of it and out of the water's surface above him—a makeshift snorkel. Shit, he was underwater. Kelly's eyes widened in terror. All senses but vision were numbed to the point of nothingness. His heart raced, and began to hyperventilate. Calm—he must stay calm. He tried to control his breathing.

Intense fluorescent light blinked rapidly into life, shining through Kelly's dilated pupils, temporarily blinding him. *Shit, that was bright.* He repeatedly opened his eyes, screwed them closed, and opened them again. The light was coming from the front like an enormous torch. Still, his vision remained blurry. He could only see shapes. What were they? Men? Those *were* men on the other side of glass. Kelly was in a tank.

The men wandered up to the tank, stared inside, and went back to the gray desks and consoles some ten feet away. Kelly looked around his aquatic prison. He was clearly naked, his genitals floating in the warm water. Concern for his current situation overwhelmed any sense of embarrassment. He examined the walls. Clear to the front but onyx-black to his right, rear, and above. He turned his head slowly to the left and peered through a transparent wall into an adjacent tank.

There was K'in, bobbing up and down in the water, limp but clearly awake. The creature looked weak, almost melancholy—nothing like the swirling lively animal to which he had become accustomed. He moved his large head in Kelly's direction and appeared to watch him. Kelly squinted in the

82

dazzling light to focus. He noticed a strange, long, black wire that was attached to K'in's head, projecting vertically out through the water into the roof of the tank. He reached through the water to his own head. A wire. He tugged on it, but it was fixed to his scalp somehow. Fuck, what was this? Where was he?

Kelly scanned the window to the outside world for a clue. Desks, consoles, men, a plain gray floor—everything looked stark, metallic, and functional. The room was definitely small. A single door behind the men looked like an elongated porthole. Pipes of various sizes ran along the ceiling. His gaze fell on a small, table-like structure in front of the aquarium, placed between his and the creature's portion of the tank. On its surface was something that looked very much like the object Kelly had retrieved for the General. Two black wires extended upward from it toward the tank and diverged after a few feet, splicing off to the left and right. *Shit!* They were hooked up to the fucking thing. Dread overwhelmed him. He kicked his feet, breathing rapidly, bubbles streaming from the regulator. *Shit! Shit!*

He stopped abruptly, every muscle in his body relaxing. A sense of ease and contentment washed over him. Kelly closed his eyes and listened to his heart rate slow to a resting rhythm. The water sloshed around his ears, lapping gently at his face, soothing him. Opening his eyelids, he lazily dragged his head to face the creature's tank. As his gaze swept across the glass front, he could see the men frantically taking notes. His field of vision reached K'in. K'in was looking at him—staring at him. Their eyes locked. Emotion oozed from the creature. K'in was scared, not for himself but for Kelly. He was reaching out to him—*telling* him to be calm. It wasn't English or any language, just a serene feeling of being at one with something. Kelly's eyes rolled back in his head. Dark—everything was going dark.

Location: U.S. submarine, somewhere in the Pacific Ocean

"How long 'til we're out of the tunnel and in the bay?"

"We've been in the bay for three hours, Mr. Tremaine."

"Oh?"

"You have no real sense of time down here, no natural light to aid your perception." The XO was sitting on his chair, hands clamped together.

"Right." He looked at his watch. It had been more than seven hours since they had left. Made sense. "So we just feel around in the dark down here? Any fool could do that. How long 'til we—"

"Sir, I've been tracking a 60 Hertz signal for a while. It has a six-line profile, light and narrow. I think we have her."

"How fast is she moving and in which direction? Has she seen us?"

The XO leapt to his feet. "We didn't move across a layer, and the TA has stayed in line; this is coming from the UUV. She seems to be moving slightly faster than patrol speed, course correction of less than thirty degrees fairly regularly but in a general westerly direction. She's sixty-five feet below us—we are in her blind spot."

"Excellent."

The XO walked across the room to the internal communications console. "Ms. Nilsson, we have the enemy sub and are tracking. Deploy the ASDS while we are still in her blind spot."

"Affirmative." Freya's voice sounded muted over the communications system. "Good luck."

"To us all, Ms. Nilsson. Out."

"Now what?" Tremaine's face was a mixture of anticipation and trepidation.

"Now we charge these fuckers like a bull in a china shop. Scare the shit out of them. We have one chance at this. We have to make it count."

There was a heavy clunk as the ASDS decoupled from the hull.

"There she goes. I hope they didn't hear that," quipped Tremaine.

"Sir, she's making a course correction, sixty degrees to port. I think she's spotted us!" the soldier at the sonar shouted.

"Fuck! All hands to deck! Move to tactical speed now! Maintain the solution, don't let her out of your sight!"

The propeller hummed as the mini-sub cruised along. Freya sat in the transport compartment of the ASDS. It was cramped inside. Six marines were with her, one in the operations section and five in the transport compartment. She was sitting in full scuba gear on a bench-like structure, awaiting her signal to exit to the chopper, or "angel" as the marines referred to it, at the surface. She'd always liked that particular term and the idea that there was a team out there ready to rescue her, should she need it—her own private army of angels with machine guns.

Her thoughts turned to Kelly. She hoped he was okay and could be rescued, too. She knew it wasn't likely, but she felt responsible for him—and Chris and Victoria. This was the first time she'd been in a real combat situation, and she'd already lost two, possibly three civilians. If she was really honest, she admired Kelly. Yes, he was a bit gung-ho, a bit sarcastic, and a bit moody, but he was brave. And he obviously took care of the people he loved—an admirable quality. *He had to survive.*

"Ms. Nilsson, we have a problem. The enemy sub has changed direction. We've been spotted. The XO has moved into attack mode. You need to get to the surface now."

Freya sprang from her seat. She blinked, dazed and confused. What should she do? Scuba gear, that's right. Get out. Get to the chopper. She sprinted into the LIO compartment, pulled on the BCD, and adjusted the straps, fastening the weight belt and the tank next.

"Okay, Ms. Nilsson, once you are away, we'll wait for the signal and then maneuver into position. We'll use the robotic arm to remove the hatch door to their lockout trunk. This will flood the sub and disable the enemy. We'll send in a team to extract the creature."

"By *disable*, you mean drown everyone on board, right?"

"Yes ma'am. Probably."

She shook her head. "Surely, only flooding the lockout trunk won't work. They can seal off compartments."

"Not with—"

"Torpedo away!"

"What?" Freya yelled, her eyes wild.

"The XO had to take her down—it's the only way."

"One hundred feet, fifty feet, twenty feet, ten … contact! The Chinese sub has been hit!" The marine at the comms station was yelling back into the LIO compartment.

"You have to go now. Go!" The marine yanked the hood of Freya's wetsuit over her head.

She glared at him, clearly pissed off. She pulled the mask's strap over her head and fixed it to her face. Freya heaved open the hatch door in the floor. It clanged against the inside of the hull as she let it go. The air pressure inside prevented water from rushing in. Placing the regulator in her mouth, she breathed deeply a few times before dropping feet first into the frigid water.

Once outside, she searched her surroundings. Three hundred feet below, she could see a blurry image of the Chinese sub as it sank to the ocean floor. A massive black hole gaped in the port side of the dull gray vessel. She watched for a few moments as the submarine slipped into the darkness. In the distance, she could see the shape of their sub. It appeared undamaged. Overhead, the ASDS moved. Freya kicked her feet and swam out from underneath it. Looking to the surface, she began her ascent. As she rose, she held a small prayer in her heart that belied her need to be strong: let Kelly be okay.

Location: Chinese submarine, somewhere in the Pacific Ocean

The tank shook violently, waking Kelly from his trance-like state. The external sounds were muffled through the water and glass, but he could make out the sound of an alarm. The men outside were struggling to stay on their feet, grasping at the consoles for support. The weight of the water around Kelly shifted as the tank moved in synchrony with room. Wherever he was, the structure was moving quickly. *Were they under attack?*

He glanced across at K'in, who bobbed up and down in his own compartment. As the water sloshed from side to side, a deep sense of confusion and fear passed from the creature into Kelly.

Without warning, the tanks twisted beyond their limits, forcing the Plexiglas to warp, bulge, and finally split open. The warm seawater spewed out through the tears, vomiting Kelly and K'in onto the floor of the room.

Kelly lay naked, sprawled out among the fumbling Chinese men, who appeared much more concerned with the current situation than with their prisoners. He flopped about on the floor and clawed at the mask on his face, but it was no use. The apparatus was strapped tightly to the back of his head, the external tubing running outward from the front and onto the floor. Clearly, it had just been a makeshift snorkel, but he could feel another tube extending downward from inside the mouthpiece into his windpipe. He flipped onto his front and lay low in the freezing water that swirled around the floor. Lifting himself onto his palms, he searched for the other end of the external pipe. He had to pick it up before it filled with water and drowned him.

In a push-up like motion, Kelly got to his knees and then his feet. Unsteadily, he stood and searched the room. He heard the heavy sound of his own breathing inside the mask and a faint gurgling sound as the other end of the hose lay in a thin pool of water.

He grabbed at the tubing and yanked it out of the water and over one shoulder in a single, quick movement. It was longer than he had hoped and difficult to manage. He swung around, now searching for K'in. The creature lay flat on the floor, his eyes darting about the room, following the panicked men and ensuing chaos. Kelly stomped with bare feet over to K'in, each step making a large splash. He knelt by the creature and put his hand on his head. K'in lifted his eyes to Kelly's. With his face covered, Kelly's eyes became an even greater focal point. They were calm and strong.

Kelly nodded at K'in—a vague indication not to worry. Be calm. Everything will be okay. He examined the wire protruding from K'in's head. It was attached, piercing the skin directly. Kelly paused. Should he remove it? Fuck it; what else would he do? He looked once more into K'in's eyes, trying to communicate that he was sorry, but this was going to hurt. With a sharp tug, he yanked on the wire. It popped upward, spurting blood from the tiny hole onto Kelly's mask. K'in's mouth opened wide, but no sound came from within. The creature shook his head, trying to shake off the pain. I know, thought Kelly, but it's okay for you. I have to do this to myself. He reached above his own head and felt for the wire. He clasped both hands around it, took a deep breath, and closed his eyes. He yanked on it, ripping it from his scalp. Kelly screamed into the mask as it tore his skin away. Throwing the wire to the floor, he stared at K'in. Okay, he thought, you took that better than I did.

A man behind Kelly shrieked loudly as a mass of seawater rushed into the room, forcing him from the doorway and crushing him against a bulkhead. Kelly had to get the door closed and cordon off the room. He left K'in on the floor and tramped over to the doorway that funneled the rushing water into the room. A Chinese man was behind the massive metallic door, trying to force it closed against the rushing onslaught. Kelly stood beside him and nodded a silent agreement. They pushed hard, but the foaming seawater pushed back harder. It was no use. There was no way that they were going to be able to close the door. The room tilted backward. Kelly and the Chinese man lost their footing and fell to the floor, sliding backward and crashing into the consoles behind them.

Where the fuck was he? He had to be deep underwater; the pressure behind that water was immense, and the room was being thrown around like a rag doll. Shit, how the hell was he going to get through this? He needed to find scuba gear. He clambered to his feet and forced a pace through the rapidly rising water swirling around his knees. His eyes fell on a single tank floating in the water, clanging against the far wall. Kelly quickened his step as best he could, wading toward it. The Chinese man, having the same thought, grabbed the tubing attached to Kelly's mask and yanked. Kelly's head twisted around as he was jerked backward and off his feet.

He coughed and spluttered as the tube filled with water. He scrambled to his feet, the spray of seawater in his eyes. He gathered up the tubing and squinted to see the Chinese man at the far wall, attempting to climb into the tank straps. Kelly realized that whatever vessel he was on, it was about to flood—and he had no air supply. He eyed the Chinese man at the end of the room and knew what he had to do. Without further hesitation, Kelly forced his way through the rushing water and grabbed the man around the head. The submariner squirmed and fought pathetically against Kelly's grip. Kelly maneuvered the man's head toward the bulkhead and jammed it sharply forward—again and again. Thick red blood spattered the wall as the soldier's skull was crushed like a hard-boiled egg. His body was limp, but Kelly kept on smashing the man's cranium against the metal corner. Frustration and anger filled his heart. Tears ran down his cheeks. Chris, his best friend, his only family—the fuckers had taken everything from him. Kelly screamed into the regulator.

K'in swam up to Kelly and pushed his body between the two men. Kelly frowned, confused and angry, but let his grip on the man go. The soldier slumped into the ever-rising water. K'in slinked backward, allowing his body to stretch outward with only his head above the surface of the water. He stared at Kelly and was understood. Kelly glanced at his defeated opponent and his own blood-covered hands. He closed his eyes, fighting back the tears, the pain. Then he looked at K'in and nodded.

He scooped up the scuba tank from the broken Chinese man and slipped the straps over his shoulders. He tightened them as best he could and clipped the waist belt together. Kelly stared at the tank's regulator and then the end of the hose attached to his face. Shit, this wasn't going to work. He was suddenly aware he was still naked and shivering. The water had risen to his shoulders now. *Think!* He had to think! Kelly shook his head once as he came to a final decision. *Going to have to hold his breath and swim for it.* He took a deep breath and tied a knot in the end of the hose as best he could.

The water was now at his chin—and freezing. Kelly ducked under and opened his eyes. Christ, it was blurry—rushing water, a veil of bubbles, and swirling notebooks. He'd give anything for his mask. Fuck it. He turned around and around, squinting to see K'in. The creature glided up beside him, flexing his body like an alligator.

K'in slipped underneath Kelly, who instinctively put his arms over the creature's neck. K'in flicked his tail, propelling them forward. Through the tight corridors, K'in whisked them along, Kelly flapping like a flag above. The creature twirled and ducked under pipes and bulkheads, dodging the floating bodies of dead seamen.

The lights overhead flickered on and off, and then they went out. It was pitch black. K'in obviously didn't need light to know where to go—at least, Kelly hoped he didn't. He imagined this was what death must be like—eerie and unnerving, a constant feeling something horrible from the bowels of hell would come out of the dark to torture you. He closed his eyes. He was cold, so cold and he had no air left. Then, he lost consciousness.

CHAPTER TWELVE

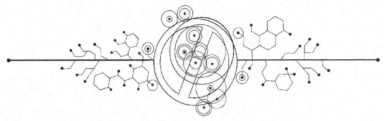

Location: Chinese submarine, somewhere in the Pacific Ocean

Kelly's grip on K'in loosened and immediately the creature stopped swimming. Kelly slipped from the creature's back and floated for a few seconds before sinking toward the corridor floor.

A dim beam of light pushed its way through the murky water ahead, swinging from left to right, a single eye searching the corridors. A frogman, wearing a completely black, full-length wetsuit and scuba gear, swam into the corridor. K'in darted to the floor and covered Kelly with his body, protecting him. The frogman turned his head-mounted torch to the source of movement. K'in's white body lit up in the dark water, his red plumes outstretched. He was on all fours, and his legs formed a cage around Kelly.

The diver touched a button on the front of his full-face diving mask. "I've made contact with the creature and possibly the male. Please advise. Over." He nodded several times. "Affirmative. Attempting extraction to the surface."

The diver swam cautiously toward K'in and stopped. For a few moments, he stared at the creature, partly in awe and partly confused as to how he was meant to *extract* the animal.

K'in forced himself off the corridor floor, pushing with all four limbs. Before the marine had time to react, the creature's hands were clamped around his head. Instantly, the diver's body went limp, powerless. K'in blinked several times, gazing into the man's eyes—feeling him.

As if satisfied the soldier was no threat, K'in let go and moved to one side. The marine treaded water, slightly bewildered, before shaking off the strange feeling and starting toward Kelly on the corridor floor.

"Affirmative. I have Kelly Graham. He's alive— but no oxygen supply and is possibly in hypothermic shock. Inform the angel. Will need assistance upon extraction. Over." The diver struggled to pull Kelly's body from the floor, the awkward shape of the tank and the makeshift hose impeding his hold. K'in ducked down to the bottom again and grabbed Kelly with all four limbs. K'in held Kelly close to his body and flicked his tail. The diver again shook his head, unsure if any of this was real. He started after the creature, trying his best to keep pace.

The animal seemed to know exactly where he was going, weaving through the corridors, navigating directly for the lockout trunk. The door to the trunk had been blown outward from inside, completely destroying any ability to form a seal to the outside world. K'in headed straight into the ascending tube that led out to the open water. His slender body, clamped to Kelly, slipped easily out into the ocean.

The diver followed suit. Looking behind him as he ascended, he saw the Chinese submarine sitting on the ocean floor, a large hole ripped into one side and the hatch opening to the lockout trunk torn away. A few Chinese soldiers had managed to climb into their ascension suits, strange-looking, orange one-piece jumpsuits that zipped completely over the head and filled with air in order to prevent nitrogen narcosis due to rising to the surface too quickly. They would be picked off by the angel overhead.

The marine contacted the ASDS again. "Be advised, creature and male have exited the submarine and are accelerating to the surface. Male is unable to make scheduled stops—decompression sickness possible. Repeat, decompression sickness possible." The diver saw the creature squeezing Kelly quite firmly as it sped upward, causing a constant stream of bubbles to escape through the loose knot in the hose.

K'in broke the surface. A strong wind tore across the water's surface, pulling large waves along. Overhead, a huge Chinook hovered, its massive rotors holding the giant aircraft approximately twenty feet from the water's surface. Freya was hanging from the side of the open door to the cargo hold. She shouted over the din of the rotors and howl of the wind to K'in, though she was unsure the creature would understand her even if he was able to hear.

"Take me closer. We need to get closer!" Freya shouted orders through her headset.

The Chinook dipped lower, swaying unsteadily as the pilot battled the side wind.

Freya hooked herself to the winch. "Drop me down. I'll attach a harness to them, and you can pull us up."

"Yes ma'am," replied the soldier closest to her.

Freya leaned backward and pushed off the floor with both feet, which were now covered in army boots rather than stilettos. The all-in-one green flight suit protected her from the cold but not the gale that seemed to manhandle her like a badly beaten flag.

She reached the water's surface where K'in bobbed along. The frogman had also surfaced and was holding Kelly's head above the water.

Freya held out the harness to the marine. "Grab it! Strap K'in and Kelly together into it!"

The frogman complied, pulling the harness under Kelly's armpits and then around K'in's forelimbs. He clipped the harness shut, pulled the strap tight, and gave the okay sign to begin winching. Freya, dangling in mid-air, twisted her body upward and relayed the message. The winch motor groaned into life, slowly pulling the three-person weight from the water.

Freya was back into the Chinook first. She quickly unclipped herself, turned, and waited with outstretched arms for the winch to finish lifting K'in and Kelly. A soldier knelt beside her and grasped the harness as it crested the floor of the open door. They released the creature first. The soldier lifted K'in and placed him gently into a makeshift plastic tank full of seawater. It was only two feet deep, and K'in rested inside with his head poking out over the lip of the tub.

Freya frantically unraveled the strap from the naked Kelly, who writhed from oxygen depletion. She drew a knife from the sheath on her left calf and hacked the end of the hose, allowing air to once again fill his lungs. Kelly's body relaxed. She knelt in front of him and wrapped his shivering body in a wool blanket and then a foil one. "You have hypothermia and most likely nitrogen narcosis. We need to get you to a hyperbaric chamber. But right now, we are going to try and remove this from your head. It seems they fixed it pretty tightly."

Freya slashed the straps. This left the hind part of the straps still attached to the back of Kelly's head but enabled Freya to begin pulling at the regulator. Kelly gagged as the tubing slid out through his throat.

"Wow, they didn't want that thing to come off, did they?" Her face was screwed up in empathetic pain.

Kelly coughed and dry-heaved awake as the remainder of the tube left his windpipe. "Fuck me. How the hell did I get involved in this shit? This is all your fault, Moby." Kelly was mockingly pointing a finger behind him in K'in's direction, though he never looked up from his crawling position on the floor of the Chinook cargo hold. He coughed hard again, swept his sodden hair backward. "Where are the others?"

Freya shook her head slowly. "Tremaine is in a sub below us. It's how we rescued you. He's going to stay there and keep in contact through a dedicated satellite link up. Benjamin and the professor were badly hurt. They were taken to a hospital. I haven't had a report for a few hours though, so I am not sure of their condition." Her voice trailed off.

"And Vicky?"

"I'm sorry, Kelly. We lost Victoria when the truck exploded." She hesitated, unsure whether she should comfort him.

"Goddammit." Kelly's voice was barely a whisper, hushed in sadness as he stared at the floor. "I'm sorry, Vicky." He wasn't sure if he'd said that out loud, but perhaps Victoria could hear him. He composed himself and lifted his head to meet Freya's gaze. "So where now?"

Freya showed him the piece of paper with coordinates written on it. "There—wherever there is."

"Okay. We need to get there now. No time for a hyperbaric. I'd know if I had NN. Moby must have done something to me on ascent."

"Are you sure you're okay?"

"I'll be fine," he said. "Just get us to where we need to be."

"Okay, but we still need to get this thing off the back of your head."

"Fine. Just do it."

Location: Peru, South America

"There it is. There's no road in. We'll have to set down about twenty miles from the coordinates you specified. The rest is on foot." The pilot had to shout over the din of the Chinook's rotors, even though Freya was wearing a headset.

"That's fine!" she yelled back. She slid the headgear off and stepped back through the cockpit door into the cargo hold.

"Kelly, we are going to have to set down a bit away from the co-ordinates. There are no roads into this place. It means we'll have to carry K'in with us—are you okay with that?"

Kelly appeared to stare blankly through her.

"Kelly?" she repeated.

He glanced over at K'in sloshing back and forth in the shallow makeshift tank. "Yeah, sorry. Still have a headache from that marine ripping the strap off the back of my skull."

"You told him to do it." Freya smirked. "Besides, that was thirty-six hours and several refuels ago—are you seriously still whining?"

"Hey, they'd used some kind of surgical staple. My head still friggin' hurts. And anyway, it's nothing compared with how much this is killing me." He rolled his shoulder slowly, screwing up his face in pain. "Right, so are you gonna tell me where exactly here is? No more conspiracy. Gotta be honest with each other from here on out. Deal?"

Freya eyed him. He seemed genuine. "Okay, deal." She shuffled round to his side and pulled out a map from a side pocket in her cargo pants. Unfolding it, she flattened it on the floor of the hold and pointed to Peru. "We are here—near the small gold mining village of Huanchumay. It's a remote part of the Carabaya province."

"I know this village. It was almost wiped out a few years back by a landslide, right?"

"I don't know. The General just sent me here. Said K'in would be safe here."

"Okay. First things first. I don't want any of these soldiers coming in with us. I know the tribes and locals around these parts—they won't be happy with these guerrillas wandering around."

"Okay, that's fine as long as you can carry him."

The chopper plummeted, causing everyone on board to reach out instinctively for the nearest object for support. "Hold on, this could get a little bumpy," the Chopper pilot called back.

The Chinook banked sharply to the left and circled around before straightening and beginning its vertical decent through the only bald space amongst the thick Peruvian rainforest. It hovered a few feet above the ground, unable to land completely on the rough and uneven jungle floor.

Kelly walked over to K'in and looked him in the eyes. K'in stared back, unable to speak, but Kelly knew the creature understood. Without a struggle, K'in allowed himself to be hoisted over Kelly's good shoulder.

Kelly stepped carefully to the cargo hold side door and peered over the edge. It must have been no more than five to ten feet to the ground, but he hesitated. *Jump*, he thought. He closed his eyes and stepped off the chopper. The journey to the ground was short, and Kelly hit it heavily. His knees bent and buckled under the weight of K'in, but he managed to stay upright.

Ignoring the pain in his legs and shoulder, Kelly opened his eyes. It was dusk now, and the jungle's wondrous shades of green and blue had faded into a mass of intertwining, black shapes. Contrasted against a burning orange sky, it was beautiful. Thick, humid air enveloped him, making it difficult to breathe.

As he surveyed his surroundings, a sense of contentment, of belonging, filled him. Kelly turned his head to address the creature flopped over his shoulder. "Is that you or me feeling that?"

K'in didn't answer.

"Probably both, huh?" It didn't matter. He hadn't said it loud enough to hear over the engine of the chopper, and the question was somewhat rhetorical anyway.

A warm hand rested on Kelly's free shoulder, a delicate touch that was contrasted by Freya's voice straining over the sound of whirring rotors. "It's getting dark fast, Kelly. We need to make a camp for the night. It'll be better to be deeper in the jungle—much harder for us to be found. But the temperature will drop quickly. I have camping and combat gear for us and thermal sheets for K'in. I imagine we have to avoid him desiccating."

"Good idea," Kelly yelled back. He slipped the creature gently off his shoulder and lowered him to the ground. "Give me some of those thermal sheets. Let's wrap him up."

Freya handed Kelly a large, silver-colored sheet. It looked so fragile as it shone and glistened like tin foil in the late afternoon sun. She then turned to the Chinook and gave an okay sign to the waiting pilot. He nodded. The Chinook rose in the air, whisking leaves and fragments of trees in its wake. She watched it grow smaller and smaller before gunning off into the distance. Freya turned back to Kelly. He had already climbed into his combat gear—dark camouflage pants and jacket, a large backpack over one shoulder, and K'in on the other.

Freya focused on the tiny screen of a handheld device. "Okay. Last encoded message from Tremaine said they are moving out of Monterey Bay. If we need him, we just have to make contact." She put the gadget back into the side pocket of her combat pants.

"Great. So, ready, Freya?" He sounded genuine and determined and even used her Christian name—all of which he had not done before.

"Are you sure your shoulder is alright?"

"Sure, I can take it. Let's move."

They trudged through the undergrowth, Freya shining a light in front, cutting through the gloom. Kelly struggled to keep up with the heavy creature and backpack on his back. The night air cooled, and the sun had been replaced by the white disc of the moon. It hung there, an orb among twinkling sequins sewn into a velvet sky. It was fortunate. Without the moon, the jungle would have been perilously dark.

An hour passed. The scenery didn't seem to change. Endless vines and trees sprawled in front of them. Freya hacked at the black limbs with a machete, slicing a path through the dense understory. She stopped. A small clearing had appeared. The jungle canopy overhead still protected them from unwanted attention, but the ground before them was treeless for at least forty square feet.

"Let's stop here," Freya suggested.

Kelly surveyed the clearing. "This seems pretty safe. I'll need to dig a hole for K'in." Kelly swung the creature from his back and gently placed him on the ground. K'in looked up at Kelly with his expressionless face. His near fully formed eyes stared into Kelly's, communicating with him. Kelly knew K'in was happy to stay put where he was.

The mud was wet and heavy as Kelly dug at the jungle floor with his bare hands. Down on his knees, he scooped chunk after chunk of earth from the same place, forming a large, bowl-shaped hole. A drizzle started and water slowly filled the ditch, causing the sides to collapse. Kelly shook his head. This could take all night. The atmosphere was damp enough. He surmised K'in would be fine. Kelly got up from his knees, now caked in soil, and trudged over to K'in. The creature stretched out his arms like a baby wishing to be picked up.

"Okay, Moby, let's go." Kelly picked up K'in by the armpits and walked back to the newly dug pit. He placed K'in inside and covered him with the insulating foil. "There. Wet and moist. You lucky bastard."

Freya looked up from busying herself with the fire and raised an eyebrow.

"Sorry. Man joke."

"It's okay. Anyway, I think I have this going now."

Two hammocks had been hung between the trees. Kelly and Freya understood the benefits of not sleeping on the jungle floor. Kelly lay there, staring through the canopy, fixated on a single star, lost in his thoughts.

"I'm sorry about Chris." Freya's voice was soft as if she did not want to disturb the tranquility of the jungle hum. "And Victoria."

Kelly took a few minutes to respond. "Me too."

"And I'm sorry … sorry about your wife and daughter, too." She was nervous, unsure how he would respond. She had learned he could be very fiery and quick to anger.

The sounds of strange jungle animals and insects melded into white noise. Kelly sighed and turned his head to face Freya, lying in the hammock opposite him.

"Chris told you about them?"

"No, he told Victoria. They thought I was asleep, but …"

"I see. Yes, I am sorry, too."

"She sounds like she was very important to you."

"She was. She is—at least, in my heart anyway. It's a strange thing, you know, to be in love with someone but so angry with them. Chris was my last piece of her, of my daughter. Now he's gone, too."

"I think he loved you very much."

"I loved him." Kelly faced the sky, fighting back the lump in his throat.

"Chris said you have bad dreams about them."

He sniffed hard. "Yeah. But lately, they've stopped or, at least, been replaced. I think it's Moby Dick over there. Somehow, we're connected. He can project emotion into me. That thing we recovered is like an amplification device. I think that's how they did it."

"How who did what?"

Kelly turned back to face Freya, who was now propped up on her elbows, looking back at him.

"His species. I asked the professor how these guys were supposed to have communicated with the ancient people on this planet given all the different languages. I think they used those orb things to amplify thoughts, feelings, and memories. The professor said in most records of these creatures, there was mention of some kind of object with them. Something about the book of Thoth and Egypt, and the round thing that Oannes guy was holding. Anyway, he was already connecting with me, but when the Chinese had us hooked up to that thing, it was so much stronger. I feel calm around him."

"Oh."

"He's like a baby. A bit like a blank slate. But imagine one of his kind that was educated. Imagine what they could have communicated."

"And that is what the professor and Benjamin wanted? To use K'in to heal the world?"

"I guess so. Though I think they lost their way and went a bit nuts. I think they figured the world could tear itself apart until only a remnant of humanity was left, making it easier to start again, making K'in's task easier. I don't know. It was a bloody, hare-brained scheme if you ask me."

"Then why are you still helping?"

"Because. Chris reminded me that it's not all about me. Izel would have helped. She was selfless. Something I failed to learn from her in life. Perhaps I can learn it now."

Freya smiled weakly. "Sometimes, you have to lose something to find something."

He looked at her for a few moments. Maybe she wasn't as vacuous as he'd thought. "Yeah, perhaps you're right."

"Good night, Kelly."

"Good night, Freya."

CHAPTER THIRTEEN

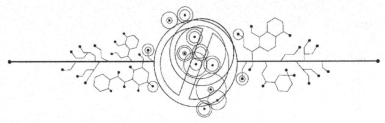

Location: A hospital, Las Vegas, Nevada, USA

Benjamin lay in the hospital bed, the monotonous beeps from the heart monitor ringing in his ears and the respirator mask smothering his face. With foggy vision, he dizzily glanced around the room until he found an open window. It was dark outside, but he could see a warm orange light flicker in the distance. In the opposite bed, the professor lay unconscious, his bandages weeping blood, the bed sheets stained red. No one was there to help. He heard the clatter of trolleys and wheelchairs in the corridor as hordes of people crashed through narrow passages and spilled in and out of rooms.

He tried to lift himself up but fell back into the bed, exhausted and broken. His thoughts turned to Freya. He'd wet her head and brought her into the church. He'd watched her grow from a baby and vowed to look after her should the unthinkable happen. He'd never expected it would actually occur. He remembered the day she came to stay with him. Skinny and awkward, her thin hair matted to her cheeks, eyes so large and wet they seemed to fill the majority of her face—she was so small, so afraid. He had worried he wouldn't feel any paternal instinct and only was doing his duty to protect her. But he needn't have worried. That scrawny little girl, the daughter of his best friend, had immediately penetrated his heart. He knew he'd do anything for her—to protect her. If he was honest, she was the reason he'd done all of this. He had no children of his own. And when Freya entered his life, his perspective changed. Suddenly, collateral damage didn't seem so collateral, and his entire life with the military seemed meaningless. He'd kept her close, and guided her from behind the scenes through the military academy, pulling various strings to ensure her position in his division. But he'd kept too much from her. Perhaps he should have trusted her—not that it mattered now.

A drunken man stumbled through the door wielding a large titanium golf club in one hand and a bottle of Jack Daniel's in the other. He swayed

99

on his feet, blinking violently as he tried to focus on the room, blood streaming from his tear ducts, making it all the more difficult. The man lurched forward, walking into the side of the General's bed. The drunkard considered the motionless patient. He surveyed the medical equipment, the bandages, and then the General's tunic that lay on the chair next to the gurney.

"You … you're a military man, huh? An army man, right?" The visitor spoke with a thick Southern drawl, made even more incomprehensible by his inebriated state. The General couldn't answer. "You're the reason for all this. You fuck-fuckers—think yer sooo clever, don't yer. Well, guess what, military man? I got me a nine iron, an' you ain't got shit!"

The drunkard lifted the golf club above his head, swaying back and forth. Benjamin closed his eyes, accepting his fate. He pictured Freya in his mind. Unable to defend himself, Benjamin closed his eyes and waited for the end to come.

Location: Peru, South America

Poked in the ribs—that's how Kelly was awoken. With an irritated groan, he shooed the prodder away with one hand, never opening his eyes. Poked again—this time harder.

"Will you fuck—" Kelly was cut short. He sat upright in his hammock and surveyed his surroundings. Ten to fifteen men surrounded him, each dressed in overly bright sports t-shirts and short pants. It was difficult to discern how old they were. Each one had the same leathery appearance to their skin and chin-length, black hair. Most were brandishing some kind of weapon, primarily old mining tools: spades or pickaxes. They looked more scared of Kelly than he was of them.

"Freya? Freya!"

"Mmm?" She turned over in her hammock and looked at her watch. "Kelly, it's four in the morning. We should wait till there's more light."

"I don't think they're going to let us wait."

Freya shot up, rolling out of her hammock onto the ground, and drew her firearm.

"Whoa, whoa, whoa," Kelly shouted. "Calm down. If they'd wanted to hurt us, they would have by now."

Freya swung the gun left and right, taking aim at each and every one of the men. They stared back at her, none of them saying a word.

K'in moved under his foil sheet. The startled men leapt back and chattered amongst themselves, apparently arguing over which one of them was to pull back the sheet. Eventually, one of the younger men was shoved forward despite his protest. He edged toward the foil-covered pit, a long spade stretched out in front of him. His eyes darted from Kelly to Freya and back to the hole.

"We can't let him." Freya said.

"Just stay calm. Relax. We're in Peru, right?"

"Right."

The man had stopped and was staring. Close enough now to lift the foil with his instrument, he was shaking uncontrollably.

Kelly took a deep breath. "*Rimaykullayki.*"

"What are you doing?" Freya demanded.

"Shhh. Let me think." Kelly breathed in again and furrowed his brow in concentration. "*Rimaykullayki. Sutiyqa* Kelly. *Inlista rimankichu? Intindinkichu?*"

The man stopped and stared at Kelly, somewhat bewildered, then turned to his comrades. They shook their heads and gestured for the young man to continue with his mission.

"What the hell did you say to them?"

"If we are in the right part of the world, then they should speak Quechua. Damn, I wish Chris or Izel were here. They could help. I'm probably saying it all wrong. Their language is pretty complicated and precise." He turned back to the man. "*Inlista rimankichu? Intindinkichu?*"

"What does that mean?"

"I think I'm asking him if he speaks English, if he even understands me. But I don't think he does."

Almost in confirmation, the man completely ignored Kelly and started poking at the sheet with his spade. The sheet moved, rustling as it did so. The foil slid back and onto the jungle floor as K'in stretched upward. His long, red plumes sprang from under the sheet and opened outward, a huge cerise fan. K'in's eyes were fully formed, glassy and black. His skin was damp and shiny but had lost its transparency and was now a milkier white. He opened and closed his mouth, allowing tiny gasps of air to fill his newly forming lungs. The man froze in fear. As his heart convulsed in his chest, he looked back over his shoulder to his comrades in a silent cry for help. K'in climbed out of the pit on all fours, his limbs clearly no longer atrophied and much more adapted to land. He padded quickly over to Kelly, his body slung low to the ground like an alligator or crocodile.

"Shit, Kelly, he's walking."

"I can see that. Don't panic." Kelly jumped down from his hammock and stood between K'in and the men. "It's okay," soothed Kelly. "He won't hurt you."

"Who are you talking to? Kelly, I hope you know what you are doing." Freya was still holding the gun, arms locked, ready to put holes in anything that moved too fast.

"Does it matter? Your General wanted us here for a reason. I'm betting these people are it. The professor said in this part of the world, Moby Dick was revered a long time ago. The South American people are one of the few groups that hold on to old beliefs. The Middle East has moved on, become more westernized. But small villages like this, they still hang on to the traditions."

One man stepped forward. He pulled off his faded hat in order to get a better view of the creature as the dawning sun's light spread around it. He was the only member of the group to have white hair. Kelly hadn't seen it before due to the man's headwear. He was much older than the rest of the group, His face full of deep crevices. The old man paused, looked at Kelly, and then stepped a few paces closer to the creature. He allowed his finger tips to lightly touch its forehead. Apart from blinking once or twice, K'in didn't move.

"Kelly?" Freya asked.

"It's okay. K'in seems fine. I can feel him."

The villager stayed in his fixed position for what seemed like an eternity. He swayed a little from side to side and then took his hand away, cutting the connection with the creature. Blinking slowly, he turned to Kelly and eyed him. A surprisingly broad smile spread across the man's face. He beckoned Kelly closer, waving his hand toward his body. Kelly obeyed and took a couple of paces forward. The elderly man took Kelly's right hand and placed it on K'in's head before putting his own left hand on K'in too. Staring deep into Kelly's eyes, he patted his own chest with his free hand.

"Yes," Kelly said. "I feel it, too."

The man nodded and turned to the other villagers. He spoke quickly, much too fast for Kelly to understand. But it at least sounded friendly. The men talked among themselves, then lowered their tools. The older man trotted back to the group. He had an almost sprightly spring in his step. He patted his colleagues on the shoulders and continued moving forward through the crowd and into the jungle. The other men followed suit as did K'in.

"Where's K'in going?" Freya asked.

"With them, I guess." Kelly shrugged and started after them.

"Wait, we need to pack these things up."

"I don't think we're gonna need that stuff. It'll weigh us down anyway."

"So we're just gonna follow them?"

"You have a better idea? The General sent us here. Let's play it out."

The sun rose higher in the sky as midday approached. The jungle was bright but quiet now. The emerald green leaves glistened with the last of the morning dew clinging to their surface. The raw untouched nature of the tropical forest apparently pleased K'in. He waddled behind the Peruvian men, his crocodilian gait causing his stubby tail to swing back and forth and his bushy plumes to bounce to and fro. His head was swiveling around as he absorbed every nuance of the new surroundings.

Sweat ran down Kelly's back and across his face. He ran a hand through his wet hair for the fifteenth time and focused on the men as they marched on up ahead, the eldest at the lead, setting the excessive pace. His mind wandered to Izel. This place made him think of her. He'd met her in a village in Argentina. He had been on a photography assignment. She was teaching English to the locals. He took her picture and strode over, cocky as ever. Made some quip or other that he couldn't even remember any more. She hadn't been impressed. In fact, she'd positively blown him off. "All brawn and no brains." That's what she'd said. Made him feel about three inches tall. He'd slinked off and sulked for the rest of the day.

For the next week, he'd watched her—how she worked with the children, how she loved them as if they were her own, and how they loved her in return. He photographed her endlessly. Each night, he'd develop the film and stare at her face—a beautiful face like that of an angel and unlike anyone he'd ever seen before. She had a halo, a glow around her.

It had taken her nearly drowning for him to get that first date. She had been swimming in the river, but the current had been too fast at the center. She'd been hauled downstream and pulled under. Kelly had been in the jungle nearby, setting up equipment for an extended capture session—time-lapse photography. Then, he had heard her gurgled cry. Kelly knew instantly it was her. He dropped his beloved camera, ran as fast as he could to the river, and dove in without thinking. He fought the current and grabbed her flailing body, dragging her to the riverbank. They had lain there, panting and out of breath. When he could speak again, he opened his mouth and said, "I just broke my camera—my favorite camera. I think that means you owe me a date." Izel lay there for a few seconds before bursting out laughing. Her beautiful face lit up. He loved her right then and there. It was weeks later that Kelly discovered he already knew her little brother, Chris, from college. That just made things all the more romantic and serendipitous to him. They were his first family.

Freya walked quietly beside him, her gaze fixed on the forest floor. She was lost in her own thoughts. Kelly glanced at her from the side, analyzing her. She seemed so different. The bolshie, headstrong woman had been replaced with a quiet, perhaps even sensitive person. Her features seemed less angular than before. In fact, she seemed almost vulnerable.

"Are you alright?"

She glanced up, her eyes wide and unsure. "I guess. I'm just questioning everything, you know? I've spent my whole life in the service of the government and never really thought about it. Now, I'm not sure of anything anymore." She released a quiet sigh and shook her head.

"If it makes you feel any better, I'm in the same boat. Spent the last few years wishing I was dead and took every crazy assignment I could on the off-chance it might kill me but never had the guts to do anything about it. Now, in the face of all this, I feel really stupid." He looked at his feet and kicked his own heels as he walked like a reprimanded toddler.

"You think K'in is okay? I don't know about you, but I'm hungry. I bet he is, too."

"Yeah, maybe you're right." Kelly picked up speed and jogged to catch the group. He passed K'in, who turned to watch him pass. Once at the head of the caravan, he slowed to match the pace of the elderly man. Freya saw

Kelly talking and gesturing to indicate eating. The man nodded and pointed in front of them. The village was close. Kelly strolled back to Freya. "We're close. We can eat in the village."

"Okay, great. I'm famished."

"Me too."

"Strange, isn't it?"

"What's that?"

"All that has happened, and yet here we are thinking about food. The human ability to move on, to do what is necessary to survive."

"I guess. We just keep on trucking. Look at Moby over there. He hasn't got a clue what's happening. But he's happy to come along anyway. And these villagers have just taken the whole situation on board. *So it's a man-sized salamander that may have telepathic powers? Okay, got it.* It's crazy."

The group crested the last green hill that signaled a break in the tree line. In front of them lay a flattened area of rich, reddish brown mud speckled with pot holes and filled with discolored water. Various shanty-style cabins were dotted around, each with a corrugated metal roof. Children danced about in nothing but shorts or a t-shirt but never both as an ensemble. They chased each other in and out of the large puddles, occasionally being reprimanded by their mothers or an older girl for unnecessary splashing.

The elderly leader of the returning troop marched into the center of this strange, little hamlet and stood on a large rock. He opened his arms as wide as he could and then loudly and purposefully cleared his throat. The people hushed. The children stopped running. He had commanded their attention. He spoke vociferously, and gesticulated wildly. Kelly strained to listen, to interpret, but the man spoke far too quickly. Until, that was, the man uttered his last word. A word Kelly did understand—*Quetzalcoatl.*

The elder swung his arms backward. The troop of Peruvian miners behind him parted like a human curtain, revealing the creature. The sharp intake of breath was unmistakable as the villagers recoiled at the site of K'in. Some of the children cried, running to their mothers and older sisters.

K'in appeared uneasy, his feet shuffling nervously. Kelly drifted toward him and placed his left hand on the creature's head. K'in ceased moving and looked at Kelly. The creature blinked slowly, calming at his touch. Kelly smiled at him, never speaking a word but communicating all the while. Everything was going to be okay.

The elder stepped down from his rock and waltzed happily over to K'in. He looked the animal straight in its glassy black eyes, searching for an answer to his unspoken question. The elder bowed his head and closed his eyes before kneeling in front of K'in. He stretched out one hand and touched the animal's forehead as he had done previously. Kelly felt the warmth and contentment course through the creature. It soothed him, too.

In a corner of the dirty courtyard, a small girl, no more than four-years old, took a single step away from her older sister. The toddler wore an ill-fitting, yellow t-shirt and nothing else. Her shoulder-length, black hair was braided into two pigtails, which stuck out horizontally as if fixed by bent wire. She took another uneasy step forward, childish inquisitiveness forcing her legs to move. With a rubbery gait, she had reached the creature within ten paces.

K'in looked at the miniature human. He was intrigued, cocking his head to one side and staring. The tot reached forward, her tiny fingers waving like branches in a breeze. Her touch reached the skin on the tip of K'in's face, on what could only be described as his nose. His skin was warm and wet, not cold and clammy as it appeared. The creature's giant plumes billowed outward in apparent joy. The little girl giggled and allowed her whole palm to rest on K'in's head.

That was the trigger. The other villagers edged closer, each one placing a hand on K'in as they reached him. The creature didn't seem to mind. In fact, with each additional person, K'in appeared to grow happier.

Freya slid across to Kelly from the spot where she had been transfixed. "What's going on?"

"Look at them. So happy, so content. And look at K'in. He seems so comfortable."

"K'in? Him?"

"I guess he's grown on me. To be more accurate, he's grown in me."

"In you?"

"Yeah, here." Kelly lifted Freya's right hand and moved it toward K'in. She resisted, trying to recoil.

"It's okay. Trust me."

Freya looked into his eyes, trying to decide whether to trust him or not. "Okay."

Kelly pulled her hand again and placed it on a free space in the middle of the creature's back, keeping his hand on top of hers in reassurance. He raised his eyes to meet hers.

"Understand?"

Freya just nodded. She could feel the kindness and tranquility pervading her, not just from K'in but from Kelly, from each of the villagers. They were all connected. She closed her eyes and absorbed the feeling, being part of a greater whole. Perfection.

A strange, low-frequency warble emanated from deep within the creature's throat. The entourage of villagers stepped back quickly, unsure if they had angered him. The creature arched his back and moved to rest almost all of his weight on his hind legs. Slowly, his head lifted upward toward the sky, the red plumes forcefully outstretched. The bright sunlight shone through the crimson, feather-like fans, projecting a halo of fire around the creature's head as he stood as tall as he could on two legs, his tail used to form a supportive tripod. K'in was upright, elevated and god-like, commanding reverence.

The elder nodded as if in agreement with K'in. He turned to his villagers and rapidly muttered a few words. Several women ran off and returned with dishes containing various fruits and vegetables. Others brought things they had obviously created in their shacks using what was available in the forest. It was time to eat.

K'in dropped back to the floor on all fours, the halo of fire dissipated. He padded over to one of the bowls held by an old woman. His nostrils flared as he breathed in the strange scent. A small child stepped beside him, dipped his hand in the bowl, and scooped out a large handful of the brown, semi-solid mush before placing it in his mouth. An obnoxious grin spread across his round face as he attempted to chew the oversized mouthful. K'in stared at him and then the bowl. Message received. K'in shoved his head into the bowl, almost knocking the old woman off her feet. Squelching noises and loud gulps could be heard from inside the pot. The villagers laughed.

"See, told you he was hungry," Freya said.

Kelly nodded. "Yeah. Well, so am I. Let's eat and then get some rest. This heat is killing me."

CHAPTER FOURTEEN

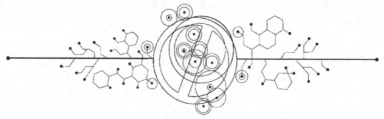

Location: A remote village, Peru, South America

The warm water swirled around Kelly's toes as he stood in the sand and stared out into the bottle-green ocean. There in the swash, they played. Two silhouettes set against the dusk red sun and orange sky. No faces or details could be made out, but he knew it was them.

Izel picked up the little one and swung her through the air. There was giggling—lots of giggling. Kelly smiled. He wanted to cry out to them, run to them. But he knew it was not the time—not now but one day. She turned to him waved.

The little one copied. "Bye, daddy."

Kelly opened his eyes and lay there for a few minutes, facing the rusted ceiling of the shack. It was the first time he could remember feeling no pain in his heart as he woke. Tears trickled from the corners of his eyes and streaked down his temples. "Bye, sweetheart."

He swung his legs out of bed and slipped back into a shabby, black t-shirt. His shoulder ached from the gunshot wound but, surprisingly, wasn't too stiff. He was already wearing pants and boots; he hadn't bothered to remove them when he had fallen into bed, exhausted. He ambled over to the doorway and out into the morning air. The dawn sun peeked over the luscious, green hills in the distance, and the sky was painted a gray-pink. Kelly admired the view from the little mud hill on which he stood, his arms folded across his chest. He loved it here.

The faint sound of laughter behind him drew his attention away from the picturesque setting. He twisted his torso to see behind him. Freya was kneeling in the dirt with five or six children bouncing around her. She caught

108

Kelly's gaze. A fleeting smile graced her face before disappearing in embarrassment and more than a little guilt for smiling at all. She turned back to the children. Kelly stared at her. This scene was all too familiar.

He looked away and focused on the villagers. They were shuffling around K'in, bathing him in a ditch they had dug. They appeared calmed by his presence—comforted. But K'in was watching Kelly. Those black eyes fixated on him. He felt anxiety in K'in—fear and apprehension. Kelly didn't know if the creature understood what was going on. Perhaps the animal sensed Kelly's own emotional state.

Raindrops speckled his face, breaking his train of thought. The children tittered and danced around, invigorated by the drizzle. Kelly and Freya looked up to the now graying sky; a thick covering of cloud obscured the heavens and the sun. Kelly closed his eyes and allowed the falling water to wash over his dirty skin. It was cool, refreshing.

He screwed his eyes shut. Then he heard a noise, familiar and unwelcome. Kelly jerked into life and shot his gaze at Freya. She was staring wide-eyed at him, the color from her already pale skin drained. It was a plane. Someone was looking for them. Kelly knew they couldn't stay there forever. Once the cloud cleared, it would be easier to find them.

Freya nodded at him, knowing his thoughts—a silent agreement. She squelched through the mud toward Kelly.

"Time to go?" she asked.

"Yeah."

"Tremaine is out there in a stealth sub somewhere, so we have transportation. Actually, trapped in a long tube a mile underwater sounds like the safest place on Earth right now. Do you know where you want to go?"

"The world is in chaos. Every major religion is up in arms. The U.S. Government is not only trying to placate the people but to avoid World War Three with the Chinese. And some kind of horrible disease is spreading over the western seaboard. Everything's fucked. Thousands of years ago, K'in's kind saved us from our own savagery. Perhaps we can help him do it again."

"Are you starting to believe all of this now?"

"At this point, I'll believe anything. We just need to get our hands on one of those devices."

"We lost ours and destroyed the Chinese's."

"I think I know where I can get another one."

"Oh?"

"I worked a lot in the Middle East. There were always nut jobs looking for various treasure—gold and whatever from Babylon and ancient places like that. Anyway, I often heard people talk about the book of Thoth. Figured it was a load of crap, you know? But what if it wasn't? What if it's another device like the professor thinks?"

"So we go to Egypt?" Freya asked.

Kelly nodded. "Egypt."

Location: A hospital, Las Vegas, Nevada, USA

Benjamin opened his eyes. He was alive. He glanced around the room, searching for an explanation of what had just happened. On the floor lay the drunken man who had been wielding the golf club moments earlier. The body was spread awkwardly, face-down in a pool of blood—an open wound in the back of a broken skull. Above the man stood a soldier in a dark green flight suit, clutching a smoking Glock 19 in his hands. It was Wiezorek.

"We need to get you out of here, sir." The soldier was out of breath, his chest heaving. His face was blackened and smeared with blood. It was unclear if the blood was his or someone else's. "I was waiting for the surgeon to return and tried to contact HQ. A mob invaded the hospital. The whole town has gone berserk! I managed to fight off three of them and came straight here for you."

The General nodded weakly and attempted to lift himself from the hospital bed, but his arms were too feeble. He collapsed backward, his face screwed up in pain.

"Shit." Benjamin's voice was muffled by the oxygen mask still sitting over his nose and mouth.

"I've got you. C'mon, sir."

Wiezorek holstered his weapon and stepped over the dead man. He pulled the mask from the General's face and heaved him from the bed. Benjamin groaned in agony. A drip bag and its metal support crashed to the floor as the intravenous line protruding from the General's right hand pulled on the poorly balanced structure. He winced.

"I'm sorry, sir. I'll have to take that out."

The General nodded.

Wiezorek released his grip on the General's left arm, leaving him to weakly hang on, one arm draped over the pilot's neck. He then reached across

110

and grasped the needle protruding from the back of his commander's hand. He tugged at it sharply, releasing it from the skin. Benjamin took in a short breath and breathed out the pain.

"Sorry, sir."

The General shook his head. Wiezorek knew what this meant: it doesn't matter. Carry on. Re-gripping the General's left arm, Wiezorek braced and lifted. The man was a dead weight. The pilot grunted in effort. "C'mon. Let's get out of here, sir."

Benjamin glanced over his shoulder as they exited into the corridor. His eyes fell on the broken form of Professor Alexander—his friend, his partner in all this mess. Damn, it wasn't supposed to end like this. The professor was meant to be the link, the one who could make the connection. Benjamin shook his head.

Taking strides as strongly as he could, the young pilot dragged the General along with him. He swung left and then right, unsure which way he was meant to go. The corridors were full of smoke and small fires burned everywhere. The acrid particles seared his eyes and stifled his lungs. He trudged on until he came to a fire-exit. Wiezorek kicked on the horizontal lock-releasing bar that lay across the door, flinging it open. Before it could swing closed, he stepped through and used his left foot to halt it on its return path. He peered down the stairwell. It seemed empty.

"C'mon, sir. Keep going. We'll make it outside and try to commandeer a vehicle."

The two men stumbled down the spiral staircase, each step labored and uneasy. As they passed each floor, the same sound of chaos grew louder and then quieted. The General's instincts took over, the hair on the back of his neck standing. Without thinking, he used his free hand to reach across and unholster the pilot's Glock. It was heavy, making it difficult for the General to do anything other than let his arm hang at his side, the weapon pointing at the floor. Still, he felt safer holding it.

Wiezorek tripped and fell into a wall. "Shit! Sorry, sir."

"You're doing fine, soldier. I'm okay. Keep going."

They reached the bottom of the stairwell and staggered through the double doors into the open emergency waiting room. Random fires littered the floor and windows were smashed, but it was devoid of activity and eerily quiet.

Wiezorek hauled the General outside through the automatic doors and searched his surroundings for the vehicle in which he had arrived. It wasn't there. At least, if it was, he couldn't see it through the night air masked in smoke and flames. It was probably burnt out.

A shrill scream penetrated the fog. From within the thick cloud, a crazed man, no more than twenty-years old and wielding a large fireman's axe, sprinted toward the General and the pilot.

With his spare hand, Wiezorek pulled a P229 from the holster at the back of his combat pants. "Stop there, sir. If you come any closer, I will open fire!"

The man ignored him and screamed again, accelerating forward.

"I said stop, or I *will* open fire!" yelled the pilot.

The man didn't need to be asked again. Two bullets quickly and powerfully punctured his chest and sent him veering off his trajectory, crashing into the side of a burning parked car. Wiezorek looked down at the smoking gun firmly gripped in the General's hand.

"We don't have time to fuck around."

"No, sir. Of course." The young pilot's heart was thumping in his chest.

"Where is the transport?"

"It's not here, sir. We will have to find another way." Wiezorek scanned the area. This was ridiculous. How the hell were they going to get through the city? It was chaos. He sighed and raised his head to the sky. It hit him. "A chopper."

"What?"

"A chopper!" he repeated. "There is a helipad on the roof of this hospital. If we can get to it, I can get us above all this shit and outta here, sir!"

"Do it, soldier."

"Yes sir, but we will have to go back into the building. I won't be able to lift you up the emergency ladder. We'll have to take the central stairwell— can't even chance using the elevator."

"Agreed. Let's move."

"Yes, sir, but ..." He hesitated. "I'll carry you. It'll be faster."

Benjamin nodded.

Wiezorek holstered his P229 and repositioned the General's arm around his neck. Grunting, he lifted the man's weight once again. The pilot shuffled through the swirling cloud of soot, ash, and smoke until he reached the double sliding doors of the emergency room. He closed his eyes and took a deep breath.

"Do it," commanded the General.

As ordered, Wiezorek slipped the General from around his neck and, in one motion, placed his shoulder firmly in the man's midriff and lifted. The General slid across the pilot's shoulders, his right leg and right arm on either side of the pilot's neck. Benjamin grabbed his own right leg to lock himself in place, brandishing the Glock in his left hand.

"Go!" the General ordered.

The pilot stomped into the open emergency room. He studied the color-coded map just inside the doorway, trying to memorize the route to the helipad. Up—he just had to go up. Scanning the room, then the map, then the room again, he identified the stairwell he needed. He shifted the General on his shoulders and marched as best he could toward the door. He pushed it open with his foot and peered upward through the stairwell. An intense heat rose through the concrete column. That couldn't be good. They had to move quickly. He took a deep breath and began to climb. Each step was a greater effort than the last. His thigh muscles burned with lactic acid. At ten stories, he had to stop.

"C'mon soldier. You can do it. Move it, move it, move it!" It wasn't much of an inspirational speech, but it was all he could think of.

The pilot gathered what energy he could and grabbed at the banister, hoisting himself up the stairs, one by one.

Somewhere between the fifteenth and sixteenth floors, there was a scream from above him. Wiezorek searched through the intensifying smoke for the source. He couldn't see anything, but it sounded close. He hacked a cough as ash particles worked their way into his lungs.

"What is it, soldier?"

"I'm not sure, sir."

"Where the hell is everybody?"

"The hospital was ransacked, sir—desperate people searching for medication for whatever it is that has infected the area. I don't think they found it. I think many made their way to a makeshift quarantine site set up in the downtown area. Perhaps—"

The pilot was cut short as something clanged and crashed down through the stairwell. A piece of the metal handrail hurtled past the men, followed by large chunks of brickwork that pummeled the stairway and exploded into a thousand fragments as they hit the ground below.

Wiezorek peered over the edge to examine the debris. As he pulled away from the edge, the limp form of a woman's body smacked on the railings in front of him, spattering blood over his combat pants before she slid and fell down the central hollow. The pilot froze in shock and could only listen to the faint sound of her limbs slapping against the stairs and metal until a final thud signaled she had hit the bottom.

"You have to move, soldier. We don't have any time." Wiezorek nodded weakly and, again, repositioned the General on his aching shoulders. He had to keep moving.

At the twentieth floor, he found the broken stairs and railing that had come apart and crashed past them moments earlier. The woman must have leaned on it before the structure gave way. Perhaps she had been trying to make it to the chopper as well.

Carefully stepping past the gap in the concrete, the young pilot pushed through the doorway and immediately fell to his knees. The General slumped to the floor and rolled onto his back. Wiezorek, still trying to catch his breath, lifted his head from the tarmac. There it was—the Bell 412 Mercy Air helicopter—a seven-thousand pound, fifty-foot-long, blue and white angel. But someone was in it.

The young pilot mustered enough strength to sprint forward. He slammed at full pace into the door of the helicopter, seized the handle, and flung it open. A rotund man stared at him and then yelled in a language the pilot didn't understand. For a brief moment, the General's words rang in his head: no time to fuck around. Wiezorek pulled the trigger of his P229, pumping two rounds into the occupant's right leg. The cockpit was sprayed with blood as the man's thigh exploded, forcing his whole body through the open passenger door. No time to fuck around, but he couldn't kill a defenseless man.

The pilot scanned the cockpit and the hold. It was now empty. He ran back to the General and lifted him onto his shoulder. He carried Benjamin the thirty feet to the helicopter and stuffed him unceremoniously into the passenger side, then slammed the door. He closed the hold and climbed into the cockpit where he froze for several seconds.

"Good job, soldier. Now let's get the hell outta here."

The young pilot nodded. "Yes, sir."

They slipped on their headgear and watched the tarmac disappear as they lifted off the helipad. Buildings became smaller as the horizon grew larger. From east to west, Las Vegas was aflame. Destroyed buildings leaked streams of vigilantes and gangs into the alleys. From high up, they looked like angry ants—tiny and insignificant.

"Where now, Wiezorek?"

"Out to sea, sir. My last communication from your team was to take you to the docks in San Diego Military Port to rendezvous with a submarine, but I think we have to go straight out to sea. Chatter was you're on the most wanted list now, sir."

"Good job, soldier."

"Ethan, sir. And no problem. Gotta stick together in these circumstances. Can only trust people in the field, sir. Those who are in the thick of it, as it were, sir."

The General nodded. "How do you intend to get us into a submarine from this chopper?"

The pilot thought for a moment and then grinned. "Splash down, sir. Splash down."

Benjamin shook his head.

CHAPTER FIFTEEN

Location: A remote village, Peru, South America

Kelly sat cross-legged and waist-deep in a mud puddle. Dirty, opaque water swirled around his bare knees. Under a bright but cloud-covered, gray sky, a warm drizzle speckled his naked torso and slicked his hair to his face. He heaved a sigh. How the hell had he gotten into this situation?

In the last couple of weeks, he'd been dragged to the South China Sea by a covert government outfit, lost his best friend, Chris, been shot, evaded a deadly virus that was still loose in California, and was now sitting in a dirt puddle in Peru next to a giant salamander whose species, according to one crazy professor, brought humans into enlightenment thousands of years ago. Oh, and to boot, the salamander thing, K'in, had formed some kind of bond with Kelly he couldn't shake—not that he was sure he wanted to.

Recently, Kelly had talked to the creature. He was a silent partner and a great listener. He would sit by the camp fire and talk for hours when everyone else had gone to bed. K'in would lie next to him in the moist ditch and appear to be attentive, staring back with empathetic eyes. One evening, Kelly had talked from dusk till dawn about his family. He'd even talked about his friend Victoria. So many people had died. It was too much to bear. But it had been cathartic to let out his emotions to someone, something, that couldn't answer back. In fact, even the nightmares and horrific images of his dead wife and child that had plagued him for many years had inexplicably stopped.

A crack of thunder rolled through the sky, rumbling in Kelly's chest. It broke his train of thought, jolting him back to the real world. He stood, allowing the brown liquid to drain from his knee-length cargo shorts. Kelly grabbed the bottom of one short leg and wrung out the water. Then the other. He wiped his torso down with both hands, swept his hair back over his head and away from his eyes, then trudged over to his little hut, patting K'in on the head as he passed.

The door was already open. Kelly stepped inside and allowed his eyes to adjust to the darkened room. Freya was on her hands and knees in the corner, the butt of a small flashlight in her mouth. She was examining a crumpled map that was sprawled out on the floor. Her hair was tied back in an efficient ponytail, and she was still wearing her black jungle gear—a far cry from the body-hugging outfits she had been wearing when they first met. Her porcelain face was even a little dirty. Kelly preferred Freya this way.

Suddenly aware she was not alone, Freya stopped her work and rocked back into a kneeling position. She looked up at Kelly. The bright light outside meant he appeared only as a large silhouette in the doorway—featureless. Still, she could feel warmth from his gaze. He had been very supportive this last week—talking with the village elder, figuring out what they had to do next, and helping her to map out their route to Egypt. She wasn't accustomed to accepting help from anyone other than Benjamin. But when Kelly did it, it didn't feel intrusive or chauvinistic.

"Hey. Raining?" Freya asked.

"About to start but not too heavy yet. We need to get moving soon. Gotta trek through the forest to get to the truck that can take us to Callao, and I really don't want to do that in dark."

"No, you're right. I was just working on the map here as we don't want to get lost."

"Any news from the General?"

"Not since yesterday before he boarded the sub. It's a good idea to keep communication to a minimum. I still can't believe he was almost killed in the hospital."

"Yeah, I was sorry to hear about the professor, though." Kelly didn't sound particularly sincere.

"I wasn't that close with him, but it doesn't help our situation very much. He held most of the knowledge in his head. I'm not sure what we'll do if we find an orb."

"When."

"What?"

"When we find an orb. You said if. If isn't an option."

Kelly was right. Was she getting soft? She was distracted with concern for Benjamin. That was for sure. "Yes, when we find one."

"Anyway," he continued. "I've been thinking. I may know someone in Egypt who could help."

Freya studied him. His tone was uneasy, and he lacked conviction. "Oh? Who?"

"Just a guy I've known for a long time. He's a bit of a brainiac—knows a lot of stuff. I think he's a professor of something or other." Kelly shuffled on the spot.

"You think? Do you know this man or not?"

"Just believe me. He'll know how to help."

"And you trust him?"

"Trust is a strong word."

"Who the hell is this person? Stop being evasive."

"Just a guy. I know him, and he knows me. Leave the details to me, yeah?" Kelly turned to leave the hut but stalled at the opening, lost in his thoughts. Kelly wasn't even sure if his friend would help. Not after everything that had happened. They hadn't spoken in years. But what choice did he have? Given the situation, there was no other way. Kelly heaved a sigh.

"You okay?" Freya took a step toward him, an arm outstretched.

"Yeah, I was just thinking about … about K'in," he lied. "I don't like your little plan with the General. I mean, handing over K'in to him and that walking fridge, Tremaine, to keep safe in the sub. It just doesn't feel right."

"You don't need to worry." Freya's tone hardened. She pulled back her hand. "I trust Benjamin."

Kelly eyed her. "You know, you're the only person who calls him that instead of *General*. What is it between you two?"

"Nothing. I just trust him." She jumped up and pretended to busy herself folding the map. She sensed Kelly staring at her. "What?" Freya asked.

"Nothing. Jeez, don't get your panties in a bunch. Your nocturnal activities are none of my concern." He turned and walked out of the hut towards his own dwelling.

Freya fumed. He could be such an asshole sometimes. If she told him, he'd feel stupid. But there was no point. She turned back to her map and stuffed it into a rucksack. Then, she slung the pack over her shoulder and marched out of the hut.

The sky was dull and gray, yet compared with the darkness of the little hut, it seemed eye-wateringly bright. It took a few moments for Freya to focus on her surroundings. She scanned the village center. K'in was sitting in his ditch, a group of children scooping up water with their hands and then dropping what hadn't run through their fingers onto the creature's back. A few adults were busying themselves with chores.

Then there was Kelly. He was talking with the village elder again. He'd been chatting away to the old man all week. She had tried to listen once or twice, but it had been no use. She could not understand a single word they said. She wasn't even sure Kelly knew what he was saying when he spoke. He was so full of shit sometimes. But his confidence—or maybe overconfidence—was part of his charm. Her admiration for him hadn't dwindled in the past few days, but she did feel she understood him better. He bulldozed his way through life, because he knew no other way. One evening, she had asked him if he had always been like that, even as a child. He had replied he didn't remember being a child. But that was all he had said and quickly changed the subject.

Freya strolled over to the men, sauntered past K'in, whose gaze followed her path. She may have been wearing jungle boots and military gear, yet she couldn't help swaying her hips. It just helped her feel a little more, well, her. She arrived at the tail end of their conversation, which was in pidgin Quechua. Kelly was frantically nodding and gesturing while speaking the odd string of words. The old man, patient as ever, was replying, speaking as slowly as he could. Sensing her approach, Kelly stopped talking.

"Don't stop on my account."

"We're finished here anyway. He was just wishing us luck." Kelly started walking away, his voice fading with his increasing distance. He turned his head back and whistled loudly. K'in sprang from his ditch and padded on all fours quickly past Freya to Kelly's side.

Freya glanced backward to catch a final glimpse of the village. In a strange way, she was going to miss it. She turned her attention back to Kelly and K'in, shifting the backpack on her back to make it more comfortable. She jogged up beside them. "What was that word he kept using when talking to you? I heard it several times."

"What word?" Kelly shrugged.

"Wa-kay-ro."

"Oh, *Huaquero*. Yeah, my Quechua isn't so good. But, if I remember rightly, it means 'treasure hunter.' In modern Spanish, it translates to 'tomb robber.' I guess you can take your pick."

"Fitting. Interesting language, this Quechua."

"Yeah, Izel thought so, too," Kelly replied without looking at her. He then pulled on his backpack toggles to ensure a tight fit to his back and picked up pace, forcing Freya to quicken her step in order to keep up.

Location: CDC quarantine, San Francisco, California, USA

Jerry Caulfield. That is what was written on the chart. The doctor examined the corpse through the plastic shield that comprised the majority of the hood covering his head, part of an all-encompassing, entirely white, protective suit. The body was twisted and contorted in every direction, a frozen effigy of torture. The sockets were blackened and the skin was gray. The chest cavity was open where the autopsy had been performed, but no organs had been found, only a mixture of liquid tissue and tar-like congealed blood—the telltale sign of hemorrhagic viruses. This was the worst way to die—long and drawn out, the body not succumbing to the inevitable for hours. It turned the doctor's stomach to see it.

The team had managed to transport the victim to the secure CDC facility, but it was no use. They had taken blood samples for analysis as fast as they could. There was no saving the man, but he could still provide them with answers. They at least knew he was patient zero.

The doctor turned away and walked across the hermetically sealed room to a large steel door. He pulled it open and stepped through into a smaller room, allowing the portal to close behind him. Immediately, he was bombarded with a fine mist, jet-powered through several hoses in the wall. He stood with his arms pointed directly upward and turned in a circle several times. The sanitation process was long and laborious but necessary.

Thirty minutes later, he was back in normal clothing: a pair of gray slacks, black shoes, and a badly pressed powder-blue shirt. He marched up the corridor, fighting with a sunflower-yellow tie that felt more like a noose around his neck. He pushed a set of heavy double doors open and entered the video conference room. The Colonel and the Secretary of State each filled a screen that projected their faces to be more than twice their actual size, giving them an even greater presence than normal. They were already mid-conversation.

"We don't know, Madam Secretary. We have several hosts with us, but by the time we take blood samples and try and replicate the virus, it and the host die. We're looking at an approximate twelve-hour cycle. It's just not long enough." The Colonel stared out of the video conference screen. His eyes were not focused on anyone in particular but had the vague look of someone staring awkwardly into a camera.

"So what you are telling me is you have no idea how to combat this or where it came from? You are head of USAMRIID. How is this possible?" The Secretary was seated at a plain metal desk in a private video conferencing room, strangely on her own. It was dark and only the light of the screen illuminated her face. She looked tired—worn out. It was two-thirty in the morning, and she had been up all night trying to engage in negotiations with the Chinese Government, who were refusing to respond to any communication. The seemingly unprovoked attack on Area 51 had washed its way through congress, resulting in furious arguments among its constituents as to whether waging war on the Chinese should be actioned immediately. She was frantically trying to reason for peaceful options, despite a strong opposing opinion from the Secretary of Defense. To make matters worse, the media was broadcasting twenty-four hours a day on some supposed secret government files on a life form that predated the human race. Files that suggested the U.S. Government not only knew about this species but were conducting active research. They had grown one in a lab at Paradise Ranch. Every conspiracy theory nut in the country had gone postal. Looting and violence was becoming more widespread. If that wasn't enough, the Vatican was constantly requesting to speak with her as well. How all this was interconnected was still a mystery. All of her usual channels had shut down. Everyone had closed ranks and was saying nothing. It had not been a good start to the day.

"We don't think it's airborne, which is a positive thing," continued the Colonel. "That means it requires fomites, touch points, to transfer it. As a result, it appears to have an R-nought of one to two. That means each person will only infect a maximum of two other people. But ..."

She sighed. "But?"

"But," interrupted the doctor. "If this is the case, then we have a bigger problem. This thing has a cycle of twelve hours in the body or on a surface. This, combined with our initial analysis of its structure, makes us think it was engineered. What's more, the only reason to engineer a virus that can only be transmitted via fomites with that short of a lifespan is to ensure two things: one, it kills quickly. And two, it stays within the populace in which it's released. In our case, it is unlikely to leave U.S. soil. It was designed to decimate a large portion of U.S. citizens."

The Colonel grunted. "Thank you for joining us, Dr. Cooper. Returning to your original question, we do think we know where it came from."

"We do?" The doctor seemed surprised.

"Yes. We think it may be linked to the current issue with the Chinese." The Colonel looked uncomfortable. He shifted his eyes to the doctor as if to ask permission to speak freely in front of the civilian.

"Get on with it, Colonel. How is this connected with my current situation? I already have a house full of officials wanting Chinese blood. If we have evidence of unprovoked biological warfare as well, I will have no choice but to recommend immediate and full retaliation." Her stern face showed she meant what she said, but her voice carried a little hope that the Colonel was wrong, that there was a way to avoid this.

"General Benjamin Lloyd headed up a facility within Paradise Ranch. This facility was conducting top secret research. It was an extremely black-boxed operation. Very few knew about it. But Benjamin and I had worked closely together for years."

"And?" She was growing impatient.

"The abridged version is this: Benjamin Lloyd, Professor John Alexander, and a small team at Paradise Ranch were conducting research on an intelligent, non-human life form. This life form was a clone of an original found frozen in Siberia by the Chinese in the 1940s. The incumbent U.S. Government at that time covertly extracted the corpse for our own research. A few months ago, General Lloyd's team learned that, back then, they had not extracted everything of importance from China."

The Secretary's face reddened, her lips puckered in anger. She exhaled slowly before speaking. "How is this connected to the current situation?"

"My information is limited, Madam Secretary. After I took on a new assignment, my connection with Benjamin and his program was weaker. What I do know is Benjamin and his team believed what the Chinese were in possession of was worth risking all-out war for. So they went into Chinese territory and retrieved it."

"What did they have?" The doctor's question popped out of his mouth. Scientific curiosity had taken over, and he had forgotten his place.

"We do not know, Doctor. We only know two things: first, they had only a short time in which to analyze it. The Chinese responded quickly and attacked Paradise Ranch. Everything was destroyed, and there was no mainframe to store the data. It was too covert to allow that."

"And the second?" the doctor asked.

"Second, General Lloyd, following his team's return to Paradise Ranch, leaked everything we know on the life form onto the Internet."

"General Lloyd leaked it?" The Secretary was confused.

"Doctor, the corpse in your morgue, patient zero, is a man named Jerry Caulfield, correct?"

"Yes."

"We have managed to trace several calls to patient zero. The trail was masked, but it used encryption codes that were assigned to General Lloyd. The source of the secret file leak came from the Internet café in which patient zero was found. It is more than reasonable to assume General Lloyd provided him with the information."

"Why would he do that? Not only is he committing treason, he's openly inviting chaos. And why would the Chinese expose him to a deadly virus?" The doctor waved his arms in distress.

"We don't know why Benjamin did what he did. It must have been related to what he found. As for the Chinese, if what was stolen was that important, then it seems they were willing to wipe out the U.S. to prevent us using it," the Colonel replied. "Besides, I assume they took our incursion in their territory as an act of war and decided to hit us fast and hard."

The Secretary slumped back into her chair and rubbed her forehead in a circular motion. A covert U.S. military strike had gone wrong, and now the Chinese wanted war. Who could blame them? Regardless of what the Chinese were doing undercover with this non-human life form, they had not attacked first. She leaned forward and peered into the camera. "Where is General Lloyd now?"

"He was originally flown to a hospital in Las Vegas, but my most recent report confirms he left the facility and is AWOL. All attempts to communicate with him have failed." The Colonel wiped the sweat from his broad, bald head. He had served in every major war in the last twenty years, but this situation bothered him more than any other.

"We need to find him. If the General and his team were that black-boxed and the President had no knowledge, then the U.S. Government cannot be held responsible. We find the General and turn him over to the

Chinese in exchange for an antivirus and truce." Her eyes were wild. She was thinking on her feet, verbalizing her inner thoughts.

"What we need to do is strike back quickly, and with everything we have. We cannot accept an attack on our own soil. It would look unbelievably weak." The Colonel spoke with the resolve of a seasoned warrior.

The doctor interrupted again. "I know I'm not a military person, but it seems reasonable to me that if we had black-boxed this operation, then the Chinese may have, too. It's plausible their government knew nothing of this either. Do we really think an attack on U.S. soil was sanctioned by the Chinese Prime Minister?" It wasn't logical—at least not to him.

"The doctor may have a point." The Secretary's face seemed to brighten.

"They haven't responded to any communication. But neither have they claimed responsibility for the attacks. If they are in the same situation as us, then they are probably trying to figure out how to avoid war, too!" She sounded almost positive now.

"And you think handing over Benjamin will be enough?" The doctor stood there bemused as the fate of a man was discussed as if he were a used piece of furniture to be given away and chopped up for firewood if necessary. What was more, no one seemed focused on the fact there appeared to be a newly discovered, intelligent life form on Earth. He wanted to ask more questions but thought better of it.

"So, what is the plan of action?" the Colonel asked.

"Colonel, you will liaise with whomever you need to find General Lloyd and bring him in immediately. In the meantime, Dr. Cooper, you will continue your research. I want you on the next available transport to USAMRIID in Maryland. You have the greatest experience with the virus so far, but you do not have the facilities. USAMRIID has state-of-the-art biocontainment facilities. Even if the Chinese are open to negotiation, we do not know if they have an antidote."

"I think I would be better placed to find Benjamin," the Colonel said. "I know him the best. And there is no need to bother the Secretary of Defense with this. I'm sure you and he are focused on preventing war with the Chinese right now."

The Secretary, already anxious about her next step, simply nodded. "Sure, okay, Colonel."

"And you, Madam Secretary?" the Colonel asked.

"I will arrange a conference with the Chinese Minister of Foreign

Affairs. I will try to stall the Chinese, keep them talking until we can find the General and find out just what the hell is going on. See why he needed to steal whatever it was from the Chinese and then release sixty years' worth of covert data into the public domain. We are not holding all the cards. You have your duties, gentlemen."

With a flick of a switch, she cut off the video conference. The faint crackle of static filled the silence in the room. But she didn't notice it. Her mind was racing and full of fragments of information that made little sense. There had to be a way of out of this. There just had to be.

CHAPTER SIXTEEN

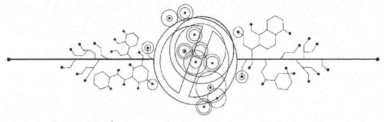

Location: Peru, South America

The red Toyota Hilux hurtled along the dirt track. Large leaves slapped the windshield as if the forest were high- fiving the vehicle, congratulating it on not falling to pieces as its suspension was tortured by the rough terrain. Their driver had said this was the easy bit. The difficult part would be out on the highway. The mountainous landscape and poor road system meant the highway was forced to wind around a thousand miles to get to Callao, Peru's largest port. A huge swath of concrete snaked from the city of Macusani, not far from where they were, round Cuzco, and then to the coast and up past Lima. With no stops, it was about twenty-four hour's drive. Although they had agreed it would not be clever to try and make it in one trip, really, they had no choice.

Freya had one arm jammed against the ceiling of the truck, the other hanging onto the thin lip of the window sill. Her feet were forced under the seat in front of her. In this position, she had formed a splayed tripod of support, preventing her skull from being smashed against the chassis. Kelly, on the other hand, bounced around the inside of the cabin. But, his relaxed manner seemed to endow him with the ability to become one with the interior, flowing with each and every bump.

"How the hell are you doing that?" Freya said, her frustration evident.

"Hmm?" Kelly absentmindedly replied.

"That. How do you not have to wedge yourself into your seat to avoid whiplash?"

"You spend enough time in these things, you get used to it. I usually go to sleep on these trips, especially if it's a long way." He shrugged and went back to his thoughts.

"You okay?"

Kelly looked up, his brow furrowed. He appeared to be irritated at being disturbed again. "What? Oh, yeah, sure. I'm just tired, I guess. A lot on my mind." He paused. "Egypt. I've not been back in a long time." He forced a weak smile.

"I've never been. Did you like it?" Small talk. She wasn't good at it, but they were going to be in this truck for a long time.

"Yeah, I was always fascinated with it as a kid. Always wanted to photograph the pyramids, and inside the tombs at the Valley of the Kings." He chuckled quietly. "Actually, when I first went, I tried and got kicked out of a tomb for taking snaps. I refused to pay baksheesh to the guard who caught me. Never made that mistake again."

"You went there a lot?"

"Yeah. Usually as a stopover to somewhere else I was going for work. But I had my ... contact there, so it was a good place to make a layover—learned a lot. Izel had taught kids out there for a while, too. She loved all the ancient history stuff. She used to talk at me incessantly about it all. She was obsessed with the pyramids, where they came from, where we, humans, came from. She would've loved all this crap."

The sudden change from rough terrain to the much smoother tarmac cut Kelly short. The truck swerved to the left as the driver struggled to maintain control. Two or three sharp maneuvers and the Toyota was once again speeding along in a straight line. "Steady there, esé."

"Sorry, Señor!" The little Hispanic man bowed his head and grimaced, thankful he hadn't killed his passengers.

"Where did you find this guy?" Freya asked.

"In Macusani. He apparently came down to trade a few bits and pieces with the villagers after driving for hours to get to them. The old man described him as crazy. Said if we needed a truck, he was our man."

"Does he know what we are carrying in the back?"

"Nope. Don't ask, don't tell. Kinda how things work down here. We're paying him enough not to ask questions."

"You do know some interesting people, Kelly Graham." Freya had one eyebrow raised and a smirk on her face.

Kelly furrowed his brow and gave her a quizzical look. Was she making fun of him, or did she think he was an asshole? He shook the thought out of his head and changed the subject. "Do you think Moby's all right back there?" Twisting his body, he peered out of the narrow rear window at the long flatbed. A heavy, green tarp was stretched across a makeshift frame, forming a tent-like structure. Underneath was a large bath tub that had been bolted to the metalwork of the Toyota. Inside was K'in. The few inches of water left from the constant bouncing of the truck were sloshing about his limbs. He cocked his head to one side, staring back at Kelly through the glass.

"Can't you feel him?"

After a moment, Kelly turned to Freya. "Yeah. Sometimes, I just tune out, though. Kinda hard to explain, but when I let myself feel him, he makes me calm, and there's no pain. It's like I'm losing them."

"Who?"

"My family. I feel guilty for feeling happy."

Freya stared deep into him. He looked in pain. "You know, K'in's influence may be a good thing for you. You have to let them go sometime." Again, she thought about reaching out a hand of comfort but couldn't make her arm muscles move.

"No, I don't." He spun back around in his seat and stared directly in front at the passenger headrest. Their conversation was over.

The beat-up Toyota grunted along the highway. It was dark now, and both Kelly and Freya had fallen asleep in the back. There were almost no lights along the road. Only the occasional passing car lit up the concrete, blinding their driver each time.

Kelly squirmed in the back but not so much as to disturb the sleeping Freya who had huddled up next to him. Even a few years as a married man had taught him how to ensure you didn't wake the woman next to you. But his efforts were in vain. The truck skidded to a hard stop, propelling them into the front seats. Instantly, both were wide awake. Freya had the Beretta in hand. Kelly cussed under his breath.

"What the fuck, esé."

"Sorry, Señor. But we have little problem." The driver nodded toward the flashing blue light in the distance. "Policía."

"Shit. We don't need this."

"What do you think?" Freya was already wielding her weapon in one hand, the other hand on the door handle. "Do we take them out?"

"Jesus, Freya. Take them out? We can't afford to have the Peruvian cops on our ass as well. We gotta lay low. This is South America. The cops here are a little more, shall we say, flexible. Watch and learn." Kelly straightened his t-shirt and stepped out into the cold night air.

Two police officers in moss-green uniforms and military style hats marched towards the Toyota, brandishing hand-held flashlights that cut through the starless night. One man was fairly thin with a large moustache. The other was rotund and clean shaven, though both looked sweaty and altogether unhealthy. Kelly strutted equally confident toward the men. Freya watched nervously from inside the truck.

"*Buenas tardes. ¿Donde estás viajando?*"

"*Buenas tardes. Estamos viajando a Callao. ¿Es algo incorrecto?*" Kelly replied.

The conversation carried on outside the vehicle, but Freya could not hear what was being said. Kelly had reached into his pocket and pulled out a wad of crumpled bills. One of the officers smiled and eyed the fistful of dollars. The other, however, peered over Kelly's shoulder at the pickup, examining the tarp. Clearly, the man figured there was something worth more than the handful of notes Kelly had offered. Had K'in moved? Could the man see? It made Freya uneasy. She could feel this wasn't going to go well. C'mon, Kelly. Tell me that charm doesn't just work on women.

The curious officer sidestepped Kelly and strode toward the truck, holding the flashlight at head height, directing its dazzling beam through the windows. Freya reacted instantly, exited the truck and blocked the officer's path. She pulled one of the Berettas strapped to her waist from its holster and concealed it behind her back. She tried a sweet smile but knew her current state, smeared makeup and greasy hair, was not going to win this man over.

Angry, the policeman barked something at her in Spanish. Freya didn't budge. Instead, she bore a stare into the back of Kelly's head, willing him to turn around. He must have felt it, because he glanced backward. Her eyes were wide and eyebrows raised. He knew what it meant. Kelly sighed, rolled his eyes, and nodded. *Now.*

Freya swiftly swung her right arm in an arc and smashed the butt of her gun into the side of the officer's head. It sent him sprawling into the passenger door of the Toyota. Before the second officer could draw his weapon, Kelly had thrown a right hook that knocked the man to the ground. Without hesitation, Kelly dropped to the road and forced his right knee into the man's neck. The officer struggled momentarily before passing out.

"Fuck! This isn't good." Kelly rubbed his head.

"We tie them up and put them in their car. Someone will find them tomorrow morning." Freya had already grabbed one of the men by his ankles and was dragging him, face down, along the road. "Quickly, before someone else comes along and sees this."

Kelly complied and hauled his victim over one shoulder. Each man was placed in the back of the police car, a large, silver four-by-four. Searching the inside, Kelly stumbled upon two pairs of handcuffs. These would do. He heaved the two men into position so they rested back to back. He cuffed each man to the other, one set of cuffs per arm.

"There." Kelly grunted as he clambered out of the police vehicle.

"But what about him?" Freya nodded to their driver.

"They'll surely check the plates and find who it's registered to."

"I'd like to see them try. It's got fake plates." Kelly smirked. "We changed them for the first leg. He can put new ones on for his trip back. Figured something like this might happen. Cops stop people for no reason. Didn't want anyone tracking the truck. Thought we could buy our way out of problems like that, but guess I fucked up there. Nice swing by the way. I'm impressed." Kelly was walking backward to the rear of the police car.

She smiled. An open compliment. Normally, they were concealed within some sort of flippant comment. "Where are you going?"

"To buy us some time. We need to hide this car at the side of the road. Don't want anyone offering assistance too early."

Freya nodded. "Good point." She reached inside the car and turned off the headlights before yanking the keys from the ignition and throwing them away into the dark. She released the handbrake, slammed the door shut, and joined Kelly at the rear of the car. He was bent forward in a braced position, palms resting squarely on the rear window.

"Ready?"

"Ready."

They strained and pushed with their legs, forcing the car to move slowly, the gravel crunching under the tires. The initial resistance waned and the car picked up speed. Moments later, it was safely concealed by a large bush. They dusted their clothes off, jogged to the Hilux, and climbed back inside.

"Go, esé."

The driver nodded nervously. "Si, Señor."

Location: Washington D.C., USA

The Secretary of State stared blankly at the reports. She couldn't read another one. Most of Nevada and California was now under control of FEMA and martial law. Despite their estimations about how this thing was supposed to spread, it was certainly causing serious damage. All arms of the military and national security had been called in to quarantine the states—no one allowed in, and no one allowed out. Hospitals were filling quickly, and the makeshift triage units were overflowing. While a General order had been issued to keep everyone in their homes, looting and opportunistic ransacking was still rife.

The President requested the Secretary keep him updated on the virus, leaving him free to offer face time with the media in an attempt to calm the hysteria. Of course, the news stations were already making huge leaps, connecting the situation on the western seaboard with the exposure of the government files on the creature. As would be expected, the President had denied it all up until recently. He didn't know the whole truth anyway. She had intended to tell him but, following another conversation with the Colonel, had decided against it. Complete deniability was what the President needed. Not for his sake but for America's. If the people lost faith in their leader and in the government as a whole, things would get a lot worse. So instead, she would deal with this quietly. She had told the President to continue keeping the nation calm. She would deal with the Chinese for now.

The Chinese were being extraordinarily quiet about the whole thing. If the U.S. had invaded Chinese waters and attacked one of their ships, why were they not declaring all-out war? Why only one attack on Area 51?

She looked at her watch. Thirty minutes until her call with them. The last one had been strange. Lots of questions and very few answers. They had clearly been hiding something, but what? She picked up the coffee cup and took another sip. *Eurgh*. It was cold.

The video conference system burst into life. He was early. That was unusual. The Secretary fidgeted with her white blouse to straighten it and tucked a lock of blondish bob-cut hair behind her right ear. Breathe. She crinkled her button nose and pushed *answer* on the screen.

The doctor appeared. Dark circles hung under his eyes and a bristly beard cast a shadow on his face. "Madam Secretary?"

She exhaled in relief. "Yes, you have more information for me?"

"Some. We have managed to slow down the virus's rate of replication by super cooling it, which is a good thing. It means we have the possibility to study it. The only issue is obtaining a viable host. The temperature we have to use is too low for the animals. They die before we reach it." The doctor had grey bags under his eyes and pallid skin. He must have landed and gone straight to the laboratory to work.

"Is there any way to confirm the origin of the virus? Can we definitively say it came from the Chinese?"

"Not at this time. We are analyzing its structure. It will be a few more hours before we can cross-reference with known biological weapons in development. But, to be honest, even when we have its structure, there is no guarantee we can say it came from them, even if it did. They may have bought the technology from another faction, or worse, our intelligence on their biological weapons program might not be up to date."

"Damn. So what is your current plan of action?"

"To figure out the genetic code of this thing, and if possible, develop something to slow it or even stop it. I'm basing my research on work originally published in early 2006. A team studying the Ebola virus, right here in this lab, announced a seventy-five percent recovery rate after infecting four rhesus monkeys and treating them with a drug class known as morpholinos. They are a type of compound that stops genetic material being translated and, thus, protein formation. Basically, it stops the virus from replicating."

The Secretary nodded.

"We essentially have two problems. One is to figure out the exact genetic code of the virus, so we can create a morpholino to match the sequence—genetic antisense. The second problem is the delivery of morpholinos into adult tissues is quite difficult. The drug has to enter the cells. Systemic delivery into many cells in adult organisms can be achieved by joining the drug with cell-penetrating peptides. But too high a dose and the patient has quite severe side effects." He paused to take a deep breath.

"What's the bottom line, Christian?"

"Time, sis. I need more time."

"We don't have time. Please, do all you can."

He nodded and then ended the call, leaving her once again in the dimly lit room, alone.

She sat for a moment, trying to gather her thoughts. Her one ally, her brother, was doing his best—not just in the lab but to be professional and give her the strength to do her job. He kept using her title—so sweet. She really needed him right now.

Her hazel eyes no longer flickered with fire for her country and her position within the government. It had not been how she had expected, and certainly, the naivety of youth had driven her along a path she was unsure she now wanted. What was the point of holding such a prestigious post if it was only to be the pretty face of America when in the presence of foreign powers? The military made all the decisions anyway, and the President took advice from them before anyone else.

The video conference system sprang into life. This time it would be them. She cleared her throat and assumed as authoritative a position as she could while seated. After a deep breath, she pressed the answer key. The video screen flicked on, revealing the image of Li Xiaoping, Minister of Foreign Affairs for the People's Republic of China. He was a plump man in his fifties with thick glasses and thin lips. As always, his face was expressionless, deadpan.

"Minister Li, it is good to see you again."

"We have no time for pleasantries, Ms. Taylor. To be more accurate, I have no time." His tone was flat.

The Secretary eyed him. In all her dealings with the man, he had never been so forward or direct. It was always a game, a battle of wits and insincerities designed to veil subtle threats. His new tact made her nervous. "I understand, but—"

He interrupted her. "Madam Secretary, what I am about to tell you is of the utmost importance and highly sensitive. The mere fact I'm divulging this information to you could cost me—well, let me say, more than my position."

"Please, continue."

"You and I both know a few weeks ago, a U.S. military group entered Chinese waters and assassinated the crew of one of our ships. In addition, this group stole an item from the crew of that ship." Again, his voice carried no emotion. Before the Secretary could respond, he continued. "This invasion was related to a project that has been in operation for more than sixty years—a project regarding a life form found in Siberia by our scientists many years ago. A life form the U.S. Government saw fit to steal from us. These attacks on China would normally result in swift and effective retaliation. However …" He paused.

"However?"

"However, I do not believe your President or ours wishes for war."

The Secretary nodded in agreement. "Of course, but—"

"Madam Secretary, I will be frank and reveal only what I need to if you will do the same." There was a crack, a slight quiver in his voice.

She hesitated. Such openness from this man was unheard of. She couldn't afford to kill this line of dialogue, so again, she nodded in agreement.

"I assume your President is unaware of these attacks. In fact, I would assume he is unaware of the project in its entirety. Given the length of this *operation*, it is likely under control of the military."

She didn't respond.

"Similarly," Minister Li continued, "our President is unaware of the last sixty years, too. Are you familiar with the Green and the Red Societies?"

"Yes, but their existence has never been proven." Secret societies? This is why he called her?

"The Green and the Red Societies are very real, Ms. Taylor. They have existed since the latter half of the seventeenth century, mainly as an underground anti-establishment faction. Ultimately, they have utopian ideals—protection of the weak and justice for the innocent. They last rose from the underground in the 1940s to fight the communists but lost. Since then, they have infiltrated the highest levels of the Chinese Government. However, over time, there has been a division in the interpretation of the ideals."

"I'm not sure how all this fits together," confessed the Secretary.

"Members of the Green and the Red Societies were part of the original team that found the life form. However, after it was believed lost—when the U.S. Government stole it—our military took over all aspects of the remaining project. Since then, we—" He stopped.

"You? You're a member?"

He didn't speak for a few moments, but then nodded. "Do you know what the creature represents, Ms. Taylor? Salvation. For us all. But we are divided as to how that salvation should be achieved. A group of us believes destruction of Western power will be the only way. Your problem is the leader of this splinter cell resides within the People's Liberation Army. He is the chairman of the Central Military Commission."

"And he authorized this splinter cell to let a virus loose in America?" the Secretary asked.

"Yes. Once he had evidence your government had the creature and had cloned it, he was determined to retrieve it and wipe out your country."

"Do you have the antidote, to the virus, I mean?" She was perched on the edge of her seat.

"No. For those of us who want to avoid war and embrace what the creature has to teach, penetration into the government is limited to peace keeping and academic posts."

"Goddamnit." She didn't mean to curse openly, but her inexperience had gotten the better of her. "I'm sorry, but then what is the point of our conversation?"

"You are young, Ms. Taylor, and untainted by the world. My research on you, your charity and humanitarian work during higher education, led me to believe you would do the right thing. We cannot afford to hide now. We need to take action." Any veil of pretense had vanished.

"What do you want me to do?"

"We know you are no longer in possession of the life form. It seems you too are unable to control all aspects of your covert operations. But do you know where it is?"

Should she trust him? Should she tell him the truth? He had been seemingly open with her. And she wanted to avoid war at all costs. "No." The word slipped from her mouth. "We are currently looking for the team that has it, but they have gone AWOL."

"That may work to our advantage. You need to inhibit the ability of your military to find the creature—for now."

"Why? So you can find it first?"

"No, Ms. Taylor. I do not want it in the hands of our military any more than in the hands of yours. Whoever has the animal is hiding it for a reason. We can only hope they also believe in peace and that it can be found through this being. Who is heading up the search for your rogue team?"

"Colonel Robertson." As she spoke his name, it was suddenly strange to her the head of the CDC would lead the mission to retrieve the creature. But she could ponder it no further as the Minister spoke again.

"You must not let him or his team get near the life form. Please, Madam Secretary."

It was the first time she had ever heard him use the word *please*. It was unbelievable. "I will investigate further, Minister Li. But what of the virus and your military? They are sure to strike."

135

"I will deal with the Chairman. Tell your President not to retaliate. Tell him we do not want war."

"Okay, I will, but—"

The Minister cut off the video conference, and once again, she was alone in the dark with a head full of chaotic thoughts. Time was running out, and although she couldn't admit it to anyone else, she didn't have a clue what she was supposed to do.

CHAPTER SEVENTEEN

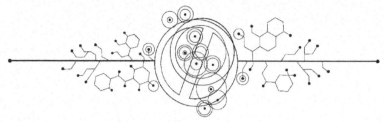

Location: Callao, Peru, South America

Kelly awoke with a start to the sound of a wet slapping on the rear window. K'in was peering through, his mouth slightly open, panting. Clearly he wanted Kelly to wake up. The playful creature had placed both hands on the glass. It took a few moments, but eventually, Kelly was able to focus on K'in's digits. They looked different. He frowned and moved closer to the animal's hands. Where was the webbing? He was sure it had been there before. Kelly touched the glass, wanting to feel K'in's skin. He looked up and caught the creature's gaze. K'in's eyes were warm, almost loving. And blue. Kelly grabbed at Freya's shoulder and shook her violently.

She protested, forcing her eyelids apart. "What?"

"Look at his eyes." Kelly sounded excited. Freya pried herself from the warm spot on the old leather seat that had molded around her. She blinked away the sleepiness and tried to focus on K'in. K'in stared back. It was strange, and although she knew it impossible, he seemed to be smiling. Perhaps she was feeling him, or perhaps it was the huge iridescent sapphire irises surrounding one-inch pupils. Like blue fire, different shades of cobalt and electric arcs of white danced within. Mesmerizing. She sat upright. "What do you think's happening?"

"Fuck if I know," Kelly replied. He was gaping at the creature.

"Señor," interrupted the driver. "We're coming into Callao."

"Make your way to the dock, pier forty-seven." Kelly kept his eyes on K'in.

"Kelly, look at me." Freya gently pulled his face her way. She concentrated on his eyes, flicking her focus between his left and right eye. She turned to K'in. "It's the same."

"What's the same?" He seemed offended.

"You both have the same color eyes. Exactly the same." She pulled her hand away and sat back, glancing at Kelly, and then K'in, and then back again.

"Don't be stupid. Look at him. They are bright blue. Mine aren't even close."

Freya surveyed him. He was right about one thing. When they'd met, his eyes had been a dirty blue, but now they had more life, more fire. "They are different too. See?" She pulled her smartphone from her jungle pants and quickly took a picture before Kelly could protest. She turned the device to reveal the display.

Kelly gasped. "What the frig has Moby done to me?" He grabbed the phone from her hand and flicked on the camera so he could see himself. He pulled at his eyelids, grimacing in as many ways as he could think of. "Am I gonna turn into a fish? Shit, after the last couple weeks, I'm surprised I haven't grown fucking gills and sprouted pink hair out of my ass."

"Nice, Kelly."

"It's all right for you. You're not the one who's gonna grow fins."

Freya shook her head and turned away, leaving Kelly to continue examining his face.

The truck shuddered to a stop. They were there. The General had been clear—they should stay in the vehicle and not expose themselves. The journey had taken longer than anticipated, and it was now broad daylight, which made it even more dangerous. Freya sat lost in her own thoughts.

What had not been made clear was how the General intended to get from the submarine to land and back again with K'in. Was he going to swim? How far inland could he come? How was he to remain undetected? She hadn't questioned him. She'd been focused on getting here. But more than that, she had been happy Benjamin was alive.

"Are we just supposed to sit here?" Kelly squirmed in his seat. His t-shirt was soaked with sweat and stuck to his chest and shoulders. "It's friggin' hot in here."

"Benjamin said to wait here. He'll come for us."

Kelly muttered under his breath. "He'll come for Moby."

An hour passed in silence. The driver had patiently kept to quiet in the front and even pulled his baseball cap over his eyes in order to take a short nap. Kelly and Freya had remained in taciturnity, not even sharing a glance. Even K'in had seemed to take the opportunity to catch up on some rest, sleeping in his makeshift greenhouse—the heat evaporating the water, creating a humid, sticky, atmosphere under the tarp.

There was a light tapping at the window. It jarred Kelly from his trancelike state. He swiveled around and peered out of the passenger-side window. A huge silhouette stood before him, the blazing sun burning brightly behind.

"Andre." Kelly laughed as he opened the car door. "Only you could block out the sun, you massive bastard."

Tremaine shook his head. "James. My name is James, dumbass." The Shadow Man was dressed in dark blue combat clothing. Huge black military boots completed the outfit. He had even found time to shave.

"Sure, sure, James. Like I'm gonna argue with you. I'd call you Nancy if you told me to."

Tremaine raised an eyebrow. "A girl's name? Says the man named Kelly."

"Hey, my family is Welsh. I'm just glad I'm not named after some kind of sheep." He shrugged and walked around to the driver's side of the vehicle.

The driver wound down the window. "Si?"

"I'm gonna need you to make yourself scarce for an hour, okay?" He handed a fistful of money from his pocket to the little man.

"Si, Señor." The man nodded and climbed out of the truck. He pulled his cap low to obscure his face, and perhaps his own vision, and scurried off down the dock toward the city center.

Freya stepped out of the vehicle and peered over its roof. "Hey, Tremaine." Her voice was gentle and warm.

"Hey," was all he offered in return. She glanced around, searching expectantly for the General. To her disappointment, Tremaine was alone.

"Well, I'm glad you two haven't lost the art of conversation." Kelly had already marched back around the Hilux and was standing beside the Shadow Man. "So now what? Where's the General? How do we get Moby into your tin can?"

"We used the ASDS to come ashore. A small crew is still inside. The General and the XO are on the sub, waiting for me to return with the creature."

"Oh," Freya said quietly. It was only meant for her but was quite audible to both men.

Kelly flicked a quizzical look at her but decided to bulldoze past the moment. "That doesn't answer my question there, Andre."

The Shadow Man glared at him.

"James, I mean James—or JT? I like JT. Suits you." He slapped the Shadow Man on the shoulder. It was like rock, leaving a stinging sensation on Kelly's palm. Kelly glanced over to Freya and shrugged.

"Okay, Tremaine. What's the plan of action?" she asked.

"We wait till dark. Then make our way to the end of pier forty-seven. We load the creature into the ASDS, and I take it back to the General. You and Mr. Graham continue on your original plan. The General asked if you needed anyone else to go with you."

"No," Kelly said. He stopped leaning on the truck and stood straight. "We can't afford to draw attention to ourselves. I can use my more *innovative* connections to get us places, but there's no way they are gonna help me with a bunch of guerrillas hanging about. Especially you, JT. Can't have you causing eclipses everywhere we go."

Tremaine fixed on Freya, silently asking for confirmation. She nodded. "He's not eloquent. But he's right."

"I'm always right. But right now, we are about to have a steam-cooked salamander in there." He pointed to the flatbed. "So where are we gonna hole up for a while? We've at least got to put this thing in the shade."

The others nodded in agreement.

"Let's put it down by the dock," Tremaine said. "There are empty boathouses there. I'm sure we can use one for a few hours."

"Good idea. Plus, I'm starving." Kelly rubbed his stomach. "Need to get some grub. You two take Moby. I'll go find us something to eat. I also have to rustle up some transport. I have a few connections down this way. How deep are your pockets again, guys? I'm gonna need some walkin' around money."

"Take this." Freya handed him a card. "You'll be able to draw some money, but you'll only be able to do it once. It's a secret account for emergencies. I don't think people will be focused on it for now, but I'm sure once it's used, flags will be raised."

"Thanks. How much can I draw?"

"How much do you need?"

"Man, was I in the wrong line of work." Kelly shook his head and meandered away. The haze of the midday heat wafted the air above the concrete upward, obscuring his outline until he was no longer visible.

Tremaine turned to Freya. "You okay?"

"Yeah, I'm fine. He's not that bad once you get used to him." She cast a glance at the path Kelly had taken, but he was nowhere to be seen.

Tremaine eyed her. "You sure you're alright? You seem … different."

Freya looked at herself and, for the first time, realized how she looked. No high-heeled shoes, no makeup, no tight-fitting dress, and her hair was so tangled that it suggested she had been dragged backward through a field. A smile broke across her face. "You know," she said. "I'm actually very okay."

"Inside joke?"

"No, just …" she began, but stopped.

"Just?"

"Nothing." It was hard to explain. Perhaps it was K'in. Perhaps it was the situation. But she was relaxed—particularly around Kelly—and there was no need to be aggressive, sexual, or otherwise. She was happy trudging around in jungle boots. Freya pulled her ponytail tight again and brushed down her combat pants, the dust flying off in all directions. "C'mon, let's get this truck in the shade."

An hour had passed, and Kelly had not returned. They had moved the truck into an old, wooden boathouse at the far end of the dock and then sat talking. Tremaine had recounted his side of events after Freya had left the submarine in Monterey Bay. She had been unaware the General had been attacked in the hospital, and the young pilot Wiezorek had saved his life. She so desperately wanted to see the General—Benjamin, her godfather. In the midst of all this, she craved security. It was exhausting being strong on the outside. Benjamin was the only person with whom she could show weakness—except Kelly. She couldn't explain it, but he made her feel safe. It was probably his unfailing confidence in whatever he did, right or wrong.

The conversation had taken all of thirty minutes—quick and concise, true to military standard and, of course, true to Tremaine. He was always to the point and didn't use more words than needed. Freya knew he really didn't like Kelly who was his polar opposite. For the most part, Kelly didn't shut up. And what came out of his mouth was usually laced with sarcasm and expletives. If you could get beyond the layers of crap designed to preserve whatever was beneath, Kelly was actually quite sweet. Sometimes she'd catch him looking at her, genuine concern and caring in his eyes. Tremaine on the other hand was a closed book. She'd worked with the man for *several years* yet, only today, learned that his Christian name was James. When they had first met, she had asked, but "Tremaine" was his only response. It was fairly commonplace to use family names when addressing colleagues, so she hadn't questioned it. And since Benjamin had personally vouched for him, everything else was moot. He was her silent partner. Like a giant Doberman forever guarding her, he never left her side. It had been that way since they started working together. She smiled. He may not have been much of a conversationalist, but she was glad he was here.

Kelly bowled into the boathouse. He swaggered over to the Hilux, looking extraordinarily pleased with himself, and rapped on the roof with his knuckles. "Afternoon in there. Not interrupting, am I?"

Tremaine stared at him through the window, his face impassive. "No, not interrupting."

Freya ignored his jibe at Tremaine and exited the car. "Did you do whatever it was you needed?"

"Yep, got us some transport to Egypt—kind of. Here." He tossed a small packet across to her.

Freya opened it to find a small, very warm sandwich comprised of white bread and some kind of meat—though it was not clear from which animal it had come. "Thanks … I think." She pried the sandwich open, hoping to better understand its contents. It didn't help.

"I got one for you, too, JT." Kelly tapped on the window and made a little wind-down-the-window gesture. Tremaine rolled his eyes and complied. Kelly tossed in the sandwich, nearly hitting the man in his left eye, before making his way around to the back of the flatbed. He uncoupled the straps holding the tarp in place and poked his head through the flap.

"Jesus, it's hot in here. Did these heartless bastards leave you to boil in here, Moby?" Kelly shook his head. He threw in the remaining package, which contained three sandwiches *sans* mystery meat, and poured a bottle of water directly into the bathtub. "Here. Drink, bathe, wallow, do whatever it is you do."

"Kelly!" Freya tapped her foot in annoyance.

He grimaced and threw a pained look at K'in. "Oops. In trouble again, Moby."

K'in didn't pay any attention. He was busily munching on the sandwiches that were quickly soaking up the water in the tub.

Kelly pulled his head from the tarp. "Yes, dear?"

"Transport, Kelly. Focus."

He wandered around to Freya's side of the truck. "Sure, right. So, how would you like to get to Egypt, pretty much undetected, in about sixteen hours?"

"How the hell did you manage that?" Tremaine asked as he leaned through the window nearest Freya, his mouth stuffed with sandwich.

"I bagged us a G650."

"A G650. You *bought* a G650?" Freya's eyes widened.

"No, no, no. Don't be stupid. I didn't think I could draw out sixty-million bucks from your account. No, I bought information as to where we can get one."

"Where?" Tremaine and Freya asked in unison.

"Well, there's a guy around here. He's, shall we say, pretty rich. But he's not exactly legal. So he won't go reporting his missing plane—you get me?" Kelly took a bite of a sandwich he had pulled from the side pocket of his combat pants. It looked warm, flaccid, and completely unappetizing. Still, Kelly scoffed it while waiting for a response.

"So we have to go and steal a plane," Tremaine said.

"Not we. Kelly and I," Freya replied. "As soon as it's dark, you need to get K'in to the submarine. We will go and steal the plane."

"Right." The Shadow Man withdrew back into the car.

Kelly frowned. "Don't worry, JT. I'm sure you'll get to steal something soon."

Silence.

"Anyhoo." Kelly pointed his flaccid sandwich at Freya. "I assume you know how to fly it?"

"I can fly it. Benjamin taught me how to fly when ..." She paused a moment. "He taught me."

"Of course, he did."

"Where is your little driver?" Freya changed the subject.

"I met him on the way and gave him some cash for a night in a hotel and to buy a new ride. Didn't want him in any more trouble than he needs to be. Someone is going to ID this truck eventually. He can just report it stolen."

"Just how much did you draw out of the account?" Freya pursed her lips, afraid of the answer.

Kelly laughed. "Enough."

CHAPTER EIGHTEEN

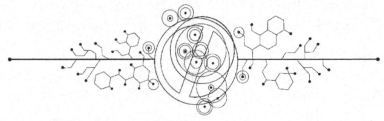

Location: Callao, Peru, South America

His watch showed three in the morning. Shit, it was early. In the gloom of the unlit boat shed, Kelly barely made out Freya's sleeping form next to him in the Hilux. She was curled in a ball, her head resting on his lap. He smiled and admired how peaceful she appeared. He moved a hand to stroke her hair but immediately retracted it as the gravity of his action dawned on him. What the hell was he thinking? He couldn't go down that road again. He couldn't get attached. It was a bad idea. Anyway, he had a wife. She was gone in body but not in spirit. He shook off the uncomfortable train of thought and turned his attention to the much larger lump, squashed in the front passenger seat. James Tremaine, Freya's disapproving sidekick. Kelly smirked, then rapped with his knuckles on the man's bald head. "Yo, JT, time to get up."

The Shadow Man lurched into life, instinctively pulling his Kimber ICQB from its holster. He swung it around and pointed it at Kelly's forehead. "Gimme a reason."

"Whoa, someone's grumpy in the morning. Relax, JT." Kelly raised his hands, motioning the agent to calm down.

Freya yawned and stretched. Then sat up. Crap, she was on his lap. Best to ignore it. Maybe he hadn't noticed. "C'mon boys, enough." She shuffled out of the car and into the cold, damp air. The chilling water vapor clung to her bare arms, making her shiver.

"Cold, right?" Kelly had also exited and was busily untying the ropes on the tarp that concealed K'in. She nodded and rubbed her hands together in an attempt to generate heat from the friction.

Kelly thought about offering her his jacket, but again, the words never passed his lips. Besides, she had a jacket in the truck—she just had to put it on. He peered through the gap in the tarp. The creature was wide awake and ecstatic to see Kelly. He puffed out his crimson gills and leapt past Kelly down from the flatbed, to the ground. He stretched his back and limbs like a newly woken dog.

"Okay, Moby, it's time for you to take a little trip."

K'in scurried up to Kelly, reared onto his hind legs, and placed his front legs onto Kelly's shoulders. Their eyes locked. A massive wave of warmth ran from Kelly's stomach up through his chest and into his head. K'in had connected. The creature smacked its tiny lips together, all the while staring into Kelly's face. K'in's eyes glowed.

"What the hell is it doing?" Tremaine stood next to Freya, his arms folded across his chest.

"Saying hi," she replied and proceeded to walk over to Kelly. She rested a hand on K'in's head, absorbing the warmth through him. The creature swiveled his head to see her and rubbed the end of his face on hers. Freya laughed, pulling away, her eyes screwed up. K'in dropped to the ground and waddled around on all fours until he reached Tremaine. The animal cocked his head to one side, deciding if he liked the Shadow Man. Evidently, he didn't. He scampered to Kelly's side and plonked down by his feet. Freya and Kelly choked back a laugh.

"Hey, we still like you, JT."

Freya erupted into a full-blown snort.

"Sure." Tremaine grunted in annoyance. "Let's just get on with this."

"Yes, yes." Freya regained her composure. "How will we do it?"

"Well ..." Kelly started.

"He's calling the shots now?"

Freya jumped to Kelly's defense. "No, but he knows where to get the plane, and he knows who we are going to see in Egypt. Ergo, he at least has a say. Right?"

"It's okay, toots, I can justify myself."

Freya huffed.

"JT, you take Moby to your mini sub. Wrap him in the tarp from the truck. You'll be faster if you carry him on your back, and much less conspicuous. We'll go get the plane. Once we're in Egypt, we'll send you another message with an update."

The Shadow Man ignored Kelly and cast his gaze to Freya. He raised his eyebrows expectantly.

She shrugged. "Seems fairly sensible to me."

"Fine." Tremaine marched over to the truck and grabbed the tarp with both hands. With a swift and mighty heave, he ripped the material from the chassis. Glaring at Kelly, he stepped over K'in and attempted to drop the tarp onto the animal's back. K'in bucked, throwing the heavy sheet to the floor, before scurrying behind Kelly's legs for protection.

"Moby! Hey, calm down. It'll be alright." Kelly bent down, rested on his haunches, and patted the animal on the head.

"You gotta go with the walking fridge here, okay?" K'in shuffled his feet uneasily.

"He's an ugly fucker, I know, but I'll come back for you. Just try not to look at him." Kelly threw a smarmy glance up at the now fuming Shadow Man and then turned his attention back to K'in. "I'll come back for you. I promise."

The animal responded and skulked around Kelly toward Tremaine.

The Shadow Man thought it looked as if it were sulking, but figured that was impossible. Animals didn't have emotions. Tremaine wrapped the heavy sheet around K'in and slung the creature over one shoulder. He stared at Kelly before turning to face Freya. "Take care."

"You too," she replied. As always, their conversations were short and not sweet.

Tremaine made an about-face and strode toward the door of the boathouse. He carefully pushed on it until he could peer through a small gap. With the coast clear, he shoved the door open and slipped through the space into the night, K'in flapping about on his back.

"Right then, we best go plane shopping," Kelly said.

They climbed into the Hilux. Kelly turned over the engine and pumped the gas with the handbrake engaged. Satisfied the battered, old vehicle was still roadworthy, he released the brake and drove up to the large doors. He crept the car forward, nudging the wooden doors open. As the hood of the car poked through, Kelly could peer out into the starless night. Tremaine was nowhere to be seen but neither was anyone else.

"Coast's clear. Let's go." Kelly pressed the accelerator, letting the truck fully emerge from the boathouse. Then, with a screech of rubber on concrete, they sped off into the dark.

Location: Washington D.C., USA

Alone in her room, the Secretary hovered over the dial button. She didn't

146

want to make the call, but she knew she must. It had been bugging her. Why was the Colonel leading the search party? It was not part of his command within the CDC. It made no sense. She'd gone back through the files on the creature and General Lloyd's and the Chinese's involvement. The facts were there. It was all true. But that was it—just bare facts, no details, and far too few files for such a project. The description of the cloning process alone comprised only a few steps. These things surely were more complicated, right? One day nothing and the next day a fully grown animal has developed? Something was missing.

On top of this, she still had the words of the Chinese Minister ringing in her ears: *Delay the U.S. military from finding the creature.* She didn't know what to do. She wanted to be patriotic. But what did that mean? She knew the answer. She had to work in the best interests of her country. That's why she'd gotten into politics—to make a difference. If nothing else, she had to find some answers.

Her finger pressed *dial* on the touch-sensitive panel. The ring tone hummed. Ten seconds passed and then twenty. She waited a bit longer, but there was no answer. Was he there? He was supposed to be available on demand.

The screen flicked on. The Colonel appeared on the screen, looking slightly irritated and completely distracted.

"Yes?" he demanded.

The Secretary found a rare moment of anger within her. "I'll thank you to remember with whom you are speaking."

"My apologies." The Colonel flashed fake smile. 'With what can I assist you?"

"Information, Colonel. Information. I have been going over the files you sent. It appears incomplete. Do you have anything on the initial cloning attempts? I can't seem to find anything."

The Colonel narrowed his eyes. "I sent you everything we could retrieve from Paradise Ranch, Madam Secretary. You know what I know."

"I highly doubt that, Colonel."

"I'm not sure what it is you want, Madam Secretary. Should your attention not be focused on the possibility of war with the Chinese and containing the virus?"

"Indeed, it is, Colonel. In fact, my discussions with the Chinese Minister went better than expected." Keeping up this level of confidence was draining. She wasn't sure if he could see through it. But she had to carry on. "And for that reason, I need you to oversee the development of the antivirus. You need to be at the CDC facility."

"Madam Secretary, you must be aware I am in the middle of tracking General Lloyd and his team. I will be leaving soon on a transport."

"Yes, about that. Why would *you* be doing that? Your position heading up the CDC does not include a search and rescue remit. Or am I wrong?"

"Madam Secretary, I know Benjamin Lloyd the best. My relationship with him will be an asset to the search team." His voice broke.

"Colonel, your place is with the CDC to oversee the antivirus development. Find someone else to lead the team. Or would you like me to inform the President you have abandoned your post at a time like this?"

He pursed his lips. "Of course, Madam Secretary. I will find someone else."

"Thank you, Colonel. Do you need assistance moving from where you are?"

"No, I'm in a secure facility in New Mexico outside the quarantine zone."

"Good." She flicked off the screen and sat motionless, adrenaline coursing through her. *God, that was nerve-wracking.*

She had managed to delay him, for a while. But she knew it wouldn't stop him entirely. She needed to do something else. But what? The Secretary leaned forward again and tapped away at her console. The video link hummed. This time the reply was quick.

"Yes, Madam Secretary? Can I help you?" The doctor stood in his lab surrounded by monitors and paperwork. His sleeves were rolled up, and his brow was laden with sweat. Clearly he had not managed any kind of rest.

"Doctor Christian, are you any closer to creating an antidote?"

"It's taking time, Lucy—sorry, Madam Secretary—but we are moving closer. At the moment, I have a problem with delivery. I have to keep the virus at very low temperatures. It means everything runs slower. It's a problem I'm trying to sort out. I just need more time."

She hesitated, but then said, "I know, I know. I'm sending the Colonel to oversee the last of the development."

"Lucy, I have been your brother for thirty-three years. You know I don't need him here. What's going on?" He stared directly into the camera.

"Christian, I need you to do me a favor. I need you to trust me."

"Okay."

"When the Colonel gets there, I need you to stall him. He wants to go after the creature on his own. I don't know why, but he isn't telling the truth."

"What has that got to do with the virus and saving all these people?"

"I said trust me. You asked me for time, and I'm asking you to return the favor. I just need to find out more. I need to go to the facility he was at. It doesn't make sense. Why wasn't he at the CDC headquarters anyway?"

Christian paused for a moment. "It's a good question."

"Exactly. I had a very interesting conversation with the Chinese Minister. I just need to investigate a little further. Get to the bottom of this."

"And how should I stall him?"

"I don't know, Christian. Just try, okay?" she pleaded. He couldn't say no to his sister. Fact was, he'd never been very good at saying no to her even when they were kids.

Christian nodded. "Okay."

"Thank you. I'll be in touch soon."

"Take care, sis." He clicked off the conversation.

Location: Callao, Peru, South America

Kelly killed the engine of the Hilux and let it roll to a soft stop. He pulled the handbrake and sat quietly. The moon overhead afforded some light. The tiny, private airfield in front of him didn't look so secure. It was unassuming and had no barbed wire. Sure, there was a wall and a gate, but that was it. In the center was the hangar and off to its right was the single airstrip. Understandably, the owner didn't want to draw too much attention. Kelly still knew in his bones somewhere in there would be a battalion of large Peruvian gangsters with very few morals and a whole lot of artillery.

"I don't like this," Kelly whispered. "I've got serious nutflies."

Freya sighed. "What?"

"You girls get butterflies in your stomach. Guys get them in our nuts. We feel them there. Nutflies." Kelly didn't look at her when speaking. It seemed perfectly logical to him.

Freya raised an eyebrow but couldn't be bothered to question his vocabulary further.

"So what's the plan?" Kelly asked.

"Well, we have the key, which means we can sneak in quietly. I don't want any bullshit from you. No charging in. Quietly. You understand?"

"You got it." Kelly saluted and climbed out of the car before mockingly closing the door as slowly as he could, clicking it shut.

Freya had already exited and was watching him, arms folded across her chest. "Funny."

"What?" Kelly shrugged, grinned, and began his crouched skulk toward the airfield's outer wall.

Freya followed behind, one of her firearms drawn and held in both hands. They rested, backs against the wall, hidden in shadow. The moon's light was not nearly bright enough to see properly. To their left, a large gate blocked the entrance to the airfield.

"Do I get your other gun?"

"It's a Beretta. And no," she replied.

"Humph."

"Does your magical key work for the gate as well or only for the hangar?"

There was a lasting silence as it dawned on Kelly he hadn't asked that particular question. "Umm …"

"Right. Of course you don't know." She held out one hand expectantly.

Kelly pulled a keyring with two keys on it from his pocket and placed it in her palm. "Here."

Freya slid along the wall, never allowing her back to leave the brickwork. She reached the gate and, following a quick glance around, tried the lock. A dull thud confirmed that this was, in fact, not the gate key. Irritated, she pulled it from the keyhole and scurried back to Kelly. "Nope."

"Damn. Well, can't win 'em all! Let's get over this wall. And I'm afraid you are going to have to give me a boost." He smirked.

"What?"

"Well, no offence, but I don't think you have the upper body strength to lift me if you go first. I'm gonna have to pull you up."

She wrinkled her nose. It was annoying when he was right. "Fine, just be quick about it." Freya holstered her gun and braced against the wall, bending her knees and locking her fingers together to create a makeshift foothold. "Okay, go."

He unceremoniously put a dirty boot in her hands and pushed up until he could reach the top edge of the brickwork. Using his free foot and the wall as a launch pad, he attempted to propel himself upward. It was to no avail. He shook his head and sheepishly placed the other boot on Freya's shoulder.

She groaned under his weight, clenching her eyelids together.

As she opened her eyes, something caught her attention. Two men were circling the truck that had been left behind on the other side of the road. She peered through the murk, trying to make out who they were. A brief scan to their left made everything clear. The police. Shit. They were radioing in the license plate. There must have been a BOLO out following the incident on the highway.

"Kelly, we have a problem."

"I know. You are way too lady-like. I need a Russian shot putter."

"Actually, our problem is on the other side of the road."

No sooner had the words left her lips than the officers spotted the would-be burglars scaling the outer wall. One man shouted into his radio while the other bolted toward them, a flashlight in hand, its beam flailing left and right with his gait.

"Fuck!" Adrenaline coursing through him, Kelly gave an almighty thrust and heaved up onto the wall. On his knees, he reached down with one arm. "Grab it. C'mon."

Freya complied, scrambling up the wall as Kelly hauled her up.

"Now jump!" he yelled.

Several bullets ricocheted off the wall as they leapt down to the tarmac on the other side. Without stopping, they charged toward the hangar, leaving the police officer cursing and unable to pursue.

A burst of yellow blinded them as a searchlight atop a small control tower erupted into life. Several men sprayed the ground with ammunition from the tower's windows.

"Run!" Kelly grabbed Freya's hand and dragged her in his wake.

She struggled to keep up, tripping every few feet and then stumbling back into his meteoric pace. They slammed into the metal doors of the hangar. Freya fumbled with the padlock, wincing and flinching as bullets squealed on the metalwork about her head. Kelly grabbed the spare Beretta from her holster and opened fire in the general direction from which the onslaught of lead was coming. His single shots were pathetic in comparison with the constant and unforgiving rain of destruction pouring down all around him.

"Got it." She threw the padlock away and shoved the sliding door upward, momentum carrying it to a fully open position.

Freya turned to leap inside but yelped as a bullet scathed her right thigh, sending her sprawling into the ground.

Kelly grabbed her and yanked her into the cover of the hangar. "Are you okay?"

"Yeah, it's just a graze." Freya pawed at the open slit in her flesh. "Damn, I bet that's gonna scar."

"Don't worry. Just gives guys an excuse when they get caught staring at your legs." He winked and then tugged at her arm once again. "C'mon, we gotta move."

The G650 stood majestically in the middle of the hangar. Kelly froze where he stood, letting go of Freya's arm to stare in awe. It was regal. More than one-hundred feet long with a wing span equally as wide, it had a long, elegant nose cone balanced by two sleek nacelles at the rear. The machine glowed pearlescent white in the dim light.

Freya had already opened the side door and was ascending the stairs. "C'mon!"

He shook off his boyish wonder and ran after her up the staircase, closing the door behind him. The interior was even more impressive than the exterior—cream leather everything, black glass tables, and wine coolers. Kelly thought these things only existed in cartoons or movies. He cursed the advantages of being a drug-peddling criminal and stepped through the door into the cockpit.

"This thing's got a Gulfstream PlaneView II avionics system. It'll practically fly itself." Freya's excitement grew as she pressed buttons and flicked switches, commanding the twin Rolls-Royce engines to roar into life. The aircraft edged forward. "Sit down. This is going to get bumpy."

For the first time, Kelly did as he was told. He strapped in and sat wide-eyed at the array of colorful monitors. He didn't know what it all meant, but he didn't have to fly the damn thing.

"Here we go." She slid a lever forward, and the jet accelerated.

As soon as the nose emerged from the hangar it was showered with bullets. The cockpit glass remained remarkably unscathed.

"Clever bastard must have had bulletproof glass installed."

"I guess," Freya shouted over the roar of the engine. She swung the plane around and pointed it down the runway. The echo of bullets on the hull shifted from the nose to the left flank.

"Punch it!"

Freya shoved the accelerator. The jet powered forward, throwing its crew back in their seats. The clatter of shrapnel waned as the plane pulled away and upward into the sky. Kelly saw the flashing blue lights of the police surrounding the abandoned truck and the infuriated skyward-firing gunmen in the tower.

"Where are we headed?"

"Egypt," Kelly replied.

"Yes, I know that, smartass." She sighed. "I meant, where in Egypt?"

"Cairo West Airport. It's about thirty-four miles outside of Cairo. They take chartered planes and business flights. I have a buddy there. We'll have no problem landing."

CHAPTER NINETEEN

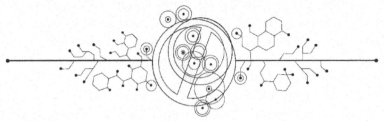

Location: U.S. submarine, somewhere in the Pacific Ocean

Tremaine stared at K'in. The strange animal lay asleep on the floor of its tank, half submerged in water. It looked different now compared with what he had seen back at Paradise Ranch. Its skin was now a fully opaque milky white. Eyelids had formed to shield its retinas from the sunlight, and its gills were a deep scarlet. They billowed outwards and then fell back to a resting position with each breath the creature took. It shook slightly, shivering.

The Shadow Man reached out one of his huge hands to touch the creature. His dark, thick fingers drew close to the contrasting white skin of the animal's head. What was all the fuss about? What did it mean to touch this thing? The temptation to make contact was overwhelming. But he couldn't. He just didn't trust it. Kelly trusted it and so did Freya. And she trusted Kelly, which annoyed Tremaine. He'd spent years protecting her, and that damn fool gets her respect in days. He grunted away the feeling and slowly pulled his hand back, careful not to disturb the air around K'in. As he took an awkward step backward, K'in jerked awake. Caught unaware, Tremaine fell and smashed onto the cold floor. K'in quickly sprang onto all fours and padded over to the fallen man. The creature positioned himself over Tremaine's body and pushed his face directly in front of the man's. He stared into his eyes, blinking as he did so, cocking his head to one side and then the other like a curious plumed bird. Tremaine stared back. His body frozen. Not in fear but confusion. What did it want? He propped himself up on his elbows, bringing his face closer to the animal's. K'in blinked again and sniffed at the Shadow Man's skin. A final blink and the animal quickly reversed, span around, and waddled back to its low-lying tank. He climbed inside and lay back down, tail folded around his body, head resting on his forelimbs.

Tremaine climbed to his feet and pulled his clothes straight. Strange little creature. It was time some other fool watched the goddamn thing. He wasn't a babysitter, or dog sitter, or fish sitter, or whatever kind of sitter there was for that thing. He marched over to the heavy metallic door and pulled it open, stepped into the hallway, and beckoned one of the submariners.

"You watch it for a while."

The soldier nodded.

Tremaine shook his head and continued along the corridor.

The XO, General, and Wiezorek were huddled around the interactive navigation table. An illuminated map of the Pacific Ocean lit the room with a faint green glow.

"Mr. Tremaine." The General acknowledged his subordinate as he entered the room.

"Sir, I'm sorry, but you have to get someone else to babysit the big fish. I think it's sick or something. It just sits in its tank shivering." Tremaine huffed and placed both hands palm down on the table. "Something's not right."

"I would agree, but we have bigger problems right now, Mr. Tremaine. It seems we are being hunted, not only by the Chinese, but by our own government. A few faithful men on the surface have kept me informed. It seems one of the original team, Colonel Robertson, has taken it upon himself to find me."

"So what's the plan?" Tremaine asked, expectantly.

"At the moment, we keep out of sight. We need to protect the creature and keep it from both our government and our enemies. We have to wait until Freya can provide more information regarding a new orb." The General motioned his head toward the XO. "Executive Officer Teller and I were just discussing options. If we found the Chinese down here, then they can find us. We are working on a strategy to stay undetected."

"And we just let Nilsson and Graham fend for themselves?" The Shadow Man's face was as deadpan as ever, but his gaze contained genuine concern.

"They will be fine. As long as the governments are looking for us and not them, they have time. It's easier for them to move undetected as it's just the two of them."

"So that's why I think we move into the Zhemchug Canyon." The XO moved the map on the table of light to hover over an image that showed a relief of the canyon as if the Pacific Ocean had been drained. "It's over two miles deep, one hundred and forty-four miles long, and sixty miles wide. It's the biggest canyon in the world. Let those Chinese bastards find us down there."

"It sounds like a plan to me. Why are we not doing it?"

"Because," interrupted Wiezorek. "We need to be in contact with our away team. And that's very difficult below periscope depth. I'm a chopper pilot, and even I know that." The young pilot fidgeted. He wanted to join the conversation—show his worth.

"It's kinda true," the XO replied. "Subs use extremely low frequency, or ELF, transmissions. The antennas required to receive and transmit these signals are thirty miles long, buried underground. Only a handful of these ELF transmitters exist, and only two of them are in the U.S. If we use them, we'll be detected right away."

"Well that's just useless," Tremaine said.

The XO ignored him and continued. "There have been attempts to bring submarines onto the U.S. Defense Department Global Information Grid along with all the other Navy ships. The High Frequency Active Auroral Research Program, which investigated using the ionosphere as an antenna for communication, was one such attempt. The idea was to excite the upper atmosphere with high-frequency radio waves, and it would then emit the ELF bands required for one-way communication with submerged submarines."

"Thanks for the techno-nerd lesson, but what I'm hearing is we can't communicate at depth, and if we bob around on the surface, we get caught. Right?" Tremaine raised his eyebrows, waiting to be corrected.

"You didn't let me finish." The XO grinned. "It's a Kobayashi Maru situation."

The General scowled. "What?"

"It's a Star Trek reference, again." Tremaine shook his head. "You and Kirk."

The XO's grin broadened. "Everyone's gotta have a role model. The Kobayashi Maru refers to an unwinnable situation. You either need a brilliant solution, or you need to redefine the problem. Kirk cheated. And so shall we."

"Get to the point, man," Tremaine said, irritated.

"My point is this: we are worried about being monitored. So, let's get monitored. Lockheed have developed a classified communication system that uses disposable buoys that jettison to the surface. They can be miles away, but we can use them to transmit to your satellite even when we are submerged. This sub has prototypes."

"What's the range?" Tremaine asked. "Surely it can't be that far? They'll still be able to pinpoint us."

"Well, that's the genius bit. What we need to do is jettison a whole bunch over a few days across a wide area. Then we use them to ping messages between themselves and the satellite. If we also spam a bunch of cell phones and devices all over the globe, it'll be difficult for them to trace who we're talking to."

A small, almost imperceptible smile broke across the Shadow Man's face. "Not bad. Not bad at all."

"Make it happen," commanded the General. "Make it happen now. I can continue to use the coded messaging that only Freya and I would understand." He hushed his voice, realizing his mistake.

The other three shot confused glances at one another.

"I will go and check on the creature. Wiezorek, you come with me. Tremaine, assist the XO with whatever he needs."

"Yes, sir." The young pilot scurried after his commanding officer, who had already stormed out and down the corridor.

Location: A small village, Egypt

His best friend stared at Kelly, not with eyes but with pitch black sockets. His face was chalk white and drawn, and gray shadows replaced his normally full cheeks. A single hole in a Hawaiian shirt pocket leaked thick red liquid. The skeletal figure raised one arm and pointed a bony index finger directly out in front. The ghoul's mouth opened to speak, yet only a chilling noise spewed forth. A noise that embodied pain and suffering.

Kelly lurched awake as the wheels of the jet touched down. He glanced around the cabin. Freya was slowing the plane, guiding it off the runway toward a small hangar to which she had been directed by the control tower. Her gaze remained dead ahead, but he could see the concern on her face.

"Your wife?"

"What?" Kelly snapped.

"Sorry, you just seemed to be having a nightmare."

Kelly sighed and shook his head slowly. "No. Actually, it was Chris. But—"

"Chris?"

"Yeah. But that's not what's bothering me. For the last couple of weeks, I haven't had dreams, not nightmares, anyway. I think they're back because I'm away from K'in."

"Oh? You think his being near you has had an influence on your psyche?"

"You know, I would have to say yes. I've had a weird, uneasy feeling since we left him with the General. I figured I was just nervous about the trip, but I think it's more. I feel—"

"Empty."

Kelly nodded. "Exactly."

"I feel it too, just a little, but I do." She considered placing a hand on Kelly's knee in comfort but thought better of it.

Kelly shook his head as if to remove the dream from his brain like a child clearing an *Etch A Sketch*. "Fuck it. We have enough to do here."

"Well, the instructions you gave worked. We were given permission to land. Do you know where we're going now?"

"It's a village just south of Cairo. My contact is there."

Freya cut the engine and switched off the display. She climbed out of her seat and followed Kelly into the main cabin. A set of small stairs dropped down from the opening. They grabbed their backpacks and took a few paces toward the exit.

As Kelly stepped into the sunlight, the bright desert sun seared his retinas. He closed his eyes in pain, but it seemed as if the photons were slicing through his eyelids anyway. He blinked and swayed unsteadily on the metal stairs.

"Are you okay?" Freya asked.

"Yeah, it's just friggin' bright." Kelly slung his backpack over one shoulder and put his free arm over his forehead to shield his eyes before stomping down the staircase in his heavy jungle boots. Freya marched after him.

A little Egyptian man was waiting by a dilapidated jeep. It wasn't open-top and looked to be sweltering inside. Kelly strode over to the man, who was dressed in a traditional ankle-length galabiya, striped kaftan, and an off-white cap of sort. Kelly muttered something to the man that Freya didn't understand. The occasional word made sense to her. She knew *Ahlan wa sahlan*, "hello," and *Izayak*, "how are you," but other than that, she was lost. Had they been in Russia, it would have been a different story.

Kelly shook the man's hand vigorously and must have told him to get into the car, because the sweaty little fellow scurried over to the driver's side and jumped in. Kelly nodded to Freya, indicating they should climb in, too.

Inside, it was horribly hot and dry. And there was no air conditioning. Freya gasped the arid atmosphere into her lungs. "How long will we be in this thing?"

"A couple of hours, depending on traffic. If we were in an air-con car, we'd probably end up with one of the local military forcing his way in to hitch a ride. You don't want that. Anyway, why? For a military chick, you're a bit soft sometimes." Kelly screwed up his face in confusion.

"I was trained as an officer after college. And my active tours have not been in the Middle East. Now frozen wastelands—they're more my thing." Freya grinned and pulled on her ponytail to tighten it. "Anyway, how come you can speak so many languages?"

"Izel was a linguist. It ran in her family, and she taught me a thing or two. And I guess on my own travels, I picked up the odd phrase. You'll do that after spending the night in a cell for mispronouncing the occasional word or two and for getting into a serious bar fight and punching a girl in the face."

Freya glared at him.

"Well, I say girl, but it was Thailand if you catch my drift?" Kelly motioned to his own groin.

"I get you. You can stop pointing now." Freya stifled the grin from spreading across her face.

Kelly shrugged. "Well, that's another story." He leaned forward and muttered something to the driver, who nodded and revved the ancient engine. A powerful stench of petrol filled the cabin as the rusty machine pulled away.

Kelly stared out the window, fixated on the yellow arches of the international fast food chain, contrasting with the out-of-focus, ancient pyramid-shaped structures in the background. He mused on the comedy of it—how those ancient monuments were probably the result of the wisdom and technical know-how passed down by K'in's kind, and thousands of years later, what have the humans done to honor this knowledge? Made hamburgers. And plonked the gaudy, ass-shaped ad right next to one of the Seven Wonders of the World. Genius. He shook his head and turned his attention back to Freya. She sat in her usual position, hands together in her lap, head down. He couldn't tell if she was awake as she was wearing a pair of aviator sunglasses.

His thoughts turned to Chris. Kelly missed him. He missed fucking about with him. They'd be wrestling in the back of the car right now, fighting to not have their own head stuck out of the window as they zipped along. Kelly smirked, but it faded quickly as his mind drifted to Victoria. She'd been dragged into this situation simply because she'd been near Kelly at the time, and now she was dead. This was all because General Lloyd's team just couldn't miss the opportunity, all in the name of connecting to the animal, K'in. Strangely, Kelly missed the weird man-sized axolotl, too. He sighed heavily, his chest hurting.

Kelly turned back to the window and watched the hustle of Cairo disappear as sand dunes filled his view. They would be there soon. He closed his eyes and exhaled slowly.

The car jolted to a stop. No sooner had it halted than Freya had flung the car door open and leapt out—perhaps expecting the external air to be cooler. It wasn't. Kelly paused, his hand on the handle but did not move. He closed his eyes and slowly breathed out, a wordless prompt to his body to get out of the goddamn car. He stepped out and was immediately confronted by the driver, who eagerly awaited his payment. Kelly rummaged in his pocket and pulled out a handful of Egyptian pounds. He handed them to the man, who scurried back to the driver's seat and powered off in a cloud of sand and dirt.

The tiny village in which they stood consisted of a few square, brick houses with flat roofs. Leather-faced people strolled by in the heat, each wearing very light clothing, with many of the women having covered heads. The people stared at the two foreigners, appearing amused, but kept to themselves and walked on. Freya looked around and then expectantly at Kelly. "So, where is your contact?"

"He'll be here. This is a small village. He works just down there." Kelly nodded along the dusty street. Freya had already marched off ahead. He trudged after her.

Before he knew it, Kelly was standing in the doorway. The small, square room was dark and dusty. Large fissures cut jagged paths through the white-washed walls, some of which were so deep, light from outside seeped through. There was no proper furniture to speak of, just an odd, rickety, wooden table with old books strewn across it. Yellowed pieces of paper with handwritten scrawl were haphazardly stuck to one wall. At the opposite end of the room, a man was standing with his back to the door. He wore sand-colored slacks and a linen shirt. His wavy, gray hair was tucked behind his ears by a pair of rectangular-framed glasses perched on top of his head. The man was busy with pieces of crumpled paper, picking them up, reading them, and then placing them on the table in front of him. Without turning, he spoke. "I heard you were in the village." His English was accurate but carried a thick Latin-American lilt.

Kelly sucked in a deep breath and held it before releasing it slowly. "News travels fast here. It's been a while."

"That it has, Kelly. What do you want?" The man still had not turned around.

"We need to talk, Alejandro."

"Do we, now?"

"I need your help, but first, I need to tell you about Chris."

161

Freya shot a confused glance at Kelly, but he ignored her, remaining fixated on the man.

"Christopher has come to his senses, has he? Finally stopped following you around like a puppy?"

"He's ... he's dead."

The man slowly turned around. His face was old and furrowed with cracks. A short white beard masked his mouth, making it difficult to judge any expression of emotion. He pulled the glasses from his head onto his nose and peered through them at Kelly. "Dead?"

"Yes. I'm sorry, Alejandro. I need to tell you how and why and—"

"So you have taken the last of my family from me, have you? First my daughter and granddaughter and now my son. I knew the day I laid eyes on you that you were bad news, Kelly Graham. My family suffers, yet you always seem to slither away unscathed."

Freya's eyes widened as the penny dropped. Izel's father.

"Look. You and I have had our differences, but I have always done my best. For Izel. For Carmen. When they died, Chris needed someone. And as always, you were somewhere else." His voice trailed off as he realized what he had said.

"I raised my children to be independent. Strong. They didn't need me. But you—for some reason, they were spellbound by you and your charm." Alejandro turned back to his work. "If Christopher has truly passed away, then he is with his family now. And you and I have no further need to speak again."

"This is why. This. You were always a cold bastard." Kelly screamed, his voice straining as he fought back a mixture of rage and sadness. "They weren't spellbound by charm or trickery—they were happy to have found someone who gave a flying fuck about them. Loved them."

Alejandro span around and scowled. "You know nothing of love. You were always too infatuated with yourself to care about anyone else. If you hadn't left for South Africa to make a name for yourself, then Izel and Carmen would still be with us." His voice was harsh but calm.

The words cut into Kelly's heart. "Fuck you, old man. This was a mistake." He turned on his heel and stormed out of the room into the bright Egyptian sun, leaving Freya standing on her own.

CHAPTER TWENTY

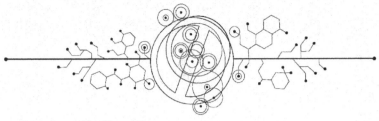

Location: A small village, Egypt

Freya continued to stand in the same spot, not saying a word. It wasn't that she didn't want to. In fact, she wanted to scream at this old man and tell him just how much Kelly had loved Izel and Carmen, and Chris for that matter. But she knew she couldn't. It wasn't her place. Besides, Kelly had said this man could help them in finding a new orb. She had to convince him to help. Freya stared at the old man. He was resting both palms on the table, his head hung low.

"Mr. D'Souza?"

He didn't respond.

"Mr. D'Souza? We need your help. I know this must be hard, but clearly, if you and Kelly harbor so much animosity, then you know our situation must be serious for him to turn to you for help." Her voice was not sympathetic, instead carrying the matter-of-fact tone she had practiced so well.

"Are you another young woman caught in the whirlwind disaster that is the life of Kelly Graham?" Again, he spoke with his back to her.

She hesitated, then took a meaningful two paces inside. "Not quite. As a matter of fact, Kelly is more caught up in my whirlwind."

The man sniffed hard and turned around. "And just what help could I be? Hmm? What possible use? I'm a professor of linguistics. Ancient linguistics to be precise."

"I'm with the military, Professor D'Souza. And I am the reason your son is dead. If we do not achieve our goal, I fear that millions more will also die." Freya stared the man in the eyes, her own steeled.

He lifted his hands from the table and raised them near his face. "Just what are you talking about, Ms. …?"

"Nilsson. Ms. Nilsson." She hesitated. "But you can call me Freya. And I'm talking about Armageddon." She pulled the mobile device from her combat pants and punched the keys until a photograph of K'in appeared. "We do not have time, professor, so I'm going to give you the short version."

Kelly sat on a small stone wall, his head bowed as he mused on the past. After he'd met Izel in the rainforest and she'd told him her name was D'Souza, it seemed like fate to him. He was already good friends with her little brother, he just hadn't known it. What were the odds? Chris hadn't talked much about his family during college but said they definitely were not like the Waltons. He had mentioned a sister but always joked she would never go for Kelly since she only dated guys with IQs higher than snails, so there was no point in introducing them. But Kelly had met her—and met her randomly in some remote part of the world. The romance and serendipity of it had taken over him. It was all too amazing. He hadn't contacted Chris about it. Izel had planned the whole event as a surprise. They were to go and visit Chris at his place in San Diego. She had told her brother she was bringing a new boyfriend she wanted him to meet.

On the plane, Kelly had been quiet. Izel asked what was wrong—whether he thought meeting family was too soon. Kelly had been serious for the first time since they'd met. He didn't think it was too soon. He was just worried about telling Chris. He didn't want his best friend to feel betrayed. All the way to the apartment in the taxi from the airport, Kelly stared out of the window, his left hand firmly gripping Izel's right.

Once there, he took a deep breath as Izel rang the doorbell. She jiggled excitedly up and down on the spot. Kelly gave her an awkward smile. As the door opened, Izel stopped fidgeting, the hand holding Kelly's went limp. Her father had answered the door.

A group of children were gathered at Kelly's feet, each one waving a rough-hewn carving in his face. All of them were chattering away in broken English, vying for their wares to be purchased. One of the children was too close and accidentally tapped his knee with a statuette of Anubis—a man with the head of a jackal. "*Imshee, imshee!*" Kelly shouted.

The children scattered.

"You know they don't mean any harm, Kelly." Freya stood ten paces away, resting her weight on one hip.

Kelly looked up. "I know that. I just have to figure out what to do next. Plus I'm not feeling too hot. Kinda sick."

"It'll be the sun. You need to get in the shade. And as for our next move, he's agreed to help us."

"I don't want his fucking help."

"Stop being a child. You brought me here because you said he could help us. You have to put your differences aside." Freya thought carefully about her next words. "What would your wife want?" As she finished the last word, she held her breath for the response.

"I guess."

Freya exhaled as Kelly shuffled off the wall and dropped the few inches to the ground. All of this was draining for him, he couldn't even be bothered to argue with her.

Dusting his pants down, Kelly picked up his backpack and trudged over to her. "Okay, where is the miserable old fuck?"

"He's still in that building, I guess. I gave him the Twitter version of what's happened. It was a lot to take in. He told me to wait outside."

"Twitter version? You know what, don't tell me." Kelly stomped past her toward the building, muttering under his breath, "Here we go."

Location: U.S. submarine, somewhere in the Pacific Ocean

Wiezorek focused his attention on the General. Even though the creature was no more than ten feet away, asleep in its tub, the young officer could not take his eyes from his superior officer. He had observed that the General was a man of few words, but something told him this leader was also a man of deep feeling. The man's face was often pained as if he carried the weight of the world on his shoulders. Over the last few days, the General had let several things slip—the odd word, the occasional facial expression or body movement. Each time it had been in relation to Agent Nilsson.

He rose from his seat and walked over to the General, who was standing, arms across his chest, near the creature.

"Sir, if I may, perhaps you should rest. I can watch the creature."

The General turned his head to face the young man. A few moments passed without a word, but eventually, he decided to speak. "How old are you, son?"

"Twenty-six, sir."

"Twenty-six. So young. I don't even think I remember being that age. It all blurs into one long war for me. But Freya, I remember her being even younger—twenty-one. It wasn't so long ago."

"Freya, sir?"

He heaved a sigh. "Ms. Nilsson."

"Oh."

"She's my goddaughter, you know. Raised her myself when her parents died."

Wiezorek remained silent.

"When she was your age, she looked at me just like you do—with respect, with perhaps even a little pride. But now ..." He hesitated. "Now, she sees me for what I am—a foolish old man."

Again, the pilot did not reply.

"Young man, she may not understand. But this being, this creature, could be the answer to all our prayers—to everything, to ultimate peace."

"Peace, sir?"

"Peace. The world is in chaos, but out of chaos, comes reason. Sometimes you have to disrupt everything to change how people think. And we are trying to change how entire nations think."

"And the creature will help us do that?"

"Yes." The General nodded. "Once the major powers have fought amongst themselves and the world is on its knees, desperate, people will be much more willing to listen—to understand."

Wiezorek mused on the General's words. Perhaps he was right. There had been many smaller wars, none of which had really changed anything. Iraq. Afghanistan. But World War II, when everything was pretty much destroyed, had changed the way people behaved. "I think I understand, sir."

Benjamin gave a weak smile. "Then perhaps all I'm doing will not be in vain." He placed a hand on the pilot's shoulder. "I will need your support. There are few people I can trust. Can I count on you?"

The young man nodded. "Of course, sir."

"I knew I could. You are a good soldier, young Ethan." The General took a final glance at the sleeping animal, its breathing rapid and irregular. "Watch the creature. It doesn't seem well. You let me know if anything strange happens, understood?"

Wiezorek stood straight and saluted. "Yes, sir."

Benjamin returned the salute and exited the room. K'in opened his eyes slightly and watched the pilot walk back to his seat. Wiezorek caught a glimpse of the creature observing him. He turned to face it and stared into the animal's eyes. For a second, he thought it looked sad.

Location: A small village, Egypt

Freya sat watching the two men. Each of them was plonked cross-legged on the ground, a small fire separating them. The orange flames lit their faces from beneath, exaggerating their already sour expressions. Her gaze fell on Kelly for a few seconds longer than she would have liked to be noticed. In one way, she found him so attractive and masculine. The way she had when she met him on the ship in the South China Sea. He was so brave and adventurous. And then there was the other side of him—the giant, defiant, toddler who threw tantrums when he didn't get his own way. She tried to give him some leeway. After all, he was dragged into this. But sometimes, she couldn't figure out if she wanted to kiss him or slap him. She smiled. Perhaps she'd do both.

Kelly sensed her staring at him and threw a glance over the fire in her direction.

Freya quickly turned to Alejandro. "Where are we going to start? We don't have much time."

"I've been thinking on that myself, Ms. Nilsson. My knowledge is restricted to linguistic issues, translations and re-translations from Greek to Egyptian and vice versa. However, your account fits with a very well-known story regarding Egypt and an advanced race that lived in or near water, as told by Plato."

Kelly grunted. "Atlantis."

Alejandro glared at him. "Highly intelligent noise, Kelly."

Freya shot Kelly a look reminiscent of a scolding mother. "Continue, Professor D'Souza."

"Where was I? Oh yes, Atlantis. According to Plato, Atlantis was a naval power, lying in front of the Pillars of Hercules that conquered many parts of Europe and Africa in approximately 9600 BC. After a poor attempt to invade Athens, Atlantis apparently sank into the ocean within twenty-four hours.

Most scholars have decided that Plato was merely telling a story, using it as an educational tool. My readings of Plato's original work have led me to the same conclusion. Until now."

"Are you seriously suggesting that we go hunting for Atlantis?" Kelly rolled his eyes.

"No, no, no, stupid boy. Let me finish."

Kelly grunted again.

"I still believe Atlantis, as described by Plato, was an allegory. However, most stories are based in some truth. From what Ms. Nilsson tells me and has shown me, there was a species that predates humans or, at the very least, existed alongside us. Indeed, there are all kinds of theories about the age of the monuments here in Egypt. Several theories suggest the pyramids align with the stars of Orion's belt, not only in their position along the Nile but also the shafts that run outward from the Great Pyramid of Khufu." He paused for breath. "The only issue is, according to these theories, these alignments are inconsistent with when we suppose the pyramids were built. Scholars generally attribute the pyramids to a period around 2500 BC. If the alternate history theorists are to be believed, these star alignments are only possible when considering the stars in their position around 10500 BC. Moreover, some of the texts I have read also refer to a great flood. In fact, there was a gentleman out here a few years ago examining the Sphinx. He claimed the erosion patterns on the statue were created by water, not wind, which suggests some credit to your story." He paused again, this time for dramatic effect. "Perhaps some ancient species was building monuments well before the Egyptians. Or perhaps they were teaching others how to build them. Either way, if such a civilization existed, and were as advanced as is believed, then it makes sense that they—or we—would want to try and store this knowledge."

"And that's what we are looking for. An orb, an object, that can link minds and perhaps even store thoughts," confirmed Freya.

"In the early 1930s, a man named Edgar Cayce popularized the idea of a secret chamber associated with the Sphinx, a Hall of Records, which was purported to hold a complete record of Atlantis. Perhaps a record of Atlantis was not what was stored, but something else was."

"So there is a hall under the Sphinx?" Freya's eyes widened in excited curiosity.

"That's bullshit," Kelly cut in. "It would have been found by now." He shook his head, a look of frustration and disappointment on his face. This was a waste of time.

"Kelly, you dragged me halfway around the world because you thought this man could help. So let him help."

"Yes, but I thought we were going to get sensible answers."

"Will you shut up? Ms. Nilsson, while Kelly is essentially correct, there are three known passageways leading into the Sphinx. One is on the Sphinx's back near its head, but it is only a short blind-ended shaft. Another is at ground level near one of its hips. But again, this shaft only leads to a dead end below the water table. But then ..." The old man leaned forward. "Then, there is an iron trap door fitted to the ground between the Sphinx's paws. This isn't a passage but a rectangular pit that was covered with a cement roof and an iron rod and sealed with a trap door during restoration efforts in the 1920s. Most people were confused as to why this pit existed. When it was originally excavated, only a few odd artifacts were found. They bore no markings and were lumped together with other artifacts, locked away in the archives of the Cairo Museum. Maybe what you're looking for is there?" Alejandro sat back and stared over the crackling embers at Kelly.

Freya rose to her feet. "So we go to the Cairo Museum and ask to look in their archives."

"It's not as easy as that, I'm afraid. After the Egyptian revolution in 2011, security has been enhanced, albeit secretly, at the Museum, and they won't be letting anyone wander around their archives. It's not only junk down there but other artifacts of great value."

"We'll need another plan." Kelly didn't look up from the floor. "And I think I have one."

CHAPTER TWENTY-ONE

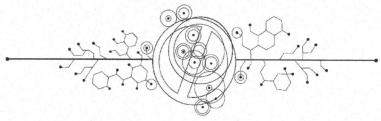

Location: Cairo, Egypt

The convoy of three dark green trucks, each with six huge wheels and wrapped in thin olive-colored tarps, sped along the dirt road, sucking up a sandstorm in their wake. The Egyptian sun beat down on their roofs, the air above shimmering in the heat. Kelly and Freya, their heads low, watched from afar in their own clapped-out vehicle. The make was no longer discernible. Dents were evident in every panel and the paintwork all but torn away by years of sand-laden wind damage.

Kelly had not been particularly clear on the plan. He had just noted that much of the content of the original museum was being moved from the Museum of Egyptian Antiquities to the Grand Egyptian Museum, located approximately two miles from the Pyramids at Giza. The Egyptian Government had already moved more than ten thousand items under high security. Today, they were moving the bowels of the old building including some of the lesser-valued objects. According to another of Kelly's somewhat questionable contacts, the item originally found between the paws of the sphinx was among them. His entire plan was to steal it, somehow. Alejandro wanted nothing to do with it and decided it was better if he wait in the plane at the small airfield.

"What now, Kelly? Hmmm? Do you even know which one we want?"

"Sure, the last one. It's the one with the lowest profile, therefore the heaviest. I'm betting it's in there."

"How very scientific of you."

"If you like that, then you'll love this. I'm thinking we use you as bait."

"What? That's disgusting. I'm not flaunting myself in front of these dirty animals."

Kelly choked on his laughter. "As sexy as I'm sure you think you are, that's not what I meant there, toots." He winked slyly. "You still have your ID on you? I doubt these guys are chatting to Interpol, so we can leverage your position with the U.S. military. We'll say you are looking for terrorists. They're distracted and I jump on board."

"You want me, an American, to stop the Egyptian military and tell them I'm looking for terrorists, most likely Islamic terrorists? I think I prefer flaunting now."

Kelly scratched his head thoughtfully. "Okay, forget that. We need a new plan."

"Indeed. What we need to do is—"

"Okay, I got it."

"I'm sure you do, but what we need to do is—"

"Hey, do you know Egypt?"

"No, but—"

"Get out of the car."

"What?"

"Get. Out. Of. The. Car. Go wait over there under that tree." Kelly waved to a solitary, crooked, withered, old tree that offered a sliver of shade from the searing sun.

She stepped out of the vehicle, slammed the door, and threw a scathing stare through the open passenger window.

"You can't do everything on your own."

"Sure. Now give me one of your guns. Sorry, Berettas." He reached out his hand, palm open.

Freya sighed, reluctantly unholstered one of the firearms and, through the window, slapped it into his open hand. "Don't kill yourself."

"I haven't died yet. Oh, and pass me that stick, will you? That big one, there." He pointed vaguely behind her.

She spun around and searched the sandy ground. A large, bleached branch protruded from a small dune. She pulled it from the sand and passed it through the window.

"Anything else, Your Highness?"

"Nope, I'm good. Okay, now go hide."

Freya watched the truck drive approximately half a mile, then stop. She frowned and shielded her eyes from the sun with one hand. The vehicle moved back and forth, turning to the right incrementally. Further beyond the convoy surged on, directly across the imaginary path of the little truck. The engine suddenly roared to life, and the wheels span against the fine sand beneath, spitting it backward. Traction took hold, and the truck accelerated.

Freya strained to follow its trajectory. Judging by its velocity and direction, it would—before she could finish her thought, Kelly's truck slammed into the side of the convoy's lead vehicle, forcing it over onto its side.

The two trucks melded together, the metal warping and twisting until each one was no longer individually identifiable. The remaining two vehicles skidded to an abrupt halt. Freya hung onto the tree, half wanting to run, half knowing not to be so stupid. Thick black smoke billowed from the wreck. She could make out the tiny silhouettes of men jumping out of their trucks and running to the rescue of their comrade. Amongst the chaos, a lone figure scurried, crouching down about the last truck. The figure climbed in. The wagon jerked back awkwardly as if the driver had no idea how to operate it. It jolted forward a few feet, then stopped, and then a few more feet. Then, it exploded into life and gunned straight toward her. Freya froze. Nowhere to run. Nowhere to hide. Within seconds it was upon her. It slammed on its brakes, stopping inches from the spot where she stood. The smell of diesel and oil filled her nostrils as she stared at the huge front grill.

Kelly poked his head through the driver's window. "C'mon! Fuckin', move it!"

Freya launched into action and sprinted to the passenger side. She flung the door open, leapt inside, and slammed it behind her.

Kelly jammed down the accelerator and yanked on the gearstick. The truck lurched. "C'mon, you son of a bitch! Move!"

It finally obeyed and powered forward, sliding and skidding as it struggled to grip the lose particles beneath its tires.

"I thought you'd ploughed into that other truck."

"Nah, I fixed the gas with that stick and jumped before impact. You didn't see me?"

"No. I was worried."

Kelly turned his head to look at her but changed his mind as the distraction impaired his already poor driving skills, causing the vehicle to veer off course. "Worried?" he asked, his eyes now fixed ahead. "About lil o' me? I'm indestructible. You know that." He grinned.

"Just drive." Freya rolled her eyes.

"Are they behind us?"

Freya leaned to peer into the side mirror. "Yes, coming up fast, and I would bet they will be radioing for help soon."

"Probably. We need to make it to the hangar," he shouted over the roar of the engine as he forced it to rev beyond its limits.

Sand flew behind the vehicle as it sped along. Kelly kept his foot pressed firmly on the accelerator, never letting up and never pressing the brake. Freya clung to the seat with both hands as he made yet another sharp swerve, the truck lifting onto two wheels before crashing back to all four. They were almost at Cairo's city limits. It was chaos. Thousands of people had poured onto the streets, many carrying makeshift flags with Arabic scrawled across the material. One flag in particular caught Kelly's eye. It had a sketch of a creature, not unlike K'in, encircled in red, a stripe through the middle.

"Shit."

"What is it?"

"It's a fucking protest."

"We can't afford to get stopped."

"Actually, this may be beneficial for us. We need to get lost in the crowd. But you gotta go back there and find the object before we hit the city. We'll have to hoof it and jack another car."

"Me. How about you. I'm a better driver anyway. You can't even work a stick."

He looked at her, then the road, and then her, again. "Okay, put your foot on the gas. Don't let up, you hear me?"

"Shut up and get out," Freya said through gritted teeth.

Freya slipped into the driver's seat as Kelly heaved himself out and through the open window. He held onto the roof and wing mirror and pulled out his legs so he could stand on the wheel arch. The wind whipped about his face and hair, while sand and grit stabbed at his eyes. Kelly squinted, almost to the point of being unable to see at all, and shimmied along the outside of the chassis. He grabbed the large straps that held down the tarp, using them as anchors.

A high-pitched whistle screamed past his right ear. He leaned backward to see the pursuing vehicle, the driver with one arm sticking out of the window, carelessly brandishing a Helwan pistol. They were firing at him. He had to move faster. He shimmied further along. Another bullet pinged off the truck's chassis.

"Fuck!" Kelly shouted in the direction of the gunman. "Son of a bitch. I gotta get inside." He shimmied around the corner so he was now hanging on to the back of the vehicle. Hurriedly, he fiddled with the straps that held the tarp closed. One came free. Then the other. Kelly scrambled inside, diving head first through the gap, narrowly avoiding the bullet that ripped through the material where his head had been. "Motherfuckers." Kelly shook off the adrenaline and searched the interior.

Bags and boxes were strewn everywhere. No system. No markings. How the hell was he meant to find anything? He didn't have time for this crap. Desperate, he clawed at everything, turning things over and spilling contents after contents onto the floor of the truck. Pieces of pottery. Jade jewelry. Papyrus. Junk. All of it, junk.

Then it hit him. A flash. Like someone had electrocuted his brain. He stumbled and fell backward to the floor. What the fuck was that? He shuddered, then heaved climbed back to his feet. Cautiously, he fumbled around, allowing his fingers to skim everything within arms' reach. A tingling on the back of his neck rose upward into his skull. Kelly focused his eyes on the object at his finger-tips. A small, black, shriveled thing, like a giant raisin.

"Is that it?" He unconsciously voiced his disappointment. He wasn't sure what he'd been expecting, but that wasn't it. But as he thought about it, it made sense. The original orb had been jelly-like. So it would probably desiccate over time.

He took a deep breath and closed his fingers around it. A surge of imagery and information penetrated his being. It surged along his arm and powered into the soft tissues of his brain. It was coming so fast he couldn't file it or make sense of it. Then the pain was too much. Kelly roared in anguish, then blacked out.

Freya slammed on the brakes, barely missing a small gathering of men who had splintered off from the rest of the protestors. Without cutting the engine, she jumped out and sprinted to the rear of the truck. Peering through the flaps, she saw Kelly sprawled on the floor, unconscious. She clambered in and knelt beside him. What could have happened? He was still breathing.

"Kelly!"

Silence.

"Kelly!"

He didn't stir. She slapped his face hard.

Kelly jolted. "What the fu—" He blinked and gazed around.

"What happened?" she asked. "Did you find it?"

"Yeah, kinda. Let's go."

"Where is it?"

"We don't need it. I'll explain later. Let's just get the hell outta here."

Freya grabbed his arm as she stood and heaved him up. Kelly swayed, steadied himself, then nodded. They jumped from the truck and scanned the desert behind them. The pursuing soldiers were gaining fast. They darted into the crowd and were lost amongst them.

"Do you know where we're going?" Kelly asked.

Freya held his hand and dragged him through gaps in the mass of people. "I just wanna hole up for a few minutes—let that guy get lost in the crowd. C'mon, in here." She yanked his arm and pulled him into a dingy little shop. The place was packed with men standing around chatting and chomping down large slabs of meat and bread. The air wreaked of garlic and spices.

"Will we be safe in here?" he asked.

"Sure, just stand with me. Act like a tourist. Keep your back to the entrance and face inward."

They stood for a few minutes without speaking. Kelly fidgeted on the spot. "The smells are killing me. I'm hungry."

"Now, Kelly? Really?"

"I'll buy something. We can't stand here and not order something." Kelly pushed his way to the counter and spoke to the man behind it. He returned holding two foil packages.

"What is it?" Freya peeled back the foil to reveal a squashed layer of dark brown meat and wilted salad in something that resembled pita bread. She crinkled her nose at it.

"It's shawarma." Kelly's mouth was already full as he spoke. "It's good. Just eat it." He took another large bite.

Freya studied it longer. It didn't look appetizing, but her stomach was empty. To hell with it. She put it in her mouth and bit down. It was actually good. "So why didn't we need the object?" She spoke quietly through the corner of her mouth, hiding the bolus of food.

Kelly swallowed. "It's weird. I touched something in there. A shriveled-up, little piece of crap. Then I got all these visions. It's like they're burned into my brain. I could see them."

"Who?"

"K'in's people. Lots of them." He smiled. "It's strange. They were there but upright and walking around. It's a bit hazy and fragmented, but again, I felt contentment, happiness. I saw a place, a city by the sea—no, not by it, almost in it. It was a partially submerged halfway house for K'in's species and

175

ours like symbiotic living."

"I wonder why you felt it and saw things no one else has. It must have been handled a million times."

"Dunno. Maybe Moby opened my brain?"

She laughed. "Yeah."

"Anyway, I know where we go from here."

"Where?"

"To the city I saw in my head. In India." He scarfed down the last of his shawarma.

"Okay." Freya finished her meal as well.

Kelly grabbed her hand again and strode out of the shop into the crowd. He hadn't noticed before, but the shop had been cooled by a fan. The change in temperature was sudden and unwelcome.

"We need to grab a car."

"No more stealing. Let's just take a cab."

Kelly laughed. "Okay, deal."

She walked to the side of the road, never letting go of his hand. With the spare one, she waved down a cab. A black and white, dilapidated vehicle that looked as if it had been manufactured and exported from Russia in the 1950s, screeched to a halt in front of them. They climbed into the back.

"Cairo West Airfield," Kelly replied.

Freya heaved a sigh. "I'll need a couple of hours sleep at the airfield before I pilot that jet again."

"Sure, of course." Kelly peered out the back window and watched the soldier that had been pursuing them search the crowd, his face contorted in exasperation.

Location: USAMRIID, Maryland, USA

"I don't care how you do it, just do it," the Colonel ordered. "We need to move them now! Do you understand? ... Good ... What? ... No, don't worry about her. She won't be in the office after this disaster. I just don't want her finding them in the next few days. Do I have to think of everything? Get her out of the picture. Hospitalize her or something. Just make it quick. This operation is much too important to allow some broad to fuck it up. Make it happen. I'll be with you in a couple of hours, then we go into the field." The Colonel slammed down the phone.

This was one big mess. What the hell had Benjamin done? He'd obviously gone off plan and AWOL. He was jeopardizing the whole operation. And that couldn't be allowed to happen. To hell with rank. Their friendship be damned. Only the project mattered. Nothing else.

Christian couldn't believe his ears. Had he really just heard the Colonel order someone to cripple his sister? He didn't care what was at stake or what the Colonel was hiding, no one was going to threaten his little sister. It was time for some serious action. But what?

He backed away from the half-closed door to the Colonel's office. He had intended on speaking with the Colonel about his sister's request, and the need to calm her and reassure her that everything was okay, that she was paranoid. But she wasn't. She was right on the money. He could only think of one way to stall the man. It would cost Christian his career and probably his freedom. He took a deep breath, stepped forward, and rapped on the door.

"Yes?" the Colonel said, annoyed.

"Ahem. Yes. Colonel, I need to speak with you urgently." The doctor stepped into the room with as much confidence as possible. The room was cold and stark. Not a picture hung on the wall or rested on his desk. He was a man with no friends or family.

"Can't it wait?"

"No, I need you to come to the lab with me. I have to show you one of the mice, following injection of the test drug. The results are amazing. I think we should move straight to human testing to save time."

"That's ridiculous. Not to mention completely off protocol. You haven't even tested in primates yet, and you want to expose humans?"

"Back in 2004, in this very lab, an investigator stuck her thumb with a needle while treating Ebola-infected mice with antibodies. A pharma company had just presented a seminar to USAMRIID on the efficacy of morpholinos for treating Ebola. When they heard about the accident, they volunteered to design and synthesize compounds against the virus to treat her if the need arose. The team worked for four straight days to generate human-grade anti-Ebola compounds. During that time, their regulatory staff worked with our physicians to gain emergency approval from the FDA to use the compounds. Five days after the exposure, the morpholino was ready and delivered to these premises."

"Yes, but it was never administered."

"I know, but we are in a more stressful situation than one infected person. I need your authorization to work with the team here and approach the FDA again to get it fast tracked. Please come look at the mice. Ten minutes. It's all I ask."

The Colonel huffed. "Okay. Ten minutes. You go to the lab, I'll join you shortly."

"Okay, thanks."

Christian shuffled out of the room and rambled down the various corridors and staircases. He was on autopilot. His mind full of his next action. It was the only way. Wasn't it? Christian hadn't actually lied; a couple of mice were showing some surprisingly good results following administration of the morpholino, but that wouldn't be enough to keep the Colonel here. He wasn't going to listen to reason. That was clear. The man was hell-bent on doing whatever he had put into motion. And he was physically much larger. There was no way to overpower him. There was only one way. He just had to trust in two little, furry rodents.

Christian was once again enveloped in his biohazard suit. His breath fogged up the inside of the plastic face-panel as he waited at the entrance to the biohazard lab. He punched in the security code using the wall panel. The door popped open under pressure. He pushed it open and cautiously stepped into another tiny room before making an about face and closing the door behind him. A sound much like an overworked drill signified the sealing of the airlock—the rapid inflation of a rubber bladder that sealed the smooth edges of the door. Christian watched the vertical banks of nozzles spraying water and virus-killing chemicals over him.

A small light shone green. He pushed the second steel door open and stepped inside the larger room. Fluorescent lights hung from the ceiling in airtight boxes that prevented microorganisms from collecting on the edges. The walls glistened from the layers of epoxy potting compound that formed a continuous seal across every surface. Electrical outlets that penetrated the seal were housed in airtight boxes and lathered in epoxy. A dull clunk sounded as the door behind him automatically shut and sealed. Grabbing the hose overhead, he connected the air supply, giving his micro-environment positive pressure.

The suit made a familiar shuffling sound, material rubbing on material, as he made his way to the Class III storage unit that contained the virus, pre-loaded into syringes. The unit was completely transparent, with two large holes in the front surface. Inside the holes were long thick gloves that pointed inward, attached at their opening to the glass front.

Christian took a deep breath. He would have to break protocol to do this. He slipped his hands into the gloves and picked up the syringe closest to him. Damn, it was cold in the unit—a necessity to keep the virus at a workable temperature. With his spare left hand, he grabbed a needle and unsheathed it from its cover. Attaching the two together, he pushed down on the plunger, forcing liquid to the tip of the needle. This was very delicate. He didn't want to force it so much that the liquid was pushed out of the end, contaminating anything it touched, but he didn't want to leave air in the needle either which would prove fatal.

With the syringe construction complete, Christian placed it down on the inner surface, careful that it did not roll away. Now it was time to break protocol. He pulled his arms from the cabinet gloves. Again, he took a deep breath. Then, he grabbed the locking clasps on the unit and popped them open. Inside, he scooped up the virus-filled syringe. He closed the cabinet and re-locked the clasps. A firm grip on his shoulder made him jump nearly out of his skin.

"What the hell are you doing?" yelled the Colonel, the loudness of his voice attenuated by his biohazard suit. "That's completely off protocol. You can't wander the lab with an exposed needle like that. You didn't use the autoclave."

The Colonel's rant melted into white noise. Christian wasn't listening. His mind was filled with only one thought—stab him. The doctor's concentration returned to the Colonel, barking and pacing, his arms flailing about in anger. Christian wasn't even sure what the man was shouting anymore. Something regarding the lab. The Colonel turned away and threw his arms wide, making some grand point about the room they were in. Christian stepped forward, wielding the syringe in his fist like a knife. He pulled it back, ready to plunge it into the man's back. He screwed up his face and closed his eyes. *Stab him!*

Christian's arm didn't move an inch. He couldn't do it. It wasn't who he was. What if the mouse data was wrong? This wouldn't slow the man. It would kill him. Christian was no killer. He sighed and loosened his grip on the deadly syringe, his head hanging low in shame for not being able to help his sister. For resorting to, for all intents and purposes, murder. He had to call Lucy and tell her she was in danger.

The doctor's eyes widened as a force pressed against the arm holding the syringe. He raised his head and allowed his gaze to follow the length of his limb to the syringe and the needle that was now lodged firmly in the Colonel's right shoulder. He must have spun, mid-rant, straight into it.

Both men froze.

The Colonel stared, eyes filled with fear, at the metallic object protruding from his suit. While his heart wished it had only penetrated the suit, his brain acknowledged the acute pain in his flesh.

"Colonel. I ..." Christian stuttered.

"You idiot. Quickly, we need to initiate an emergency protocol. Get me to the BPCU. Begin blood tests. Run RT-PCR for virus RNA."

Christian just stared at him, unable to speak, unable to move.

CHAPTER TWENTY-TWO

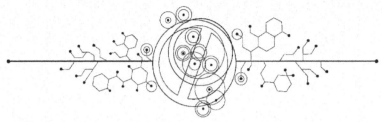

Location: G650 jet, somewhere over India

The jet slipped through the thin wisp of cloud covering the cobalt-blue sea. Kelly stared outward, his chin resting on his palm, his elbow wedged into the small porthole frame. It seemed he spent much of his time these days just staring out of small windows, absorbing and appreciating all of the things he'd taken for granted before. Long slivers of golden coastline and emerald-green palm trees carved their way through the still ocean. He'd missed the ocean so much. It had only been a few weeks away, but he could imagine the salty sea breeze whisking over his face.

He turned his attention to his female pilot. She was sitting upright, her gaze fixed on the horizon ahead. But, even in that position, somehow she looked elegant. Kelly watched her closely. She wasn't moving a single facial muscle. Her porcelain-like skin was as smooth as ever, though covered in soot and dirt from their ordeal. She looked like a mixture of a fearless Amazonian woman and an afraid little girl. He mused on her relationship with the General. What was it with those two? He was old enough to be her father. Could they be involved? He shook his head gently, disagreeing with his own question. No, it was something else.

He hadn't noticed, but they were already descending into Bhavnagar airport, a small operation forty miles from the bay of Cambay: their destination. The flight had only been three hours since the jet was unbelievably fast. Lucky for them, the Bhavnagar tower had agreed to an emergency landing, courtesy of Freya's ability to leverage her military position. News of their outlaw status clearly had not reached this part of the world.

"When we land, we're gonna have to dump this jet. We can't afford to use it anymore. Someone's gonna come looking for it—the drug lords or the authorities. We'll take a cab and hole up in Ghogha. You sort the diving equipment, I'll get some rest." Freya smiled weakly. She hadn't had any

181

proper sleep since they had left Lima.

The tires screeched as the jet set down. Moments later, they were veering off the only runway in the airport and being escorted to an old hangar. Before Freya had even parked, Kelly had unbuckled himself and climbed through the cockpit door into the main body. There, on the chair- cum-bed, was Alejandro, curled up asleep under a sheet. Kelly sighed. The crusty old bastard looked peaceful, but as soon as he awoke, it would be another barrage of insults. There was just no convincing him how much Carmen and Izel had meant. Fuck it. Kelly prodded him—hard.

Alejandro woke with a start and a snort. "What?"

"Time to go, old man."

"Come on, Alejandro." Freya gathered up their bags. "Let's go."

"You realize we are going to have to pull a fast one here?" Kelly put his hands behind his head and stretched.

"I know," Freya replied.

"A fast one? What do you mean?" Alexandro's eyes were narrowed as he pondered what harebrained scheme Kelly was plotting now.

"We got landing permission based on the need for an emergency landing. We need to make a sharp exit."

"Kelly's right, I'm afraid."

Alejandro sighed.

They trudged down the stairs of the jet and were met by a lone, semi-official-looking man in an off-white uniform.

"Are you okay?" the man asked in a thick Indian accent.

"Sure," Freya said, smiling.

Kelly stepped slowly behind the man and then hit him across the back of the head with the butt of one of Freya's Berettas. He fell to the floor in a crumpled heap. Alejandro winced in empathy.

"When did you take one of my guns?" Freya put her hand on the empty holster attached to her belt.

"Sticky fingers." Kelly winked and handed it back to her.

Freya couldn't help but smile. "C'mon, let's go."

They exited the hangar and snuck around the side of the building, heading toward the nearest highway. It would be a bit of a trek, but they weren't about to hail a cab in the airport. They'd have to grab one en route.

Location: Washington D.C., USA

182

Lucy stared in disbelief at the television. The news reporter was nodding away and talking in the strange way news reporters do, delivering short punchy sentences and emphasizing certain words. The irritating woman's bright red lipstick and shock of golden, curly hair would normally have distracted Lucy from the story. Normally, she would be berating the reporter for being a bimbo and reducing an important profession to breasts and eyelashes, but not today. Today, she was fixated on every syllable.

> *"Top story again. The Chinese Minister of foreign affairs, Li Xiaoping, and the chairman of the Central Military Commission, Xi Jintao, have been killed in an explosion at the Ministry of National Defense compound. Minister Li apparently entered the so-called August 1st Building with an explosive device strapped to his body and detonated it in the office of the chairman. The reasons for this action remain unclear. However, an emergency meeting of the CMC has been called."*

Lucy switched off the television and slumped back in her Chesterfield armchair. Her eyes were fixed wide open, and her hands were white-knuckled as she grasped the arms of the chair. What the hell had he done? He'd said he was going to take care of the situation. She hadn't thought he meant this. This was a disaster. Was it really the only way? Perhaps he wanted to show her he meant what he said. Perhaps it was a gesture to jolt her into action. Or maybe it was a trap. Maybe it would all be traced back to her somehow.

She marched out of her lounge, down the corridor, and into her home office. Flicking on the green Tiffany lamp, she searched the messy oak desk for her telephone. Where the hell was it? She needed to call her brother. She needed advice, and there was no one else to ask. Damn. She swept the papers from her desk in frustration.

A dull *thunk* confirmed the cell phone had hit the ground. Feeling amongst the fallen papers, she found it. Before she could dial, it sprang into life, the image of her brother's face on the screen. Startled, she almost dropped it but managed to regain her grip.

"Christian. That's so weird. I was just going to call you."

"Hey, are you alone?"

"Yes. I need to speak with you. Something awful has happened. I need advice." Her statement was met with silence. "Hello? Christian?"

"I'm here."

"Did you hear me?"

"Yes, I heard you. What is this bad news?"

He sounded oddly nervous, thought Lucy. "Remember, I told you I had a conversation with the Chinese Minister, right? Well, what I didn't tell you is he disclosed to me that a secret Chinese society has infiltrated their government and a splinter of this faction is hell-bent on stealing the creature and wiping out the U.S. He told me he would try and stop the leader of this faction, and in return, I had to stall the Colonel. Well, he kept his word. He just blew himself up in the leader's office." Again silence. "Christian?"

"Yes, I'm sorry. I'm here. Sis, I can tell you that you kept your end of the bargain, too." His voice trailed off.

"You managed to stall him?"

"You could say that. He's not going to be chasing anyone around the world."

"You're a genius. How'd you do it?"

"I injected him with the virus."

It was Lucy's turn to be silent. For the second time that day, she was stunned.

"Lucy? Sis?"

"You did what?" Her tone wasn't angry, more exhausted.

"It was an accident. I was going to do it when I overheard him say he was going to hospitalize you. Get you out of the way. But then I couldn't do it. The Colonel backed into the needle. There was nothing I could do."

"Where's he now? What's his condition?"

"He's in quarantine. He's signed off on immediate human trial of the anti-virus, using himself as the guinea pig."

"If he dies, you will be convicted of murder."

"I told you it was an accident."

"Then manslaughter at best. God, what have I gotten you into? Okay, I'm coming to you. I need to speak with him face to face before he ... well, just in case he—"

"Dies?"

"Yes."

"Okay, but watch your back. He was on the phone when I overheard him. Someone might be on their way to you right now."

"I'll call my security—"

"No!" he shouted, causing Lucy to pull the phone away from her ear. "What if one of your security guys works for him? Just get out of there. Come here."

"Okay. I can be there in an hour or so." She pulled the phone from her ear to click it off but hesitated and placed it back. "Christian?"

"Yeah?"

"I love you."

"I love you, too, sis."

She ended the call and slipped the phone into the inside pocket of her blazer. After a deep breath, she tried to calm her nerves. Okay, move. Lucy scurried around the room, picking up the papers and placing them back on the table in an attempt to make things appear as calm as possible, because she most certainly was not calm. Her pulse raced. Her hands trembled. She had no idea who to trust. The Chinese Minister? The Colonel? Right now it had to be her instincts. And her brother.

A hard rapping at the door shocked her into alertness. Who the hell was that? Lucy grabbed the handbag on her office chair and the car keys that were in the bowl on the sideboard. She thought about finding her coat but decided better of it.

The rapping at the door became louder. "Madam Secretary?" called the voice through the door.

Moving as quietly as possible, Lucy crept out of the office to the kitchen and into her garage. Should she take the car? They'd see it, surely, and follow her. But how else would she get away? She pondered her options for a few seconds. Her neighbor. She could ask her neighbor.

She scurried to the back door and snuck out. Carefully, she tip-toed through the wet grass to the small gate at the end of the yard. She flicked the clasp and pushed the wooden door open before quickly making her way down the path to the nearest house.

The gate to her neighbor's yard was locked. Lucy hitched up her skirt and awkwardly vaulted the gate into the garden. Her stockings caught on a protruding nail and tore a massive ladder in the silk. She pulled at the ladder and shook her head. No time to waste now. Looking all around, Lucy hurried to the back door.

She rapped on it, lightly at first, afraid someone other than the occupants would hear. But no one answered. She needed to knock harder.

Lucy took a deep breath and rapped once more.

Moments later, George appeared at the door, pulled back the curtain to the glass, and gazed outward, his brow furrowed. "Lucy?" His voice was muted through the door.

"George, I need your help." She mouthed words so he could read her lips.

Bolts and locks clunked and clacked before George opened the door. He was a rotund black man in his early sixties. His face was a mass of gray hair and beard, and he wore a pair of thick-rimmed glasses balanced on his nose. "Lucy, child, it's freezing out there. Come in, come in. Why are you using the back door? What's going on?" He ushered her into the back porch and closed the door.

"I don't really have time to explain, George. But I'm sure you've been watching the news."

"Yes, of course. The whole world's gone crazy. Seems safer to stay indoors if you ask me." He fiddled with his cardigan and shuffled into the kitchen. "Can I make you some tea?" he called between rooms.

She followed him, not wanting to raise her voice in order to answer. "No, George. No, I just need to borrow your car. I'll bring it back, but I need to go to my brother."

"Is something wrong with your car?" he asked, confused.

"No, no. But everyone knows my car and the plates. I need to go unnoticed for now. Please, George." Lucy's voice cracked.

"Sure, Lucy. It's okay. Of course." He rummaged in the pocket of his slacks and pulled out a set of keys. "Here."

She clasped the keys and his hand within her own. "Thank you, George. If anyone knocks on your door, don't answer it. Stay inside."

"Okay, Lucy, okay." He smiled weakly at her.

The Secretary shuffled toward the door to the garage, glancing through the windows as she did so. Time to get the hell out of here. She climbed inside the large SUV and clicked the door shut. The key slid into the keyhole and turned smoothly, bringing the engine to life. Thankfully, it was quiet. A click of the small remote attached to the sunshade initiated the garage door mechanism. It glided upward. Lucy slowly pressed the accelerator, moving the car forward. She paused at the entrance to the road, glancing left and right. A hundred feet or so away to the right, a black sedan was parked outside her house. A man in a dark suit, standing in her doorway, was talking into a cell phone. She crept the car forward and eked it onto the road. Careful not to gun the engine, Lucy pressed the accelerator and slid away.

Location: Somewhere on the Indian Ocean

The pathetic, little, wooden boat spluttered over the ocean surface, the makeshift outboard motor choking and coughing petrol fumes. Alejandro steered while Kelly struggled to climb into the cheap wetsuit and keep his balance in the small of the bow.

"This is ridiculous. How the hell are we meant to do this properly?" grumbled Kelly.

"Alejandro got us this boat. And it's inconspicuous, paid for in cash from a local, and there's no paper trail. It's perfect." Freya began unbuttoning her combat pants. "You boys wanna look away?"

The old man, embarrassed, slowed the boat so he could turn his head away without causing an accident. Kelly ducked his head down and stared at the old, wooden boards that comprised the bow. His urge to catch a glimpse of her perfect naked form was overwhelming. He bit his bottom lip.

By the time Kelly had resolved to look up, Freya had already slipped out of her pants and t-shirt and into the wetsuit, pulling it up and over her shoulders. "Okay, you can zip me up."

Kelly raised his eyes to see Freya's bare back turned to him. He yanked hard on the zip, pulling it upward. Damn, even her back was elegant and alluring.

They skimmed along for another ten minutes before Alejandro cut the engine. The small vessel bobbed on the surface, the sun reflecting off the ripples. The smell of salty air filled his nostrils and filtered to the back of his throat. He could almost taste it. But the annoying Hispanic accent of his father-in-law brought him crashing back to reality.

"This should be it."

"Are you sure, old man? We don't have GPS."

"This is India. GPS isn't something every local fisherman happens to have in his kitchen. Besides, I was on the ocean before you were born, Kelly Graham. I was told roughly where we needed to be, and this it. Trust me."

"We should trust him, Kelly." Freya put a hand on his shoulder in reassurance.

"Fine." Kelly pulled the ill-fitting scuba mask over his head and snapped it into his face. "Fuck knows whose dirty, smelly, bacteria-filled mouth has been around this regulator." He shuddered.

Freya laughed. "Now who has issues with putting things in his mouth?"

Alejandro restrained a smile. "Okay, last item." He handed Freya a balled-up piece of metallic mesh.

"What is it?" Freya asked as she unraveled the item to reveal two sleeves joined in the middle with black straps.

"They're Neptunic sleeves," Kelly replied. "Essentially a budget anti-shark suit."

"I'm afraid it's all I could find, young lady."

"Do we really need this?"

Kelly nodded. "Yes. There's bull sharks in these waters. Nasty fuckers. The old man used his head. But no gloves?"

"And what about Kelly?" Freya asked.

The old man shrugged. "As I said, all I could find."

"Put it on, and let's get wet." Kelly sat on the side of the boat and then fell backward into the water, disappearing beneath the surface.

"Be careful down there, young lady." Alexandro's voice carried a tone of genuine concern.

"I'll be alright." She pulled the sleeves over her wetsuit and fixed the straps. Then, with Alexandro's help, she lifted the tank onto her back before pulling the mask over her face. "Kelly's the best diver I know. He'll look after me."

The old man gave her a pained look but said nothing.

Freya popped the regulator into her mouth, sat on the edge of the boat, and then dropped back-first into the ocean. Alejandro watched the bubbles dissipate. It was difficult to explain, but he'd grown fond of Freya. She was, in some ways, very much like his daughter. And just like Izel, she was besotted with that blithering idiot, whether she wanted to admit it or not.

Kelly peered through the electric-blue water. Despite the clarity of the Indian Ocean, the cool waters attenuated light quickly. He couldn't see more than a couple of hundred feet in front of him—not that he was really concentrating.

The last twenty-four hours played in his mind. It had been strange. Alejandro had meandered his way into town to organize the boat and diving equipment that they would need. In the cramped room of the dingy hotel they had managed to find in the little Indian town, Freya had crashed out on the one tiny bed, tired from piloting. Kelly, quite rested already, had sat awake, his back propped against the wall, watching her sleep, breathing slowly. Her eyes, even when closed, were beautiful. He was unable to look away. Despite her strength and ability to look after herself, he couldn't help but feel a deep need to care for her, to watch out for her. He had been so intently observing her he'd failed to notice Alexandro's return. The old man had coughed to signify his presence, startling Kelly. "Leave her alone." That's what he'd said. Kelly had thought about arguing but decided the old bastard was right. She was better off without him. Instead, he'd sighed and asked for details on Alexandro's success in town.

Freya elegantly glided in front of Kelly, breaking his train of thought. Her slender body slid through the water with grace and ease. She must have sensed his stare, because she turned her head to face him and gave a huge, regulator-filled grin. Kelly stifled a laugh.

He turned back to his equipment to check their depth—sixty-five feet. They were at the sea floor. It wasn't very deep, but this was where it was supposed to be. He motioned his right arm to get Freya's attention. He then signaled for her to look down and keep her eyes open. She gave the okay sign.

As they swam a little further, the structure came into sight just as Alexandro's information had indicated. A large horseshoe-shaped wall, three-feet thick and six-feet tall, spanned more than two-hundred-fifty feet in diameter. Other than that, it was unimpressive—just an old stone wall. Surely, if a team had already been down here, they would have found an orb? Kelly pulled himself along the bottom, sifting through the sand, picking up each stone he came across. He shook his head and looked across at Freya. She seemed to be having similar poor luck, pointlessly rummaging through silt and mud. He swam across to her and pointed in front, indicating his intent to look on ahead. She nodded and watched as he flicked his fins, disappearing into a haze of ocean and sand particles.

Freya returned to her treasure hunt. All she found were rocks and the odd tin or soft drink can. Ugh, it was disgusting. Even the ocean wasn't safe from humanity. She reached the outer edge of the stone wall and swam along, keeping close to it. Her gloved fingers prodded into each crack and crevice, not that she could feel anything through the thick material. Her mask was beginning to fill with water. She thought about Kelly's instruction and began the mask clearing procedure.

Pressing the palm of her right hand against the top of her mask so the bottom released a few millimeters from her face, she exhaled hard through her nose, forcing the water out. A stream of bubbles crashed about her head in a white-water curtain. As it cleared, a small metallic glint protruding from beneath one of the huge stone bricks caught her eye. She clawed her way to it, then started digging in the sand. The fine silt clouded up around her, obscuring her view. Using only her limited sense of touch, Freya kept tunneling under the wall. The familiar shape of a box began to form under her fingers. She dug beneath until she could grip the box with both hands. Tugging hard, she released the cuboid object from its hold in the silt. The billow of sand cleared.

She stared at her treasure. It was a small chest, copper-colored with a green oxidized coating on its surface. She smiled. Could this be it? Could there be an orb inside? The excitement power through her. She raised her head to see if Kelly was nearby, but he wasn't anywhere to be seen. She swam in a circle. The inability to hear or feel anything was unnerving. She only had the power of sight and that was restricted to a straight line in front of her for one hundred fifty feet or so.

The light above her dimmed. Freya frowned and raised her head to investigate. Above her, the huge shadow of a shark glided by. She knew her mask would magnify any object, but still, the thing looked huge. Its blunt snout and thick body looked positively primeval—the perfect predator. Panic set in.

Damn, where was Kelly? Clutching her treasure, Freya lowered her head. She searched for the knife strapped to her right calf. Before she could find it, her gaze was met by the cold stare of reptilian eyes. A sea snake was inches from her face, rippling its body to hold its position. Its eyes were fixed on hers. She froze, holding her breath. Freya shifted her focus from the uncomfortably close predator to the shadow lurking behind it. Oh God. The shark?

It was Kelly. A brief feeling of relief washed over her, but it was snatched away by the searing pain of fangs plunging into her left hand. Freya gargled a scream through her regulator and dropped the box, letting it fall to the sea floor. The snake shot off into murk as Kelly tore through the water toward her. Her breathing slowed and her limbs grew heavy. Her eyelids slid closed. She blinked before her eyes closed one last time.

CHAPTER TWENTY-THREE

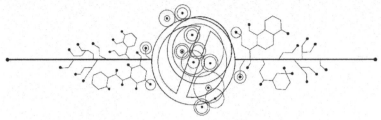

Location: A hospital in a small village, India

The haze of unconsciousness lifted. Freya was laid on an unsteady, broken, hospital gurney. Light blue sheets were tucked tightly at her sides, with only her arms remaining free. Various wires and tubes protruded from pale limbs that were bruised at the point of needle entry.

The sound of labored breathing droned in her head. For a moment, she wondered what the hell the noise was and then realized it was her own heavy exhalation into a ventilating machine. Sluggishly, she pulled at the mask, trying to pry it from her face. Kelly's hand gently rested on hers, preventing the action. She rolled her eyes upward to see his familiar smiling face gazing back at her. He looked exhausted, drained. His usual, healthy, tanned complexion was pallid and sickly. Dark circles had formed under his now gray, dull eyes.

Kelly shook his head slowly. "Don't try and get up. And don't pull the mask off. You're lucky to be alive. That was a Jerdon's sea snake. Pretty powerful venom in those things. They cause asphyxiation through diaphragmatic paralysis. At least, that's what the Doc says. Basically, it stops you breathing, and you suffocate."

Freya nodded once.

"So, I hope you don't mind, but I had to suck on your arm for a bit there to try and get rid of as much of that poison as possible." He chuckled, but his frivolity was cut short by the onset of a coughing and wheezing fit.

She stared at him, her eyes full of concern.

"I'm fine, I'm fine," he lied. "Anyway, you're the one in trouble this time, not me."

Raising a spare hand to her arm, Freya felt for the fang marks. She winced as her fingers lightly skimmed across the two puncture wounds in her otherwise perfect flesh.

"Don't worry. I don't think it will scar."

"Di … did we find it? Was it a device?" Her voice was weak, each word a concerted effort to push from her lips.

"No. At least not a device that we were looking for."

She scrunched her nose as if to ask, what?

Alejandro waltzed into the room and sat by Kelly's side, though he did not extend the courtesy of actually acknowledging his son-in-law. He was still dressed in his linen shorts. It seemed his outfit was just as useful in India as it was in Egypt.

"What we have found, young Freya, is something that may still be of help. It's an Antikythera mechanism." It was the first time either Freya or Kelly had heard the old man express any kind of emotion. For it to be joy was a surprise to them both.

"What does that mean?" Freya could barely catch her breath to ask the question.

"The original Antikythera mechanism is an ancient mechanical computer, thought to be built around one-hundred years BC and designed to calculate astronomical positions. It was recovered in 1900 during a diving expedition just off the coast of the Greek island Antikythera," began the old man. "But its significance and its complexity were not understood until many years later. Jacques Cousteau even visited the wreck for the last time in 1978 but found no additional remains of it."

"I've heard about this. There were a bunch of us that did a dive on the Antikythera wreck. It's a huge galleon. We didn't find anything." Kelly stared at the old man, who still did not acknowledge he had spoken.

Alejandro continued. "The device is remarkable for its level of miniaturization and complexity. The recovered device had more than thirty gears, although it was badly corroded. It has been suggested there may have been as many as seventy-two gears, each with tiny teeth—small triangles. When a date was entered via a crank, the mechanism calculated the position of the sun, moon, or other astronomical bodies, such as the known planets. This device is so accurate it even compensates for the elliptical, rather than circular, movement of the heavenly bodies. It had more than two thousand markings on it, and I was part of one of the teams that helped verify the translations—quality control, if you will."

Freya nodded again but was still confused as to what this had to do with the device they were looking for.

"It has long been debated that a device of such complexity could not have been just thought up and built in the space of a year or even ten years. To start with, understanding the paths of the sun, moon, and planets would take many, many years of recording—particularly to establish the elliptical orbits. It suggests there was prior knowledge, ancient knowledge, like the kind you believe to be passed down by your aquatic friend."

"So?" Kelly said. "How does this help us? All you've found is another high-tech cuckoo clock. And?"

The outburst grabbed Alexandro's attention. "As always, dear boy," huffed the old man, "you are jumping the gun. The mechanism that young Freya recovered is in perfect condition and doesn't have Greek markings. It has Mayan ones." Alejandro reached inside the bag he had rested at his feet and pulled out an object approximately the size and shape of a standard shoe box but made of bronze, not cardboard. The mechanism had three main dials, one on the front and two on the rear of its longest sides. "I have done a cursory inspection. From what I can decipher from the text, the outer ring, here, is marked off with the days of the Mayan calendar. The front dial carried three hands. One showed the date, and two others showed the positions of the sun and moon. The front dial also includes a second mechanism with a model of the moon, displaying the lunar phase. There are also references to Mars and Venus in the inscriptions. The lower back dial is in the form of a spiral, which, if like the original device, means it might predict eclipses. But here is where it gets interesting." He shifted the box around and placed his index finger on a row of symbols. "Here, it refers to the visitor, Viracocha, who comes at each lunar eclipse."

Freya's eyes widened.

Kelly leaned forward on his chair. Could it be? Had they found a device that was supposed to predict the coming of K'in's kind?

"This would explain almost every civilization on Earth and their obsession with the stars and planets. Although many writings refer to gods and other deities originating from the stars, it is very likely this is merely a corruption of the original intent—to predict the next encounter with the knowledge-bringers." Alejandro took a breath.

"But, what is a high-tech cuckoo clock with Mayan markings doing in the Indian Ocean? And how does this help us find what we're looking for?" Kelly had grown impatient. The old man was rambling again. They had no time for this.

"There are markings on this I have never seen before. I don't know what they mean. Symbols that look familiar, yet don't. I have a colleague who is up in Siberia near the Altai Mountains. She has an interest in rare symbology and languages. If I could send her pictures of this—"

"No!" Freya snapped, having mustered enough breath. "No, I don't trust sending anything through email, or fax, or whatever. If we move, we need to rendezvous with the General first. He needs to see this. There's a port in Vladivostok."

Kelly pulled a map from the side pocket of his sand-colored combat pants and spread it roughly across Freya's legs. "Okay, so how do we get there?"

"We'll need to get to Lhasa—here, in Tibet." She propped herself up on her elbows and pointed weakly to the city that was almost directly north of India. "We can take the plane there. But from that point, we are better off taking a train to Beijing, then Harbin, and then on to Vladivostok." She slumped back on the gurney, having exhausted her energy.

Kelly admired her. Even on death's door, she could give commands. "Okay. I assume we'll need visas to get through Russia. I'll go into town. I'm sure I can find help." With that, Kelly scooped up the map and left.

"How are you feeling, my dear?" Alejandro placed a hand on her blanket-covered knee.

"Okay. Tired. But we need to keep moving. I can't stay here. I'm sure Kelly can get us some visas—even if they're fake. He's resourceful."

"Kelly Graham is not always right, young Freya. Believe me. He's hot-headed and rash. He's the reason that—"

Freya cut him short. "I know what you will say. But it's not his fault."

"I suppose he told you that?"

"Actually, I overheard your son telling someone else about Kelly, Izel, and their daughter. Kelly doesn't really talk about it."

"The reason he doesn't talk about it," scowled Alejandro, moving his hand away from her leg, "is because he doesn't want to tell the whole truth. Carmen was not his daughter."

Freya frowned. "What? But I heard Chris. He said Carmen was Kelly's daughter."

"Kelly Graham is no more related to my granddaughter than you are, Ms. Nilsson. Kelly met Christopher when he was just beginning college. Chris was so intelligent. Kelly was in his mid-twenties and a mediocre student at best. His final year crossed with Christopher's first. He was supposed to be a mentor. Instead, he dragged my son around bars and got him into trouble. After twelve long months, Kelly left for work in South America. I thought I was rid of the man, but as fate would have it, he met Izel."

"Oh."

"Izel was teaching there. It was her lifelong dream. A dream she could not fulfill, given her daughter, little Carmen, was only a year old."

"Wait. Izel already had Carmen? If Kelly was not the father, who was?"

"A remarkable young man named Paulo. He passed away before Carmen was born—just died in his sleep one night. So tragic. He was a good man—strong, educated, and kind. Izel was distraught." He paused and furrowed his brow. "When Carmen was born, Izel didn't bond with her. She told me once that she just saw Paulo in the baby. For months, she couldn't cope. So I took over the situation. I sent Izel away to clear her mind, so she could come back ready and able to care for her daughter. Instead, she brought home Kelly Graham. I loved my daughter very much, but she always needed a man in her life. I never understood why."

Freya eyed him, feeling the anger in his voice. How could he not see it? Clearly, she sought from men the love he was unable to show. "So why does Kelly refer to Carmen as his daughter?"

"Despite my protests, Kelly and Izel married within six months of meeting, and he adopted Carmen as his own. Izel would not listen to reason. Carmen was told Kelly was her father, and I was not allowed to mention Paulo. Ever." Alejandro shuffled in his seat.

"You know, there is another way to look at this." She tried propping herself up again. "Kelly loved both your daughter and your granddaughter. And he misses them both more than I think even he lets himself admit. To take on someone else's daughter as his own is a big thing. Trust me, I know what I am talking about." Freya hadn't thought it possible, but perhaps now more than ever, she had a connection with Kelly. He had a strength in him that only Benjamin had shown.

The old man changed the subject. "Get some rest, young Freya. If you are to travel, we need to get you out of here. The emergency team allowed you in, but soon, they will start asking for identification and details."

Kelly shook the hand of the little Indian man, secretly exchanging a large number of folded bills. The man expertly received them and placed them in his pocket in one silky movement before scurrying off to a scruffy, little moped and speeding off in the direction of the town center. Wandering slowly back toward the hospital, Kelly paused at the emergency entrance. It was a horrible, old, and decrepit building but obscure enough to be concealed from prying eyes for now. He hated hospitals. They freaked him out. He hadn't been near one since he'd had to identify Izel's body. He closed his eyes and took in a deep breath. His mind wandered back to his first meeting with Alejandro.

As the door opened, Izel stopped fidgeting. The hand holding Kelly's went limp. Her father had answered the door. He glared at Kelly.

"Papa?" Izel feigned delight. She took a step forward and kissed him on the cheek. "Papa, what are you doing here?"

"Christopher mentioned that you were bringing home the love of your life. And you didn't think to mention this to me?"

"Love of your life?" Kelly was agog.

"Papa, I hadn't … well, told him yet." Her tone was hushed and embarrassed.

"And just what is it you do, young man? Hmm?"

"Papa, we're still on the doorstep."

Chris came barging out from behind his father. "Kelly? Kelly Graham?" Chris had short hair, unbleached at the time, and was sporting one of his baggy, light shirts over khaki shorts.

"Hey, esé."

Chris stared in disbelief. Then he punched Kelly hard in the mouth. Blood trickled from Kelly's lip.

Kelly raised a finger and touched the open wound, licking the crimson liquid from his fingertips.

"Kelly Graham, the degenerate womanizer you slummed with at college?" Alejandro stormed into the house, muttering in Spanish.

"Feel better there, esé?" Kelly raised an eyebrow, still nursing his lip.

Izel remained frozen on the spot.

"Yep. Figured we'd get that out the way and get on with our friendship. What d'ya reckon?"

196

Kelly smiled at him but winced in pain as the wound opened. "You got it, Paco." He slapped his friend on the shoulder and stepped inside the apartment.

Location: U.S. submarine, somewhere in the Pacific Ocean

Pinging. That was all that could be heard inside the control center of the submarine. Pinging. Hollow and empty. The sound of sonar. Searching for another object. Another submarine. But there was nothing. Deep below the surface within the trench, there was only the cold dark ocean. Not so much as a whale had swum by. The XO had his hands placed on the shoulders of his sonar operator, who was intently concentrating on the consistent pinging in his headset.

"Anything?" the XO asked.

"No sir, we're alone down here."

"Good."

He patted his operator's shoulders and walked back to the chart table in the center of the room. On the surface of the electronic map were six digital flags, indicators of where they had deployed the series of communication buoys. They had spent the last two days drawing out an incomprehensible path within the Pacific Ocean to ensure no pattern or direction of travel could be discerned from where the buoys surfaced.

The XO stared at the map. The harsh white light from underneath illuminated his face, obscuring his good looks. His chiseled features cast shadows in awkward and unpleasant shapes.

"Teller, how goes the signal scrambling?" The General sidled up to the XO and rested his elbow on the table.

"Good, sir. If they have managed to detect with whom we are speaking or even decoded your messages, then they haven't shown their hand. So far so good." He shrugged his shoulders. "All we can do is guess, really."

"Sir, we have an incoming transmission from the buoys," the communications officer called over his shoulder. "I'll patch it through to you."

The electronic map disappeared and was replaced with a line of green-glowing text. Teller stared at it, but the code didn't mean anything to him. It read: *z*13**2te99*va6ch**ay3**a82g.

"What does it say? It's not standard military code."

"It's a cipher. I taught Freya how to create one when she was young—er. It's unique to her." The General paused again. "We need to go to Russia. Head to the east coast."

"Won't it be easy to crack?"

"It's a standard thirty-nine character Beaufort cipher, but they don't have the keyword. They may crack it, but we'll still have time on our side."

"General, if anything should happen to you, we would be unable to communicate with Ms. Nilsson. Should you not tell at least one of us the keyword?"

Benjamin studied the XO's eyes. The man had come this far. Perhaps he should be trusted. Given the situation, the men aboard the submarine were the only people Benjamin could trust. The General pulled a pen from an inner pocket of his jacket and grabbed the XO's hand. He turned it palm up and scrawled *Father* across it.

Teller quickly glanced back at the code. Working the keyword into the equation, it read: *o*to**ladiv*stock**two**ays*. It was still coded, so he calculated the missing characters using the keyword again. Now, the message was clear: *Go to Vladivostok. Two days.*

Teller nodded. "Aye, aye, sir."

"Good. Now, we need ..." The General trailed off, distracted by the loud clanging of heavy boots echoing up the corridor.

Wiezorek burst into the room, completely out of breath, almost falling into the command chair. "Creature ... breathing ... stopped." wheezed the pilot.

"What?" Benjamin barged past the officer and ran down the corridor, bouncing off the oncoming Tremaine.

"What's going on?" called the Shadow Man after him.

"Follow me. K'in has stopped breathing."

"Ah, shit." Tremaine started after his commander, lumbering down the narrow space.

The XO and pilot were left in the command center.

"Do we have a medic on board?" the young pilot asked.

"Nope, this is a skeleton crew," Teller replied.

"Damn. I'll go, I have some basic field, triage training." Wiezorek blew out the last of the carbon dioxide in his lungs, hoping the lactic acid in his muscles would also dissipate, and ran after the other two men.

"I'll just stay here, then!" yelled the XO.

K'in lay in his low-lying tank. He was motionless. His eyes were dull, matte orbs, and his gills were flaccid and drained of color. The General clambered through the porthole into the room and instantly dropped to his knees. He pulled at the animal's arms, but its dead weight fixed its body to the floor. Benjamin put his head to K'in's chest, listening for a heartbeat. There was none.

CHAPTER TWENTY-FOUR

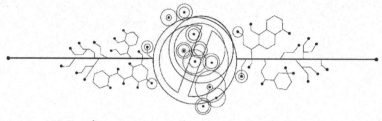

Location: U.S. submarine, somewhere in the Pacific Ocean

"Fuck, fuck, fuck!"

Tremaine almost tripped over the lip of the doorway as he careened inside. "What's wrong with it?"

Benjamin looked up at Tremaine. "I have no goddamn idea. It's a fucking corpse."

"Excuse me." The young pilot stepped in, pushing past Tremaine. "If its heart's stopped, we need to start it again."

"Tremaine, out of his way." bellowed the General. "Here, soldier."

Wiezorek knelt by K'in and bent to listen for a heartbeat. Still nothing. He put his ear to the animal's mouth. K'in was not breathing. "We have to start CPR."

Tremaine grunted. "How the hell are you gonna do CPR on a fish?"

"The same way I'd do it to you," Wiezorek replied.

"General, help me turn it over."

They groaned as they heaved K'in's heavy body onto its back. The pilot then placed both hands, one on top of the other, on the animal's chest and pressed while counting.

"One, one thousand, two, one thousand, three, one thousand. Breathe!" He grabbed K'in by the end of his snout, covering the tiny nostrils with his palm. He enveloped the tiny mouth with his lips and blew as hard as he could. The animal's chest puffed out momentarily.

He listened for a heartbeat, but there was no sound.

"Dammit." He restarted the cycle, pumping and breathing into K'in's mouth over and over. It was no use.

"Why don't you shock it with the paddles?" yelled Tremaine in frustration. He grabbed the defibrillator from the wall and pulled out the electro pads. The young pilot ignored him and continued with the CPR.

"Defibrillators don't work that way. They are used to shock the heart into asystole. We need to get the heart started," the General replied.

Exhausted, Wiezorek slumped onto his hands. "I can't do it." He shook his head.

"There has to be a way," yelled the General.

"Maybe you're going about it the wrong way." The XO stood in the doorway. "Sorry, but I had to come down."

"You have a suggestion, Teller? Out with it," Benjamin ordered, his face red.

"Aerate its gills. Breathing into its chest may not be enough. We use dehumidifiers on these subs to remove moisture from the air. Its gills are probably dried out."

"Shit, you're right. They need to be wet to work." The General leapt to his feet. "We don't have anything deep enough to submerge it in."

"Maybe we do. Tremaine, help me lift it." The XO pushed his way into the room and grabbed K'in by the front limbs, dragging it upward.

Tremaine dropped the defibrillator and jerked into action. Moving to the rear of the animal, he grabbed its hind limbs and lifted. "Lord, this thing is heavy."

"Stop complaining. Follow me." They shuffled as quickly as possible out of the door and down the corridor, Wiezorek and the General following closely behind.

After a few minutes, they reached a thin, metal ladder at the end of the corridor. "We have to go up," yelled the XO.

"General, you go up, and we'll push from below. You pull."

Benjamin nodded and squeezed past. "Wiezorek, you're with me. It'll take two of us."

They ascended the ladder and then bent down, their arms hanging through the hole. The XO heaved K'in upward, Tremaine pushing from the bottom. Benjamin and the young pilot grabbed the flapping forelimbs and pulled. Finally, with an immense amount of grunting and cursing, the four of them managed to elevate the cumbersome animal onto the next level.

Out of breath, the XO called up to the General. "You're at the lockout trunk. We have to put it inside." He scrambled up the ladder and, once again, grabbed the animal. "Heave."

They slid K'in over the lip of the porthole and into the lockout trunk.

"Now what?" the General asked.

"I gotta get into scuba gear to perform CPR in the trunk."

The XO grabbed one of two scuba tanks that were lying in the trunk and climbed into the straps.

"Wait. You aren't going to put on a wetsuit?" Wiezorek asked.

"We don't have time." Pulling the mask over his face, the XO stepped into the lockout trunk with K'in and closed the door behind him. The others were left outside with no window into the trunk and no way to observe. They just had to wait.

Inside, it was cramped. Various wheels that opened valves adorned the walls. The exit tube, big enough to allow a man to pass through, filled much of the space and a thin metal ladder ascended from the floor into the tube toward the hull of the submarine. Teller, his face covered and the scuba regulator in his mouth, opened the valve to fill the lockout trunk. Freezing water sprayed inside, foaming and swirling as it filled the space.

The XO bit down on the regulator mouth piece and screwed his eyes shut as the icy water crept its way up his legs, his thin polyester coveralls providing little insulation. Fighting the excruciating feeling of knives stabbing at his skin, Teller lifted K'in from the floor. It was easier now that the water was buoying the animal's weight. He splashed water onto the creature's gills and moving the stalks in a waving motion.

The space had now fully filled, and Teller was completely underwater. The frigid water stiffened his muscles, but he fought the urge to give up. Using one hand, palm outward, he pushed on K'in's chest, holding the creature against the wall. With his spare hand, he pulled the regulator from his mouth and placed it in the creature's mouth. He pressed the purge button on the front of the regulator, sending a burst of air down K'in's trachea, although most of it seemed to be forced into the surrounding water. He put the regulator back into his own mouth and then, with his feet against the wall behind him, began compressing the animal's chest—once, twice, three times. He then put the regulator back in K'in's mouth for some air and repeated the cycle over and over again.

Teller's legs quickly became tired. The combination of freezing water and lactic acid drained him of energy. Come on, you giant fucking salamander, come on! Teller growled into the regulator and extended his legs, shoving the animal as hard as he could against the wall, crushing its chest.

K'in spluttered into life. Confused and in pain, the animal flailed its limbs and flicked its head wildly about the trunk in an attempt to understand its environment. But the panic was momentary. Within a few seconds, the familiarity of the seawater and comfort of almost-weightlessness calmed him. K'in blinked a few times and then stopped, staring into the eyes of the XO.

To Teller, the locked gaze of K'in seemed to last forever. The animal's black, now glassy, eyes were warm and comforting. The XO forgot the pain of the cold water and let his body relax. K'in was alive. He'd managed it. A weak regulator-filled smile graced his face. With a feeling of contentment, he reached across and turned the valve to pump out the water.

Outside, the three men waited anxiously. The low hum of a pump grabbed their attention, making each one of them shuffle on their feet in expectation. After a few minutes, the hum stopped. There were various clanging and banging sounds from within the trunk and then the sound of the door lock moving. The porthole swung open. Inside lay the shivering XO, completely covered by K'in, who appeared to be keeping the man warm.

The General sighed in relief. "Get the XO some new clothing and something to warm him up."

"Yes, sir." Wiezorek ran off in the direction of his bunk.

"Good job, Teller. Good job. Let's just get to Russia and out of this goddamn tin can."

Shivering, the XO nodded in agreement.

Location: USAMRIID, Maryland, USA

The biocontainment patient care unit looked strange to Lucy—and not at all like it could contain a virus. It was a large plastic structure with orange pillars and supports and thin, transparent walls. The whole construction comprised three rooms: two airlocks in sequence leading to the main chamber with a bed for the patient. Christian had explained the entire thing was maintained under negative pressure with an increasing pressure gradient from airlock one to the patient room. Equipment for patient care was placed outside the unit. Cables and flexible tubes for artificial ventilation or suction were passed through the walls.

"He's in there?"

"Yes," Christian replied.

"He doesn't look so tough anymore."

"I guess not."

"When it comes down to it, all men are just human and vulnerable to the tiniest of viruses." She paused, reflecting on the situation. "Does he know?"

"No, I haven't told him yet. I was going to, but then you arrived." Christian wiped his brow.

She hesitated, her hand hovering on the glass in front of her. "Don't. I want to speak with him first."

Christian nodded. "Sure."

"Face to face."

"You'll need to suit up."

"Of course." She searched the small room before her gaze fell on the biohazard suits hanging on one wall.

"You want me to come in with you?"

"No, no. I'll do it. Don't worry."

"Okay. I'll go to the observation area and watch through the window. There's an intercom on the other side. If you need me, I'll be here. The glass is mirrored on the other side, so you won't be able to see me, but I'll be here."

"Thanks, Christian."

The doctor left the room, leaving Lucy to change. She slipped out of her clothes and into the one-piece biohazard suit. Christian had once told her that normally each person would have their own suit. They would prep it, pack it, and maintain it themselves, never trusting another person. But she had to make do with someone else's. She hoped he or she was meticulous with the care of it.

Lucy paused nervously at the large steel door but, eventually, managed to pluck up the courage to push it open. Briskly, she walked toward the first airlock of the BPCU and stepped inside. Looking outward through the plastic, the world looked warped and strange. She thought it could not be very comforting for a patient in one of these things.

She made her way through the second airlock and into the main chamber. There, the Colonel lay. His breathing was labored, skin gray, and eye sockets sunken and dark. It was a struggle for him to pull his own eyelids apart. His eyes rolled about like marbles in his skull until he finally found focus on her face.

"I suppose you think this is some kind of karma?" His voice was barely audible.

"Not really, Colonel. While I cannot say I'm amused you thought it prudent to have me put out of action, and might consider this retribution, the fact is I need you to live long enough to tell me what the hell is going on." She kept her voice cold and empty of emotion.

"Long enough?"

"Yes, Colonel. Long enough. The doctor will fill you in. It's not my place. But I need information from you. They say dying men tell the truth. Suppose you tell me the truth, Colonel?" She steeled her eyes on his.

"The truth? About what?"

"Why did the Chinese Minister of Foreign Affairs beg me to stop you from finding General Lloyd and the creature? And why did he then blow himself and the head of the military commission to holy hell? To ensure his own government didn't find them either? And why you? Why were you chasing the General? What're you not telling me?"

"There are many things you don't know, Madam Secretary, many you don't need to know, and many you don't want to." His eyelids slid closed and then opened slowly, fatigue draining him.

"Oh no, Colonel. I *do* want to know. Very much so. And I want you to tell me, or I will convince my brother in there to hold off on any kind of treatment for you."

"Brother?" The Colonel's eyes glassed over.

"Yes, brother. I took our mother's maiden name. It's not something we advertise. Given your little plan to hospitalize me, I don't think it would take much for me to convince him."

The frail man darted a glance at the large mirror, the one-way glass, at the opposite side of the room. Did she mean it? Could he risk it?

"Why were you heading up the search team to find General Lloyd? Why would the Chinese Minister commit a bombing to prevent the Chinese from finding him?"

"Because," he began, "the creature General Lloyd has with him is the only one that worked as we expected. It is the only one that reached maturity and was able to perform tasks. It has massive military application."

"The only *one*?"

"There were others. But clone five was the one that worked. Benjamin Lloyd had obtained a device that allowed us to communicate with it. He stole it from the Chinese, but they attacked the base, and it was destroyed."

"But that doesn't explain why you wanted to be the one to find him. What interest do you have in this?"

"I told you I used to work with Benjamin, but it wasn't entirely true. I was part of the clone project team with him. Following the success of the K'in clone, there was a separate project set up to militarize the cloning process.

Benjamin was skeptical, so when I took on the position as head of the CDC, I continued the research, utilizing the new resource at my disposal."

"Your own private project?"

"In a way. But nothing is that isolated. I had funding and supporters, particularly in New Mexico." He stopped talking. He hadn't wanted to give away that particular piece of information.

"You're talking about Dulce base? I thought that was a myth."

"That's the point."

Lucy skipped over the topic. "General Lloyd didn't want to continue with the military application, did he? So, instead of handing it over to you, he gave the creature to the world?"

"Yes. It would seem he lost his nerve and decided to become a hippy, but the human world is not ready for that. And if we did not maximize the opportunity, then our enemies would."

"So the Chinese Minister also felt so strongly that his government should not maximize this opportunity that he killed himself to slow them from finding it?"

"It would seem so."

"Two distinguished men, respected in their countries, were so afraid of what would happen if either of their governments were able to militarize the clone that they risked everything to prevent it. It would seem to me it may be you who is misguided, Colonel."

"Benjamin Lloyd is no hero. He caused world chaos." The Colonel hacked and spluttered through his mask. "The only reason to release the information publicly is to instigate a war. He wanted to bring the world to its knees."

"To what end?"

"Who knows? You've read the files outlining the theory. The clone's species brought intelligence to humans. Perhaps his crazy sidekick, Professor Alexander, convinced him the world would be better if it was brought back to the Stone Age, and the clone could exert some kind of influence."

"That doesn't make a lot of sense."

"No, it doesn't. What makes sense is to ensure we alone hold the creature and are able to harness its abilities."

"It's a living animal, Colonel, and your little experiment is over. I will see to that. This creature, whatever it is, needs protection from the world. And perhaps, we from it. I will be dispatching my own search team to find the General."

"You think it will be that easy? The General has sent out a splinter team. We don't know if the creature is with him or them." He grimaced, his throat dry from too much talking.

"He's trying to divide our resources, to send us chasing more than one team?"

"Perhaps. Or perhaps he's searching for something—something like the object he stole from the Chinese and then destroyed. I've told you all I know." He coughed again, spraying spittle onto the inner plastic of the mask. "Send in the doctor."

"Oh, there won't be any need for that, Colonel." Lucy turned and walked away. "You won't be going to hell any time soon. Just a jail cell if I can help it. The morpholino is working. You'll live, at least long enough to face a judge."

Lucy stormed out of the chamber and into the second airlock. An overhead shower applied foam to the surface of her suit. She stood there fuming, her anger consuming her. Although the shower sequence only took twelve minutes, it seemed like a lifetime. Her mind raced—she'd been threatened, her brother put at risk, and the U.S. Government was conducting nonhuman experiments and invading Chinese territory. Furthermore, the Minister had killed himself and the head of the Chinese military. It was a mess. She was sure the President didn't know, but she could not go to him yet. She had to have proof, otherwise no one was going to believe her.

The shower stopped. She pushed her way into airlock one and fought her way out of the biohazard suit, grunting as her arms got trapped in the sleeves. She threw the suit into a crumpled heap on the floor, marched out of the airlock, dressed in only the specialized underwear, and up to the intercom interface.

"I'm ready to leave, Christian."

"Did you get what you needed?" His voice crackled through the speaker.

"Yes. Seems I need to go to New Mexico."

"Okay. By the way, I have initiated wider testing of the morpholino. I think we should be able to bring it to the General population in a day or so."

"Good, very good. Well done, Christian." She sighed and turned back to the Colonel who was grunting and coughing in frustration. "Now, time to finish off this little experiment. Boys and their damn toys."

CHAPTER TWENTY-FIVE

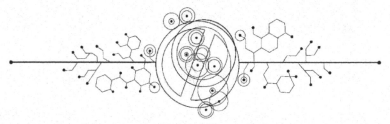

Location: Somewhere on the Trans-Siberian Railway

The old train rattled along the tracks with the three unlikely companions inside a cabin. They had bartered their way onto a very long truck ride to Lhasa, where they then boarded the train that would take them to Harbin and the trans-Siberian Railway to Vladivostok.

Kelly was the only one awake. Freya was back in her combat gear and propped up by one elbow, wedged into the window frame, still recovering from her tangle with the sea snake. Alejandro sat opposite them, curled up in a ball, underneath Kelly's jacket that the old man had refused for a full hour before finally accepting it when the frosty morning air had bitten just a little too hard. Looking about the rickety old car, Kelly spotted an old, beat-up guitar perched on one of the parcel shelves above Alejandro. Carefully, he rose from his seat and fetched it down. It had holes in it and was missing the first E string, but he turned the machine heads until he could get a decent set of chords to reverberate inside its hollow interior. It had been ages since he had played. In fact, the last time he could remember was floating down the Amazon with Chris. Kelly sniffed away the lump in his throat and strummed quietly, singing in the softest voice he could.

"I don't believe,
The world would understand,
Or people would want to see,
The boy beneath the man,
So I hide the inner child,
Avoid another's touch,
And play the endless fool,
So rejection won't hurt too much."

"I didn't know you played," Freya said. She was fixated on Kelly's performance.

He snapped back to the reality of the cabin, embarrassed that she'd heard him. "I don't really. I taught myself a long time ago, but I'm still crap. Anyway, didn't your agency have records on me? I mean, you found me, right?"

"Actually, we did research, but there was surprisingly little on you. Your records only had any substance once you went to university, and that was also late if I remember correctly?"

Kelly eyed her. He didn't like being questioned. And he was not used to telling anyone anything about his personal life. He'd been surprised Chris had talked about Izel in the Chinook while they traveled to Area 51. Perhaps he'd felt Victoria was a friend. He turned back to the expectant face of Freya and sighed. "My mom ran off with another man a year after I was born. For as long as I can remember, I had to help my dad through. He turned to drinking to cope, and that meant I pretty much had to fend for myself. He wasn't abusive or anything, just useless. By the time I was fourteen, I'd grown tired of looking after him, so I left home. I traveled about, taking odd jobs and letting the breeze blow me where it wanted. My travels eventually took me through Mexico and into South America. I took pictures wherever I went. I was fascinated by photography. For a while, I settled in Rio and took up freediving and underwater photography. I sent a few pictures off to National Geographic, which were bought. After a while, they got interested in my work, and I started doing more things for them. They paid for me to go to college, where I met Chris." He squirmed in his seat. "Anyway, what about you? You never told me what was up with you and the General."

Freya sat motionless for a moment considering whether to answer. But she decided if he could open up, then so could she. "My parents died when I was thirteen. My father was in the military and was good friends with Benjamin and his wife—so much so that they were my godparents. By the time my parents passed away, Benjamin and his wife had already divorced. I don't think he knew what he was doing, but he agreed to fulfill his duty and bring me up on his own. He did a pretty good job. He's the reason I'm in the military."

Kelly fidgeted in his seat, embarrassed for having previously suggested a sexual relationship. "Sorry."

"It doesn't matter. These things happen. I was really too young to know them well. And Benjamin has been a father to me. I think this is why all this has gotten to me so much. I never expected him to lie to me." She turned away to hide any outward expression of vulnerability.

"You know, in his own twisted way, he was trying to protect you." He hesitated before finishing his thought. "Like Izel for me. When Carmen died, Izel didn't tell me. I don't think she knew how to break it to me. Probably thought she was doing me a favor."

Freya turned back to Kelly. His usual sarcastic expression had melted into one of understanding and empathy. He was starting to open up. Should she push it further? "Alejandro explained something to me. I know that Carmen wasn't yours."

Kelly froze. He focused his stare on Freya, searching her face and eyes for her intention. He'd already started to tell her things. There was no point in trying to avoid questions now. "No, Carmen wasn't mine. In fact, when I met Izel, she didn't tell me she had a daughter. I didn't find out until I met her father for the first time. Chris, my friend from college, he was her brother. We crossed paths during my final year. He had no idea I was dating her. We had gone to his apartment to surprise him. Well, he was so surprised he punched me." Kelly laughed and rubbed his jaw where it had been struck. "But for Chris, that was the end of it. Her father met me at the door and instantly disapproved. At first, I thought my college exploits had preceded me, and I just needed to do some damage control. So when he turned tail and stormed back into the apartment, I followed him, keen to set the record straight."

Freya nodded. "Then?"

"Then, I almost tripped over a baby crawling across my path. I looked down, and the tiniest little brown eyes stared back at me. I hoisted the li'l one up. The kid beamed at me, bit of drool swinging from her gummy grin." He smiled and swallowed away the stone in his throat. "I asked, 'What's your name, bright eyes?' Chris replied on her behalf that it was Carmen. I opened my mouth to congratulate the old dog on his baby-making skills when Izel interrupted and said Carmen was hers. For a few seconds, I was silent, stunned. I looked into Carmen's eyes and suddenly saw Izel staring back at me. I asked where the dad was. Alejandro shouted that he was dead."

Freya nodded.

"At the time, I didn't even hear how the guy died. I was too busy staring at Carmen. It was as if the little rug rat had stuffed a knife into my chest, opened it up, and crawled inside. She was a beautiful piece of the woman I loved so much. There was never any question. Izel and I agreed Carmen would never be without a father, and one day, we would tell her the truth." Kelly sighed again, exhausted from opening his innards to another person.

"And that's why Alejandro dislikes you? Because you took on the role of the father?"

"In part. He loved the real father. And I was apparently no match. Things got worse between us, and in the end, we just stopped talking. I did quite a bit of work in Egypt, and Izel would come with Carmen and see Alejandro, but I always steered clear. When my jobs there stopped, so did our visits. I think he resented that."

Freya simply nodded again, unsure of how to respond. Kelly looked hurt and vulnerable, but she knew better than to try to comfort him, to get closer. She had pushed him far enough.

The landscape was bleak under the pale moonlight. Miniature shacks speckled the horizon, each shadowing its own little plot of farmland. An intensely pot-holed forest track whisked by the train window, only visible due to the moon's reflection off the water-filled, mini craters. Whenever the train stopped at a station, a small gaggle of women appeared from nowhere. They shuffled up and down the train, touting a strange collection of gifts for sale. The items changed as the journey progressed, beginning with more traditional Asian items, such as paper lanterns and decorated bowls, and moving to more bizarre items, including fake Fabergé eggs and full crystal chandeliers. These latter items signified the transition into Siberia.

Alejandro stirred under the jacket, then sat up. The cold air made him shiver, so he grasped at the jacket and pulled it tighter around him. He should have accepted Kelly's offer to buy warmer clothing while in India.

He blinked away the sleepiness from his eyes and looked across at his fellow travelers. Kelly was asleep, head tilted back, mouth open, and snoring. He twitched slightly and moaned, his brow wet and his skin pale. What else could he expect from the man? He was a useless brute with a wit as dull as the knuckles he dragged along the ground. Once again, Alejandro had been pulled into this slack-jawed idiot's stupid world. He shook his head and turned his attention to Freya. She, on the other hand, was graceful and elegant. She was sitting upright with her hands in her lap and her eyes closed.

Her mouth was definitely not open. Her long ebony hair and slender frame reminded Alejandro of Izel or perhaps who Carmen may have grown to be. The past was such a tragedy and all Kelly's fault. And now he was about to do it again to another woman. The young lady had said it was her fault and Kelly was dragged into this, but it seemed trouble followed this man everywhere.

"You know, it's rude to stare." Freya spoke without opening her eyes.

"Oh, oh, I'm sorry. I didn't mean to, young … I was just thinking," stuttered the old man.

Freya opened her eyes and let them adjust to the darkened cabin before she spoke. "You know, Kelly isn't as bad as you may believe, Professor D'Souza."

"Alejandro, please."

"Okay, Alejandro."

"You don't know him like I do. He doesn't care who he hurts as long as he is moving forward and pretending to be Indiana Jones."

"I disagree, Alejandro. Over the past few weeks, I have spent a lot of time with him. He cares very much who he hurts." She changed her position to be a more relaxed one and bent forward, elbows on her knees and hands clasped together. She was still weak but strong enough to support her weight. "Did you know when we first asked Kelly to dive for us and collect the original orb, he wouldn't let Chris go with him?"

Alejandro grunted. "Probably wanted all the glory."

"No, he said it was too dangerous and he was only willing to risk his own life."

The old man didn't respond.

"Also, did you know Kelly has very bad nightmares about Izel and Carmen? Their death haunts him. He's been unable to let go."

Alejandro still didn't respond but cast a brief glance at Kelly.

"He does care. He just doesn't know how to show it."

"And that's why he's grunting and snorting now?"

"Possibly. It's strange. K'in seemed to become very fond of Kelly. They bonded, I think. Kelly's nightmares stopped for a few weeks, but since we've separated from K'in, they've returned. And he seems to be getting sicker."

"He didn't say anything."

"He wouldn't."

Alejandro nodded thoughtfully and sat back in his seat, pondering this new information. "Perhaps."

Freya mirrored the man's posture, leaning back in her own seat. "So, tell me. This friend of yours, why is he up there, and what is he doing?"

"She's searching for artifacts frozen in the ice. She's part of a team chartered to excavate in the Altai Mountains. There have been a lot of mummies and corpses found in that region of Siberia."

"Any idea what they're looking for?"

"She never really said, but I do know she's a bit eccentric and believes in some of the more unconventional theories. She still believes that Hapgood's theory of earth crust displacement may have some credibility."

"Earth crust displacement?"

"Charles Hapgood was a professor of the history of science at Keene College in New Hampshire. His research led him to study many early maps of the world. He found several of these maps appeared to show a southern landmass very similar in shape and size to Antarctica."

"Okay."

"Now, although various explorers visited the islands to the south of South America in the seventeenth and eighteenth centuries, Antarctica was not officially discovered until 1820. Hapgood thought these maps, which were believed to be copies of much older ones, depicted Antarctica as it would have looked before it was covered in ice. For that to be true, the original maps would have to have been created by an advanced civilization many thousands of years ago. I have to say, his work is highly debated."

"Well, what you suggest would fit with our thoughts on K'in and his advanced civilization."

"Perhaps, although you told me K'in is aquatic. A need to draw paper maps of Antarctica may not have been strong. In any event, Hapgood argued Antarctica did not lie in its current position at the South Pole but about thirty degrees further north. In the 1950s, he developed a theory called Earth Crust Displacement. He suggested the tectonic plates shifted violently, relatively quickly, and as one over the liquid inner of the Earth. Hapgood claimed this resulted in Antarctica moving from a temperate climate to a polar one. Even Albert Einstein supported this theory. He wrote a foreword in one of Hapgood's books. It has even been suggested this could account for the large number of animals found flash frozen in Siberia."

"The original corpse from which we cloned K'in was found frozen in that part of the world. Could it be?" Freya's eyes widened.

"I don't know. Many people have refuted his theory. Our understanding of geology and how ice moves under pressure has advanced since then. Some scientists still maintain the continent has been under ice for millions of years. Others argue Hapgood may be correct and say they have evidence Antarctica had free-flowing rivers on it a mere six-thousand years ago. I've looked at the original maps myself, but it does not help me to draw any conclusions."

Freya slumped back in her seat, disappointed.

"But I digress. The point is, young lady, if anyone can help us, it will be Minya Yermolova."

CHAPTER TWENTY-SIX

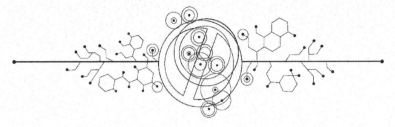

Location: Vladivostok, Siberia

Kelly snorted awake and drove his head into the cabin wall. Freya laughed. Even Alejandro had to suppress a smile.

"We've been trapped in train cabins for days, and I'm so tired of getting harassed by annoying little shits trying to force their wares on me," grumbled Kelly.

"Just be glad we've had our own car all the way. Everyone else has had large men who smell like pickles traipsing in and out." Freya screwed up her nose at the thought of the vinegar-soaked stench that had become ever present as they penetrated further into Siberia.

"You've got issues with food. Anyone ever told you that?" Kelly shook his head.

Freya wrinkled her nose. "I just never got used to the cuisine out here."

"I must say, I still think traveling all the way to Vladivostok is a little inefficient. Minya is based in the Altai mountains, more than twelve-hundred miles in the other direction."

"I know, Professor D'Souza. But it's the best place to rendezvous with the General and then travel together. Think of it this way. You'll get to meet K'in." Freya smiled at the thought of seeing the creature again.

Kelly huffed loudly. "Yeah, I wonder what Moby will make of the old goat."

Freya shot him a scathing look. Alejandro didn't take any notice.

The wheels of the train squealed as its brakes ground on them. The carriage lurched and swayed to a halt. A voice from overhead barked something that was garbled through static and crackling. It was almost impossible to discern between the different languages: Eskimo-Aleut, Mongolic, Paleosiberian, Siberian, Turkic, Russian, Tungusic, Uralic.

"This is it. Vladivostok." Freya stretched out her slender arms and yawned. "Let's go."

"How the hell do you know that?" Kelly asked.

"You may be at home in the Middle East, Kelly Graham, but now you're in my backyard."

"You speak Russian? You never said."

"We don't all need to brag twenty-four-seven. Anyway, Sherlock, this is the last stop, and so it must be Vladivostok." She winked, tightened her ponytail again, and stood.

The three travelers groaned, stretched, and collected their backpacks. Kelly picked up the old guitar and slung it over one shoulder.

"You taking that, too?"

He shrugged. "We have another four-day drive from here to Altai. Gotta keep you entertained somehow, right?" With that, he waved her in front of him, a mock act of chivalry.

"Thank you."

She stepped forward and out of the carriage, but her stride was cut short as she almost crashed into a large man dressed entirely in black. Freya's gaze began at his boots and rose slowly upward until it met the unsmiling face of Tremaine. "How the hell did you get here so fast?"

"We've been moving toward the east coast of Siberia for quite a while. You forget, that sub is fast."

"Well shit, JT!" Kelly stepped forward and weakly patted the Shadow Man on the back.

Tremaine ignored him.

"Where's the General?" Freya asked, scanning the train platform.

"Not here. We have a secure building not far away. Old contacts from the Cold War, when Vladivostok was a military base, helped out the General. It seems Mr. Graham is not the only one with *friends* in low places."

"Oh," was all she said.

"So we meet the creature now?" Alejandro directed his question at the new man in front of him.

"You must be Professor D'Souza. Yes, we will make our way now."

216

Tremaine pointed beyond a handful of people shuffling around the platform to a battered old car in the distance.

"For once, can we take a car that doesn't look like it belongs on a scrap heap?" Freya threw her arms in the air and stormed off in the direction of the vehicle.

Kelly scanned the faces of the other men and shrugged. "Hey, don't look at me, it's not my fault. I stole a private jet. You boys need to step up your game." He started after her, the backpack bouncing on his shoulder.

Tremaine calmly followed and climbed into the driver's side of the car. His bulk pressed against the roof, door, handbrake and steering wheel. He was not comfortable. Kelly sat up front in the passenger seat, while Freya and Alejandro sat in the back.

"You want me to drive, JT?" Kelly asked.

"No," he snapped. "I drive." With that, Tremaine shifted the gear and pressed the accelerator. The car grunted and choked but eventually lurched forward.

Kelly stared out the window. He had not been in this part of the world before and wasn't sure what to expect. As the vehicle meandered through the streets of Vladivostok, he found it decidedly boring. Besides the odd ex-soviet statue, it seemed much like any western city he'd ever visited. In Egypt, at least things were different enough to be interesting. He huffed loudly like a bored child. Then, it dawned on him. They were moving away from the coast. "Hey, JT. Where are we going? I thought you guys parked your sub at a port or something?"

"No, we used the ASDS to come ashore, but we needed something much more secure. This is an ex-soviet city. We're being careful. That port deals with Korea, Japan, and *China*. We have a secure location."

"The fortress," Freya said. "You're using the fortress."

"Yes."

"Fortress, what fortress?" demanded Kelly. Perhaps this place was going to be more interesting than he thought.

"That one." Freya pointed out the car window.

Kelly followed her outstretched arm. In the distance among the green hills, he saw several small, concrete buildings. "That? That's not a fortress.

It's a couple of sheds." He huffed again and shook his head.

"You of all people, Kelly Graham, should know not to judge a book by its cover." She stared at him, boring her point into his head. "Vladivostok literally means 'to rule the East,'" she said. "Since the late nineteenth century, this city was designed to be a huge fortress. Originally, it was wood and mud, but before long, concrete structures were built."

Kelly smirked. "Was it built by three little pigs?"

"No, smartass. Actually, it was a Colonel Velichko, ranked among the world's best engineers at the time, who made major changes. Well, him and General Lieutenant Vernander in 1910, but—"

"Did you read a book called, I Love Vladivostok?" Kelly asked.

"No, I completed my thesis on the history of Vladivostok. From a military point of view, it's very important."

"Look, lose the history lesson. What's your point?" Kelly rubbed his temples to convey his boredom.

Freya huffed. "The point is this: most of its structures can withstand heavy artillery, and it has numerous underground passages. Vladivostok fortress has pretty much no parallel in the world, which makes it the perfect hiding place."

"So this whole town is one giant fortress?" Alejandro asked. He'd been listening intently.

"Yes. It's a tourist trap now, but the General has called in a favor. It's closed to the public for a few days," Tremaine replied.

No one spoke for the next thirty minutes as the car gunned up into the hills toward one of the concrete buildings. The battered, old vehicle ground to an uneasy halt. The odd collection of travelers exited and stretched their stiff limbs, grunting and moaning as they did so. The sun was bright, and the grass surprisingly green, but a sharp, stinging wind blew across the hilltops.

"Fuck me, it's cold," Kelly complained. "Can we not get inside?"

"Good idea." Freya nodded. "Down here." She pointed down a dark hole that vanished into the hillside.

"Let's go." Tremaine marched to the front of the group and disappeared inside the tunnel.

Freya clicked on her flashlight. "Follow me."

Kelly and Alejandro complied, taking up the rear of the line.

After a long walk along the uninviting tunnel and an awkward descent down roughly hewn rock stairs, what lay before them was not what Kelly had been expecting. To start with, there were no bats. There were supposed to be bats in these places, screeching out of the dark and scaring the crap out of people. But there were none. And for that matter, it wasn't dark either.

Bright light bulbs on the ceiling drowned the walls in an unhealthy yellow hue. Kelly examined each room and tunnel as they passed through. Stalactites decorated the underground system, and some paths were impassable due to wide pools. The air was saturated with vapor so staying down here was not really an option, yet it was ideal for K'in, thought Kelly. The other odd thing was the old rooms were strangely lavish, echoing the zeitgeist of Stalin's elite. Although the place was in horrible disrepair, Kelly sensed the ghosts of the past and imagined the elegance of what had been. Parquet flooring, carpets, oak-paneled walls, and gilded door handles graced the interior. Old suits of armor, telegraph and radio equipment, even dusty books by Lenin lay on the tables. The group approached a final large room. Kelly's innards began to warm with a familiar feeling. K'in was close.

The group stepped into a room that had once been used as a cinema, a map of Primorye now replacing the projection screen. Several chairs lay haphazardly on the floor. In the corner in a deep puddle lay K'in, quiet and solemn. Kelly stopped and scanned his environment. The General and two other men stood in the opposite corner, discussing something. He watched as Freya and Tremaine made a beeline for them. Then, he eyed Alejandro. The man was fidgeting on the spot and rubbing his hands.

"Come with me, Alejandro. There's someone I want you to meet." Kelly strolled toward the creature.

Alejandro followed.

As the two men approached, K'in became alert. Like a dog that had waited all day for its owner to come home, he excitedly scrambled onto all fours and vaulted toward Kelly. The sheer force of the animal colliding into him sent Kelly sprawling. Alejandro jumped backward, afraid.

K'in had Kelly pinned to the floor and was bouncing up and down on his chest, blinking furiously. Alejandro watched in amazement as, in a matter of seconds, the animal's eyes morphed from pitch black, to a deep, oil-like purple, and, finally, to an iridescent blue. Kelly laughed and wrestled with the giant salamander.

"Whoa, okay, Moby, chill, chill! I gotcha."

The ruckus attracted the attention of the others, who wandered over, curious.

"Astonishing," remarked the XO. "The animal has been positively catatonic the whole time. Now look at it."

"Yes, and look at its eyes." The General clenched his jaw in concentration, unhappy with the situation.

"He did that before," Freya said. "His eyes changed and so did Kelly's."

"Huh?" Kelly looked up, struggling under the powerful animal as it grappled with him. As his gaze met Freya's, the electric blue of his eyes shone outward.

The General leaned slightly closer to his young protégé, Wiezorek. "Keep an eye on them."

"Yes, sir," the young man replied.

After a few minutes, Kelly managed to pry himself free and clamber to his feet. He looked at each of his audience in turn. "What?"

"Nothing, Mr. Graham. Sort yourself out and then join us in the next room. You will need appropriate gear to travel to Altai at this time of year, so we've taken the liberty of providing you with the necessary kit," the General said.

"Sure." He patted the dust down from his clothes and marched after the group. K'in padded after him.

"Freya, you have the device from India?" the General called over his shoulder.

"Yes."

"Good. Bring it with you. I should like to inspect it."

"Yes, sir." She shifted the backpack on her back, feeling for the weight of the object inside before following the rest of the group, her head hung low. Benjamin seemed cold and distant. Her heart ached.

"What do you want me to say, Freya?" the General asked.

"That you are pleased to see me. That I did a good job."

"I am pleased to see you. And the job isn't over," he replied.

"This damn mission. It's all you care about. I hope it's all worth it in the end." Freya turned on her heel and stormed out of the dimly lit room, barging past Wiezorek.

Benjamin stood silently in the gloom.

"General?" Wiezorek shuffled nervously in the large, arched doorway.

"What is it?" Benjamin didn't turn to face the officer.

"The Trekol is ready, sir. I thought you should know." His voice trembled.

"Good. Then we should make our way soon. We've spent a night down here in this atmosphere. It's more than enough." He turned and eyed the young soldier. "Something wrong, son?"

"No, sir. Well, I mean, yes, sir."

"Out with it, soldier."

"May I ask, sir, what we will do about Mr. Graham? He seems quite volatile. If all of our fates rely on this creature who is connected to him, it seems the mission is compromised."

"I would agree with you, young Ethan. The creature has formed some sort of bond with him. Until now, it's been beneficial to have him around. But he's an idiot. I can't let him fuck things up. Once we have what I'm looking for in my possession, I need him removed." He gave a communicative nod to the young pilot.

"I understand, sir."

"Good. Freya has grown fond of the imbecile, too. When it comes to it, we can't allow her emotions to compromise the mission." He walked past the soldier to the doorway.

"Does she know?"

The General halted. "Does who know what?"

"Agent Nilsson—Freya—does she know you did all this for her?"

Benjamin backed up to be face to face with the young man and glared at him. "What did you say?"

"I'm sorry, sir. I meant no offense." Ethan took a step back, pulled a small leather wallet from his pocket and opened it. Inside was a picture of a young, red-headed woman holding a newborn child. "His name's Connor. He's three-months old." Wiezorek beamed with pride. "When the Chinese attacked, I had to make a choice. To make sure I did everything I could to ensure his safety. And I trust my team. I trust you, sir. I know you're doing the right thing."

The General sighed. "No, she doesn't know." He stared the young man in the eyes. "But you are right. I would do anything for her."

The two men stared at each other for a few seconds, then turned on their heels and marched toward the light of the doorway.

Kelly stood in the cold wind, a large, down-filled coat enveloping his muscular frame. The rabbit fur-lined hood was snug around his head and face. Tremaine stood to his left. Both men stared at the Trekol—a massive, snow-white vehicle with six huge, pillow-like tires. To Kelly, it looked much like a Land Rover crossed with a caravan. Despite its huge size and ability to easily seat eight people, it only had three doors. Two side doors for the driver and front passenger and a small, rectangular porthole-like door in the rear.

"What the frig is this?" Kelly asked.

The Shadow Man beamed with pride. "It's a Trekol."

"Well, *obviously*."

"You have no idea what a Trekol is, do you?"

"Not a goddamn clue, JT."

"I have no idea what she sees in you," Tremaine muttered under his breath. "It's a specialized vehicle for traversing terrain in arctic conditions. Its body is made of fiberglass and can withstand temperatures from minus seventy-five to one-hundred-forty degrees Fahrenheit. This monster weighs two and a half tons. Its special tires leave no rut and don't damage the topsoil. Hell, I could run over you, and you'd be fine."

"I'm sure you'd love that." Kelly raised his eyebrows and patted his freezing body in an attempt to keep warm.

"I'm sure I would."

"So what's the deal there, JT? You got the hots for Freya or what?" Kelly kept his eyes on the truck.

The Shadow Man took a step toward Kelly. "I was assigned to keep her safe by the General. And that's what I do. If that means kicking your dumb ass to do it, I will."

Kelly turned his head to face the Shadow Man. "You've been doing a grand job of that. If I recall, I saved her ass several times on this little trip."

Tremaine inhaled, puffing up to even greater proportions.

Kelly sighed. "Look, James."

The use of his Christian name took Tremaine by surprise. He held his breath.

"I'm a dick. We both know this. But she's been good to me. I won't hurt her. In fact, quite the opposite. If you haven't noticed, she's been looking a bit despondent. Probably on account of the fact the General hasn't been very, shall we say, fatherly."

"Fatherly?"

Kelly eyed him. Perhaps he didn't know of Freya's relationship to

Benjamin. "Well, supportive as a leader. He's a bit blinded by this situation. He's kinda single-minded. Anyway, I reckon if she's got both of us watching out for her, it's gotta be better, right?"

The sudden change in Kelly's attitude blind-sided the Shadow Man. He frowned, then exhaled, nodded once, and backed away.

"Right."

Having seen the display of testosterone from a distance, Freya had decided to interrupt the two men. "What are you boys clucking about?"

"Nothing," they replied in unison.

Freya raised an eyebrow.

"James and I were just having a chat. Man-to-man."

"You're calling him James now?"

"That's his name, right?" Kelly frowned at her as if he had always been so polite and friendly with the Shadow Man.

"That it is," she replied.

Kelly shrugged and slapped the Shadow Man on the shoulder. "See ya in there, JT." He sauntered toward the Trekol. "C'mon, Moby."

K'in came bounding out of nowhere, crashed past Tremaine's legs and caught up with Kelly before slowing and waddling by his side.

"That didn't last long," Freya said. "The politeness, I mean."

"He's not so bad." Tremaine nodded as if he were deep in some internal discussion. He then trudged after Kelly. "I'm driving," he called backward.

"What was that all about, young Freya?" Alejandro asked as he wandered up beside her.

"I have absolutely no idea."

CHAPTER TWENTY-SEVEN

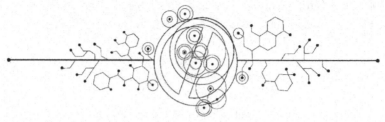

Location: In the Trekol, somewhere in Siberia

The massive vehicle raced over the topography without ever slowing—not for fallen trees, or huge boulders, or anything else that stood in the way. Its enormous pillow-tires rolled over everything, which Kelly thought was particularly fortunate, because he'd never seen terrain in a country change so much in one journey.

Through his tiny window, his gaze was met by broad and boundless views of steppes, luxuriant taiga thickets, strange desert expanses, jagged snowy peaks, and beautiful tundra. It was as if he were turning the pages of an atlas.

As they approached the Altai Mountains, a myriad of small rivers, fed by the nearby glaciers, became ever more present, cutting through the scenery. Spruce, cedar, pine, and fir accompanied the streams, dotting the landscape.

On their infrequent stops, Kelly took the opportunity to observe the variety of wildlife. Bear, lynx, Siberian stag, snow leopard, and hundreds of species of small birds. K'in would sit beside him and look wherever Kelly looked, mimicking his movements. Kelly had thought how much Izel, Carmen, and Chris would have loved this place.

One thing that didn't seem to change very much was the weather. Although there were spells of blue sky that broke through the gray, snow-laden clouds, the temperature never rose above fourteen degrees Fahrenheit, and an ice-cold wind penetrated through even the thickest layers of clothing. Kelly had taken to wearing his huge, arctic jacket even when in the truck. He was definitely not cut out for this weather. He wished to be back in Peru, Egypt, even Hell at this point seemed appealing.

It had been more than three days of bounding over the countryside without much conversation. Freya wasn't as vocal as usual. She only spoke when the General spoke to her. She seemed stiff and uncomfortable.

Similarly, Tremaine was quiet, but then again, he never really said much at all. It was likely he was concentrating on not crashing the vehicle. Kelly didn't fancy driving three days in a row, so he had decided the Shadow Man deserved at least a little respect for his diligence.

The young pilot, Ethan Wiezorek, looked downright scared. His eyes were permanently pried wide open like a rabbit trapped and hypnotized in car headlights. Perhaps more annoyingly, the infant soldier kept watching Kelly from the corner of one eye. What did the little shit want?

Then there was Executive Officer Teller. Now this guy was funny. At least, Kelly thought so even if no one else laughed. The guy had a thing for *Star Trek* and would make a Kirk reference at every given opportunity. A military nerd might seem odd, but it worked. At one point in the journey, he'd told Tremaine he would make a good Klingon as he was a grumpy bastard. Kelly had snorted out loud, and even Freya had stifled a chuckle. The Shadow Man, on the other hand, had just glared at the XO and then focused back on the road ahead.

Finally, Alejandro. The old goat was less than a foot away from Kelly yet didn't say a word to him. Instead, he was fixated on the Antikythera mechanism, constantly playing with it, toying with it, moving the dials on the outside, and watching the others move in synchrony. On the last day of the trip, he had some kind of epiphany and waved it in front of K'in—a vain attempt to engage the animal and see if some kind of deep-seated, pre-programmed knowledge of the device existed in him. It didn't. K'in had just stared at him with an almost human look of absolute confusion on his face. Kelly had laughed at the attempt. For a world-renowned linguist, the grumpy fucker had absolutely no idea how to communicate with the animal. Kelly had reached out and patted K'in on the head, an unspoken apology for the sheer dumbassery of his father-in-law.

Kelly blinked away his daydream and let his eyes focus on the world outside. He hadn't noticed, but a snow storm had completely enveloped the Trekol. The white-out forced Tremaine to slow the vehicle to a crawl, but he refused to stop completely.

"Can you even see where the fuck you're going?"

"Can you not backseat drive?" the Shadow Man snapped.

"Okay, okay. Jeez, keep your panties on. I'm just assuming we actually want to get where we're going. Which reminds me, do you have an address or something?"

225

"Professor D'Souza gave us the rough coordinates of the archaeological dig site. It should be coming into view soon," Freya replied.

"Oh good. I guess they aren't using tents up here—too friggin' cold—so billets or something?"

"How about a Kharkovchanka?" The XO nodded toward the windshield.

"A Karo-what-now?" Kelly raised an eyebrow.

"A Kharkovchanka," Freya repeated. "One of those." She pointed in front of them.

An enormous, bright-red mass emerged from behind the curtain of sleet and snow in the distance. It looked like an oversized shoebox with four small windows cut into the narrowest end and was seated on giant black caterpillar tracks. It was gargantuan.

"Kharkovchankas were exclusively manufactured in Kharkov for arctic expeditions. Each one has a five hundred and twenty horse-power V12 diesel engine. It's fourteen feet wide and more than thirty feet long." The XO spread his arms wide, mimicking the dimensions of the monster vehicle. "The cab usually seats six people. The rear is hermetically sealed and divided into multiple compartments. Back in the day, these compartments often comprised a bunk room, galley, head office, and comms room. But I guess that could easily be adapted for other work."

"What the fuck is it with you people? You're like goddamn walking encyclopedias." Kelly huffed and turned to K'in. "I suppose you're gonna suddenly open your trap and recite War and Peace word for word?"

K'in just gazed back at him.

"Russia still represents a significant threat to national security, Mr. Graham. Just because you do not hear it on the news, does not mean that it's gone away. Understanding your enemy is the first step in defeating him." The General hadn't even turned around to respond, instead speaking into the ether. Perhaps he was reminding his subordinates.

"Your contact is in there, Alejandro?" Kelly asked.

"I assume so." The old man was transfixed on the gargantuan Kharkovchanka. Its massive form loomed larger and larger in the windshield.

"So, professor, how do we make contact?" called the General over his shoulder.

"I guess, we knock." replied the old man. "She will be surprised to see us. I wasn't allowed to make a call ahead."

"Rightly so. Okay, professor, you, Tremaine, and I will go and introduce ourselves. Freya, you stay here with the creature, Mr. Graham, and the rest of the team. Do not come in after us. We'll come for you. Understood?"

"Yes, sir." Freya nodded.

The General, Tremaine, and Alejandro climbed out of the Trekol. The blistering, cold wind tore inside the vehicle, freezing the occupants. Tremaine struggled against the wind, forcing each door closed in turn.

"C'mon," The General bellowed over the howling wind and trudged off in the snow toward the Kharkovchanka.

Tremaine trod up behind Alejandro and placed a reassuring hand on the old man's shoulder, a signal he would be right behind to support the old man on his slog through the less than favorable climate.

The three men stomped awkwardly on. It took almost ten minutes to traverse the fifty feet or so, in the ever deepening snow, to the mobile archaeological base. Having reached what appeared to be the outer door, the General rapped on it with a gloved hand. The sound was muffled and barely audible to the General in the howling wind, let alone to anyone inside. He reached inside his coat and pulled out his Beretta. Then, using the barrel, hammered on the door. This time, the sound was dull and metallic but at least loud. He waited for ten seconds, but nothing happened. He tried again and again, nothing. Turning to Alejandro, he shrugged. As he raised his gun for a third attempt, he was halted by a high-pitched screech as the door's locking mechanism was released. It swung open.

A tall bearded man stared out of the doorway. He glanced at each of the three men and then shouted something over his shoulder. A woman appeared. Her strawberry-blonde hair blew about her face in the crosswinds. She squinted to see her visitors through the bluster of snow. Shaking her head, she frantically waved at the men to come inside.

The men did not need to be asked twice. They ascended a short ladder and climbed in. The bearded man closed the door behind them. It clanged shut, signaling their safety—at least for now.

Minya studied the three men, each with his hood pulled up around his head and face. She said something in Russian. Her almond eyes flared and her high cheekbones flushed red. The old man quickly slipped back his fur-lined hood and pried the goggles from his face. The other men followed his lead.

Minya stared for a few seconds, unsure she was really seeing the man in front of her. "Alejandro?" Her accent was definitely Russian but not stereotypical, not Muscovite. It was slow as if the words and syllables were rolling from her lips, rather than being spat.

"Minya, I apologize for my unannounced arrival, but I wouldn't come if it weren't urgent."

She threw her arms wide, a smile breaking across her face, and hugged the old man, kissing him several times on the cheeks. "Alejandro, *kak ty la?*"

"What did she say?" the General asked.

"She asked how he is," Tremaine replied.

"Minya, English please, my colleagues are American."

"*Da!* Of course! Alejandro, why are you here? How did you get here? I thought you were in Egypt."

"We brought him here. I am General Benjamin Lloyd. This is my associate, Tremaine. Is it just you and him?" Benjamin pointed unceremoniously at the large, hairy man standing in the corner of the compartment.

"*Da, da.* Just us. Winter months. All others have gone home." As good as her English was, the epiglottal H sound in her pronunciation was unmistakable.

"Good. We have more colleagues in the vehicle outside. I would appreciate it if we could bring them in here before they freeze to death. Then, I will explain why we are here."

Minya glanced at Alejandro for reassurance. "More?"

He nodded at her.

She nodded back. "*Da. Ilari, idt I sobriat ljudej.*"

Before the General could ask, Tremaine was already translating. "He's called Ilari. She just told him to get the others."

"Wait," the General commanded. "Tremaine, you go with him. Wrap our cargo in the thermal sheets and bring it here."

Tremaine lowered his head in obedience and marched after the Russian. The two men wrapped themselves up in their arctic gear—Ilari in bright red in order to be found and rescued if he were lost and Tremaine in crystal white, so he could be hidden at all costs. The rear door was flung open, and the two men disappeared into the blizzard. The portal clanged shut behind them.

"Alejandro, my old friend, please explain what is going on." She folded her arms across her chest and raised her perfectly shaped eyebrows expectantly.

"Professor D'Souza is merely a victim of circumstance in this instance," the General said. "But if you allow me, I will explain why we are here and with what we need your help. Professor, the device please?"

The old man shuffled off the backpack and dropped to his knees. He rummaged around inside and pulled out the Antikythera mechanism.

"This is why we are here," the General said. "And why we need your help."

The inside of the Trekol's windows had fogged up with warm breath. Kelly sat huddled in the back, muttering and patting his arms and body. The cold did not agree with him.

"What's wrong with you? Surely, a big macho man like you doesn't mind a little cold?" Freya asked.

"It's fucking cold, that's what's wrong. You think it's a coincidence I spend my time in equatorial climates? Warm is good. This is shit." He shook his head and huffed out a cloud of moist breath.

"Well, you know …" the XO began.

"If you quote Kirk, I swear to God I'm gonna rip off my frostbitten arm and beat you to death with it."

"Well, actually it was going to be Spock, but I imagine a similar response." He laughed.

Freya and Wiezorek glanced at each other and stifled a smirk.

A rap on the outer hull broke the frosty atmosphere. The XO stepped over K'in and opened the rear door. Two large figures stood there, one in red, the other in white, both shivering and being pummeled by every form of frozen water.

Tremaine pulled down the zip of his hood to reveal his mouth. "We gotta move inside. Temperature is gonna drop."

"Affirmative." Freya pulled the goggles onto her face and the hood over her head. "Let's move. Tremaine, you grab K'in. You'll be fastest with him in this snow. Everyone else, follow my lead." She climbed through the group and dropped out of the rear door into the snow, a crisp and satisfying crunch under her feet.

The Shadow Man scooped up the foil-covered K'in and sprinted off in the direction of the giant mobile base. The Russian in red followed suit.

Kelly laughed. "Jesus, he can really move when he wants to."

"Don't just stand there," yelled Freya over the howl of the wind. "Follow him."

The others didn't need to be asked twice. Kelly and Wiezorek ran off into the blizzard, their sight fixed on the red coat in front of them.

The XO exited last and closed the Trekol door behind him. "Ready?" he yelled.

"Ready," Freya shouted back.

"Wait, wait, wait, you're serious? This is incredible. Do you know how long I have been waiting to see this?"

"You knew it existed?" Alejandro furrowed his brow.

"*Da!* Of course. The Antikythera mechanism is old, but this one looks older. The theory was Archimedes invented the device, but it was too advanced. We never found any evidence of predecessors or previous attempts. It never made sense he could create something so accurate on first attempt. There had to be older versions."

"Can you read it?" the General asked.

"Well, these symbols look familiar, but I would need to study this more. Where did you find it?"

"In India, amongst some old ruins, less than sixty-five feet underwater."

"That doesn't make sense. Most of these markings are Mayan." She paused. "But these, these are not, they look like proto-cuneiform symbols from Sumeria."

"From the Kish tablet? I'm sure I would've seen that." Alejandro shook his head.

"The Kish tablet? What is that?" the General asked.

"The Kish tablet is believed to be very first example of writing, albeit very crude writing," Minya began. "The tablet records ridding of insects from a piece of land. The last line on tablet reads, 'he made it bright,' believed to refer to a ceremonial purification of a field."

Alejandro nodded. "Of course, every linguist knows this."

"Yes, but these things are all interpretation, and often wrong. Look here." She ran her finger along the pictograms around the largest dial. "At this point, here, the symbols are almost identical to the Kish tablet. But these things are always about context. When reading here, it does not say, 'he made it bright,' it says, 'and he brought light.' But I do not understand why."

Alejandro uttered a single word to the General. "K'in."

The General nodded in agreement, his lips pursed in thought.

"K'in? What is K'in?"

As if on cue, the doors to the Kharkovchanka opened with a screech. The frozen travelers clambered inside as quickly as they could. A whirlwind of snow and ice blasted in with them, forcing Minya, the General, and the old man to cover their eyes.

Ilari slammed the door shut, killing the miniature storm dead. The ice crystals dropped to the floor, and the cutting wind failed. Minya lowered her arms back to her sides and studied her new guests.

In one corner, there was a young woman, her jet black hair slicked to her face with frozen water. Next to her were three new men, two clearly military from their stance—tall and straight, even when drenched. The last one was a civilian shivering uncontrollably. Tremaine stood at the front of the group holding a limp form wrapped in a thermal foil.

"You have someone injured? We need to make him warm." She stepped forward to help. Tremaine stepped back, still clutching his package.

"It's alright, Tremaine. Show her."

The Shadow Man took two steps forward and cautiously dropped to the floor. He placed the foil-covered body in front of him and unwrapped it, revealing a frigid, pale animal.

"This, Ms. Yermalova, is K'in." The General folded his arms. Minya stared for a few seconds before slowly dropping to her haunches. Her eyes darted as she inspected the animal. Cautiously, she reached one hand out to touch it.

K'in skulked close to the floor and hid behind the shivering legs of the frozen Kelly.

"Don't feel bad. It seems the creature has a thing for Kelly, here. None of us can figure out why." Tremaine shook his head.

"What is it?" Minya's gaze was fixated on the gap between Kelly's legs.

"Well, I could try to explain, Minya, but I think the General and his colleagues would be best placed. I'm so sorry I brought them here, but you were the only person I could think of who may have a clue about the device, and ..." the old man rambled quickly.

"Alejandro, it's okay." She tried to soothe him. "Your friends are cold. We should make them more comfortable inside. Then, they can tell me all about the problem." She stood and waved for them to follow her into the next compartment.

CHAPTER TWENTY-EIGHT

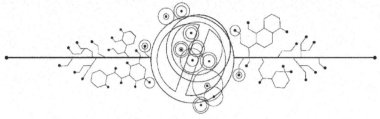

Location: Inside the Kharkovchanka, Altai Mountains, Siberia

The group sat around the table in Minya's small and claustrophobic meeting room. The chairs could only pull away from the table enough for each person to squeeze in. There were not enough chairs for everyone. Kelly had offered to sit in the corner with K'in as he'd wanted to keep an eye on him.

For the next thirty minutes, the General and Freya recounted the last sixty-odd years of history just as it had been told to Kelly, Chris and Victoria—almost word for word like the pair had memorized a rehearsed speech. Or perhaps they had heard Professor Alexander spout it so often it was ingrained into their minds.

The rest of the group hugged their plastic mugs of hot black tea and cautiously munched on various pickled vegetables and kholodets, the unidentified meat in jelly. Minya had apologized, saying they only had food that would last for a long time in the depths of Siberia. Kelly laughed as Freya turned her nose up at the food and sipped on her tea.

Minya nodded along while glancing at K'in and Kelly in the corner every so often. She also studied the General and Freya, taking in each word they spoke, digesting everything, analyzing the situation.

"Which brings us to now. We need to find a new orb. Kelly and Freya thought that it may have been in India, but they only found that device. We were hoping you may be able to help. Perhaps you could lead us to an orb." The General's eyes were a little wider than normal—a look of hope on his face. Perhaps she could help.

"Well," she began. "I have good news, and I have bad news."

Kelly groaned. "Of course"

Alejandro threw him a scathing look before returning to face Minya. "Please, start with the good news."

Minya cleared her throat. "Earlier, when you showed me device and I

233

read inscriptions, I could do this, because it was not first time I'd seen them."

"You've seen them before?" Alejandro asked. "Where?"

"On another object. Something we found here in the Altai mountains." She nodded to Ilari, who disappeared out of the room. He returned carrying a perfectly cube-shaped metal box, slightly bigger than the Antikythera device. It was tarnished and dented but clearly heavy as Ilari struggled to set it down on the table.

The group stared at it. Even Kelly craned his neck to see.

"We found this, twelve miles away, buried in ice. We don't have technology here to scan the interior, but I am sure it is hollow."

"Do you think there's something inside it?" Alejandro stood, palms on the table, as he inspected the box.

"The book of Thoth."

"Fuckin' knew it." Kelly hadn't meant to voice his inner thought, but it was loud enough to make the whole team glance at him. He shrugged.

"Why do you say that, Minya?" the old man asked.

"Look here." She heaved the box around. On one side were several rows of symbols. The top row seemed separate from the other four or five below it. Each row was also completely different from each of the others. "Here, the top row, it looks like the symbols on your device, no? 'He brought light.'"

Alejandro nodded. "Yes, and here, we have Mayan, and here, Egyptian." He pulled his glasses to the tip of his nose and then translated, reading as he went. "The god's ... knowledge ... is not ... meant ... for ... humans to know."

"*Da, da.* Exactly."

Alejandro sat down, stunned. His face blank as his mind kicked into overdrive.

"Why is that important?" the XO asked.

The old man snapped back to reality and swallowed. "The fictional Book of Thoth appears in an ancient Egyptian story from the Ptolemaic period. The book, written by Thoth, is said to contain two spells. One allows the reader to understand the speech of animals." He glanced at K'in. "The other allows the reader to perceive the gods themselves. The Egyptians believed such knowledge was not meant for us. There are many stories of humans who try to steal the book of Thoth and are punished for doing so."

"Can we open it?" Freya asked.

"Don't open it." Kelly sighed. "Don't you guys watch movies? Every

234

time some dumbass opens a mysterious box something bad happens."

"This isn't the movies, Kelly." Freya shook her head in exasperation.

Kelly shrugged. "Hey, don't say I didn't warn you."

"Minya, have you been able to open it?" Alejandro clasped his hands together in anticipation of the answer.

"Not yet, but," she began, "if I may?" Minya reached for the Antikythera device.

The General nodded in approval, and Alejandro handed it to her.

She placed the device into a rectangular depression at the top of the box. A light click sounded from the union of the two objects. She then moved the largest dial on the front of the smaller mechanism.

K'in fidgeted, swaying from side to side and making a low-frequency warble.

Kelly frowned at the creature. "Hey, guys?"

His bid for attention went unheard. Minya moved the dial slowly and carefully. "Here, I align the symbols to make them show the coming of the gods." As she spoke the final word, the larger box clanked open. One of the side walls had been hinged and now sat slightly ajar.

K'in was becoming more agitated, nudging Kelly with his nose and blinking furiously.

"Hey, guys. Moby's not happy over here."

They weren't listening.

Minya carefully pulled back the box door and peered inside. A familiar blue-green glow emanated from inside. An orb, much larger and more complex than the one at Paradise Ranch, showed a vastly intricate network of vessels through its transparent skin—a neural network.

K'in reared onto his hind legs, raised his head in the air, and let out a strange gargling sound. Every member of the group jumped in their seats and turned to face the animal.

"What the hell is it doing?" the General demanded.

"I don't fucking know, but I've been trying to tell you for the last five minutes he ain't happy."

"Keep it still—we need to make it bond with the orb," the General said.

"It? He's not an *it*, K'in is a he. Just back the fuck off, all right. You ever been attached to one of those things? Well, I have, and it's no fun. He's scared, so just fuck off!" Kelly shielded K'in with his legs.

Wiezorek leapt to his feet and pulled a P229 from its holster in the back of his pants. He pointed the gun at Kelly's head. "Do as the General says, Mr. Graham."

"Oh, put the peashooter down, John Boy. Does your mommy know you have a gun?"

"Wiezorek, put it down!" Freya stood between the young officer and Kelly.

Tremaine picked up the conjoined devices in his arms and slowly backed away toward the door.

"Wiezorek," Freya shouted, before calming her voice. "Ethan, put the gun down." She lowered her hands, hoping he would mirror her movement.

He didn't. Instead, he took a step forward and jerked his gun. "Do as the General says."

With lightning speed, Freya reached into the back of her combat pants, released one of the two Berettas, and pointed it at the young pilot.

Simultaneously, the XO drew his own weapon and pointed it at Freya. "Now, Ms. Nilsson, you might wanna calm down. This could get messy. Why don't we all just relax?"

"Freya." The General took a step forward and then hesitated, trying to quiet his voice. "Freya, put the gun down."

"Why? So you can shoot Kelly? I don't think so."

"Freya, it's me. Trust me," he pleaded.

"How can I? I don't know who you are anymore." A lump formed in her throat, but she swallowed it away and steeled her resolve.

Kelly watched her nervously. He eyed the second Beretta strapped to her belt.

"Stop this," Minya yelled. "You have bigger problems."

The General glared at her. "What the hell are you talking about?"

"I told you. There was good news and bad news. Bad news is I am funded by the Chinese government. I radioed them two days ago that I found something. They're coming."

An explosion tore through the back of the room. Metal and plastic warped and ruptured as the door ripped from its hinges and slammed into Tremaine. His skull was crushed by the force, his body was thrown to the ground like a rag doll. The devices he'd been holding smashed into the floor, shattering into their various components; cogs, wheels, and levers flew everywhere. The orb spilled out from inside the box and plopped onto the floor. Its translucent skin split open, releasing the fluorescent liquid.

Several men in white combat gear rushed into the smoke-filled room, yelling and screaming in some Chinese dialect. Their gas-operated, Type 79 automatic machine guns were the only things visible in the smog.

Kelly pulled the Beretta from the back of Freya's pants and pointed it directly out in front of him.

"Alejandro, Minya, Ilari. Get behind me." Freya ordered.

A single shot echoed out from the smoke. Ilari yelped and then fell silent. His body slumped to the floor, next to Tremaine. Kelly grabbed Alejandro by the scruff of his shirt and yanked him behind the group near to K'in, who was crouched down. Minya had dived to the floor and was crawling to the same spot.

Kelly tried to see through the debris and soot, with no success. He could only feel the fear emanating from K'in.

A Mexican stand-off. The Chinese soldiers, the General, the XO, and Kelly's group all pointed their weapons at each other. The problem was that Kelly was severely out-gunned. He had only one pistol, which he held nervously, his arms shaking. Conversely, the three Chinese soldiers in front of him were holding machine guns, and the General, XO, and Wiezorek to his left were brandishing two side arms each.

Freya was standing to Kelly's right, just a pace back, still clinging to her weapon. She was using her legs as a human shield to protect K'in, Alejandro, and Minya, who were crouched low to the floor, their eyes flicking from person to person. Tremaine and Ilari's broken bodies lay in the middle of the death circle.

The atmosphere was thick with adrenaline. Kelly watched the tiny clouds of warm breath from each person puff rapidly into the freezing air. His heart beat fiercely in his chest, and he guessed everyone else's did the same. He closed his eyes for what seemed like an eternity. K'in was scared, so very scared. Kelly had to admit, he was terrified, too. How the hell were they going to get through this? One twitch or one murmur and all hell would break loose. It couldn't end this way. He wouldn't let it. He couldn't lose someone else—not again. He had to save Freya—at all costs. The images of Carmen and Izel filled his mind. Each image stabbed him like a knife in his heart.

Perhaps it was his inner monologue distracting him, or maybe she was too quick, but Kelly had failed to notice Freya had lunged forward. Too late, from the corner of his eye, he watched the scene in slow motion. Her arms outstretched, Freya launched herself at the Chinese men. In millisecond-response time, the soldiers opened fire on her. Automatically and without thought, Kelly retaliated. The bullets seemed to move so slowly that he could perceive their trajectory and velocity. He watched several of them spark and ricochet off the internal metal walls. To his left, the General, Wiezorek, and XO had dropped to their knees, presumably to avoid the mid-level spray of ammunition and counter attack with kneecap-destroying shots.

Then, the scene suddenly jerked forward and joined the realms of normal space and time. Smoke and debris filled the room, obscuring all sense of orientation. The awful sound of lead tearing through human flesh was accompanied by pained gargling that echoed all around. A shrill scream ended the onslaught. Kelly, still standing in the same position as he had for the entire gunfight, gazed around. In the haze, he could make out the moving shapes of the General and XO—they were still alive. But Wiezorek was down—sprawled lifeless on the cold floor. Fuck. The stupid little shit was too young to die.

Kelly scanned to his right. The broken bodies of the Chinese soldiers were strewn about the floor. All were dead. But where was Freya? He couldn't see her. He called out, but there was no reply. He dropped to the floor and scrambled about on his hands and knees in the gray, gun-derived mist. Frantically, he felt around until his hand fell on a slender leg. "Freya!"

"I'm here." She coughed.

He continued to feel his way about her body until he encountered something warm and liquid trickling down her torso. His heart stalled, and his stomach knotted. No, not again—this couldn't be happening. Angrily, he waved his arms and swept away the smoke so he could see. As it cleared, his tear-filled eyes found a river of blood pouring across Freya's combat pant-covered legs. No. Not her. Why not him? How had he survived again? It wasn't right. But as he studied her, the whole scene came into focus. Following the crimson stream to its origin led him to K'in, lying on top of her, panting weakly. Blood flowed from several open wounds gouged into the animal's side. For a fraction of a second, Kelly was relieved that Freya was unscathed. But it was instantly snatched away as his mind comprehended the cost of her survival. "What happened?"

Freya lifted her head and, under K'in's weight, forced herself onto her elbows. "I don't know. I tried to make a run for one of the Chinese soldiers, but K'in leapt and pinned me to the floor. He covered me with his body. He saved me." Her voice was thick with shame and guilt.

Slowly, Kelly hoisted K'in's body and pulled him off Freya, freeing her. He rolled the creature backward so he lay face up in his arms. Kelly rocked K'in back and forth like a child. "I'm sorry, Moby. I'm sorry." Kelly's voice was soft, virtually imperceptible.

The room was silent. Kelly sensed the other people, those that survived, gather around him—the General, XO, Minya, Alejandro, and Freya. He hugged the broken animal close and gazed around. Death was everywhere—Tremaine, Wiezorek, Ilari, and the Chinese soldiers. A hand rested on his shoulder. It was Alejandro. Kelly raised his head to see the old man, whose face was no longer scathing or disappointed, but sad and empathetic. He knew Alejandro could feel him through K'in. Looking into his father-in-law's eyes, Kelly's strength finally waned. He broke down. He cried for K'in, for Izel, for Carmen, for Chris, for Victoria, for every dead person in that room, and for all he had held inside for so long.

K'in lay gasping like an exposed fish in Kelly's arms. The creature opened and closed his mouth as if he wanted to speak—to say something to Kelly. His eyes were no longer blue and bright but were once again black, dull, and empty. He stared at Kelly. Kelly stared back, and in that moment, he knew why K'in had done it—why he'd saved Freya. As K'in exhaled for the last time, Kelly's the hope for the world and his own salvation slipped away into darkness.

In the murk of his own sorrow, Kelly could hear a new commotion erupt around him as a group of soldiers spilled into the room. The U.S. search team had found them—not that it mattered anymore. Kelly ignored their screaming and bawling of orders to drop all weapons and kneel on the floor. He forced their voices from his head so they sounded muffled and distant and clung to K'in's lifeless body, holding it as close as he could. It was all over now. It was done.

CHAPTER TWENTY-NINE

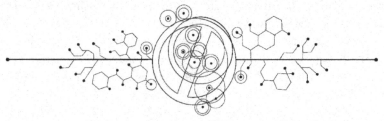

Location: A small Island, somewhere off the coast of South America

The sun was bright on his face, warming and soothing. In contrast, the cooler sea water lapped about Kelly's ears as he floated outstretched. He dropped back into the crystal-clear water and dove several feet. Thousands of tropical fish parted like a submarine curtain, granting him the ability to pass through the cacophony of color and life.

Reaching the slope of the beach, he climbed out of the wash and pushed his wet feet into the hot sand. It felt wonderful as the grains wedged themselves between his toes. The spit of land was deserted and only green, tropical trees dotted the vast expanse of white. He picked up his towel and a large pair of yellow fins he'd left next to a nearby rock and trudged down the coastline toward his shack.

The white painted wood dwelling had a thatched roof. It stood on stilts three feet off the ground. *Impressive.* He'd built it himself. He climbed the stairs and opened the front door. The interior consisted of two rooms: one to sleep in and the other to sit in. There was no television, no radio, and no link to the outside world at all. Near the yellowed mattress, laid haphazardly on the floor, were a fishing rod and spear.

Kelly flopped his wet body onto the bed, allowing the seawater from his shorts to soak into the dry sheets. He lay there for a few moments, his long, chestnut-brown hair stuck to his forehead and a graying beard starting to show on his face. He thought of all that had happened in the weeks leading up to and after their capture by the U.S. search team.

Most of California and parts of the surrounding states had been decimated by the virus. Some doctor, a Dr. Cooper, working for the CDC and a Colonel in the U.S. military had been turned into national heroes. Apparently, the Colonel had volunteered to be infected with the virus and receive the experimental treatment. The media had been fed some bullshit story that it had been a rogue mutation of Ebola that had come in on a flight from Africa. There was no mention of the Chinese whatsoever, or the attacks in the South China Sea, or at Paradise Ranch—it was as if they had never happened. Kelly wasn't sure how the Americans had been able to avoid World War III with the Chinese but figured it was none of his business. He didn't want to know. Given all the secrecy he had encountered, he didn't rule out anything, not even collaboration between the two countries.

What really bothered him was every trace of K'in had also been erased. The released government files were reduced to a childish prank dreamed up by two tech guys called Jeremy and David, *Google* nerds. The panic had subsided, and the religious groups had taken no more than a few weeks to calm down. It seemed the human community was in no way ready to face the truth. It was easier to swallow the lies and pretend they were and always would be the apex life form on Earth. But Kelly would always know.

With K'in's death, Kelly had also lost a part of himself. It wasn't easy to explain to anyone, but he was empty. Sure, the sickness that resulted from being away from K'in had subsided. But that wasn't it. It was more like he had been shown paradise for a brief moment, and then it had been ripped away. After that, nothing felt the same. Food didn't have the same taste. Drink never quenched his thirst. He was empty.

Kelly sighed as thoughts of his hollow soul turned to Freya. She had asked him, with wide and expectant eyes, to stay a while in Washington. She was to be removed from the field to do more executive things. This new position had been a gift—a last act of respect by the U.S. Government for the General before he had been taken to prison for his part in the whole debacle. Kelly had refused the invitation. It wasn't because he didn't want to stay. He did. It was just, in his heart, he knew he still wasn't ready. Guilt over Izel remained, and as much as he wished he could let go, it wasn't fair to Freya to live in the memory of his dead wife. Freya had said she understood, but Kelly could read in her face she was disappointed. Better to hurt her a little now than a lot later.

Anyway, he wanted to be as far away from civilization as possible. He hadn't been fond of it in the first place, but now, he disliked it more than ever. He'd figured something should come from K'in's death. So he'd moved to a remote part of Peru, somewhere he could do some good—help the villagers build schools, or fish, or mine, or whatever they needed. Kelly could never replace K'in, but he could at least do the right thing—do something that would make his own life have meaning again, real meaning. He had imagined he would not be allowed to live without supervision or, at least, would need to report to someone somewhere at regular intervals. But it seemed the General, in an altruistic moment, had vouched for everyone on the mission—Kelly was free to go.

Kelly and Alejandro had been allowed to leave and continue with their lives, never speaking of what they knew. The fact that both men preferred to live in third-world countries and away from any laptop or mobile device probably factored heavily in the decision. As for the rest of the General's ragtag gang. With K'in dead, they had all been reassigned. Since the General had taken full responsibility, it had been decided they were merely following orders. The U.S. Government sure did like its scapegoats.

Like most evenings, this inner monologue ended as it had begun in the morning: with Izel, Carmen, and Chris. He wasn't a religious man, yet it helped him cope to imagine them all together in a better place—wherever that place may be. After everything that had happened, it was impossible to refute anything—even the possibility of an afterlife. He only hoped if one did exist, his decision to do good for others and himself would bode well. Still, at least they were at peace even if he never would be.

Kelly reached behind his head and pulled a small, silver tin from under a large, crumpled pillow. He laid the tin on his chest and opened it. The cold metal tightened his skin. Rummaging within, he pulled out a wrinkled envelope. It was already open, ripped at one edge. Kelly pulled the single piece of white paper from inside. On its surface was a barely legible scrawl in black ink.

I forgive you.
A.

Location: Dulce Base, New Mexico, USA

The black sedan pulled up to the barn. A light wind whipped up the dry, red dirt into eddies that disappeared into the powder-blue sky. Both passenger side doors, front and rear, were flung open. Two large men, dressed in similar black suits with white shirts and black ties, stepped out. Each wore a small earpiece attached to a spiraled wire that disappeared down the back of their shirt collars. The rearmost man walked around to the other side of the car and opened the remaining passenger door. A pair of willowy legs slid out. Lucy stood and straightened her pencil skirt. She nodded to the secret service agents. They sidled up close to her and marched alongside toward the rickety-looking structure.

A stout-framed man, dressed in a loose, button-down shirt, was already waiting at the large double doors. He walked briskly to meet her. "Good afternoon, Madam Secretary." He seemed quiet and friendly enough with an easy disposition. Yet he spoke and moved with deliberation. "I know why you are here, but—"

"I want to see them, Dr. Parnham," she replied.

"Yes, I understand. But—"

"You can either show me now, or I will have you arrested, and I will find someone else to show me. As you are the director of science here, I would rather you did it."

"Yes, ma'am." He sighed and turned on his heel. "Please follow me."

The group entered the barn. Inside, it looked very much like any other. Bales of hay, an unused tractor, picks, shovels, and other assorted equipment long past having any practical function were strewn about. It even smelled authentic—damp, old, moldy. But she knew it was just a front for Dulce Base.

Dr. Parnham pulled a small, plastic remote control from his pocket and held it out in front of him. He pressed the only button on its surface. The groaning and familiar whine of machinery seeped from beneath the old floorboards. A square section of the floor depressed a few inches and then slipped apart. A small, metallic elevator rose from within the dark hole, stopping when it had reached its maximum elevation.

"Your colleagues will need to wait here." The doctor glanced over his shoulder at the secret service agents. "Don't worry, gentlemen, she will be perfectly safe."

Their deadpan faces told him they were not convinced.

"I'll be fine, wait here. Call in that I am going into the base alone."

The men gave a single nod. One pulled a cell phone from his suit pocket and walked away, dialing.

Lucy and the doctor stepped inside the cramped elevator. He pressed his index finger on a small plate on the inside to confirm his identity. It worked. The doors glided shut, and the elevator descended.

There was an awkward silence. Neither one wanted to speak. She was nervous to be there, and he was uncomfortable with her presence.

As they descended, Lucy thought about the cover-up. It was so infuriating. Some governmental department even more covert than the CIA had intervened and cleaned up everything. The President had told her the situation needed to be dealt with, but for now, they had to calm the public and ensure peace with the Chinese. He'd said there would be an enquiry into everything, and he'd promised he'd get to the bottom of it all personally. That had been three months ago. Nothing had happened. Perhaps more important things had taken precedence since the clone was dead and the team that had conducted the experiments at Paradise Ranch was disbanded.

For Lucy, it wasn't enough. The Colonel had said he had supporters in New Mexico at Dulce Base. In a last visit with General Lloyd before he was dragged off to jail, she'd asked him about Dulce Base. He had paused, staring at her, and then whispered an address in her ear. That was all she needed.

Lucy turned back to the doctor at her side. "So, is it true?"

He peered down his nose at her. "Is what true, Madam Secretary?"

"The rumors about Dulce Base."

"And what rumors would those be?"

She took a breath. She wasn't one for gossip or urban myth, but her line of questioning was, at least in part, driven by the need to fill the silence. Deep inside, she guessed she also had a morbid curiosity. "The rumors that this place has seven levels, each worse than the last. The first few levels are benign. But on level four, you have human research in paranormal areas. On level five, there are supposed to be captured aliens. And level six, which I heard is called, 'Nightmare Hall,' holds the genetic labs with animals and humans that have been *altered*. I dread to think what's on level seven." Lucy trailed off. She half expected a guffaw, a scoff, or even a smirk, but his face was unmoving.

"Much of what you've heard is of course garbage—scaremongering by conspiracy theory nuts. But all rumors have their roots in some fact. We do have multiple levels. And level seven houses our advanced genetic labs, which is where we're going now."

The elevator slid to a halt. The doors parted and Dr. Parnham exited. Lucy followed. They marched down a narrow corridor, lit by widely spaced spotlights in the rock-hewn walls, and disappeared into a small room.

As the Secretary entered, her line of sight was immediately drawn to four glass tubes standing in the middle of the room. Each was at least three feet wide, more than six feet tall, and filled with rose-colored liquid. Each contained a strange, balled-up form.

Lucy stepped close to the tubes and peered inside one at a time. Each creature was the same yet different. One was small, about the size of a cat. Its skin was grayish and rudimentary stalks protruded from the back of its head. The gills were pale. Another animal was slightly bigger than, perhaps as large as a toddler. Its limbs were fully formed, but its strange pear-shaped head had no stalks at all or eyes for that matter. The last two creatures were both as large as fully grown men with long head stalks and full, blood-red gills. Vestigial eyes could be made out, but the animals were clearly blind. All of them hung lifelessly in their glass coffins.

She examined the small plates at the top of each tube—*I, II, III, IV.* Lucy turned to the doctor. "They're all dead."

"One to four are dead, yes, but not six."

"Six?"

"Yes, six. You discussed seeing them all with the Colonel, correct?"

She hesitated for a split second, knowing she had to lie. "Of course."

"So," he continued. "Six is at the back in the larger tank. Six is different from the K'in clone. For clone six, we spliced in human DNA. The original idea was to try and speed up the process of communication. Military application was also considered. It was completely separate to the K'in program. General Lloyd and his team thought it had died—this was the Colonel's pet project."

The Secretary narrowed her eyes and studied him. He didn't seem menacing or evil, just simply a man who followed orders. She turned and peered around the glass tubes. There at the end of the room was another larger tank. She stepped cautiously around the tubes and toward the end of the room until she was a few feet from the tank. "It's in here?"

"Yes, but don't get too close. Six is different. It has *behavioral* problems." He moved two paces forward but stopped. "It's why the military application program was put on hold. Our staff here even gave it a name—Wak. It's Mayan for six. Given it has issues, Wak seemed appropriate."

She gave him a quizzical glance. "Behavioral problems? Issues?"

The aquarium glass rattled as the massive animal slapped its entire weight on the inside of the transparent prison wall. The creature could only be described as muscular—as if it had received anabolic steroids. The sinews were visible under its translucent, white skin. A huge plume of black gills adorned the six long stalks on its angular, trapezoidal head. Large, fully formed, deep red eyes stared intensely at her—studying her. As it floated there, it repeatedly hit its massive head on the glass. Lightly at first, but as the seconds passed, the hammering became harder and faster as if it were a severely unwell psychiatric patient.

"Behavioral problems," the doctor repeated.

A cold chill passed through Lucy's body as the blood drained from her limbs. As she turned her head away from the strange animal to steady her nerves, something else caught her eye. Another tank in the very corner of the room. Inside hung another form. She narrowed her eyes to focus, but it was still too far away.

Slowly the Secretary walked toward the tank. As she drew closer, the form inside became clearer. It was a young woman, hanging naked and motionless in the water. A black oxygen mask covered her mouth and nose, the corrugated hose rising up and out of the water above her head. Long, mousey hair swirled in slow motion in the water around the young woman's face. The left side of her body was badly burned; charred skin twisted and gnarled along the length of her torso and down her leg. Her left arm, however, was a strange, milky white color. Her fingers appeared almost fetal.

"Who is this? What happened to her?"

The doctor picked up a chart and flicked through the pages as he spoke. "She was caught in an explosion a few weeks ago. She was found nearly dead in the wreckage of a large, semi-articulated truck just outside Las Vegas. She had third-degree burns on one side of her body and had lost her left arm from below the elbow."

"What is she doing here? Why isn't she in a normal hospital?"

"The wreckage was caused by a Chinese attack helicopter. She was picked up by our military."

"She's connected with the Chinese attack?"

"We believe she was part of General Lloyd's original team. However, we have been unable to identify her. Her limbs were so badly burned we couldn't identify from fingerprints, and half her face was mangled. All we found was part of a driver's license in her pocket. She's not a U.S. citizen, that's for sure. All we know is her name is Victoria."

"And you used your techniques here to grow her a new limb?" Lucy studied the woman's grotesque arm.

"Yes. We applied our learnings from the cloned creatures. It was a successful human-creature hybrid and the best place to start."

"She's growing a creature's arm?"

246

"Kind of. We aren't sure how this will turn out."

"You aren't sure?" Lucy repeated.

"There are effects. Side effects."

"Side effects?"

The thumping on the inside of Wak's tank became louder—loud enough to draw the Secretary's attention. The animal had increased the ferocity of its head-banging onslaught. A long, jagged hairline crack squealed its way through the glass.

A thud in the woman's tank pulled Lucy's gaze back to the aquarium in front of her. The woman inside was convulsing, her limbs flailing and knocking into the tank wall.

"What's wrong with her?"

"Like I said—side effects. We used tissue from Wak to grow her new limb, but it seems she's connected to it now." His voice trailed off.

The woman's juddering ceased, leaving her once again to hang seemingly lifeless in the water. Lucy moved closer and peered inside, trying to see under the swathe of hair that covered Victoria's face. Closer still. The hair glided to the side, revealing Victoria's now open eyes. They were crimson—no iris, no sclera, no visible pupil, just crimson—and boring a cold stare deep into the Secretary.

"This can't be good," Lucy said under her breath.

"No, Madam Secretary. It certainly is not."

CHAPTER THIRTY

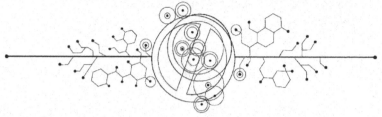

Location: Dulce Base, New Mexico, USA — One Year Later

The drone of the internal alarm was deafening. On. Off. On. Off. It wailed like an injured child into the thick smog that quickly filled the facility. Overhead lights flickered and fizzed while electrical cables torn from their fixtures sparked and crackled.

Freya hoisted her head from the cold floor, her skull still ringing. Her eyes stung from the acrid smoke, and her breathing was labored. She couldn't stay where she was. Her attacker was still in the room with her—somewhere.

With a grunt, Freya shoved herself upward and supported her weight on her good ankle—the other was badly twisted, maybe even broken. Blindly, she limped forward, her arms outstretched to feel for a wall. She'd lost her Beretta and didn't have time to search for it. Her knees clanged into the metal frame of the bed. *Shit. That hurt.*

She tried to focus on the task at hand rather than on her burning ankle and now throbbing knee. Behind her, the smoke was a lighter gray, and the light from the tank illuminated the thick atmosphere. That meant she was dead center in the room. If she circumnavigated the bed, the door would be ten feet in front. Using one hand to guide her around the cot and the other to feel out in front, Freya hobbled on.

A scuffle in the corner.

Freya froze. Her heart beat fiercely in her chest. Freya squinted, hoping to see something—a shape, anything—but there was nothing. Breathing out her fear and controlling her nerves, Freya hopped forward again. *Almost there.* Her fingers left the safety of the bed frame. *Ten feet to go.*

A clang—this time from the opposite side of the room.

Shit. Have to dash for it. Freya clenched her jaw, bracing for the pain of trying to run on her damaged ankle.

Whump.

Before she could take another step, Freya was thrown clear over the bed.

She smashed into the floor and slid to the back of the room amongst the illuminated smog. Before she could regain her composure, Freya was lifted by the neck of her shirt and thrust against the cold aquarium. Her head thumped on the glass, sending a ripple of sound through the water inside.

From within the dense smoke, the sickly, drawn face of a woman appeared. The sunken, crimson eyes, hidden behind a mass of limp, blonde hair, bored a stare into Freya's soul. The woman's teeth were bared. The animal instinct within her giving only one command—kill.

Freya squirmed against the vice-like hold. As she struggled to free herself, a menacing shadow entered her peripheral vision.

Wak swam up from within the aquarium to the glass and then slowly sank down to Freya's level. It gazed outward, fixed on the women. A powerful seizure gripped the animal, forcing its head to turn to the side, and its eyes to clamp shut. It lasted a few seconds before letting loose its painful hold. The creature then banged its head on the tank's glass—over and over.

"Victoria—" Freya's sentence was strangled off by one of the woman's strangely powerful hands.

A brief, controlled explosion blew in the door to the room. It crashed and rattled about the floor. Behind the smoke, Freya heard the voice of a soldier calling her name.

"Ms. Nilsson, are you in there? Are you okay?"

Victoria hissed in anger and tightened her grip on Freya's throat, squeezing out her last gasp of air.

"Ms. Nilsson!"

Freya kicked in the air, desperately writhing as her body fought asphyxiation and lungs screamed for oxygen. Then, there was only darkness—peaceful, quiet, eternal.

CHAPTER THIRTY-ONE

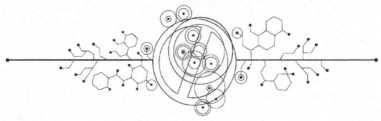

Location: Lima, Peru, South America

Heavy clouds emptied their burden upon the small, grassy knoll. The raindrops were large and made slapping sounds as they fell on the already-sodden soil. Beneath the veil of water, three figures stood hunched around a rectangular hole. Each was dressed in black or gray, which appeared black with the wetness of the rain. The lead figure was holding an umbrella and reading in Spanish from a small book. The other two had not sought the shelter of umbrellas, instead allowing the rain to envelop them.

Kelly peered out from under the mat of hair covering his face. The water that filled his ears and the frequent rumbling of thunder overhead meant he rarely heard what the priest was saying. There wasn't much the holy man could say that would offer any kind of comfort anyway. The fact that only he and Minya, who had flown in all the way from Siberia, were at the service spoke volumes. Alejandro had always been a loner.

In the last twelve months, the old man had taken to writing relatively frequently to Kelly. He never wrote about anything meaningful like Izel, or Carmen, or Chris, or even about K'in and the ordeal in Siberia. No, instead, it was about the old man's latest academic work—translations and discoveries of some sort.

Kelly had rented a post office box that only a few people knew about in a nearby village and had never expected it to be used, especially not by Alejandro. It had been two months before Kelly had bothered to check the box. There had been four letters from the old man inside. At first, Kelly had not known what to make of them. He wrote back, more out of a sense of duty than anything—duty to his dead wife and daughter and duty to his brother-in-law. But as the letters flowed, the underlying reason for Alexandro's contact became clearer. The old man had stage four cancer and wasn't sure how much time he had left. From the tone of the letters, Kelly got the feeling Alejandro, despite himself, saw his ex-son-in-law as his only remaining family.

In a strange way, Kelly felt the same.

Through the cloak of rain, he stared across at Minya. Minya, the only friend of Alejandro whom Kelly had ever met. Even that meeting had been brief—a few hours in a remote part of Siberia more than a year ago.

The woman stood silently, her hair, now dyed auburn, dripping wet. Her almond-shaped eyes were closed in reverence. She was a difficult woman to read—emotionless. Her facial expression was flat and unmoving. Perhaps she didn't speak Spanish and therefore couldn't understand the prayers. Perhaps she simply required no comfort. Either way, the scene was quite uncomfortable, a flash into Kelly's own future, reminiscent of some dark Charles Dickens novel. He imagined his own funeral. No family. No friends. No one to mourn.

The priest finished his speech, closed the book, and strolled over to Minya. He spoke quietly to her before moving toward Kelly. Placing a hand on Kelly's shoulder, he mumbled something inaudible and then sauntered off in the direction of a little church shrouded in a curtain of rain.

Kelly sighed. Alejandro was gone—his last tie to the D'Souza family. He grunted away the fear of having to truly start again. The rain was still smacking the ground around him.

He focused on Minya, who was now walking in a tight circle. She held an umbrella in one hand, had a cell phone sandwiched between her right ear and right shoulder, and a finger wedged into her left ear to block out the ambient noise. Kelly frowned. He hadn't heard a phone ring or noticed where she'd pulled an umbrella from. Then again, he had been lost in his own thoughts. He watched her nodding over and over.

He meandered his way back to the worn out, blue Toyota pickup, yanked open the door, climbed in, and shut it behind him. Kelly shivered and shook off the rain, his wet hair flailing about.

For more than a minute, he sat in a motionless daze. The rain slid down the windshield, obscuring the outside world from him. Inside the truck, he was safe and blocked off from the pain of life. He cursed himself for thinking about it again. He needed to go see a shaman. It had been more than a week since his last session. He needed the escape.

The engine of the truck growled into life as Kelly turned the key in the ignition. He shifted the stick and pressed the loose accelerator. The gears groaned as the wet tires struggled to gain traction on the drenched mud. Eventually, they found some grip and pushed the vehicle forward.

Minya came to stand in the deep, wet tracks Kelly's truck had dug just seconds earlier, watching it speed off into the distance. She frantically waved the cell phone aloft in her right hand. *Yebat.* He didn't see her. She put the phone back to her ear. "He left. *Ya ne znayu. Da, da, Charasho.* I will try and follow him."

Location: Hong Kong, China

The Shan Chu walked to the window and stared at his reflection. The darkness of the night sky transformed the tall glass of the high-rise office window into a full-length mirror, though the colored lights of the Hong Kong skyline obscured his image. He stared into his own cold, black, narrow eyes, formulating his next move.

He turned on his heel to face the two men who stood on the other side of the large oak desk. Their nervous demeanor, shuffling awkwardly on the spot, belied the confidence their crisp designer suits would otherwise convey. Neither one raised his head, each instead choosing to keep his gaze fixed on the floor.

The man by the window stepped around the desk, stopping when he was within arm's length of the closer of the two men. In one smooth motion, he pulled a meat cleaver from a concealed holster at the back of his suit jacket and sliced twice. The first cut separated the man's left ear from his head. Blood poured from the open wound. The second slice, anticipating the man's reflexive response of clutching at the gory orifice, severed his left hand at the wrist. The man screamed and dropped to the floor. Blood pooled around him. His companion shook and shivered violently but didn't move from his position.

"It seems to me," began the Shan Chu, "you do not understand my instruction in our mother tongue. Perhaps if I speak in the ugly, basic American language, you will comprehend. Maybe with one ear, you will learn to concentrate on my instructions better." His voice was deep and menacing. His accent, while of an East Asian persuasion, was not easily associated with any one country.

He cleaned the customized blade with a silk cloth he had drawn from his jacket pocket. The thick blood smeared across the smooth metal and pooled within the ornate dragon etched along its length. He focused his concentration on meticulously mopping up any remaining fluid from the engraving while talking to the sniveling men. "You failed to obtain the creature at Paradise Ranch. Then, when you did capture it, somehow the American amateurs were able to reclaim it from you—from within one of our own submarines." He kept his voice level, never looking back at them. "Even when I organized the release of the virus in California, tying up their resources and politicians, you were unable to find this band of misfits or the creature. Only when I learned of their arrival in Siberia did we have another chance to take it from them. But again, my gift was squandered. Your buffoons managed not only to get themselves killed but also to kill the creature and destroy the orb." He fixed an icy stare on the men. "I needed them both. We have no choice now. Our control of the People's Army has been lost. I will travel to America and make contact with the 14K there. Wan Kuok-Lóng is the Dragon Head in Chicago."

The unscathed subordinate dared to raise his eyes. "But," he began nervously, "the 14K in particular is difficult to control." He stuttered and then stopped talking, regretting his outburst.

The Shan Chu stepped over the bloodied man lying on the floor and pressed the cold sharp steel of his machete under the other's sweaty chin. "Are you questioning me, Ping?"

"No, no, of course not, Shan Chu." Fear danced on the glassy surface of the man's eyes.

"Good." He lowered the blade, leaving a shallow gash in Ping's chin. "Speak with Wan Kuok-Lóng's Straw Sandal. Tell him I will come soon. We must regain what is rightfully ours. Now go. And take Bao-Zhi with you."

Ping, frightened and sweating profusely, nodded and grabbed his crying friend and heaved him across the carpet. As he exited through the large double doors, he didn't turn his back to his superior.

Left alone in his office, the Shan Chu placed his machete on the table, straightened his dark, one-buttoned suit and slicked back his long, black hair. Elegantly, he strode across the room and opened the intricately-carved double doors of a large rosewood cabinet. Inside was a small black screen. He pressed his right thumb against it. The glass flickered into life, displaying nine electric blue Chinese symbols. He tapped several of them and stood back. From within the cabinet, there was a faint click followed by a hiss as the false back slid downward. An iridescent blue light lit the Shan Chu's face, casting strange and unearthly shadows across it.

This time, we will be successful.

Location: Lima, Peru, South America

Swirling patterns of color penetrated the darkness. The smoky trails were bright and comforting at first but became intense and dark all too soon. Crimsons, burnt oranges, and deep purples replaced the yellows, blues, and greens. A deep-seated feeling of menace spread through him as the vision shifted.

The swirls became geometric shapes that moved in unison with malevolent intelligence and definite direction toward him. They twisted from two-dimensional to three-dimensional structures that seemed to fall away into a darkness that sucked him in, yanking on his insides as if he were riding a rollercoaster. He swallowed his fear and fought back the nausea. *I will not be afraid.*

In an instant, the shapes melded together, the color draining from them until only a white mass sat in the darkness. The shape rose and fell like the chest of a sleeping child. As he focused harder on the gelatinous form, he observed the beginnings of limbs and a head. Slowly, the shape dribbled into its final morphology.

K'in, the man-sized salamander-like creature padded in slow motion toward him, his red fan of gills bobbing with his gait. Bright blue eyes shone from the middle of his face. The sight of the animal pushed any last remnants of fear from his heart.

Other forms, humans and K'in-like creatures, emerged from the darkness. Walking slowly and calmly toward him, their hands were outstretched, wanting—needing—to make contact with him. He held out one arm in reciprocation. A feeling of complete release washed over him.

Kelly's stomach convulsed, forcing the vision from his mind and a watery liquid from his insides. He leaned over and vomited all over the wet patch of mud on which he sat. He folded his arms across his midriff and nursed his aching gut while swirling saliva around his mouth to extinguish the acrid taste. He fell on his side and rested his head in the warm dirt. The rain, now more of a light speckle, wet his face.

"Hello, Mr. Graham." The strong Russian accent, with its epiglottal *h* sound, was familiar.

Kelly pried his eyes open and looked up. Against the painfully bright, white sky was the dark silhouette of Minya. Her sodden red hair stuck to her head, and her hazel eyes threw a cold, judgmental stare. He couldn't quite figure her out. She cared enough about her appearance to dye her hair and wear some makeup, but that was where her femininity seemed to end.

"Ayahuasca tea?" she asked.

Kelly nodded. "Yes, Ayahuasca tea."

The visionary brew comprised the vine of *Banisteriopsis caapi* and the leaves of shrubs from the genus *Psychotria*. It was a foul-tasting concoction that had been used for millennia by the people of Peru for its divinatory and healing purposes. It also always made Kelly throw up.

"The shaman seems to have a better constitution than you." Minya waved a hand at the old man who sat opposite Kelly, cross-legged on the ground.

Kelly groaned. "He's had a lot more practice."

The shaman, dressed in a brightly-colored poncho and equally gaudy wool cap with earflaps, squinted quizzically at Kelly.

Grunting, Kelly lifted his face from the muck and translated Minya's comments into his best Quechua. He then flopped head-first back into the mud.

The old man laughed out loud, his leathery brown skin creasing into a thousand folds with a huge smile, before clambering to his feet. He shuffled across to Kelly and patted him on the head. "He has not found his Huaca," the old man said.

"His what?" Minya asked.

But the man did not reply and simply meandered off into the forest.

Kelly closed his eyes and groaned again, rubbing his aching stomach. It brought Minya's attention back to the grousing man at her feet.

"Man, you are like big child. You realize the tea contains high dose of DMT?"

Kelly nodded. He was well aware of this fact. Every batch of tea was different and contained different concentrations of DMT. Each time he drank it, the visions were more or less intense. But each time, it was like an escape—like he had been lifted as he had when he had been connected to K'in.

Despite Kelly's efforts to become engrossed in various community projects in the little village—building schools and helping the residents fish—he had never felt settled, never felt truly calm. Since his separation from K'in, there had been a chasm in his chest—bigger than after the loss of Izel,

Carmen, and even his best friend, Chris. It was something beyond love and beyond friendship. All he knew was the Ayahuasca tea was the only way he escaped the emptiness. And his relationship with it was beginning to border on dependence.

"I have never consumed the tea myself. You are okay?"

"Sure, I'm fine," Kelly lied. "I throw up every time. You get used to it."

"You do not seem to get used to it, Mr. Graham."

He opened one eye to view her. That calculating stare hadn't diminished. She was analyzing him. "Perhaps you're right. By the way, thanks for coming to the funeral."

"Alejandro was a friend. You know, he wrote to me many times in last year."

"Yeah, to me, too."

"He mentioned you."

"Oh, really? What'd he say?" Kelly forced a chuckle. "Actually, scratch that. I don't think I wanna know."

Minya smiled weakly. "Not all bad."

"So, back to Russia for you?"

"Siberia. But no. I need to go to U.S.A."

"Oh?"

"*Da.* And so do you."

"Hey, look, I like you and all but hitting on me at a funeral? You Russians are quick off the mark."

Minya stared at him, her face deadpan. "Siberian. And I do not hit on you, Mr. Graham." This time she purposefully emphasized the *h*. "I had phone call. It was for you."

"What?"

"It was the U.S. Secretary of State."

"The Secretary of State? What'd he want?"

"*She* said she needs your help and perhaps even mine. She said it was quite urgent. Something to do with Ms. Nilsson."

Kelly sank into his thoughts. It had been a year since he'd seen Freya. Was she alright? "Sure, right. Did she say what happened? Is Freya okay?"

"I do not know. I am not Secretary, Mr. Graham." Again, Minya's response was unemotional and matter-of-fact. "There is truck waiting for us in town. It will take us to airport."

His stomach fluttered at the thought of seeing Freya again, a feeling that turned to nausea at the thought of her possible demise. He nodded and hauled himself off the ground with an overly loud groan. "Okay, let's go."

"*Da, Charasho.*"

"Christ," he said, flicking the hair from his face yet again. "You got any scissors on you?"

CHAPTER THIRTY-TWO

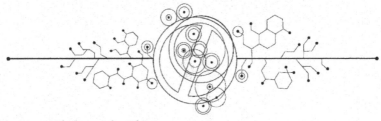

Location: Vladivostok, Siberia

Polkovnik Sasha Vetrov paced the damp room, occasionally stopping to pick up a piece of garbage, examine it, and put it down. His highly-polished black boots sparkled in the dim overhead lights while his olive-green, heavy wool uniform blended into the surrounding moss-covered walls. A light-green, peaked cap was tucked under his left arm, expertly held in place even while he completed his inspection of various objects.

He raised his head and scanned the room with narrowed eyes. The atmosphere was strange—even for him. The Stalinesque parquet flooring, oak-paneled walls, and gilded door handles were no longer grand. Instead, they just served as a reminder that Russia's glory was very much behind her.

The Polkovnik picked up one of the wooden chairs that had been laid on its side and took a seat, staring at the projection screen that had once been a map of Primorye. He wasn't even studying it, just lost in his own thoughts.

He and his associates had followed the story of the clone closely, albeit watching from a distance. The Chinese and American governments had squabbled like children over the creation—a great power and the last of the ancient civilization. Russia's Federation Council and State Duma had been quite clear on the issue—let the West and the East decimate each other.

But their war had spilled into his homeland. So now he was involved. And his instructions were non-negotiable: collaboration was the key. Fighting the Americans and Chinese simultaneously wasn't an option. His government had chosen a side, and he was bound by command and honor to stand by this alliance—no matter how much he hated it.

The Polkovnik's anger boiled over. He leapt from his chair and grabbed it before flinging it at the back wall as hard as he could. His roar echoed around the room, followed by the hollow smash of wood on brickwork.

No one came to investigate the commotion. The soldiers knew this about their Captain, their Polkovnik. He was passionate. And God save the man who dared get in his way when he was frustrated.

Sasha straightened his uniform, picked up his hat from the floor, and then made his way to the long stairway that led into the cold air outside. As he stepped out of the gloom into the fading starlight of dawn, his nostrils were still flaring. The crisp atmosphere of Vladivostok calmed him. He surveyed the myriad of lights emanating from the boats on their moorages, harbor cranes, and hundreds of colorful houses clinging to the slopes of the hills. While they were primarily Soviet buildings, they appeared organic against the background of an urban landscape that was punctuated with gothic cathedrals.

Having left the catacombs of the fortress, his phone regained its link to the satellite and hummed in silent mode within his tunic pocket. He stopped walking and dug around inside for it. After a short struggle to pry it from his tight-fitting uniform, he opened its clam-shell case and answered. "*Da?*"

The voice on the other end spoke for a few minutes. The Polkovnik stood silently, absorbing the information. Without speaking another word, he ended the call and signaled another officer in a similar green uniform to come to his location.

The soldier walked briskly forward. "*Da, Polkovnik?*"

Sasha barked something in Russian, indicating a westerly direction with an outstretched arm and pointed finger.

"*Da, Polkovnik.*" The junior officer nodded, turned about face, and marched off.

Sasha's attention was drawn back to his beloved town. Oddly stretched on knolls that slipped into the sea, Vladivostok was considered one of the most picturesque cities in all of Russia. Indeed, while its rich military heritage was well known to the locals, the town's rustic beauty had become quickly recognized by foreign tourists, who descended upon it like vultures. Thousands of camera-wielding, fat Americans flocked and flapped around the city, using its unique geography to photograph the breathtaking panoramas and the white-winged yachts that slowly rocked in Zolotoy Rog Bay.

He watched the people below scurry about their daily lives, going in and out of small buildings and cycling through alleys. They were unaware of what had happened here and were oblivious to the danger that lurked within their streets. The people were open and friendly, never losing their sense of humor or passion for what could be—a testament to the struggle of their ancestors. It was his job to protect them and shelter them from foreign enemies—at all costs.

He turned and stormed toward a caravan of four black, special-purpose, armored assault vehicles. The Polkovnik admired them as he approached the lead truck. He had been lucky to obtain them. These prototypes, codenamed Ansyr, were designed to support special operations, patrols, and reconnaissance. Each thirteen-foot-long, wedge-shaped vehicle was capable of operating successfully in temperatures ranging from minus forty-nine to one-hundred-twenty degrees Fahrenheit and at altitudes of up to one-thousand feet. Most importantly, the lockable inter-axle and cross-axle differentials and all-wheel independent suspension meant it could cross any terrain. He would need it where he was going.

The door slammed shut with a satisfying heavy clunk. Sasha nodded. The driver nodded back. With a fierce growl, the engine rose from its slumber and powered the monstrous vehicle forward.

Location: Dulce Base, New Mexico, USA

The wheels of the massive Chinook touched down. The side door slid open with a substantial thump, and Kelly dropped onto the dusty ground, closely followed by Minya. Both were dressed practically in utility pants, heavy boots, and loose-fitting t-shirts. Each had a large backpack slung over a shoulder.

A dusk sky had ignited the powder blue of day, though within a few hours, it would be extinguished by the wash of night. Out in the desert, there was no light pollution. The stars shone brightly and were even visible against the dying light of the sun.

Kelly pulled the aviator sunglasses from his face. He saw the dark silhouette of a large structure sitting like a lifeless lump in the distance. It was all too familiar—the chopper ride, an unfamiliar and desolate place, the apprehension, and the U.S. Government being as clear as mud—again. He shook his head.

"Nutflies," he said, under his breath.

"*Stoh?* I mean, what?" Minya asked.

"Nothing. I just got a bad feeling."

From within the haze of the dying evening heat, a man approached them, dressed in formal pants and shirt, his necktie pulled away from the collar.

"I'm Dr. Parnham," the man said.

Kelly frowned. "Where's Freya?"

"Ms. Nilsson? She's inside the facility," the doctor replied, appearing thrown by Kelly's abrupt greeting.

"Facility? I don't see a facility."

"There." The doctor waved an arm behind him toward an enormous, red farmhouse about a hundred yards away. Its silhouette revealed a dilapidated and unmaintained building. Its huge doors squeaked in the strong breeze.

"Wow, budget cuts, huh? Before it was Paradise Ranch. Now it's just Ranch." Kelly chuckled at his own joke. No one else did. "Jesus, doesn't anyone have a sense of humor anymore?"

"*Da*," Minya replied. "But I wait for you to say something funny."

The doctor smirked.

Kelly rolled his eyes. "Oh, I give you gold, and her line gets a laugh. Just take me to Freya."

"Of course."

Kelly and Minya followed the doctor to the farmhouse. The massive wooden doors were pulled back to reveal an elevator in the middle of the straw-strewn room.

"Of course, more secret bases. Where are we now?" sighed Kelly.

"Dulce Base," the doctor answered.

"Great."

The group stepped inside the cramped elevator and allowed the doors to slide shut behind them. Thankfully, the small tube descended quickly so the uncomfortable silence didn't last long. When they arrived at the required level, the doctor side-stepped through the opening doors into the rock-hewn corridor, not wasting a second more in the claustrophobic box. Obviously, he was not a fan of small spaces. He drew a breath and beckoned his guests to follow.

Minya and Kelly cautiously stepped out and examined their surroundings, but nothing gave away what might lie ahead. The interior was simply a red-brown rock cave with evenly-spaced halogen lights hanging overhead. They followed the scientist down the poorly lit passageway until they reached a small, metallic door.

The doctor tapped at a flat-glass security pad embedded in the rock and waited for the door to pop open. "In here." He waved his arm into the now-open doorway.

"Going for the dungeon look. Nice. Not very original, but I like it."

The doctor ignored Kelly's comment and ushered them through the portal.

The familiar white-walled and hermetically sealed room reminded him of his time at Paradise Ranch—the first time he had met K'in. Even the smell, clinical and sterile, was the same. "I stand corrected. Seems you guys have a standard creepy lab blueprint everybody follows."

"Kelly?"

The voice was soft and alluring—and not to be trusted. He smiled in relief. That was just how he'd felt the first time he'd heard it.

Kelly side-stepped the doctor to see Freya standing in front of him. With no need for field gear, she was once again in business attire: a black pencil skirt, a high-collared white blouse, and fitted suit jacket. Her jet-black hair was pulled back into an efficient ponytail. He also noticed her right ankle was bound in a tight support.

"Kelly, it's good to see you." Freya smiled as she inspected him. "New haircut? You look … grown up."

He rubbed his newly shorn, crew-cut hair. One of the soldiers in the chopper had carried a set of clippers to keep his head efficiently shaved. It had seemed like a good idea at the time. Besides, the wet mane constantly in his face was pissing him off. "Yeah, I was due."

"The haircut or growing up?" She folded her arms and smirked.

"Probably both," he replied. "So what's the emergency? Why'd you drag me all the way out here? I'm sure the army isn't in the business of letting you use their choppers to get me up here for a date."

"No, Mr. Graham."

Kelly didn't know this woman's voice. "And you are?"

Lucy stepped toward Kelly, moving a lock of blonde hair behind her ear before offering her hand for him to shake.

"I'm the Secretary of State, Lucy Taylor. I called you here."

"No shit," exclaimed Kelly, shaking her hand vigorously.

"You'll forgive me. I don't tend to follow politics. There's no TV with cable where I hang out, ya know?"

"Of course, Mr. Graham, I understand. I apologize for bringing you here on short notice, but we do need your help."

"Well, it was a sneaky move making me think Princess Freya was in trouble to get me up here." He winked at her. "But now you have me here, what's the emergency? Let me guess, you found aliens from Mars and thought it would be a great idea to give them CPR, and now they're running around in giant tin cans with legs, blowing shit up?"

The group stared at him, perplexed.

"*War of the Worlds*? H.G. Wells? No?" Kelly sighed. "Forget it. So, what's up? Why me?"

"It's a little complicated, Mr. Graham. In the last year, I have been trying to uncover and close down any part of the program that was linked to the cloning of the creature you knew as K'in. I was appalled at how our government had behaved, causing war with the Chinese and exposing our citizens to the virus. Not to mention the ethical and moral implications of bringing an extinct intelligent species into the modern world and then trying to use it for our own ends."

Kelly frowned and studied the woman. A politician with morals? Really? He indicated for her to continue.

"I have managed to shut down most of the program and exposed some pretty high-profile people in the senate. It's all but discontinued—apart from this one piece."

"Out with it, lady. What are you talking about?"

"The creature K'in was not the only clone."

"Yeah, I know this. There were four before him. Professor Alexander told me. They didn't work."

Suddenly, Kelly became aware of his surroundings. He focused on the tall glass cylinders behind Freya and the Secretary. He stepped between the women and peered inside the tubes, examining each of the grotesque forms, gnarled and twisted. They looked like K'in—kind of. "Holy shit, is this them?" He studied the plaques. "One, two, three, four."

"Yes, that's them." Freya put a hand on Kelly's shoulder. "But ..."

"But? But what?"

"There was a sixth."

Kelly took a deep breath and then sighed loudly. "Jesus, another poor, scared animal wondering what the hell is going on?"

"Not quite," the doctor replied.

"Wait, are you talking about?" He cast his mind back to the discussion with Professor Alexander at Paradise Ranch more than a year before. He'd seen a file on the computer screen that had been quickly hidden from him.

Even then, he'd known it contained something to do with military application. "The fusion folder."

"Yes," the Secretary replied.

"Oh shit, where is it?"

The doctor pointed beyond the cylinders to the large tank at the back of the room.

Kelly looked at each of the others' faces in turn, his own furrowed with worry. Strangely, Minya appeared calm. She was quietly absorbing all the information.

Taking another deep breath, Kelly made his way to the aquarium at the back of the room. Inside, a dark shadow slowly swam up to the glass window and then stopped and hung there, staring at him. Kelly studied it, his eyes wide as he examined its sinewy flesh, huge blood-red eyes, and massive black gills. His stomach knotted and his concentration waned. It was horrible, like a demon from a childhood nightmare.

"That is not like K'in."

"No, Mr. Graham. This is Wak." The doctor was now standing beside him.

"Wak? Why does it look different—from K'in, I mean?"

"Wak is the result of combining the original animal's DNA with human DNA. Fusion."

"Fuck me. It looks pissed." Kelly raised one eyebrow. "What's wrong with it?"

"It has behavioral problems," Freya said, who had now joined the two men.

Kelly scoffed. "No shit. Wait a minute, you want me to bond with this thing? Like I did with K'in? You're outta your goddamn mind."

"No, no, nothing like that," Freya said, shaking her head.

"In fact, it's already bonded with someone."

Kelly span around and looked her straight in the eyes, his face pale. "Not you?"

"No, not me."

He sighed in relief.

"This isn't going to be easy for you to hear, but …" Freya swallowed.

"But?"

"It bonded with Victoria."

"Victoria? Victoria who?" he asked, puzzled.

Freya gave a weak nod as if to will him the answer.

"Vicky? But she died. What the fuck are you talking about?"

"She was found in the wreckage of the truck in Las Vegas, dying. Our team picked her up. They had no idea who she was. There was no ID. All they knew was she wasn't American. She was a perfect candidate." Freya had her palms outward, trying to calm Kelly.

"Candidate for what?" Kelly's voice grew louder with his frustration.

"She was near-dead and badly hurt. She'd lost one of her arms. The work with Wak had led to the possibility of limb regeneration. They saved her."

"Where is she?"

Freya stepped to the side to reveal another tank in the corner of the room. Kelly ran past her and almost fell into the glass wall. He gazed at the woman suspended inside. She was wearing a short, black, neoprene wetsuit and a mask over her face that fed her oxygen. Her eyes were closed as if she were asleep, and her hair swirled about her head. Kelly searched for signs of injury to her arms but found none.

"Get her out of there."

"We can't," the doctor replied. "She needs to spend a couple of hours in there every day. It calms her."

"Calms her?" Kelly asked.

"Yes. Kelly, Victoria may not be like you remember her. She didn't take the news of what happened to her lightly. Using the animal's cells to save her … you remember what happened at Paradise Ranch."

Kelly thought back to the incident. Victoria had been so angry. Her beliefs torn apart in front of her. "Of course, I remember. She's probably freaked out. These sick fuckers stuck cells in her from something she hated with every fiber of her being."

"They didn't know, Kelly. They just—"

"I know, they just saved her."

"She didn't remember anything for a long time—she was calm. But then, things started coming back to her. She started asking for you and Chris. When we didn't bring you, she became angry. As she became angry, so did Wak. Eventually someone will get hurt." Freya trailed off and swallowed nervously. "It's why they brought me in. She asked for me, too. I told her everything that had happened, but she wouldn't believe me. She just got angrier and angrier."

"I'm surprised you didn't just kill her and it. Isn't that what you people do?" Kelly directed his question at the Secretary and the doctor.

"I am in charge of this now, Mr. Graham. And as I told you, I do not agree with the fundamental amorality of all this." Lucy swept her arm around the room. "Wak is a living being, and Victoria is a woman with rights. I want to find a way to deal with this."

"And what do you want from me?"

"Victoria's been asking for you over and over. We're hoping she will be more cooperative if you talk with her," Freya replied.

Kelly turned back to the tank and placed his palm on it. For a few minutes, he said nothing, instead choosing to stare into the cold water. "I'll talk to her—but on my own. I don't want your lot freaking her out."

"Thank you, Kelly." Freya placed her hand on his shoulder again.

"Sure."

"Just one thing. She has a bit of a temper, so be careful."

Kelly laughed for a second but stopped when Freya didn't reciprocate. "Really?"

Freya lifted her bandaged ankle a few inches to show Kelly. "Really."

CHAPTER THIRTY-THREE

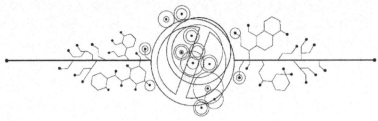

Location: Blagoveshchensk, Russia

Sasha sat in the waterfront bar, staring across the river at the Vegas-style lights. He'd been waiting for several hours for his contact to arrive. The whole feeling of this place was so un-Russian it hurt his sensibilities. While his uniform offered him some protection and even respect from his countrymen, the Chinese who lived here gave no such preferential treatment. Blagoveshchensk was reluctantly twinned with Heihe, and only the small Amur River separated them. These intrinsically linked cities sat on the border between Russia and China. And Sasha hated it.

Across the water in Heihe sat the Yuan Dun shopping center, its name written large enough to be seen clear across the river. The lights of downtown Heihe were reflected in ripples of the river's surface. As far as Sasha was concerned, both cities were dirty and chaotic. Heihe was nothing more than a Potemkin village—a bauble the Chinese government lavished money on solely because of its location.

Here, perhaps worst of all, ordinary Russians and Chinese could cross the border, and foreigners freely moved in and out. It was an outrage.

He sipped the vodka in the shot glass and scanned the room. A mixture of Russians, Siberians, and Chinese filled the seats—yet never sat together. There may have been free movement, but no one nationality trusted another.

From within the crowd, a man approached the Polkovnik. Unlike everyone else in the bar, this man was Middle Eastern. His thinning hair revealed a shiny scalp, and his skinny build seemed almost inhuman. He hastened toward the Russian.

Two FSB agents stepped down off their stools and blocked the man's way. Finishing his vodka, Sasha tapped his men on the shoulder, signaling they should let the sickly-looking man through. They grudgingly parted but stayed close.

"You have what I want?" Sasha asked.

The skinny man stared momentarily. The Russian's accent was difficult to place. It almost had an American quality to it. But he ignored it and continued with his business. "You have what I want?"

"You have what I want?" replied the man.

"Do not test me. If you have what I came for, you will get paid. If you have wasted my time, I will kill you."

A flash of realization passed across the Arab's face. He was not in a position of power. He pulled an envelope from his jacket and handed it to the Polkovnik. "Here."

Sasha ripped open the letter and slid out a small piece of paper. Unfolding it, he surveyed what was clearly a photo of a map of Western Russia covered in Cyrillic scrawling.

"On paper? Really?" the Polkovnik asked.

"Yes," the man hissed. "You of all people should know the dangers of the digital age. Didn't your government recall all the typewriters used during your wars to prevent tracking of certain documents? Sometimes the old ways are the best."

"If it were the old days, you would not be paid in money, but in fewer internal injuries for cooperating."

Color drained from the pathetic man's face.

Sasha tapped the photograph. "And you are sure this is where I will find what I'm looking for?"

"Yes, of course. You doubt me?"

Sasha didn't respond.

"Of course. You think I need you chasing me, KGB man?"

"FSB. And what about those it belongs to … chasing you?"

"They have more morals than you. They would at least kill me quickly, Russian."

Sasha narrowed his eyes. That was probably true. He gave the okay nod to the soldier on his left.

The skinny man was handed a small satchel, which he snatched away with his bony hands and duly inspected. Satisfied with his payment, he bowed sarcastically and scurried out of the bar.

The men stared at the Polkovnik in expectation.

Sasha downed his vodka in one and held the map so they could see.

"*Yebat*," said one.

Sasha nodded. "*Da. Yebat.*"

Location: Dulce Base, New Mexico, USA

Kelly sat at her bedside, watching her sleep. The team at Dulce Base had removed Victoria from her aquatic prison more than an hour ago, but she hadn't woken up yet. She was in a small space on the other side of the tank that held Wak. The aquarium was transparent on both sides, creating a water-filled window from the room they were in to the lab that contained the deformed, deceased clones.

Swirling in the cold water of the aquarium was the creature, Wak, its red eyes piercing the blackness that surrounded it—watching Kelly. Its movements were calculated and menacing like a jealous partner pacing a room. Kelly didn't like this creature. It was nothing like K'in.

He turned his attention back to Victoria. Her hair was drying in a matted mess, stuck to her forehead and shoulders. White sheets were wrapped around her body, leaving her arms free. Her breathing was shallow, punctuated by the occasional gasp and muscular spasm.

Kelly understood all too well the bond with the animal was powerful. He gently brushed the hair away from her face. At least K'in had been peaceful and childlike. This new thing seemed malevolent.

He thought back to the attack on Paradise Ranch and how Victoria had been so offended at the thought of a non-human species being intellectually more advanced than humans. She couldn't believe a life form had possibly given humankind the ability to build great societies with morals and rules. The thought that God had not bestowed these gifts, but something else, had attacked the very core of her being. She'd flipped, stolen a gun, and raced to kill K'in. Only, she couldn't do it. Yet, by some sick twist of fate, the Chinese had attacked the base, sending Victoria off-kilter so much so she'd accidentally pulled the trigger, sending a stray bullet bouncing around the hermetically sealed room—a bullet that had come to rest in the chest of Kelly's best friend in the world, Chris.

Vicky hadn't meant to kill Chris. It wasn't her fault. Kelly knew that, but he couldn't help resenting her for it. He swallowed the lump in his throat. She was just passionate about her religion.

Kelly paused on that thought. It was strange. He'd known her for several years and the topic of religion had never come up. Had she always been that fanatical? He couldn't remember. If he was honest, he had been too busy grieving Izel and Carmen at the time to pay any attention to anyone else.

A light moaning broke his train of thought. He sat silently and watched Victoria stir and stretch her arms. The creature was now quite still, watching them.

Victoria blinked in the harsh light of the fluorescent tubing overhead. The synthetic yellow haze that lit the room made the intensity of her now-red eyes appear even greater.

Kelly took a short, sharp breath and quickly exhaled it away through pursed lips. He hadn't seen her with her eyes open until now. No one had warned him. She looked so different. The warmth of her gaze was absent, replaced by a crimson stare.

"Kelly?" Her voice was weak and croaky but still carried that gentle English accent.

"Hey, Vicky. Yeah, it's me."

"How did you find me?"

"Freya, Ms. Nilsson, called me. Said you've been asking for me."

"Yes." She sat up, then, realizing she was naked, gathered the bedding around her chest and held it close. "Yes, they won't let me leave. They said Chris is dead, and that it was me who shot him. And that after the first creature, they made another one, and it's attached to me. Kelly, what's going on?"

As Victoria's excitement grew, so did the vigor of Wak's swimming within its aquatic prison.

Kelly kept the strange animal in his peripheral vision but didn't allow his focus to break from Victoria. He rested a hand on one of her bed sheet-covered legs and spoke as calmly as he could. "It's a long story, Vicky. What's the last thing you remember?"

"We … we …" She frowned, trying to dredge up memories from deep within her psyche. "We had collected something from the bottom of the ocean—some kind of round, gelatinous thing. We were brought back to America. To a military base by Ms. Nilsson and the big black man."

"Tremaine."

"Yes, him. They showed us a large creature, a huge amphibian thing like the one sitting in the tank over there." She pointed at Wak without making eye contact with it. "They told us it was a clone of some ancient species, and … and that it …" She grasped at the air close to her neck, searching for the crucifix that had once hung there.

270

"And its species had brought humans from savagery to civility," Kelly said, finishing her sentence.

"I was angry. I remember running, but the rest is a blur. They say I shot Chris." Her voice broke, tears streaming down her cheeks.

"That's not strictly true," Kelly began. "It wasn't your fault. You were very angry, yes. You took a gun and ran to the aquarium—you wanted to shoot the animal, shoot K'in."

"K'in." She sniffed and nodded.

"You never got the chance. Before you could pull the trigger, the place was attacked. In the explosions, you fell and accidentally fired the gun when you hit the ground." Kelly cleared his throat. "The stray bullet must have ricocheted off something before it hit Chris."

Victoria burst into full-blown sobbing, burying her face in the sheets that were clutched in her hands.

"Vicky, it's okay. It wasn't your fault. It was more than a year ago."

She sniffed hard. "A year?" Her voice seemed harsh and angry now.

Wak began swirling again.

"Yeah. We tried to escape the attack in a truck, but they chased us and blew the shit out of us with a missile. I was taken hostage with K'in. When I was rescued, I was told you hadn't made it. I only found out a couple days ago you were still alive."

"You all left me for dead." Her voice rose another octave.

"No." Kelly pulled his hand from her leg. *Shit, here she goes.* "No, I told you I was captured. The truck was totaled. Everyone thought you'd been killed."

The expression on Victoria's face relaxed. Kelly heaved a sigh of relief.

"Then what happened, Kelly? What's been going on for the last year? Why don't I remember anything?"

Kelly proceeded to recount his adventure. How it had been a rogue faction of the Green and Red Societies—a Chinese cult—that had attacked them at Paradise Ranch. How the cult had released a hemorrhagic fever virus into America to kill thousands of people. How, after their truck had been destroyed, he and K'in had been captured by the cult and taken prisoner in a submarine. Freya had mounted a rescue and flown them to safety in Peru.

After some moments of contemplation, Victoria said, "Where is K'in now?"

Kelly sighed. "He died."

"He?"

"Okay, it. Whatever. K'in is dead."

She stared at him. "How? What? How did it die? Did you kill it?"

"No, no, no." Kelly waved his hands as if to wash himself of the responsibility. "We didn't stay in Peru long. At the time, we figured maybe we should finish what the General had started."

"What did he start?"

"This is all backwards. Let me start again." Kelly shook his head in frustration. "The General was scared. What you and I pulled from the South China Sea allowed humans to communicate with K'in. It was an orb, made of, well, fuck knows. It looked like Jell-O. Anyway, the General and the professor had decided such power should not sit with any particular country's military. So, his plan was to release the knowledge of K'in's existence to the world. He knew it would cause chaos. He—they—believed after the chaos, K'in would be able to once again bring peace like his species did before." He rolled his eyes. "Saying it out loud, it sounds pretty stupid."

She nodded vigorously. "Yes, it does."

"Anyway, things were crazy. There was the virus, the Chinese were after us, and the U.S. Government was after us too, since the General's little plan had been, let's say, not endorsed by the powers that be."

"So, what happened?"

"We left Peru. We stuck K'in in a submarine with Tremaine and the General to keep him—it—safe while Freya and I flew to Egypt. We were looking for another orb—to perhaps create peace."

"You, Kelly Graham, went on a hunt around the world for some kind of voodoo item to save mankind?"

"Yeah, forgot you know me so well—or knew me. Things change."

"For her?"

"Her who?" Kelly asked, feigning ignorance.

"You know who. The military woman."

"Freya? No, not really." *Perhaps.* "Anyway, from there, we ended up trekking round half the frickin' world looking for an orb. Through Egypt, India, and Russia, where we were finally getting somewhere and thought we'd found something that could help us, but the Chinese guys caught up with us. There was a gunfight and K'in was killed, protecting Freya."

"It protected a human? That animal? Why?"

"Long story. The big fish wasn't as bad as you think. Anyway, that was like a year ago. But it seems the Secretary of state has been attempting to put an end to the cloning program."

"But it wasn't the end?"

"No. It would seem a parallel program was running. And while our General, perhaps misguided, was attempting to solve the world's issues, someone else was trying to create an army of some kind." Kelly waved behind him at Wak.

"I knew it. I knew it."

"I'm sure you did, Vicky. But right now, we gotta figure out what to do with you and … that."

"They told me they used it to help me—to save me." She shuddered and rubbed her own arms.

"I don't know how they did it, Vicky. I'm no scientist. I was just told you were badly injured—very badly. One guy said you lost one of your arms."

Victoria pulled her hands from her chest and nervously inspected her arms. "Lost one?"

"The animals can regrow limbs. They used cells from that *thing* to help you—to replace your limbs and repair damaged skin and organs." He softened his voice as if the gentle tone would somehow mask the painful truth.

"But I don't want it in me, Kelly. Take it out." She sobbed. "Take it out."

Kelly quickly put his arms around her and pulled her close to his chest. "I know, Vicky, I know. I'm gonna try and help you. I don't know how yet, but I will."

"I have dreams, you know," she whispered. "I see things—strange things. And I can feel it, Kelly. The creature, I feel it in my head, in my heart. It wants to leave—to escape—so badly. It hates it here."

"I know," he soothed, rocking her gently. "I know what you mean. It was the same for me with K'in."

Victoria pulled away to look him in the eyes. "Really?"

He nodded. "Really. K'in had quite a hold on me. In a weird way, I kinda miss him."

"Him?" Victoria's expression soured. "It's a thing. And I want this thing out of my head. Out, Kelly."

"Hey, I know. I'll find a way, okay? I will. Let me go talk to these guys. I'll see what I can do." Kelly brushed the hair from her forehead again. "In

273

the meantime, you do something with this mop you call a hairdo."

For a moment, Victoria forgot her predicament and was embarrassed by her appearance. "Sure." She sniffed, then grabbed a thick length of her hair and started braiding it.

Kelly winked and headed to the door.

Freya was waiting in the other room, pacing back and forth. It had been a long time since she'd last seen Kelly, yet it seemed like yesterday. All those feelings and the closeness that had been forming a year ago all rushed back, clouding her thoughts and judgment. After Siberia, she'd put herself out on a limb and asked him to stay, but he was never going to. The stubborn jerk wouldn't admit he felt anything. But she'd thought making the first move would make it easier. It didn't. He'd shot her down and ran away to some stupid little village or island in the middle of nowhere—such a child.

She shook her head in determination. She didn't have time for this. Where the hell was he, anyway? He'd been in there with Victoria for hours. Freya stormed toward the door but was cut short as Kelly bowled out first.

"Kelly ..."

"Hey."

An uncomfortable silence.

"Did you get anywhere with her?"

"Kind of. She's pretty messed up. You know how much she detested K'in. The whole theory of his kind violates everything she believes in. And you guys went and pumped her full of it." He slumped on a nearby metal chair and rubbed his face in frustration, exhaling loudly.

"I know. I never said it was right." Freya took the seat next to him and placed a hand on his shoulder. Damn, why did she feel the need to mend this man?

"All she wants is to be rid of it. Is there a way?"

Freya shook her head. "It doesn't work like that. She's got the creature's DNA within her. It's not just the arm. And it seems to be spreading, rewriting code. We're not really sure what the deal is. But to help her, we need cooperation. She's got a direct link to Wak, too. We know she can feel it, but she's not talking."

Kelly sighed. "She did mention that. She can feel it. Said it wants to leave—that it *needs* to escape."

"Did she say where it wants to go? Or is it just a desire to escape?"

"No idea." He shrugged. "She needs rest right now. I'll talk to her again later, see if she can tell me more."

"Okay."

"I tell you one thing. She ain't gonna be happy about this thing being stuck in her. I gotta give her something—perhaps we can break the bond between her and it at least?"

Freya thought for a moment. "It's possible, I guess. Distance worked for you and K'in. Perhaps it will work for her, too."

"Maybe, but her bond is different. We should speak with the Doc and find out if there's any danger."

Freya nodded. "Makes sense."

CHAPTER THIRTY-FOUR

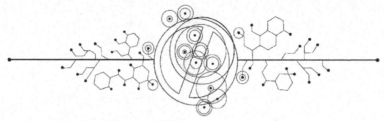

Location: Chicago, Illinois, USA

The black sedan slid along the highway, leaving Chicago airport, and headed into the city. Massive and densely packed glass buildings cut across the perfectly blue sky. Each pane reflected the building next to it until no individual structure was discernible. Instead, a mosaic of windows on a colossal scale lay before the Shan Chu.

The engine was barely audible over the clamor of his thoughts. Try as he might to channel his energy, he knew what lay ahead was going to be difficult, and it preyed on his mind. The Triads' similarity and ancient allegiance were not going to work in his favor here. They didn't function like that. They were not like the western Mafia. There was no ultimate father figure. Each Triad faction was autonomous and had its own profit and loss account. And did not, under any circumstances, answer to another faction. This was their main failing—something they could have learned from the westerners. They could embrace their common and noble heritage and become an unstoppable force on the planet.

Both the Triads and the Green and Red Societies had been born of an initial uprising against the tyranny of the Manchu Emperor in the Qing Dynasty almost three hundred years ago. The resistance force was known as the Tian Di Hui, the Heaven and Earth Society. However, as it had spread through China over time, the group had splintered and become known under several names. The San He Hui, the Three Harmonies Society, had been referred to as Triads by the stupid British authorities in Hong Kong. It had stuck.

Another faction had been the Red and Green Society. They had been more intelligent—more cunning than their San He Hui brothers. With the help of overseas Chinese and the Japanese imperial families, they'd managed to overthrow the last emperor and install Sun Yat Sen in his place. The Shan Chu clenched his jaw with anger at the thought their success had been in vain. The war with the communists in Shanghai some seventy years ago had driven them underground again.

So, the San He Hui pranced around in the public eye, flaunting their criminal activity and their decadence—the fools. The 14K were the largest San He Hui in the world, and the sub-faction of Chicago had grown particularly powerful. Their main sources of revenue—drugs, money laundering, and illegal alien smuggling—had enabled them to assemble a large army, much larger than was typical for these thugs. And now, their spawn, the second-generation gangs, were clumsily making their deals on the streets—*idiots*.

In the shadows, the Green and Red Societies had been plotting—and infiltrating. Yes, some of the members had involved themselves with the San He Hui, but many members had been at the very highest levels of the Chinese Government—until recently. Minister Li had fucked that up and put his moral beliefs ahead of the greater cause, killing Chairman Xi and stopping the Societies from taking the creature from the Americans.

The creature was theirs. They had found it in the first place, and the Americans had stolen it. But he would succeed. He would take the power and use it to unite the Triads, the San He Hui, and the Green and Red Societies all over the world—to destroy the Americans, the white supremacists.

The trick would be taking control of the 14K to start with. It was their lack of loyalty he planned to use. Frequently, members of one faction would leave for another that seemed more prosperous. Greed would be what he wielded—greed and fear.

The car rolled to a stop, interrupting his boiling anger. He breathed slowly, channeling his emotion into the task at hand. *Take control of the Chicago 14K and then all of the 14K sub-factions.*

There was a brief click and the door swung open. The Shan Chu stepped out into the brisk Chicago air. He pulled his overcoat collar up around his neck and slipped on his tailored leather gloves.

As he glanced around, his nostrils flared in disapproval. They were at some run-down building in the heart of Chinatown. Despite their power, the high-profile arrest and imprisonment in Macau of Wan Kuok-koi, the Dragon Head, had resulted in factions all over the world lowering their public profile. Perhaps this was a good thing, but it was no excuse for such disgusting abodes.

A short, stocky man, his demeanor shrewd and careful, approached him.

He bowed briefly to the Shan Chu.

"Of course. The Straw Sandal. The liaison."

The man seemed startled that the Shan Chu had chosen to speak English.

"We are in America, are we not, Straw Sandal?" continued the Shan Chu, sensing the man's confusion.

He nodded. "Yes, Shan Chu. You have had a long journey. You must wish to rest."

"No," the Shan Chu said. "I only wish to speak with Wan Kuok-Lóng. Now."

"Shan Chu, I beg your indulgence, but your visit is unexpected, and we are not prepared. We have many issues we must attend to first. Local business is our first priority." He smiled, though it was more threatening than placating.

"Local business," the Shan Chu replied, nodding. "Fair enough."

In a single movement, he pulled his razor-sharp machete from under his coat and sliced off the man's arm at the elbow. Blood sprayed the concrete sidewalk, and the air filled with a curdling scream as the man fell to his knees, clasping the severed stump.

"I would call this local and quite the priority, wouldn't you, Straw Sandal?" He almost laughed at the end of his sentence.

The whimpering man scurried off into the decrepit building, leaving a trail of red behind him. The Shan Chu waited patiently—nonchalantly—brushing dust and lint from his coat.

Moments later, a much rounder man appeared, his face contorted in anger. His blue suit stretched across his stomach, barely able to stay buttoned. "Move inside," he shouted.

"Gladly," the Shan Chu replied. He signaled to his driver, to stay where he was.

Once inside, the rotund man stomped off down a corridor and into a large room that had been fitted out like an office, though the decor appeared to be mock-Chinese—an American reproduction of what the westerners believed China looked like. A desk of deep red wood sat in the middle of the room, set against a backdrop of ancient-looking sepia-colored oriental paintings that covered the entire back wall. A random room-separating piece, completely superfluous due to the fact it was just wooden latticework and, thus, didn't separate anything, was plonked a few feet from the desk. A lone lamp, its base forged to resemble a Ming vase, adorned the monstrous bureau.

"You have become a parody. You are not San He Hui. You are Triads— American Hollywood stage props. Look at you. You are even fat like an American. You disgust me," the Shan Chu said, waving his arms about the room, pointing at the gaudy furniture.

The fat man slumped into the chair behind his desk. "Who do you think you are? You may associate with high society in China, but you have no power here. This is America, and here, I hold all the cards."

"This is America, but you don't hold all the cards. You control a small part of one city. You play second fiddle to the Italians. You are nothing, Wan Kuok-Lóng. You are fat, old, and lazy, and there is more to be taken." The Shan Chu sat in the chair on the opposite side of the desk, purposefully provoking the man.

"I do not listen to you, Jia-nghù Tsai. Yes, I know who you are. You are not even Chinese blood. You are Japanese. You bring shame to the Green and Red Societies." He laughed long and loud, looking at his bodyguards standing on either side of the only door in and out of the room.

"Yes, my family is Japanese," Jia-nghù Tsai replied. "But you pathetic Triads were not complaining when my Yakuza ancestors helped you overthrow the Manchu Emperor. Some Yakuza took positions within the Green and Red Societies to facilitate order." He grinned. "You Chinese can't be trusted to run things on your own."

"But you are not with your Yakuza brothers now, Jap. You are alone. And I am not."

The door swung open, allowing ten Triad soldiers to file in. They constructed a human circle around him, Wan Kuok-Lóng forming the critical link.

Jia-nghù Tsai closed his eyes and concentrated on the minute sounds and air movements that informed him of the position of every man in the room. He slowly slid his eyelids open and stared coldly at the Dragon Head.

"Why are you here, Jia-nghù Tsai?"

"To give the 14K an opportunity."

"An opportunity for what?"

"World domination."

The Dragon Head laughed. "You are out of your little Japanese mind."

"I am in possession of a great power—one that will allow me to control a magnificent weapon, a weapon the Americans have but do not understand.

I will take it and use it against them." He calmly crossed his legs and straightened his tie, allowing his words to sink in.

"You are crazy. And the 14K is under my control. We have built an army and wealth through my leadership. I will not lose everything to follow your crazy ravings. Go speak with your Yakuza scum, Jap."

The Shan Chu sighed. "I do not have time to educate you, ignorant pig."

Before Wan Kuok-Lóng could respond, Jia-nghù Tsai had sprung over the desk and somersaulted over the man's chair. He tucked the blade of his machete firmly under the Dragon Head's throat and pressed a hand on the back of his head.

"Let me make this simple. I need your army, and I need them now. We will go to New Mexico and take the weapon from the Americans, and with it, destroy them. Then we will use this power to unite all the Sen He Hui across the globe and establish a new dynasty. Mine." His eyes flared with passion, his voice straining with rage.

The Triad Leader choked. "This is madness. Dreams of gold and a time past."

"It is a time coming, Wan Kuok-Lóng. But you are too stupid and Americanized to see it. I am of the old world, and I will lead your men to great honor and wealth." He eyed the room, ensuring that each soldier's gaze was met.

The Triads' resolve waned. They threw confused glances at each other.

"I am the Dragon Head here. The 14K follow me."

The Shan Chu turned his attention to his captive and calmed his voice. "Yes, Wan Kuok-Lóng. There can be only one Dragon Head."

The Shan Chu pulled on the machete with sharp and deliberate force, slicing through the Dragon Head's neck muscles, trachea, and carotid artery. Wan Kuok-Lóng's eyes bulged from their sockets as he choked on a voiceless scream. Blood spattered down his chin and across the desk in thick globules. The Shan Chu released his hold, dropping the Dragon Head lifelessly onto the bureau with a dull thump.

After climbing onto the desk, Jia-nghù Tsai stood with his feet on either side of his victim's head. He fished inside his overcoat and pulled out a transparent, sealed, plastic bag that contained a strange gelatinous orb glowing with a furious cobalt light. He held it aloft, his eyes wild. "I will lead the 14K to victory. To power."

The Triads looked on in awe and fear, unsure of whether they should move against the insane man. They eyed each other nervously but knowingly, making a silent agreement. Clutching their knives, swords, and side arms, they edged with deadly purpose toward him.

Location: Dulce Base, New Mexico, USA

Lurching from her deep slumber, Victoria yelped and fell from the bed, smacking her knees and palms on the cold tiled floor. The pain burned through her stinging skin into her very bones—through her forearms and thighs, surging into her spine.

She collapsed into a heap, the thin, sweat-soaked hospital gown clinging to her skin. Victoria sobbed deep breathless cries of frustration and fear. The nightmares were so vivid, so strong. But they weren't hers. They were the animal's. The animal's overwhelming desire to escape was primal, without rational thought or language, just pure emotion—pure rage.

The door to the room hissed open. Dr. Parnham and Kelly rushed in, practically falling over one another to get to her. They fired lots of questions. Was she alright? Was she hurt? Could she hear them?

She could hear them, but their voices were muffled and distant as if she were watching the scene from outside her own body. They kept screaming, but she couldn't answer. She was too weak.

Victoria tilted her head and rolled her eyes so her gaze fell upon the ever-swirling form of Wak. It was bouncing off the inner walls of the aquarium as it bolted from one side to the other. It stopped mid-stroke and locked its gaze on hers. Its deep red eyes drew her further and further into its mind. She exhaled and slumped into unconsciousness.

CHAPTER THIRTY-FIVE

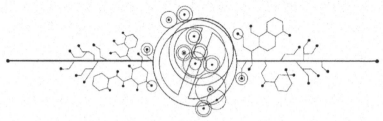

Location: Dulce Base, New Mexico, USA

Victoria's weightless form hung in the cold water of the stasis tank—relaxed, serene. At least, she seemed that way. But Kelly knew better. Each twitch and every spasm told another story. In her mind, she was fighting with the animal, Wak. Placing a hand on the cold glass, Kelly sighed and closed his eyes, allowing his mind to drift back.

Victoria had been a young, polite, and quite naive woman when Kelly had met her. It had been on an assignment for the BBC, a UK television broadcaster famed for its cutting-edge wildlife documentaries. They had been filming mating elephant seals in Peninsula Valdes, Argentina. It was pretty dangerous work. The producer had requested Kelly's expertise with the underwater filming and photography.

Bowling into the camp, he'd literally bumped into Victoria as she ran about her business trying to impress the director. Kelly caught her as she fell over her own feet. The young woman squeaked but never actually thanked him before running off.

Laughing, Chris had joked about yet another woman falling at Kelly's feet. It hadn't gone down well. Izel had been buried barely a year earlier, and Kelly was still not dealing with it well. In fact, this had been his first job since then. He'd only taken it because Chris had badgered him into it.

For the next few weeks, the team had camped on the rough, gray shale coastline, the cold sea lapping at the shore. They had waited and watched, keeping their distance all the time.

Elephant seal mating is no picnic. The beachmaster battles between males, measuring up to fifteen feet and weighing close to six thousand pounds, were often fierce—and fatal. Victoria had taken to following Kelly about. Seeing he was revered by the team for his underwater photography skills and tendency to charge in where angels feared to tread, she decided he was a good role model. Every move he made, she was there watching, noting it down.

Early one morning, eager to show what she had learned, Victoria rose before everyone else, grabbed Kelly's camera and crept down to a clump of rocks that overlooked a herd of seals. She'd been busily snapping away and not paying attention to her surroundings—or to the angry, two-ton male that was bounding toward her. Before she could react, the animal was upon her, trumpeting an awful battle cry, its massive form rearing up.

By sheer fortune, Kelly had woken to pee. Tramping awkwardly in bare feet across the jagged gravel, he'd heard the elephant seal and saw it vaulting along the coast—directly toward Victoria.

Quickly, and quite painfully, he raced across the shore, grabbing a flare gun along the way. He shoved Victoria from her spot and dropped to his knees in front of the seal. He screamed at the top of his voice, pointed the flare gun toward the sky, and pulled the trigger. A combination of the deafening bang, the screeching flare, and the final bright explosion of red and white had been enough to warn the boisterous animal off.

Nursing his lacerated feet, Kelly muttered under his breath about how stupid she had been. When he noticed his beloved camera in Victoria's grasp, the mutterings became outright ravings.

She burst into tears, clasping the crucifix dangling on a thin silver chain around her neck. Completely ignoring Kelly's ranting, she had blubbered thanks to God for sending the crazy American to save her.

The clip-clopping of high heels on the tiled floor snapped Kelly back to the present. He spun around to see Freya gracefully gliding into the room with a cell phone firmly glued to one ear.

Freya smiled and gently nodded. Then her gaze flicked to his, her eyes glassy.

"You too. Of course. Okay, see you soon." Freya quickly ended the call.

"Anything important?" Kelly asked.

"No …" She hesitated. "Not really. What happened in here?"

Kelly eyed her suspiciously. "Vicky had an episode. The Doc put her back in the tank to calm her. I think her bond to that crazy ass thing in the other tank is getting stronger."

"I agree. Her mood swings have been getting progressively worse. Initially, we put it down to the fact she was getting her memory back, but I think it may be something else."

He nodded. "My bond with K'in was pretty strong, and that was only a matter of weeks. She's been hooked up to that thing's psyche for a year. Frig knows what's going on in her head."

"I think it's more than in her head." Dr. Parnham strolled toward them, drying his hands on a towel.

Kelly grunted. "What are you talking about?"

"Well, I thought I saw something when you picked her up just a moment ago. So I checked when I put her in the tank."

"And?" Kelly demanded, his frustration building.

"Her fingers have webbing."

"What?" Freya asked.

"Yes, I thought it strange, too. Mr. Graham, when you were bonded with clone five, did you notice any physiological changes?"

"Not that I remember. Though …"

"Yes?"

"My eyes did change color—remember, Freya?"

She nodded thoughtfully. "Yes, but actually, in that case, it was more like K'in was taking on your features. K'in's eyes changed from black to blue. Yours just became bluer, I guess."

"Yeah, that's true."

"Well, I think it's the opposite way around for Victoria. Perhaps you, Mr. Graham, were the stronger of the two in the bond. But in this case, it is most definitely not her." The doctor waved a hand at the tank holding Victoria and then glanced at the tank holding Wak.

The animal was staring at him, all four limbs pressed palm-outward against the glass. Its head ticked two or three times in an awkward shudder to the left, its eyes squeezing shut for those few, brief seconds before it once again locked its stare on him.

Kelly raised an eyebrow. "I don't think it likes you, Doc."

"Would you like me if I kept you in an aquarium all day, every day?"

"S'pose not. Anyway, what's the deal here? Vicky's changing. It's gone beyond re-growing her arm, right?"

"Right. I think the bond they have has activated dormant genes—ones we weren't aware of. I don't think it's just in her. I think it's in Wak, too."

"I'm sorry, Doctor, what are you talking about?" Freya cocked her head, quizzically.

"You may or may not know we learned the K'in clone was neotenous."

"Oh, sure. That means it adapts, right?" Kelly nodded as he spoke, hoping for reciprocation.

The doctor nodded back. "Basically, yes. The K'in clone developed the ability to see and breathe in air when it was removed from water for any significant period of time. Having studied Wak now for some time, I'm not sure we had it right. I don't think it's neoteny, I think it's full metamorphosis."

"You mean that thing is gonna turn into a giant fucking butterfly?"

"No, no, Mr. Graham. But I can use butterflies as a way to explain." The doctor pulled a pad and a pen from his lab coat pocket and positioned himself between Kelly and Freya so they could both see what he was sketching.

"Here's an egg, and here's a caterpillar. Here's a chrysalis, and here's a butterfly."

Kelly nodded. The drawings were simple and childlike but conveyed the message clearly.

"Okay. A caterpillar is a juvenile form of a butterfly, right?" He circled the caterpillar. "They have high levels of juvenile hormones running around inside them that are not present in such high quantities in the adult butterfly. They keep the animal in a young state. Moreover, there is a specific gene, the broad gene, which allows the formation of a chrysalis. If this gene is blocked, knocked out, the caterpillar never becomes a butterfly. The hormone levels remain the same."

Freya sighed. "So?"

"The point is this—genes are turned on and off to control what happens both inside and outside the animal. During the transformation of a caterpillar into a butterfly, a whole host of genes are activated and hormone levels change, completely altering the animal's morphology. Something has to trigger this. It can be environmental like with K'in, or it can be something internal—a body clock of sorts."

"You think their bond is turning on certain genes," Freya said.

"Yes, and not only in Wak but in Victoria, too, since we used the animal's DNA to grow her a new arm."

"So Victoria is changing?" Kelly asked.

"I'm not sure. I've been monitoring her hormone levels, and they've been fluctuating wildly over the last few weeks. The development of webbed fingers would suggest whatever changes she's going through are manifesting externally now."

Kelly rubbed his temples in frustration. "This is fucking nuts. We've got to get her away from that thing. If it's the bond that's doing it, then we separate them."

"And then what of the animal, Mr. Graham?" Lucy had just stepped inside the doorway and caught the tail end of their discussion.

"What the fuck is it with you people waltzing in on other people's conversations?" He huffed and turned back to the doctor. "As I was trying to say, Doc, we separate them. But that won't be enough. Victoria kept telling me it wanted to escape but not just randomly. It has a particular direction in mind. Maybe it's like a migratory thing? What if we let it out, supervised, or sedated, or something? See where it wants to go? We could leave Vicky here."

"That is actually not a bad idea, Mr. Graham." Lucy raised her eyebrows and fixed an expectant gaze on the doctor.

He shook his head. "I agree in principle but letting the animal take the route it wants would mean we'd have to let it loose. How would we supervise it? How would we stop it from running into a populated area and hurting people?"

"What if it understood it was being escorted?" Kelly rubbed his newly shorn hair.

"I'm sorry?" the doctor asked.

Lucy took a seat. "Please explain, Mr. Graham."

Kelly paced the room. "When I was bonded with K'in, he seemed to understand me. He even listened to instructions I gave him. I'm not saying he could speak or understand English, but he got what I meant. Perhaps it would be the same with Vicky and the psycho salamander in there. If she explains to it we are willing to escort it where it wants to go, maybe it'll be calmer?" He stopped pacing and examined the other faces in the room. Only the Secretary seemed enthused.

Lucy stood. "I think it's worth a shot."

"Madam Secretary—" the doctor began.

"Dr. Parnham, until now, we have had no other plan, and right up to the point Mr. Graham walked in, we couldn't even get the young woman to talk to us rationally—"

"Kelly, please. I'm not a Mr. Graham. It's too formal."

"Okay, Kelly. Anyway, we have enough military personnel at our disposal to be able to form an escort, and you, Doctor, should be able to devise a safety protocol, a way to disable the animal without hurting it, should we need it."

"I guess, but I'd want it sedated the whole time."

"That would be sensible."

"So, I will need to talk with Vicky?"

"A helpful suggestion, Mr.—Kelly."

"Okay, come get me when she wakes up. I need to catch up on some sleep." Kelly started toward the door but stopped mid-stride. "Where's Minya?"

"On the surface, smoking if I remember correctly. We don't allow it down here," the doctor answered.

Freya narrowed her eyes.

"I wouldn't worry, Ms. Nilsson," Dr. Parnham said. "We're in the middle of the desert. There's nowhere to go and no one around for a hundred miles."

"I suppose so."

The desert wind whipped about the end of the cigarette, snatching the ash and casting it into the air. With squinted eyes and through the stinging smoke, Minya watched the orange sun disappear behind the horizon. She sucked the last of the nicotine she could and flicked the butt away into the sand. Clasping a small plastic device in her other hand, she glanced once more at the short message, took a deep breath, and pressed send.

CHAPTER THIRTY-SIX

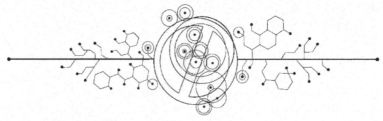

Location: Chicago, Illinois, USA

The Shan Chu stared at the advancing Triads, ensuring he made eye contact with each one. They looked scared but determined. If he wasn't careful, they would attack en masse. And even with his skill, it wouldn't be an easy fight. He placed the bag containing the glowing orb back inside his coat and raised his machete high in the air.

"My brothers. We may be from different families, but we are brothers. Brothers by honor, by code."

Their advance slowed.

"Too long have we lived in the shadows. Our great ancestry lost, our power forgotten. After restoring the true emperor to power, our people were cast aside." He jumped down from the desk to the floor in a cat-like motion before stowing his blade and calming his demeanor. "My friends, now is the time. The Americans are weak. Their economy is poor. Their President would rather show his love of trees than a strong arm to his enemies. Even as we speak, their military prepares to destroy the last chance of great power. Because they are afraid."

"What is this power?" chirped a voice from within the crowd.

"An ancient power. Older than even our own lineage." The Shan Chu's eyes flared with excitement. "Knowledge, my brothers, knowledge. It is the ultimate power. The ability to know your enemy, to be inside his head, and control him."

"If the Americans wish to destroy it, then perhaps it is not a power we want. Our lives are good. We have all we need—power, money, women. What is the point of this? The Americans and our government have waged wars for years, yet we remain."

Jia-nghù Tsai circled the desk, exposing himself to the men and to a possible attack—a show of trust.

"Is this all you wish for?" His eyes narrowed, and his gaze scanned the room. "Taking scraps from the table of other nations? Your Chinese brothers are more than a billion in number, yet they live in squalor, confined to a single country in the world. Those of you who have escaped bow to the laws of the westerners. We should create our own laws. Our ancestors developed medicine and technology while the westerners groveled in their own filth. Now we must rise again. And with this power, we can."

A large muscular man dressed in an all-black suit, his head shaved, stepped forward. He wielded a large knife more than twelve inches long. "You say the Americans have this weapon. How are we few men meant to take it from their army, their military?"

The Shan Chu stepped forward to meet the man. While not as wide, he was taller and could still command a fearsome presence. "The Americans are stupid. They are covertly dealing with their issue. There is no army, merely a handful of men. Besides ..." He circled back around, pushed the dead Dragon Head from the chair and sat in his place. "I have an employee in their ranks. I know what they know. I move when they move."

The man sneered at the Shan Chu. "You come into our house, kill our Dragon Head, wave a plastic bag with a glowing bauble in our faces, and expect us to march on American soldiers to regain a power that was held centuries ago. You are crazy, Jap. You cannot even prove such power exists."

"Can I not?" the Shan Chu replied, one eyebrow raised. "What is your name, soldier?"

"Wei Xin," the man snapped back.

"So, Wei Xin, you are not afraid to experience the power?"

The man shuffled on the spot. "You said the Americans have it."

"Oh, indeed, they have part of it—a creature, a being of immense strength and capability. But I have the other half, which will allow true bonding with it."

"The Americans reported on this a year ago," said another. "It was a hoax."

"Oh, no, I assure you it was not. Let me demonstrate."

He retrieved the bag from his coat and placed it on the desk. Then he pulled it open, its zip-lock-like seal peeling back. "Place your hand inside, Wei Xin. Or are you afraid?"

The soldier glanced around the room at his Triad brothers, their expectant faces spurring him on to show no fear. He grunted and stepped quickly forward, thrusting his hand into the bag to clutch the gelatinous orb.

As quick as lightning, the Shan Chu shot his arm out and grabbed the soldier by the throat, completing the circuit between the orb and the two men. "Feel me penetrate your mind, Wei Xin. You cannot escape me."

The soldier whimpered as the stabbing pain of another person piercing his consciousness overwhelmed him. Fear consumed his very being as he failed to defend against the mental onslaught, his memories being forced from his synapses and torn from his mind. His eyes widened and tears streamed down his cheeks as the Shan Chu ripped open his psyche.

Flashes of the Shan Chu's mind popped and crackled in the Chinese soldier's visual cortex—images of death, torture, scorching deserts littered with corpses, withered and burned human figures crawling on their hands and knees, and disease-ridden children running feral through garbage. There was a river of blood flowing through the center of a crippled city of broken high rise buildings. It was truly a dystopian vision that would have disturbed Dante himself.

"True discipline," the Shan Chu began, "means having a strong mind. Complete control." His snarl became a menacing grin and he released his grip on the soldier, who slumped to the floor. "Only I have the strength to bond with their biological weapon."

The men stared in absolute fear and awe.

He scanned their scared faces. "Our victory was already written centuries ago, brothers. And now it comes to pass. Their own god has decreed it."

"God?" replied one of the Triads sheepishly.

"Yes, my feeble-minded brethren. The westerners' own prophet, Ezekiel, described a great war between two global power blocs that will occur in the end time." He jumped back onto the table for theatrical presence and held his arms aloft. "Son of man, set your face against Gog, of the land of Magog, the prince of Rosh, Meshech, and Tubal, and prophesy against him, and say, 'Behold, I am against you!'" His eyes flashed wildly. "Persia, Ethiopia, and Libya are with them. Gomer and all its troops. And the house of Togarmah from the far north and all its troops."

The men stared blankly at the raving lunatic.

"My simple friends. The prince of Meshech and Tubal is the leader of our neighbors to the north—the Russians." A huge, creepy smile broke across his face. "And you must know Persia is now Iran. And of course, the African nations need no introduction. But most importantly, Gomer and the house of Togarmah. Gomer, my friends, is Asia itself. It is us. A coalition of the oppressed was foreseen to destroy the westerners."

Again there was low murmuring among the men.

The Shan Chu sprang back down to the floor and walked among the bemused Triad members. "The coalition is already formed. We are already strong. And soon, we will have what we need to destroy them all—starting with the Americans."

"The creature?" offered one man.

"Yes, the creature. But first, I have another surprise for our American hosts. I am going to reset the world, starting with the U.S."

He broke into maniacal laughter that convulsed his whole body. The Triads laughed nervously with him.

The phone buzzed in his pocket. The Shan Chu ceased laughing abruptly and withdrew it. He clicked it open and read the short note:

> *Wait. Situation changed. It will be gift wrapped. Come to Dulce Base ASAP.*

The Triad leader put the device away and smiled a cruel smile. "Fortune favors the bold, my friends."

Location: Dulce Base, New Mexico, USA

He sat motionless on the floor, his back pressed uncomfortably against the frame of the bunk. Even with the bright phosphorescent lights switched off, patterns and strange swirls formed in the darkness. And with them, morbid sounds emerged from the walls to fill the awkward silence. *Clear your head. Think straight.*

Kelly sipped the hot tea again, swallowing what he could, and then braced his empty stomach for the scorching liquid and ensuing feeling of nausea. He concentrated on his plan. He hadn't been completely honest with the Secretary or, for that matter, Freya. But they would never agree to it, so there was no point in telling them. No, instead, he would just do it. He'd switch the bond from Vicky to himself. The Doc had said it. Vicky wasn't the strongest of the pair. She couldn't deal with it—but he could. If he could get the crazy ass thing to switch its bond to him, they'd have a much easier time of transporting it to wherever the hell it wanted to go.

Getting it to switch—that was going to be the tricky part. He had no idea how to do that. Physical contact like he'd had with K'in seemed the most logical way. He'd have to wait until he could get close enough to it and then would grab it and hold on till it surrendered—well, something along those lines. It would all become clear when the time came—hopefully.

The familiar mixture of fever-like symptoms washed over him as the tea took hold. It was a struggle to keep his eyes open, so he decided it wasn't worth fighting it. He crossed his arms over his aching stomach and tilted his head back.

A cacophony of colors swept over his retinas, zooming out of the nothingness behind his eyelids. The strange shapes and lines pulsated and weaved. It reminded Kelly of being a child when, lying in bed, he would rub his eyes extra hard to generate such vivid imagery. From within, the dancing light and shapes hummed softly. Kelly focused on it, screwing his eyes shut, willing his hearing to improve or the sound to grow louder. It was a voice—a woman's voice. She was calling his name, gently at first but then with more urgency and annoyance.

Freya shook Kelly by the shoulders. "Kelly," she yelled impatiently.

He dropped the metal cup from his hand. It clanged and pinged about the floor, spilling hot tea everywhere.

"Wh ... what?" Kelly dragged his mind lost in some far-off place.

Thankfully, the lights were still off, saving him from the searing pain of white-hot light stabbing through his dilated pupils.

"It's Vicky. She's awake."

"Oh, shit, yeah, of course." Kelly groaned and hoisted himself from the floor, swaying unsteadily.

"Hold on there, cowboy." She grabbed him by the arm and helped him take a seat on the bunk.

"Thanks."

"What's going on, Kelly? Hmm? What's with the tea?"

He met her gaze, her eyes full of genuine concern. "Just helps me relax, ya know?" He winced, cradling his stomach, fighting back the nausea.

"I know you better than that, Kelly Graham."

He sighed. "You know what this is?"

"No."

"It's Ayahuasca tea. The various peoples of South America used it, use it, to ..." He paused, embarrassed.

Freya raised her eyebrows. "To ...?"

"To induce spiritual revelations. To work out their purpose on Earth, how to be the best person they can possibly be. They call it a rebirth."

"Feeling lost?" She placed a hand on his knee.

"Maybe. I dunno." He rubbed his short hair again. "After Siberia, after K'in died, it was like I was left with a hole in my chest. I figured that maybe I needed to do something for someone else—something altruistic. I helped build schools and wells and worked with the locals. I even answered the old goat's letters. Nothing really helped."

"Yes, I'm sorry about Alejandro."

"Doesn't matter." Kelly skipped past it.

"Anyway, you started using the tea? Because you thought it would show you the way?"

"I guess. But it didn't work like I expected. I mean, it does feel like an escape, like the hole is filled briefly. But I haven't received a revelation. I just keep having weird dreams—often with K'in in them."

"You see K'in?"

He nodded. "Yep. The shaman told me people who drink the tea can also make contact with various spiritual or extra-dimensional beings who act as guides. He thinks K'in is still with me."

There was a lasting silence.

"Do you?" Freya asked softly.

Kelly scoffed. "No, of course not. Our link was biological from being physically in contact. You know I don't believe in all that crap." He jumped up from the bed.

Freya eyed him. He didn't seem as sure as he pretended to be. "Kelly—"

A hollow metallic knocking cut Freya short.

"Sorry to interrupt, but Victoria is awake and asking for Mr. Graham." Lucy stood half in the room, half out.

"Sure. We should go." Kelly marched out and down the corridor, quickly followed by the Secretary.

Freya picked up the small metal cup and sniffed the contents. The foul smell filled her nostrils and the back of her throat. *Ugh, it's disgusting.* She placed it back on the small bunk side table and started after the other two.

Victoria sat in the uncomfortable, square chair. Its lack of padding and the thin material of her medical gown combined to make the experience of sitting there even worse. She absentmindedly twisted and fiddled with her hair, forming yet another braid to accompany the mass already adorning her head. Behind her, Wak swirled and glided in its tank, never removing its fixed stare from the woman in the dry world.

The hiss of the door snapped Victoria from her fugue state and halted Wak from its constant swimming. The animal placed all four limbs on the glass and peered out. Its head twitched violently to the left, its eyes squeezed shut. When the seizure ended, Wak returned its focus to the outside.

Kelly bowled into the room. "Hey, Vicky. Okay, we got a plan. You up for listening to me for a few minutes?"

She squirmed in the chair and eyed the doorway, waiting for another scientist to come through to poke and prod her.

"I'm on my own," Kelly said. "Just you and me." He perched on the edge of the nearby bed.

Victoria smiled weakly, though her crimson eyes were unable to convey any real emotion. "You have a plan?"

"Yep. Came up with it myself." *Sell it to her, Kelly.* "You told me that thing in there wants to escape, wants to go somewhere—somewhere specific."

"Uh-huh," Victoria replied in a hushed voice before bowing her head and turning her shoulder to hide her face from the animal.

"Well, we're gonna let it."

294

"What?" Her head shot up, and she stared Kelly directly in the eyes.

He steadied himself and consciously kept her blood-red gaze. "Look, when I was attached to K'in, the other clone, distance really made a difference. The bond became much weaker. Maybe if we put some distance between you and it, we can free you from it."

Victoria frowned. "You'll just let it go? But it's crazy. Look at it."

"We want to escort it. Give it room to move but be by its side. See where it wants to go, but—"

"But?"

"But we need you to tell it."

"No. I'm not going near that thing." Victoria violently shook her head.

"Listen to me." Kelly jumped up from the bed and grabbed her shoulders. Then, he got down on his haunches to meet her at eye level. "Listen, you're the only one the psycho salamander will listen to. With the other animal, K'in, he—it—understood me. Not necessarily through language, but he knew what I meant. I need you to tell it we are going to let it go where it wants—escorted—on our terms. If it farts and my nostrils are offended, it's back in the fish pond."

She stared at him. Her sclera-less eyes made him nervous. He couldn't tell whether she was trying to figure him out or was deep in her own thoughts.

Victoria turned her head to look at Wak. It was very still, pressed firmly against the glass as if listening to their conversation. Clumsily, she rose, her bare feet on the floor, and shuffled with her head down toward the tank.

Kelly watched her intently. She reached the glass and stopped, her head still slung low. Kelly watched as her shoulders rose and fell quickly with nervous breathing. Victoria took a final deep breath and exhaled before facing the animal. She clutched at the space where her crucifix used to be. Remembering it wasn't there, she grabbed one of her hair braids instead.

Wak lowered itself to meet her, eye to eye.

There was a lasting silence.

Kelly sat again on the edge of the bed, careful not to make the mattress springs groan.

"You understand me, don't you?" Victoria wasn't asking.

Wak didn't move.

"I know you do. I can feel you do. That must mean you know I despise you, too. I hate that you're in my head, in my body. You make me feel sick. And I want rid of you. Do you hear me? I want my life back."

Kelly strained to listen. She was speaking too quietly—like she didn't want him to hear.

"You want out of here. I can feel you're trapped. You want to escape. So we both want something. These people will let you go where you want. They will take you. And I will be rid of you. We both win. If you fight, it will be back in the tank for you. Do you understand me?"

Wak stared at her through the glass. She breathed away her fear. It understood. She couldn't say how she knew that, but she did.

Victoria turned slowly to face Kelly and nodded sheepishly. "Okay."

Kelly nodded back. "That was very brave, Vicky."

"Can we get out of here? I don't want to be in the same room as it anymore."

"Of course."

She shuffled to him. Kelly placed his arms around her shoulder and walked her toward the door. Upon opening it, they were met by a guard and Freya standing in the corridor.

"Sir, the woman cannot leave. Doctor's orders."

"Pal, you best get the fuck outta my way. I ain't gonna ask twice." Kelly clenched his jaw and shot Freya a look she knew well.

"It's alright, she can't run anywhere. Let them go." Freya stepped aside.

Kelly walked Victoria through the gap and gave Freya a nod of both gratitude and confirmation that Victoria had done as asked.

Freya watched as the pair trundled away down the dark passageway.

"Something wrong?" Minya asked.

The Russian's silky accent didn't startle Freya, but she had been so intently watching Kelly that the woman's presence was unexpected—unwelcome.

"No, I just don't trust him. Something's not right. I know Kelly." Suddenly aware she was voicing inner thoughts to someone she wasn't really acquainted with, Freya snapped back to give full attention to the Russian woman.

"Can I help you with something?"

"*Da.* I was just wondering when you intend to move creature."

"Tomorrow, first thing. We're prepping a team. We'll move at first light." Freya eyed her. "Why?"

"I wonder if you really need me. Until now, I have not been much help."

"Actually, we'll probably need you more than ever. You are an expert on

CHILDREN OF THE FIFTH SUN

languages and, if I remember, some of the more *adventurous* scientific theories. Wherever the creature wants to go, I imagine it will be quite specific. Your skills will be needed, Dr. Yermalova."

Minya pursed her lips but did not respond.

A faint buzzing broke the tension.

Realizing it was her cell phone, Freya fished around inside her jacket pocket. Having retrieved it, she held it up briefly—the universal sorry, phone gesture—and walked away.

Minya could only make out part of the conversation. Someone was coming, and whoever it was didn't make the American woman comfortable. In fact, she sounded more stressed.

CHAPTER THIRTY-SEVEN

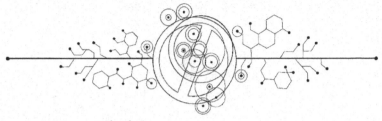

Location: Grozny, Chechnya

Sasha sat in the Ansyr as it gunned along the dusk-lit dirt road, past derelict apartment buildings, on the outskirts of Grozny. The battered moonscape of this province bore no resemblance to the city center. Thanks to regular financial transfers from Moscow, Grozny now flaunted a 32-storey luxury hotel, designer boutiques, karaoke bars, and scantily clad women tottering around in high heels. But here, the aftermath of the separatist wars with Russia could not be hidden. The sight of piles of broken cars atop one another and poorly dressed children cycling through the garbage sickened Sasha. But this was where his mission had led him—to the Chechen Mafia.

One of the largest organized crime groups operating in the former Soviet Union, the Chechen Mafia's sphere of influence now extended from Vladivostok to Vienna. Originally fighting for Chechen independence from Russia, their purpose was now blurred. For Sasha, it was still not clear whether they fought for an independent nation-state or were more intent on continuing regional instability.

The Chechens had gained support from the Islamic world. Fighters from many Arab countries had volunteered their services. Intelligence reports even suggested some militants wanted to establish an Islamic state across the North Caucasus. Sasha even had tried to link Chechen insurgents with Al-Qaeda but with little success.

Besides standard organized crime activities, car theft and money laundering, the mafia had now become involved in trafficking Chinese immigrants and the illegal sale of nuclear material such as plutonium and uranium. It was due to the latter activity that Sasha now approached one of their facilities. He needed what they had.

The vehicle ground to a halt, spraying gravel from beneath locked wheels. Swiftly, the Polkovnik and his men exited and spread out in formation, weapons in hand. Their stealthy advance belied their enormous builds as their huge boots failed to disturb the rubble underneath them.

The sky had now darkened, offering additional cover and allowing the night-gear-clad men to creep between the shadows. In quick succession, the troops surrounded the gray-walled compound. Covering every exit and blind spot as they moved, the team surged silently into the inner courtyard. Sasha followed quickly behind. The giant metallic double doors pushed open relatively easily. No one was inside. Sasha signaled the first wave of men in. They scurried inside and took up positions behind concrete pillars and large pieces of industrial machinery. Still, there was no one to be seen.

The Polkovnik stepped cautiously into the cavernous room and surveyed his surroundings. In the center of the derelict-looking space sat row upon row of tall, cream-colored, metal cylinders. The makeshift construction was at least ten tubes wide and easily one hundred long. One thousand tubes daisy-chained together, stood on end like the bristles of a giant toothbrush. Sasha knew this machine was nothing so innocuous. It was a series of gas centrifuges, each containing toxic uranium hexafluoride and designed to separate atoms with weights of 238 from those with 235. The latter being required to create a nuclear bomb.

A clang in the corner of the room jolted Sasha from his study of the gargantuan mechanism. He pulled his firearm and signaled to his men to be on alert; they were not alone. With adrenaline rushing through his body and his heart beating fiercely, he rounded the corner of the machine and pointed his gun straight ahead.

A skinny black cat bolted for the exit, startled by the Polkovnik's quick movement.

"*Yebat,*" he cursed under his breath.

A lone bullet squealed off the metal piping next to Sasha's head and ricocheted before becoming embedded in the concrete of a nearby wall, debris spraying across the cold floor. Sasha instinctively ducked and yelled a command to hold fire. They could not risk puncturing the cylinders and releasing the radioactive gas. Single, controlled headshots only.

The team circled around the machine to approach from the rear. Another barrage of ammunition and shrapnel shattered through the room, exploding brickwork and screaming off the metal cylinders. The Russian team took cover behind the pillars and the uranium centrifuge in hopes their assailants would exercise a little more caution around the radioactive elephant in the room. They did not. Instead, a hand grenade was tossed between the cylinders.

One Russian soldier scrambled underneath and forced his arm through a tight gap in the metal framework holding the contraption together. He strained and growled as he struggled to place his fingers around the deadly device. Sasha held his breath.

Moments later, the soldier jumped up from the ground and lobbed the grenade as hard and as far as he could through the doors to the outside. It exploded midair, blasting the doors off their hinges but miraculously did not affect the centrifuge. Sasha exhaled in relief.

These guys were not Chechen. They had to be fundamentalists—willing to blow themselves and their whole operation to hell if they needed to. He gathered his thoughts. How to do this? It was dark. And their enemy's shots were pretty accurate. That would suggest night-vision goggles. Crouching to the floor, he signaled to his lead soldier: disorientation. The man complied and relayed the silent message via hand gestures to his comrades. A few seconds later, the entire crew had taken the black cylinders from their belts and waited patiently. Sasha nodded once.

In unison, the Russians pulled the pin on their flash grenades, counted to five, and tossed the grenades straight in the air before covering their faces. A massive, blinding, magnesium-white light exploded in the air—an Earth-bound supernova.

Screams from the Chechens filled the room as their night vision goggles amplified the intense burst of light, burning their retinas. The Russians seized their opportunity and stormed around the centrifuge into the room behind, stomping on and pistol-whipping Chechen Mafia thugs in their path.

A single man, tubby and Middle Eastern, was backed against the far wall, a Kalashnikov in one hand and a grenade in the other. He said something in an Arabic language that none of the soldiers understood, but it was panicked and accompanied by the waving of the grenade.

Sasha walked calmly into the room and between his soldiers. The man's ranting became more enthusiastic and his gesticulations more overt. Without even breaking his gait, Sasha put a bullet in the man's shoulder, which exploded in a mess of flesh. The man screamed and slumped to the floor, dropping the assault rifle. Sasha crouched down to eye level with the whimpering man and pried the grenade, pin still in place, from his hand. This mafia member definitely didn't look Chechen or, for that matter, Russian. "*Ty govori 's' po-russki?*"

The man didn't answer but turned his whimpering face away in defiance.

Sasha held out one hand. One of his men placed the pommel end of a knife into it. Swiftly, Sasha drove the blade into the top of their prisoner's knee. The man screamed as blood poured from his wound.

Sasha kept hold of the pommel and stared into the man's eyes. "English, then? You understand if I twist this knife, how much it is going to hurt?"

The sweaty, whimpering man nodded.

"Good. Where is the warhead?"

The man sniveled some more and hesitated to provide an answer.

The Polkovnik twisted the blade a quarter of an inch to the right.

The prisoner cried out as the wound opened, and the tip of the blade ground against his femur.

"Did you not understand the question?"

"Yes, yes!" the man replied, panting and crying. "There is no bomb. We were not finished. We only just distilled the gas. Right … right now it's the uranium metal."

Sasha sighed and raised his eyes to meet the gaze of his men. "This is good news. Moving the metal is much easier than moving an entire warhead. Where?"

The man nodded toward the back of the room, where a large, industrial-looking chest sat on the floor.

Sasha peered back over his own shoulder. "In the trunk?"

"Yes, yes. It's in there."

"Thank you." He stood up, shot a glance to the soldier next to him, and marched off toward the chest.

The clap of gunfire echoed in the room, but Sasha didn't flinch. He was too focused on the prize.

He approached the chest and stared down at it before pulling out his cell phone. He pressed a single digit and raised the phone to his ear. "I have it. Yes, it is transportable." As Sasha spoke, his attention was drawn to three words haphazardly painted across the front. *That's not possible, is it?* He had not been expecting this. They read: *TEAK AND ORANGE.*

Location: Dulce Base, New Mexico, USA

The dawn sun slid upward into the sky, dividing the view into three disconnected horizontal bars: the black sand, the orange-red streak above it, and the powder-blue sky presiding as the uppermost layer. But it offered no warmth, and the cold breeze whipped over the dunes.

The caravan of four HMMVWs, each furnished with an M134 minigun operated by a lone soldier, created a square defense net around the entrance to the barn. A team of ten heavily armed troopers, dressed head-to-toe in desert combat gear, filled the gaps between the vehicles. Within the circle of safety stood Lucy, Freya, Minya, and Victoria, who were huddled up to Kelly. They waited for Dr. Parnham to arrive at the surface. He was to be escorted by two armed guards who were ordered to kill the animal that would accompany him, should it be necessary.

"Do you think it's going well?" Kelly asked.

"I have no idea, Mr. Graham—sorry, Kelly. We are taking a huge risk, but I am really not sure what choice we have at this point." Lucy wanted so badly to find a humane way to deal with the situation, but her gut told her this venture had a high chance of going sour.

"How will they bring animal to surface?" Minya scanned the opening to the barn, hoping to see movement inside.

"This will be the relatively easy part. A small, tube-like aquarium will be brought up in the elevator. Wak will be inside. The difficulty will be when it is released to roam free."

Kelly glanced at the Secretary. She was a brave woman—naïve but brave. Going against the grain and trying to do some good was not at all how he had imagined a politician to be. And for his part, it worked in his favor. Once the animal was loose, Kelly would make his move.

The elevator slid up through the floor of the barn. Kelly craned his neck and strained his eyes to see just a little better. He unconsciously held his breath as the doors glided open. Dr. Parnham was standing inside—alone. Kelly huffed in disappointment.

The doctor fiddled with his ill-fitting tie and stepped out onto the dusty ground. The elevator doors closed with a faint whoosh. The elevator then disappeared back underground.

"Doctor?" Lucy asked, expectantly.

"It was too small inside for me, Wak, and the guards. And they wouldn't leave me alone with it, so they're coming up behind."

On cue, the elevator hissed out of its hole in the ground again. The doors slid open, revealing two armed soldiers, one either side of a thin, water-filled, transparent tube. Wak was squashed inside, its bulky frame pressed against the glass.

"Nice, guys, piss it off before we even start. Look at it!" Kelly pointed at the animal.

"We're working on a bit of a tight timeline, Mr. Graham. We didn't have time to prep the delivery system. You wanted to move quickly, yes?" The doctor's tone was laced with sarcasm. Following this idiot's idea was not what he had in mind. But the Secretary's instructions were clear.

"Look, pal. You ever been hooked up to a giant salamander?" He didn't wait for an answer. "Well, I have. We need Vicky away from this thing ASAP. We ain't got time to follow all your dumbass protocols."

Victoria fidgeted on the spot, her frightened gaze fixed on the animal.

Kelly backed off the doctor and put his arms around her. "It'll be alright. Psycho salamander is going on a trip."

Freya watched in anticipation. Adrenaline coursing through her veins. She shifted her weight to feel for the Berettas strapped under her jacket.

"You know, this is nuts. I'm really not comfortable with this." The doctor had sidled up to Lucy.

"I know, Doctor, but what else do you suggest? If we try to leash the animal, I think we'll anger it and cause more damage. We need to give it some room, and let it follow its instincts."

"And what if its instincts are to kill you?" the doctor asked.

Lucy didn't answer. She didn't want to consider that.

The doctor gave Lucy a last glance, a silent plea for reason. But she didn't make eye contact. He sighed and started toward the glass tube. He stopped in front of it, and exhaled slowly. He caught the eye of the guard on the left, a blonde man a little older than one might expect in a low rank. "Tom, right?"

"Yes, sir. Tom Radley, sir."

"When I open this, you'd better be ready, Tom."

The soldier smiled. "I got this, sir."

The doctor reached above the tube to the two-inch high, black ring that crowned the top. He pulled back a small panel and punched a few large keys in specific succession. "There. Here we go." He stepped back and to the side.

A sharp sibilant sound filled the air as the seal on the tubing ruptured. A previously unseen seam appeared along the exact vertical center of the glass. The two halves parted but only by a crack. A blade of water sprayed from the thin slit, slowly emptying the tube of its contents until, all too soon, the animal inside was resting with its hind legs on the floor and its forelimbs pressed against the inner transparent surface.

A faint clunk ended the expulsion of water, and the glass doors slid backward, following the contour of the tube. Wak fell forward heavily onto all fours. For a moment, it seemed dazed—confused—but then it passed. Quickly, it padded forward into the dawn light. It squinted, protecting its eyes, before scanning the horizon. Each and every one of the humans watched it with fascinated and worried stares.

"Are we ready?" Lucy asked.

"As ready as we'll ever be," Freya replied. "Okay, people, give it some room!" She waved her arms back, indicating the soldiers should back off.

The doctor, frozen to his spot, breathed as quietly as possible, not wanting to draw attention. Wak stepped cautiously forward. One step at a time. It scanned left and right until its search found her—Victoria.

Her stomach knotted as the animal's stare bore into her. "Kelly, it's staring at me." She shrank back into his embrace.

"I know, I know. It'll be gone soon."

It came a step closer, but then, a powerful spasm took hold of it. Its neck twisted to the side, and its eyes screwed shut.

Kelly decided its epileptic fit was his chance. It's now or never. Kelly launched himself at Wak, his arms outstretched to grab it by the gills. His right hand managed to grasp a filament, but his left missed, slapping the animal in the back.

"Kelly, no!" screamed Freya.

The soldiers immediately focused their aim, their trigger fingers twitching.

Kelly wrestled with the animal as it flailed its head. "Bond with me, you ugly fucker!" yelled Kelly, struggling to keep his grip.

With a powerful hand, it grabbed him by the throat and flung him like a rag doll into the dirt. Kelly lay there, rolling on his back, struggling to breathe through his crushed trachea. Wak snapped its sights back to Victoria and bounded toward her.

"Fire!" Freya ordered.

The soldiers obeyed, unleashing a firestorm on the animal.

Lucy shrieked. "No!"

With speed unknown by any human, Wak pounced, slid and darted amongst the ammunition. It leaped at the nearest soldier, grabbing him by the head. The man screamed as the immense creature pulled on his skull until his neck broke.

The firing stopped. Everyone froze. Wak surveyed the circle of men. Freya, breathing heavily, eyed her men. *Shit. What to do?* There was no more time to think.

Having sized up the opposition, Wak moved swiftly and in calculated succession through the ring of soldiers. Necks were crushed, spines snapped, and abdomens ruptured as the animal tore through the humans with its powerful arms.

The soldiers fired wildly but never hit the animal.

A young man who had been operating the minigun atop a Humvee slumped off the roof, leaving Wak in his place. It sat there, perched on all fours, surveying the remaining humans from its elevated position. The last few soldiers fixed their sights on the animal but stayed still.

Kelly clambered to his knees, still nursing his throat. "Jesus." He wheezed. "Yo, Tom, I thought you had that?"

The soldier shrugged sheepishly.

"What the hell, Kelly?" Freya whispered.

"I was trying—"

"Forget it. Just stand still, dammit," she ordered through gritted teeth.

Kelly did as he was told.

"Now what?" Lucy said, her eyes wide, absorbing the carnage around her.

The animal dropped from the roof of the Humvee to the ground and again eyed the statue-like humans. It padded slowly forward toward the cowering Victoria.

"Kelly?" Victoria's voice trembled.

"Vicky, don't move." He edged in her direction.

Wak, spotting Kelly's movement, accelerated forward and locked Victoria against its body with one hand. With the other, it blocked Kelly's attack and shoved him away, once again into the dirt. Carrying Victoria, who had now passed out, Wak sped off past a truck and into the desert. The woman, clutched to its side, flapped like a child's toy, her braids flailing in time with the animal's gait.

For a long moment, no one spoke.

Freya's eyes had glazed over as had everyone else's. The sheer overwhelming speed with which Wak had dispatched the entire team and stolen Victoria was beyond belief.

As always, Kelly was the first to break the silence. "We gotta go after her."

"How, Kelly? How? It murdered our whole team. You wanna go after it, just us? With what? One vehicle? God damn it, Kelly!" screamed Freya in frustration.

"Look!" Kelly shouted. "That thing was never gonna let her go. I did the only thing I could think of, all right? It was a bad call—"

"Bad call? It's a massive fuck-up! Look around you."

Lucy emerged from her stupor. "This isn't going to help anyone. We have to calm down and regroup." She marched to the doctor who was standing, quite limp, in the doorway of the elevator in the barn. "Doctor, can you track it?"

He shook his head slowly. "No."

"What?" Freya said.

"We tried to implant a tracking device before, but its tissue rejected it— actually, it expelled it. That's why we had a whole team to follow it. Oh, God."

"Give me a goddamn truck, then. I'll follow it. Just gimme the—"

The deep growl of an engine cut Kelly short as a jeep careened onto the scene, spraying dirt everywhere. The engine stalled, stopping the vehicle dead. There was a lasting wait. Minutes passed before the driver's door swung open. Against the now fully risen sun, the silhouette of Jonathan Teller emerged. He slipped his cell phone back in his pocket and marched toward them.

CHAPTER THIRTY-EIGHT

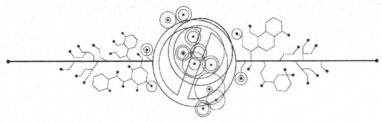

Location: Dulce Base, New Mexico, USA

Minya sat on a creaky bed that was placed against the back wall of the room they had given her to wait in while they reformulated their plan. The Americans were hospitable enough, but she'd never really liked them. They were loud and annoying—everything she hated about being around people. Plus, they traveled the world making a nuisance of themselves. It was uncomfortable being near them.

Kelly was particularly annoying. A sincere word never seemed to pass the man's lips, just snide or sarcastic jibes. Alejandro had warned her about him, but she hadn't fully understood just how infuriating Kelly was. Sometimes, she got the feeling he was deeper than his outward appearance, but it was fleeting. His protective layer of bullshit was so thick, she almost didn't believe there was room for anything underneath.

Still, protection was something that made sense to her. Keeping the past hidden was vital. No one would understand. How could they? She did what she did to survive.

She had been initiated into criminal life at a young age as a drug mule for her uncle. In those days, young girls weren't necessarily suspected of packing a kilo of cocaine in their satchels. She hadn't wanted to do it. In fact, she loved school and was a child prodigy. She excelled at languages and in science, though it hadn't mattered at that point.

At the age of sixteen, she'd gone to jail but not just any jail. Her skills had landed her in a remote Gulag prison. A remnant from the first half of the twentieth century. As with all Soviet plans at the time, the Gulag prisons were initially devised to weed out counter-revolutionary and criminal elements, imprisoning those who stood against communism. The system put the prisoners to work—correction by forced labor. And if you had special skills, you went to a special prison.

But the system was quickly abused and became a substantial economic pillar in Soviet society. As time went on, the prison camp conditions became worse and worse, particularly in the north. Almost three million people died in the prisons before they were *officially* dissolved in the late fifties. But a few had remained in the outskirts.

The conditions were disgusting and freezing temperatures in tiny shacks with no food compounded her depression. The camp had prisoners from across Russia, Siberia, Uzbekistan—everywhere. The guards used her to communicate with the prisoners, and the prisoners used her to communicate with each other. And they all wanted to buy and sell contraband.

For two years, she avoided rape, using her language skills to talk her way out of situations or making sure she was always working for the prison master as late as possible—until her eighteenth birthday. On that day, one of her cellmates had offered to tattoo a rose on her shoulder. It was an old tradition in the Gulag prisons. A symbol for young prisoners, showing they had lost their innocence to the penal system. The ink had been made from melted down boot heels mixed with urine. A dull needle then punctured her flesh over and over to form a crude flower under her skin. She had cried herself to sleep that night—until one of the guards had come into her cell. Apparently, there was another tradition for those young girls who spent their eighteenth birthday in a prison. She hadn't even fought him. At that point, she had given up all hope and just let it happen. She couldn't even remember his face.

The next four months had been a blur. Her memory of that time was fragmented and distorted. She had lived like a zombie, moving through her work and chores day-to-day without really engaging with the world. Though she never had the energy to cut her own wrists or create the noose to hang herself, she wished for death. But this was already hell. There was no point in swapping it for eternal damnation. Nothing would change—until *he* came.

He'd been known to buy labor from the Gulag prisons. After all, it was cheap for the outsiders, and the prisons needed funding now the government had all but abandoned them. On the day she had been lined up with a few of the other prisoners—stock to be chosen from for an important job—he walked in and, having taken one look at her, decided he wanted her to work for him. Not only that, but he'd paid to get her out under the condition she work for him and do whatever he asked of her.

There had been no second thought, no pause. Perhaps God had shown mercy. Perhaps it was fate. However it came about, it was an opportunity.

Minya brushed her red-brown hair across the back of her head and fished out the communication device from her pocket. There were no new messages. There had been no contact for a few days. It was unlike him. He always checked in. It worried her. She scowled, stuffed the device back into her pocket and paced the room. She hated it here. Not only was she stuck with many people she didn't like, but they were deep underground, too—maybe that's why she couldn't receive his message. Plus, it was claustrophobic, and she needed a cigarette.

The guards had been pretty lax about letting her topside. But then again, where would she go? They were in the middle of the New Mexico desert. She brushed her hair back once again and stomped out of the room and down the corridor. Upon reaching the elevator, she was met with the same soldier she saw every time she left. He'd introduced himself as Tom Radley. It had been difficult to place his age—not that she cared. He was overly familiar and wore an annoying grin every time he saw her. Did he know who she was? His poor attempts at flirtation, commenting on her "beautiful almond eyes" or "amazing bone structure only Russian women have" had fallen on deaf ears. For one thing, she was Siberian. For another, she hated ninety percent of people—especially men.

"Evening, Ms. Yermalova," Tom said, beaming.

Minya eyed him and gave the weakest smile she possibly could.

"Cigarette break?"

"*Da*," was all she could be bothered replying.

"Sure. You want me to go with you? That creature could still be up there."

"No," she replied and then decided to add, "*Spasiba.*"

"Okay, as always, five minutes before I come get you."

Minya nodded and stepped into the elevator.

The door hissed closed behind her. It lifted quickly upward, and then jerked to a halt. The doors slid open, revealing the cool desert. Its orangey sand spread out for miles and miles in a lonely expanse. She loved the peacefulness.

Stepping outside, Minya lit up a cigarette and took a long drag. The nicotine seeped through her lungs and into her bloodstream, instantly relaxing her. It was a habit she'd picked up in prison and ended up relying on—she hated that.

She pulled the communication device from her pocket and glanced at the screen—still no message. *Yebat. Bistro! Bistro!* Where was he? Minya sucked on her cigarette again. Why the hell was she here? She didn't want to be. She should be back home. But this was what she deserved for getting caught up with the Chinese. She was tied to them by the funding of her last dig in Siberia and now to the Americans through a chance encounter a year ago.

She glanced at her watch. Already six minutes had passed. *Damn.* She huffed, took a last drag of her cigarette and flicked the stub off into the sand before stepping back inside the elevator and descending back underground.

Location: Somewhere on the Rio Grande, Texas, USA

The enormous creature slipped out of the river and onto the shale bank. Dark stones littered the soft silt and extended back ten or fifteen feet to meet the dense tree line. Rows and rows of tree-filled mountains were painted against the cloudy, blue sky. Wak laid Victoria on the ground and slinked off a few feet to sit by itself. Keeping guard, it breathed heavily and rested its aching muscles.

A light, chilly breeze licked at the river's surface and across Victoria's wet skin. She shivered and opened her eyes. Her head was laid in the shale, her body curled up in the fetal position. She glanced around. Where was she? Where was the creature? Had she passed out again? Sitting up, she concentrated harder on understanding her environment. They were still following the river, but the air carried another scent—salt. She lifted her nose and closed her eyes. The power of the scent was strong. It filled the back of her throat so she could almost taste it. The sea. They were close to the sea. It was comforting like home. She inhaled through her nostrils, filling her lungs to capacity. Holding the wonderful atmosphere in her chest, she opened her eyes. Opposite her, she saw the creature mimicking her movements exactly. Its chest puffed out, full of sea air.

Victoria exhaled quickly, her fear leaving her as the air did. Was she enjoying the experience or was the animal? Which were her thoughts and emotions, and which were its? It was so hard to tell—to separate. She clutched for her invisible crucifix and then her braids. What did the animal want? To escape to a place she did not know? But for some reason, the closer they got, or perhaps the farther away from Dulce Base, the less scared she became. It was inexplicable and abhorrent. The mere fact she was attached to this monster was vile. Why had God forsaken her? What had she done? Was this punishment for the wrong she had done in her life?

The grating of stone on stone drew her attention to the animal. Wak had begun to stalk toward her. Slowly, cautiously, Victoria shuffled away, just a few inches. But the animal came closer. Its deep red eyes studied her, noting every curve and flaw of her face. Victoria's insides burned as the animal's mind penetrated hers, its emotions pouring into her very being—fear, anger, sorrow.

Victoria frowned. Sorrow? The animal could feel sorrow? For what? Its actions? For killing those men? For invading her soul? She stared further into its eyes. "What do you want?" she whispered.

Wak backed off slightly and sat on its rear end, its front legs straight like a dog. Victoria found this odd, even amusing. She cocked her head to the right. Wak copied her. She cocked it to the left. Again, the animal mimicked her movement. Was it trying to communicate?

A powerful seizure gripped the animal, its neck muscles spasming, pulling its head to the side. Its eyes screwed shut as if the pain were excruciating. Victoria felt the fear in the animal and the confusion. It didn't understand its seizures. They frightened it.

For a brief moment, Victoria's heart ached in sympathy. But the feeling was snatched away as the seizure ended, and once again, she sensed anger emanating from the beast. It added to her own anger. Why had this happened to her? She had been a good Christian all her life. Sure, everyone slipped sometimes—made the odd mistake or was unable to control their thoughts. But she'd kept her lust for Kelly under control—for years. And that had been before she'd learned about his deceased wife and daughter.

After Kelly rescued her on the beach from the elephant seal, she'd become a little infatuated with him. He was both a mentor and an object of desire. He flirted and was cheeky but never crossed the line. She'd always supposed this was because he respected his teacher-like status. Of course, now she knew otherwise. He had been grieving his loss.

Victoria remained still on the shale shore. She watched Wak. It stared at her as if it knew she needed rest before it was to continue. Of course, it would continue, and she, of course, had no say in the matter. It would drag her along. At least, that was how it had been up until now. Yet, as she rested, a morbid curiosity formed. She needed to see where the animal wanted to go—where it wanted to take her. If this was truly God's plan for her, perhaps she should see it through.

Her stomach growled, breaking her chain of thought and startling Wak. She wrapped her arms around her midriff, trying to muffle the sound, almost embarrassed. Wak focused its attention on her and then on the river. Swiftly, it darted from its spot and plunged into the running water.

Victoria hesitated. Where had it gone? Had it been frightened off? She craned her neck to see farther, scanning the river's rushing and foaming surface. The creature burst from within the river, spraying Victoria in a foam of water. It landed expertly in front of her. Her heart leaped into her throat, and she froze on the spot, glued to the gravel beneath her.

In its mouth, Wak held a large fathead catfish. Over three feet in length, it was a mottled gray color and sported a multitude of whisker-like projections on its snout and lower jaw. It flapped and struggled, gasping for oxygenated water. Wak crunched down on the animal, and the struggling ceased. Victoria turned her head away in disgust.

Wak dropped the catfish onto the shale in front of Victoria and, using its nose, nudged the lifeless creature. It wanted her to eat it. Victoria stared at the slimy teleost and then at Wak. The huge beast's face looked almost hopeful as if this gift would endear it to her. She frowned. What was the behavior from this animal? Altruistic or manipulative? Either way, it suggested intelligence. As she mused on the possibility she was anthropomorphizing the animal, her stomach growled again. This time it hurt.

She looked at the fish. She couldn't eat it, could she? It wasn't even cooked. But even as she argued with herself, she clasped her hands around it and lifted it to her mouth. Without thinking, she bit into the wet flesh and tore a jelly-like chunk from the carcass. The cold, uncooked meat slipped around inside her mouth until she allowed it to slide down her throat and into her stomach.

As she raised the fish once more for another bite, she caught sight of her fingers. They looked *different*. She pulled her hands away from her face and studied her digits more closely. There was something between her fingers, sticking them together. She dropped the catfish and pulled at the thin film of material between her first knuckles. It was attached. Panicked, she pulled harder at each one. It was webbing—her skin had webbing!

Victoria let out a bloodcurdling scream. "No! No! What's happening?"
Wak blinked, its face contorted in confusion.

She screamed again, but it was drowned out by the sound of rotor blades
slicing through the air. An Apache attack helicopter dropped out of the sky
and hovered no more than ten feet from the ground. Four soldiers dropped
out, their machine guns aimed at Wak.

"Don't move," the leader yelled over the drone of the helicopter. "Tell
it not to move."

Victoria instinctively put both hands in the air. "It doesn't listen to me!"

The soldiers, dressed entirely in black, their faces masked by camouflage
paint, edged toward the animal. With an incredible thrust of its hind legs,
Wak launched itself at the Apache and landed inside the hold that had just
contained the soldiers. The animal stomped its way to the pilot. Unable to
fire on their own chopper, the soldiers watched helplessly as Wak twisted the
neck of the pilot until it snapped. The helicopter span out of control and
immediately smashed into the river, its rotor blades hacking at the river bed
until eventually jamming.

The military team sprinted into the water after their comrade, searching
for the creature. It was gone. They scanned the wreckage, their guns always
following their line of sight, but they didn't see it. A gurgled scream pierced
the quiet only for a moment, and then there was silence—another soldier
gone. The remaining men circled the destroyed Apache, watching the others'
backs. It was to no avail. Wak, with incredible strength and speed, pounced
on each man in rapid succession, ending their lives before a single shot could
be fired.

Panting heavily, it plonked itself into the shallow water of the river and
stared at Victoria, its chest heaving. She dropped to her knees and sobbed in
desperation. There was no escape.

Location: Dulce Base, New Mexico, USA

In the control room at Dulce Base, Teller stared at the screen. Static stared
back. Sending in a strike force from Laughlin Air Force Base had seemed like
a good idea. He had made an educated guess the animal would use a major
river to move quickly, but needed to rely on satellite imagery, which was
always delayed. It was just good fortune Laughlin was so close. Or perhaps it
was bad luck. The speed at which Wak had taken out the Apache and the

team was astounding. All those lives. Gone.

The room was deathly quiet as each person struggled to comprehend the events they had just witnessed. Lucy and Dr. Parnham stood paralyzed at one end of the room, fixated on the large monitor. Kelly and Freya sat bemused at the opposite end. Minya was standing by the door, her arms folded across her chest. No one wanted to speak.

"That didn't go quite according to plan." Kelly couldn't bear the silence any longer.

"No," Teller replied. "I knew we should have taken it out from the air."

"That's not the objective, Mr. Teller," Lucy said. "We brought this animal into existence, and it deserves our respect."

"What about my men? Didn't they deserve respect?"

Lucy didn't reply. His argument was hard to refute.

"This won't get us anywhere," Kelly said. "We need to keep our distance, and let this thing run its course. Get a team in there and follow it."

"That will not be as easy as you hope. We can track it by satellite, but a new team is at least twenty-four hours out. If anything were to happen to Ms. McKenzie, there would be little we could do."

"Well, that ship has sailed, hasn't it, Captain Kirk?"

Teller calmly turned to face Kelly. "I believe our current situation is the result of your little escapade, Mr. Graham. Correct?" He raised one eyebrow.

"Hey, at least I'm doing something." The room fell quiet again.

"Kelly—"Freya began.

"Ah, fuck this." Kelly stormed out of the room toward his bunk.

"He's a liability," Teller said.

"He has his uses," Freya replied.

"I go find him," Minya offered, stepping out of the room after Kelly— anything to be away from the room full of people.

"No, I'll go," Freya said. "I don't trust you."

CHAPTER THIRTY-NINE

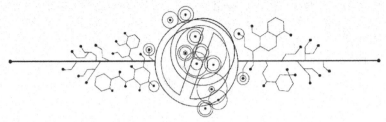

Location: Dulce Base, New Mexico, USA

Freya watched Kelly through the doorway. He was drinking that goddamn tea again—lost in his own thoughts, his own world. He still wasn't free of the pain of losing his wife and adopted child and now K'in as well. That had been the last straw. The bond between them had been strong. When K'in died, saving her, it had broken him.

She slid into the room, careful not to wake him, and cautiously sat on the floor by his side. His eyelids were fluttering. He was probably visualizing some crazy hallucination. She softly stroked his shorn head. The stupid man—for all his strength, he was the most lost person she knew. Yet when it came down to it, he was there for Victoria in her time of need. And he'd been willing to sacrifice himself to Wak for her. Always the hero.

He jolted awake, snorting.

Freya recoiled and let out a tiny yelp. She clenched her jaw and hit him in the arm. "You asshole, you scared the shit out of me!"

"I'm, uh, sorry." Kelly rubbed his head.

"What did you dream about this time?"

"Hair."

"What?"

"Hair," he repeated.

"Are you joking?"

Kelly wet his lips. "No, I saw hair. Lots of it. It was weird. The hair turned into ropes, and then I climbed the ropes and came to a huge place filled with blue light. Then I woke up." He held on to his stomach and groaned.

"You're not going to vomit, are you?" Freya asked, shifting away.

"I'll try not to." He feigned a smile. "Anyway, what do you want?"

"I just came to see how you are. I know this is all very difficult for you. I just wanted you to know I appreciate it." She put a hand on his knee.

"I don't think your boyfriend appreciates my help," retorted Kelly. "Or you touching me, I'd imagine."

Freya backed off. "Look, I'm just trying to be a friend."

"I don't need friends."

"Yes, you do. Everybody does. It wasn't so long ago that we …"

"Didn't take you long to move on though, right?"

Freya tightened her lips in frustration. "I asked you to stay."

"And I told you I couldn't."

"Then there was no reason to wait, was there?" Freya's eyes widened, waiting—hoping—for a crack in his stubbornness.

"But with the Star Trek nerd? Really?" He coughed and held his stomach, grimacing.

"Jonathan Teller is a brilliant man. He was transferred to the NSA after his skills in our little escapade were recognized. After some pretty intense testing, it turned out he's hyper-intelligent. In terms of warfare strategy, at least—"

"The guy that pulled a gun on you in Siberia?"

"He was doing his duty."

"Duty?" Kelly huffed. "Well, some guys put career first."

"And some guys stick around."

Damn. "He still has a thing for green women and guys with pointy ears," Kelly snapped.

"Everyone has something."

"Hey, whatever floats your boat. None of my business." He tried prying himself from the floor, but nausea overwhelmed him.

Freya's nostrils flared. "Whether or not you like it, Kelly Graham—"

"Not?" Kelly interrupted.

"What?"

"You said not."

"Well, yes, but I don't see—"

"Knot! Jesus, I'm stupid." He palm-slapped his own forehead and scrambled to his feet before tearing out of the room and down the corridor, leaving Freya dumbfounded and alone.

Teller stepped into the room, almost having been mowed down by Kelly, and clicked his cell phone off. "Where the hell is he running off to?"

Freya sighed. "I have no idea."

"Should we follow him?"

"I guess so. Whatever it is, it got him off his near-to-vomiting ass. Who was that on the phone?"

"No one important. After you, sweetie."

Freya groaned as she climbed to her feet and sauntered out of the door. "I told you not to call me that."

It was an easy taunt to deflect her question. He squeezed the phone in his fist and followed her down the corridor.

The couple meandered along the hallway, searching each of the rooms for Kelly, until they eventually found him outside the door of the security office, arguing with the guard.

"Look, pal, this whole thing is above your pay grade, so how about you just be a good little boy and let me in, huh?"

"Not interrupting, are we?" Teller asked in his ever-calm tone.

"I was just explaining to GI Joke here that I need to get inside the security office."

"It may help if you could tell us why you need to get in there, Kelly," Freya offered.

"The knots," Kelly replied.

"We're gonna need a bit more than that, I'm afraid," Teller said.

Kelly huffed in exasperation. "The knots," he repeated. "The knots in her hair. I don't know why I didn't see it before."

"Oh, sure, now it's clearer." Teller shrugged and shook his head.

"Just let us in, corporal. It's okay, we'll be with him," Freya said.

The young officer took a step to the side and swiped his card through a reader. The door lock popped. Kelly immediately snatched the door open and raced inside, startling the on-duty soldier, a rotund man in his mid-fifties, who looked like part of the furniture as if he had been at the facility long enough to have seen most things.

"Can you bring up footage of Victoria in the last few days?" Kelly asked.

The old soldier stared at Teller, who had followed Kelly through, and awaited instruction.

Teller nodded, indicating the officer should comply.

"Sure," he said, spinning in his chair and punching the keyboard in front of him. "What time frame do you want?"

317

"Just the last couple of days. I need a clear shot of her head from several angles," Kelly replied.

The soldier adjusted his wire-framed glasses and tapped in instructions, resulting in various images appearing on the multitude of monitors in front of him. They were stills of Victoria in the laboratory. She'd clearly been pacing, which had allowed the various cameras in the room to capture her from multiple angles.

"Okay, zoom in on that one and that one." Kelly's index finger left smudge marks on two of the screens, one showing the back of her head and the other showing her from the front. "Do you see it?" He shot a hopeful glance at Teller and Freya.

They leaned forward and stared harder.

"What are we looking at?" Freya asked.

Teller stood upright and rubbed his clean-shaven chin. "They're quipus."

"Exactly," exclaimed Kelly.

"Okay, boys, let the rest of us play," Freya said. "What are quipus?"

"Talking knots," Teller replied. "Very clever, Mr. Graham. It seems you do have uses."

"What are you talking about?" Freya demanded.

"Quipus." Kelly beamed, proud of his discovery and of redeeming himself. "Quipus are used as a three-dimensional, knowledge-recording system. Historically, they were used in Andean South America. Back then, a quipu was made of a bunch of colored thread or string twisted together to form a cord. The cords used knots of different sizes, colors, and spacing to encode information. Numbers, mainly."

"There's information in her hair?"

"Yes. My dream was trying to tell me, but I didn't see it. She's been subconsciously tying braids and knots in her hair."

Teller stepped up to the screen and began typing away.

"Can you decode it?" Freya asked, hopefully.

"I don't see why knot." Teller grinned at his own pun.

"That was lame, Teller," complained Kelly. "This guy? Really?" He glanced at Freya.

Freya scowled back at him.

Teller ignored the comment and carried on typing. The images on the screen became wireframe and colorless. The outline of Victoria's hair was isolated and pulled out from the still on its own. Then, with a few more key punches, the hair schematic was stretched flat, much like a map of the world being peeled from its spherical mount and flattened into two dimensions. He typed a few more key words, accessing a secure server, and stepped back.

"Is that it?" Kelly asked, somewhat disappointed.

"I've accessed the NSA's code-cracking program using quipus as the main decryption unit. Quipus are a base-ten positional system. It shouldn't be long."

As if on cue, numbers appeared below the various braids in Victoria's hair: *1 9 6 8 3 3, 9 8 8 5 0 0.*

They stared at the screen.

Freya squinted her eyes and cocked her head. "They're coordinates."

Teller nodded. "You're damn right. 19.6833 north by 98.8500 west."

"Jesus, why do you guys make me feel like I belong in remedial class?"

Teller and Freya exchanged an amused glance.

Kelly sighed. "Okay, brainiacs. Where do the coordinates point to?"

"Let's see." Teller tapped into the system again, bringing up a geolocator. He punched in the coordinates. An image of the globe spanned quickly and slowed over Central America. It zoomed in over Mexico City and then slightly south before coming to rest over a barren wasteland, punctuated by crumbling buildings that appeared uninterestingly square from the limited aerial view.

"Where is that?" Freya asked.

They studied the map for a few moments.

"Teotihuacan," Kelly said softly.

"You know it?"

"Yeah." Kelly nodded. "I was supposed to do a job down there. Chris wanted to go, but I didn't. So we never went. Selfish, really."

"Oh," was all Freya could say.

Kelly thought of his best friend. The pain in his chest returned. Shit, he missed him. He shook the thought from his head. "That must be where they're going."

"Okay, but why there?" Freya turned to Teller for an answer.

"Hmm. I'm not up-to-date on this one. But that's what the Internet is for, right?" Teller keyed Teotihuacan into a general search engine.

"You're Googling it? So much for the NSA." Kelly turned to Freya and mouthed, *this guy?*

Freya rolled her eyes.

"Sometimes, Mr. Graham," Teller began without breaking his concentration on the monitor. "You need to consider your best sources of information. This place is not exactly high on the NSA's watch list."

The screen filled with references to Teotihuacan. Teller scanned them, opening up various websites and personal pages. His eyes moved rapidly as he absorbed the information at lightning speed and then moved on.

"Okay. It seems that Teotihuacan was a large city in Mesoamerica during pre-Columbian times. Thought to have been built around 100 BC and lasted until around the 7th or 8th century AD, yadda yadda yadda ..." He scrolled through more. "Seems to be a lot of conspiracy theory and alternate history sites dedicated to this place. Some debate on when it was actually built, and no race of people was attributed to building it" More scrolling. "The name *Teotihuacan* was given to the place by the Aztecs long after it was built. It means 'the place of the gods' or 'where man met the gods.'"

"Stop! That's gotta be it—where Wak is taking her. C'mon." Kelly was already halfway out of the door.

"Wait, Mr. Graham." Teller put a hand on Kelly's shoulder but then dropped it, not wanting to anger him. "It's a massive tourist trap. I'll contact the local authorities in Mexico City and clear the site first. Then we can track them by satellite, ensure that really is their destination."

Kelly nodded. That made sense.

"Okay. And I want Minya with us. We brought her along on this little trip because she knows about this kind of stuff," Freya said. "We may need her to translate something."

"I'll find her," Kelly replied.

"Affirmative." Teller moved toward the door, his hand already fishing for his cell phone. "I want to move on this immediately. I need everyone prepped and ready in an hour. Grab the last of the team based here as well. We'll need them. Understood?"

Freya nodded. "I'll inform the Secretary."

Kelly gave a mock salute and marched out of the security office. Teller tried to follow suit, but Freya called after him.

"Jonathan?"

He paused, his hand still in his pocket, clasping the cell phone. "Yeah?"

"Have you spoken with my godfather? Do you know how he is?" She smiled weakly, hoping for good news.

General Benjamin Lloyd was still serving his sentence for his part in the original cloning debacle. He'd refused to see Freya, saying he was ashamed enough. Teller had used his influence in the NSA to keep tabs on the old man for her. He even convinced the General to allow Teller to visit once in a while. But recently, news of Freya's only family member had been thinner and thinner.

"No," Teller replied. "I gotta make a phone call. Can we talk about this later, sweetie?"

She wrinkled her nose at hearing the pet name again. He only ever used it to placate her. He may be around in body, but his mind was always elsewhere. "Sure." She offered him a weak smile.

He winked and slipped out of the door, pulling the phone from his jacket.

CHAPTER FORTY

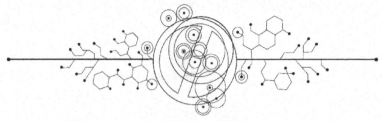

Location: 14K convoy, leaving Illinois, USA

The Shan Chu sat alone in the back of the truck. His brow was furrowed, and his eyes were closed as he tried to focus on his task. It was difficult to separate the hatred in his heart from his objective as the two were intertwined. He had been born into the Green and Red Societies. He knew no different. They were his family. When he had been seven-years old, his father had died in a gunfight in Hong Kong over a feud with another member, a pure-blood Chinese, a Red Pole, an enforcer—a dealer of death. His Japanese heritage had once again been a point of contention.

This enforcer had taken the son of the man he had killed as a prize and personal slave. For the first few years, it had been hell. He suffered savage beatings and humiliation at the hands of the pure-bloods. But as time had passed, he had proven his value. His abilities had become well known among his clan. He was first involved in collecting debts and protecting money for the Red Pole, and his reputation as a tiny assassin spread quickly. His unassuming size meant he was able to get close to his victims before he pulled out a small blade. Careful to kill only the family members of the individual who owed money, he always collected the debt.

His first kill, the young wife of a dry cleaner who wasn't paying his protection debt, was easier than he had ever imagined. He had simply wandered to the front door of her home and knocked on it. When she'd answered, she offered a smile at the small boy before her. He'd calmly asked if she was the wife of the dry cleaner. She'd nodded enthusiastically and enquired whether the boy had left something in their shop. He had plainly informed her that her husband owed his master money and she should give it to him. The woman's smile had faded and her tone had become that of a scolding mother.

This had irritated him and encouraged him into action probably faster than he would normally have chosen. The blade sliced across her pale exposed flesh with great speed. The woman crumpled to the ground, weeping and clutching at the wound that would not close—no matter how hard she pressed.

He stepped over her, grabbed her by the hair and dragged her wailing into the house before closing the door behind. He searched the house, but as it turned out, the couple really had no money. So he slit the throats of their three dogs and left. Two days later, the dry cleaner paid his debt.

There was no remorse, no guilt. In fact, all he could think about was his next kill and the feel of warm blood spraying onto his hands and face. Yes, this was his calling. He was Jia-nghù Tsai, the Tokyo Boy.

At the age of twelve, he was initiated into the brotherhood. The youngest member of his clan to undergo the ceremony, he readily sacrificed a pig at the altar of Guan Yu. He gulped the wine mixed with thick porcine blood so feverishly that much of it spilled over his face and tunic. With a crazed look in his eyes and his clothes stained red, he marched under the arch of swords held aloft by his Red and Green brothers while he recited the thirty-six oaths.

Now, more than twenty years later, he was the leader—the Shan Chu. And he was close to achieving the goal given to him by his father and his father's father—kill everyone who stood in the way of their ultimate supremacy.

A light buzzing pulled his gaze toward the cell phone on the seat next to him. He scooped it up and read the text.

Change of direction. Teotihuacan. They will be exposed. There will be a gap in the perimeter.

The Shan Chu rapped on the shoulder of his driver and gave the new directions. The man nodded and radioed to the rest of the convoy before checking his mirror and veering off at the next exit. The Shan Chu pulled on the sleeves of his jet-black Mao suit with gold-threaded buttons, rotating his shoulders. He didn't like unforeseen changes to the plan. The short communications didn't allow any explanation. On top of that, he had not heard from his team who had been tasked with obtaining the uranium. This made him nervous. He didn't like relying on foreigners in his coalition to do their part—their job.

He settled back in his seat and watched the desert sand whip past in the pale moonlight, contemplating. A thin and malevolent smile spread across his face. There was no need to fear. He had taken control of the situation now.

Soon, he would wield the power. He would have ultimate control.

Location: U.S. Chinook, somewhere over New Mexico, USA

Gunning along the skyline, the Chinook cut through the air, churning the cotton-like clouds as it went. Inside, the crew was decidedly quiet except Teller, who was completing his final transmission for the day with the Secretary, shouting loudly into his headset over the drone of the engines.

"Yes, Madam Secretary. We'll update you as we know more. Thank you. I wish us luck, too. Over and out." Teller lifted the cans from his ears and off his head, resting them around his neck. "Shit."

"What's wrong?" Freya asked.

"We have a problem."

"Which is?"

"Okay, so you remember how the Green and Red Societies were behind the viral attack on the U.S., and they were behind the attempts to retrieve K'in, the original clone—right?"

Freya nodded. "Sure."

"Well, it seems their leader has raised his ugly head and is coming for us."

"Hang on, I thought the military leader, the one who was killed by the Minister, was the source?"

"No." Teller shook his head. "He was a powerful pawn but nothing more than a pawn. The guy we thought may have been behind all of it is an international terrorist called 'Jia-nghù Tsai'—'the Tokyo Boy.'"

"Tokyo Boy? The Green and Red Societies are Chinese. What's the connection?"

"We believe his real name is Masamune Sagane. A great-nephew of the late Professor Ryokichi Sagane, a nuclear physicist at the University of Tokyo. Sagane was one of the scientists who studied with the Americans who created the atomic bomb."

"Okay."

"A little-known fact is that prior to dropping the bomb on Nagasaki, we dropped several instruments within which were copies of a letter to Sagane urging him to educate the public about the horrific effects the bomb would have. The professor received the letter a month after the bombing." Teller shook his head, imagining the destruction it must have caused. "The power of the atomic bomb could easily have been in the hands of the Japanese, but it wasn't. From his point of view, they had the ultimate weapon in their hands but lost it to the Americans. What is worse for Jia-nghù Tsai is a member of his family had it within his grasp and lost it. I don't have to tell you what that bomb did to the people of Nagasaki."

"What's that got to do with anything? Jonathan, you know I hate it when you're cryptic."

Teller huffed. "Let me finish. Look, Jia-nghù Tsai wasn't even born during World War Two, but at this time, Ryokichi Sagane's brother, Jia-nghù Tsai's grandfather, was about sixteen-years old and living in Manchukuo. It sits right in the East, overlapping Russia and China. In 1945, the Russians abrogated the peace treaty between them and Japan and launched a full-scale attack on Manchukuo."

"Every officer knows about the Manchurian Strategic Offensive Operation. Jonathan, I swear to God."

"Listen," he snapped. "Within three weeks, the Russians had wiped the Japanese out. Mothers were forced to kill their children and themselves rather than face the terrorism and rape the Soviet soldiers inflicted."

Freya squirmed.

"Jia-nghù Tsai's grandfather was orphaned during the fighting. He escaped and was picked up by the Green and Red Societies. He had several children of his own, all of whom were brought up within the Triad family. One of them was Jia-nghù Tsai's father. Hate was passed down from generation to generation. From birth, Jia-nghù Tsai has been indoctrinated to hate all foreigners. And he's been searching for the ultimate weapon, one even worse than the atomic bomb, to wipe us out."

"He thinks Wak is the ultimate weapon?" Freya said.

"Well, that's what we thought he was after. But—"

"But what?"

"The Secretary just told me the Chechen Government reported finding an illegal uranium enrichment plant on the outskirts of Grozny, and it's been completely destroyed. They had all the set-up to produce weapons-grade uranium."

"You think he's making a warhead?"

Teller shrugged. "I don't know. They tried to wipe us out with a virus a year ago. Perhaps this is their second attempt."

"A single nuke wouldn't do that."

"I know. Doesn't make sense to me either. And not only that. I mean, why Chechnya? China has enough power to wipe us out if they chose." Teller shook his head at the thought of a billion Chinese people being pissed at the U.S.

"The power the Green and Red Societies had within the Chinese Government died with the suicide bombing by the Minister. He took out the head of the People's Army, remember?"

"True," Teller said. "There was a bunch of dead Chechen Mafia guys left at the plant. They have been growing strong links with Islamic terrorist groups. Maybe it's a cross-border collaboration."

"But you just said the Chechens were dead?"

"Sure. But this guy is crazy. It could be a deal gone bad, or maybe he stole their material. Either way, he would have had help getting his thugs in and out of Chechnya. Not an easy task—unless they were local or local enough."

"Shit," was all that Freya could say before turning to stare thoughtfully out of the window.

Teller rubbed his hands together, processing the information in his head. He scanned the interior of the helicopter, studying his traveling companions. Kelly sat on his own at the end of one of the makeshift benches, his head tilted backward, resting on the padded wall. His eyes were closed, but Teller couldn't tell if he was asleep or not. Opposite him lay Minya, curled up in a ball, a light-gray jacket twisted around her torso and pulled slightly from her shoulders. She was snoring lightly, which was quite amusing to him since he wasn't sure he'd ever heard a woman snore before.

He then eyed each of the twenty-strong team he'd rounded up from the base. Dressed in black combat gear, they sat silently facing forward and mentally prepared themselves for whatever may come. They were good men, strong men, and he hoped they would be able to stand against the creature—unlike those who died along the Rio Grande.

It dawned on him he didn't even know the names of most of the men he had essentially stolen from Dulce Base. The only reason he knew Tom's name was he'd heard Kelly shout it out loud. In the end, only his mission mattered, and soldiers were expendable. First rule of strategic warfare—calculate collateral damage. At least, that was what he was supposed to do. It was difficult when emotions were involved.

His gaze was inevitably drawn to Freya. She was now in fatigues and heavy boots yet had one leg resting on the knee of the other—ever feminine. She was staring listlessly out of the porthole, her eyes flicking quickly as she focused on an approaching object, watched it zip by, then focused on a new object, and repeated the cycle.

Since he had arrived at the base, Freya had been a little odd. Or perhaps it was since Kelly had arrived. That man messed with her head. After Siberia, and Kelly's departure, Freya had been removed from the field. She'd been given a desk job in Washington. That was where Lucy Taylor had begun working with her. Considering Freya's involvement and experience in the situation, she was the perfect person to act as Lucy's right hand in dismantling the cloning project.

Similarly, Lucy had brought the project to the attention of the NSA. Teller, although their newest recruit, also had experience in the situation and was assigned to the task. He'd walked into the Secretary's office. The crest of America was emblazoned on the carpet, patriotic flags hung on the walls, and a large oak desk rested by the window. But his focus had been drawn to something else in the room—someone else—Freya.

He'd only ever seen her in field gear. Now, she wore a fitted skirt and collarless white shirt, and her hair was silky smooth and pulled into her signature ponytail. Her green eyes flashed in the evening sunlight that cut through the office windows.

She gracefully walked toward him, a huge bright-white smile on her face. "Officer Teller," she remarked, offering her hand. "Fancy seeing you here."

"Ms. Nilsson," he managed. "So nice to see you."

"I thought you'd be on a five-year mission." She laughed. "You know, to seek out new life and—"

"New civilizations?" he said, finishing her sentence. "Turns out I'm not into green women, just women with green eyes."

She nodded, her smile broadening at his clever—if comical—line.

It hadn't taken long for them to start dating. He liked her a lot. What's not to like? She was strong, interesting, and beautiful. He'd done his best to keep a relationship and work balance and even managed to help her by checking on the General, her godfather. This act of compassion had been the start of something bigger. His meetings with Benjamin Lloyd had become more and more frequent over time, and less and less about Freya. The more Teller learned from the General regarding the clone program, the more things made sense. In retrospect, Benjamin had realized his mistake and understood trying to enlighten humans was simply impossible. Instead, he had helped cause chaos and war, which was quite the opposite of what he had set out to do.

Thus, the General had begged Teller to end the program at all costs. He had reminded Teller it was his duty to defend his country against all enemies, foreign or domestic, even if it meant sacrifice—collateral damage. As a strategist, it made sense to Teller. It was logical. And logic was what was needed, not emotion.

That was why he'd had to distance himself from Freya. He was so close, and he couldn't let emotions get in the way right now. When it was over, he could concentrate on her. Right now, the mission was top priority. *The needs of the many outweigh the needs of the few*—a lame line from a TV show to some, a mantra for strategic warfare to others.

Freya dragged her gaze from the window as she sensed Teller staring. "You okay?" she asked.

"Yeah, sure. Just sorting out the events in my head. Our next move."

"Can't believe we're back in this situation. Feels like square one." She sighed.

"A little bit, I guess," agreed Teller.

"He asleep?" She nodded at Kelly, his neck awkwardly bent backwards, his mouth slightly open.

"I think so." Teller chuckled quietly. "Man, there's a photo op, huh?"

Freya smirked. "Be my guest. He'll be pissed when he finds out."

Kelly jerked but didn't wake. Instead, he squirmed in his seat, adjusting his head into a more comfortable position. Occasionally, his eyelids fluttered and clenched, and his limbs shook.

"Quite the dreamer," Teller remarked.

"Actually, it's probably nightmares."

"Ah, yes. I read your report. His dead wife, right?"

Freya nodded. Yes, at least he cares enough to be distraught she's gone.

"Is that what the tea is all about?"

"The Ayahuasca tea? I think so. At least in part." She shuffled to properly face Teller. "I think losing K'in was a breaking point for him. He's been trying to escape the loss."

"Well, he'd best stay out of the way. We can't have another incident like back at Dulce Base."

Freya thought back to the submarine in Monterey Bay more than a year ago. Teller had considered Kelly a secondary requirement to their mission even then. He had fired a torpedo at the Chinese sub, knowing Kelly was inside and might drown. He'd calculated the odds of success. It was what he did, and he was good at it. Emotions didn't come into it.

To her left, there was a man overflowing with emotion and in front of her, a man who seemed devoid of it at the flick of a switch. "He figured out the quipus, didn't he?"

Teller stared at her for a moment. "I guess so. Sometimes I just wish I had a Taser set to stun, you know? To shut him up."

Freya stifled a laugh. "Get in line."

The chopper banked sharply, waking Kelly. "Shit," he blurted. "I felt like I was falling. You guys have got to drop that," he mumbled, before rubbing his head and stretching. "I'm just Kelly."

Teller reached out a hand. "John," he said. "I don't think we were ever properly introduced."

Kelly shook his hand. Indeed, even in Siberia he had never asked the man's Christian name. He'd just enjoyed Teller's pokes at Tremaine, the grumpy bastard. Kelly hadn't thought about him in quite a while. They hadn't seen eye to eye, but Kelly respected Tremaine and his stalwart, almost Spartan demeanor—he was honorable. The world was a poorer place for his death. Kelly quickly changed the subject. "We there yet?"

"No, not yet. Soon, though."

There was an uncomfortable silence before Teller spoke again. "So, I guess you're our resident expert on being linked up to one of these beings. Anything you can tell us?"

Kelly eyed him. "Well, I hear you're a genius. Don't you know?"

Teller smiled. That must have come from Freya. "I'm just a nerd—with a good jawline, of course." He laughed, tilting his head to an imaginary camera and smoothing his chin.

Freya laughed as well. He could be cute when he wanted.

Kelly didn't respond.

Clearing his throat, Teller rephrased his question. "How about this? Can you give me your perspective?"

Pursing his lips, Kelly thought for a moment. "Okay," he said. "It's hard to describe, really, being linked up to it. I was whole. But I didn't realize that until after."

"After?" Teller asked.

"After K'in died. It was like the hole that had been left by the death of, well, everyone I loved had been temporarily patched. Then the Band-Aid had been ripped off and it was worse." He shook his head. "I did a lot of stuff trying to fill it in the last year. Lots of stuff for the locals, ya know? Maybe giving would make the hole go away. You know what I think? I think—"

He was stopped short by Minya, who bolted awake. Her eyes were wild as she searched the room, unsure of where she was.

"Ah, you're awake," Teller said.

Kelly eased backward against the wall, uncomfortable with another pair of ears listening to his inner thoughts. He watched as she fiddled with her jacket. As she pulled it straight, he caught a glimpse of a blue marking on her right shoulder.

"We were just talking about what it's like to be joined to one of the creatures," Teller said.

Minya acknowledged each person with a glance and sensed they expected her to say something. Don't make them suspicious. "There is school of thought," she said, breaking the quiet. "Called the Binary Soul Doctrine. It is perhaps the closest humanity has ever come to a single world religion."

Teller narrowed his eyes and Freya leaned forward.

Minya had their attention. "This doctrine," she continued, "has been present in many cultures from dawn of time. Thousands of years ago, peoples and tribes from all over globe believed almost the same thing—human beings possessed two souls."

Kelly's ears pricked up, though he was careful not to show an outward sign that his interest had been piqued.

"This can be seen in the earliest writings of Egypt, Greece, Israel, Persia, India, and even China." She placed her hands together in a meaningful gesture. "Greece called these two souls *psyche* and *thumos*. In Egypt, it was *ba* and *ka*. In Christianity, they are called the *soul* and *spirit*. The list is endless. *Ruah* and *nefesh*, *urvan* and *daena*—"

"We get the picture," Kelly interrupted.

Freya shot him a disapproving look.

Minya continued. "However, one version of the doctrine will be of interest to Mr. Graham."

"*Kell-y*," he enunciated. "Kelly, not Mr. Graham."

Freya rolled her eyes.

"The ancient Toltec civilization of Mexico believed whole world comprised two equal but opposite forces. They called it *Omeyocan*. It means 'place of duality.' They thought each man, woman, and child had two mental halves: the tonal and the nagual. For them, the purpose of human existence was to integrate them."

"Jeez, I thought you said I'd be interested," Kelly said. "Do you know what men like? Are you single?"

"I'm interested, Minya," Teller said.

She huffed, unsure of whether she should continue.

Kelly waved his hand in an *okay, go ahead* gesture.

She cleared her throat, feeling a nagging desire for a cigarette, and continued. "The terms nagual and tonal appear in other Mesoamerican belief systems. There are many studies and many interpretations, but often, a nagual was considered a human who could transform into an animal. In tonalism, which is sometimes linked to nagualism, all humans were believed to have an animal counterpart to which their life force was connected."

Kelly shifted on the bench.

"It seems these beliefs may have had some basis in truth if the creatures like the one we chase and the creatures you tell me existed thousands of years ago bonded with humans."

"Is that what it felt like? Like having another soul?" Freya was focused squarely on Kelly.

He opened his mouth to speak, but before words could follow, the chopper dropped sharply—and then dropped again.

Teller frowned as he put on his headset. What's going on?" he asked, cupping the microphone with his hand. He nodded a few times and pulled off the headset again. "We're here. Strong crosswinds. Gonna be bit of a choppy decent. Hold on."

"We land?" Minya asked.

"Looks that way," Kelly replied.

She nodded. "Okay." *Soon, it will be over. I won't have to be among them anymore.*

CHAPTER FORTY-ONE

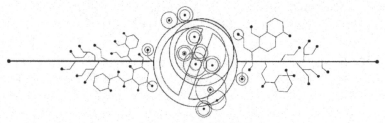

Location: Somewhere on the coast, Gulf of Mexico

The small rodent struggled in the iron grasp of Victoria's webbed hand. It squeaked and wriggled as much as its tiny body would allow until a final press of her thumb snapped the little thing's neck. Victoria crammed the entire mouse into her mouth and forced it down her throat, swallowing hard. She gasped as it cleared her esophagus, unblocking her airway. She scanned for more amongst the reeds of the estuary on which she crouched.

Her hunger burned inside, radiating outward from her stomach. The feeling was hard to describe. It was like a primal force of pure emotion egged her on to survive at all costs.

That small morsel had not been enough to quell it. But there wasn't anything else around. She had no idea where she was, never mind where she should look to find more. Yet, she was compelled to follow the creature, Wak. The monster no longer carried her, instead it merely slowed its pace. When they had transitioned from the river into the ocean, the massive animal had dragged her along as it swam. For how long, she could not be sure.

Dodging all contact with humans, it dove under the waves and hid in the shallow littoral waters whenever it felt the threat of a person. It had seemed odd to her that it avoided human contact. She had presumed it would want to kill. But no, it was fixated on a destination. She could feel that much. Exposure would likely mean failure.

After a day or so of swimming, they clambered into an estuary. The brackish mud deepened as they approached a port of some kind. Large ships carried massive metal containers in and out, their cargo delivered and taken by gigantic cranes. It was a hive of activity which made Wak uncomfortable. Strangely, it made Victoria uncomfortable, too. She was wary of the people and confused by their actions. She was constantly ready to surprise them—to attack them—in order to escape if necessary. But it hadn't been necessary.

Wak had been methodical, working the edges of the estuary. Wherever they were headed, there was no rush, only blind determination.

A ripple in the water drew Victoria to the edge of the mud, where freshwater and seawater mixed. She stared at her own reflection, obscured by miniature waves rolling across it. Her hair was no longer in braids. Instead, it fell about her face in a greasy, limp mess. Her pallid skin was clammy and smeared with dirt and grime. Crimson eyes stared back at her. But she wasn't repulsed. The reflection didn't feel like hers. It was someone else staring back—watching her. No, she was still inside this shell, this creation—somewhere.

God would find her. God would protect her. Wouldn't he? Perhaps not. She'd been defiled by the scientists and infected with the flesh of an animal. But she had to hold on and believe such things were sent to test her.

She closed her eyes and tried to remain calm, concentrating on the dark behind her eyelids. It wasn't calming. The nothingness was unnerving, scary even. Her heart beat faster, harder, drumming on her insides. Her breathing quickened, and her muscles tensed. She opened her eyes to see Wak beside her, also panicked and breathing rapidly, a look of anxiety on its face. She followed its gaze to two men who had spotted them and were walking their way.

"Hey!" one of them called. "Are you okay, lady?"

Victoria didn't respond. A mix of emotions emanated from Wak—a conflict between the desire to run and the thought of killing the men to protect itself. Fight or flight. But, why was it conflicted at all?

"Hey, lady? Are you okay? What's that thing?"

The men were now no more than fifty yards from them. They had stopped walking, studying her and the creature.

Victoria chose to run, turning inland as fast as the mud would allow her. Wak hesitated for a second and then bolted after her. But their limbs became trapped in the mud, sucking them into the bog.

The men, confused and assuming the animal was chasing her, followed, wielding a large screwdriver and wrench. Being much more suited to working in that environment, they quickly moved between rocks and areas of solid earth.

Victoria saw the advancing men would likely reach Wak first. She should have been glad—relieved. Perhaps they would save her. Instead, she was afraid—afraid they would hurt the animal—and then anger. Her anger turned to an uncontrollable rage.

She made a complete U-turn and trudged toward the men. They watched her, confused. A primal scream poured from her mouth as she leaped on the first man, driving him into the mud. With both knees on his stomach, she pounded at his head over and over until his weeping stopped and his skull caved in.

She looked up to view the other human, but he was already dead. Wak's massive hand was laid flat over the man's crushed face, his body contorted in an awkward upward diagonal from the mud.

Victoria's shoulders heaved with her breathing—with the rush of adrenaline. She searched the horizon through the lank hair that fell over her face. She searched for something else to kill. Inside, she knew she should feel guilt, but all she could find was bloodlust. Hunting—killing—felt good.

Location: Teotihuacan, Mexico

The cool desert wind whipped by the large green tent, flexing its thin walls. Gritty particles of sand sought out every gap and crawled their way in, filling the dwelling at a glacial pace. The orange disc in the sky was descending, taking with it the warmth of the day, leaving only the cold of the exposed land.

Still fully clothed, Kelly tossed and turned in his sleeping bag. His garments twisted and wedged themselves between the creases of his elbows, knees, and groin, making it difficult to be comfortable.

He huffed loudly and sat upright. This wasn't going to work. He couldn't rest anyway. It had been almost two days of waiting. He was thinking about Victoria and wondering if she was all right. Their chance meeting on the Amazon, more than a year ago, had resulted in her being dragged into this. Actually, her competitive nature had dragged her into this. Her need to prove she was every bit as good as her teacher-cum-rival. He hadn't asked at the time, but he was sure that was why she'd volunteered to come along on their little jaunt to the South China Sea in the first place some twelve months ago.

He thought back to their early time together. After he'd rescued Victoria from the elephant seal and she had followed him around for months on end, the flirtation had become more of a rivalry. When it had become clear he would never actually make good on his quick quips and cheeky remarks,

Victoria had channeled her energy into being just as good at her job as he was. And she was—at least at the photography. But she was never the diver he was. His freediving skills were unparalleled and highly desirable for taking pictures of marine animals that were easily scared by the exhaled carbon dioxide from standard scuba gear.

Eventually, she'd gotten bored and gone off to do her own thing. He hadn't seen her for a few years until she'd turned up that fateful day on the Amazon. He heaved a sigh. Somehow, it was all his fault. People connected to him just seemed to get hurt. Anyone who loved him ended up dead—Izel, Carmen, Chris, and now Victoria was as good as ... Fuck this. He needed tea.

Kelly stood up, grabbed up his satchel containing the Ayahuasca tea, flicked open the flap to his tent, and marched into the citadel. Compared with the toxic atmosphere of nearby Mexico City, the air around Teotihuacan was crystal clear. The night sky was a purple wash with a million white and blue stars that lit his surroundings. He peered down the Street of the Dead and admired the Pyramid of the Sun, set slightly to the east of the avenue, and the Pyramid of the Moon, which sat at the extreme north. The citadel, where they had decided to camp, sat in the middle of the two and a half mile long road. Though it was normally surrounded by gray-green scrubland, at night everything appeared to be eerie blue.

To his left, about one hundred feet away, was the Chinook, almost camouflaged against the dark sky. Directly in front of him, Freya and Teller sat huddled around a military issue stove on which Teller was cooking something.

"Something interesting?" Freya called from her seat.

Kelly blinked, jolted back to reality. He had stared at her for a few moments too long. Freya—she was so beautiful. Her huge, green eyes lit up every time she saw him. He fought back a smile and quenched the warmth that had begun to creep over his heart. No, she was better off with the *Star Trek* nerd who sat so loyally next to her.

"Kelly? You okay?" Freya's expression had become one of concern.

He restarted his march toward the group. "A camp? Really? We gonna cook S'mores and sing 'Kumbaya?'"

Teller glanced up from his pan, which held a few small hot dogs. "My men are patrolling. And we need to eat. Survival isn't about sitting here sucking on ants. If the creature is coming, I want us fit and ready."

His argument was hard to refute.

Kelly plonked himself on the ground and kept silent. At least for a few seconds. "So what's the plan?"

Teller gave Freya an awkward glance.

"Tell him," she said.

Kelly frowned. "Tell me what?"

"We have a complication," Teller said.

"Complication? Is that military speak for *giant fuck-up?*"

"Not a fuck-up, Mr. Graham. A problem."

"Spit it out."

Teller took a deep breath. "You remember how we pissed off the Chinese, took the clone, tried to steal the orb, and they ended up kidnapping you and releasing a virus into California?"

"Vaguely," Kelly said.

"Well, the people behind all of that are part of a Chinese cult. And it seems their leader has taken a shine to our little outing. He's coming for Wak."

"Good luck to the crazy bastard. We can't even find it."

"That's not all. We think he has a nuclear weapon, too."

"Oh, fan-fucking-tastic. I do love things super complicated and world-endingly dangerous." Kelly leaned back. "Look, right now, all I give a shit about is getting Victoria back. Have you been able to track her?"

"Satellite tracking showed us she and the creature exited the Rio Grande into the Gulf of Mexico and popped up again at Tampamachoco Lagoon, which is just down the coast. But satellite is only good when we have daylight and something in orbit in the right position. We lost them."

Kelly screwed up his face in confusion.

"Something wrong?" Freya asked.

"Tampamachoco Lagoon. It's more than one-hundred-fifty miles from here. They'd have to hoof it, which just doesn't seem right."

"Agreed," Teller said, still poking at his cooking. "It's pretty mountainous between there and here. There must be something we're missing."

"You didn't think about their route when you knew where we were going, oh brainy one?"

"Yes, I did. But this is where our information led us. The creature is not proving to be dangerous unless provoked. We have tracked as best as possible by satellite. Logic dictates we stick to the plan."

"Tom and the other soldiers are circling the perimeter." Freya pointed and drew an imaginary circle around the camp. "We'll know as soon as Victoria and Wak turn up." She paused, then added, "Don't worry."

Kelly nodded absently. He didn't like Teller all that much, but the man wasn't stupid. He at least deserved respect.

"Kelly?"

"Yes, Freya?" he replied.

"I was just talking with Jonathan about K'in's species and how his kind is supposed to have given us civility. You are the only person to have been linked with one of them or, at least, the only one who can talk about what you've learned."

"You asked me about that earlier."

"No," Teller said. "We asked what it was like being connected to K'in. Freya is asking about the wider perspective. What has the whole experience taught you?"

Kelly clenched his jaw, irritated at being interrogated again. "What have I learned?" he began, his tone implying, *do you really want the truth?* "I learned that ..."

Minya watched the three Americans talking by the campfire. She hated being there. It was so mentally exhausting. It was cold and she needed the warmth of the fire, but she just couldn't bear being part of their plebeian conversation.

She carefully took a seat at the edge of the circle, far enough away that their voices were muted but close enough that the camp fire gave a little comfort. In her hands, she toyed with the small black communication device that stayed on her person at all times. But her warm solitude didn't last long. It was interrupted by the loud and obnoxious voice of Kelly.

"Quite the spot they picked, huh, Minya?"

"Hmm? What?" She fumbled with the transmitting device and stuffed it into her pocket.

"Here, the Street of the Dead. Seems oddly fitting. Don't you think?"

"Oh, *da*. It is."

"Street of the Dead?" Freya repeated.

"*Da*, it is what this place is called. To opposite end of avenue, you have

337

Pyramid of the Moon. And over there, the temple of the feathered serpent."
She pointed to a temple at the far eastern side of the citadel.

"Feathered serpent," Freya said. "Just like K'in."

Kelly bobbed his head in agreement, though his attention was fixed on
Minya, who squirmed.

After a moment, Kelly leaped to his feet. "Want a walk, Minya? You can
go on about the archaeological crap if you like."

She eyed him suspiciously. His lopsided smile. His overconfidence. He
annoyed her. But then again, would it be worse than sitting with a whole
group of Americans? Perhaps not. "*Devai*."

She climbed to her feet and trotted after Kelly, who had already started
toward the temple of the serpent.

Freya stared at them. Teller watched Freya.

As they trudged toward the great stone monument, Kelly decided they were
far enough away that he could now speak. "You okay, Minya?"

"What?" she snapped, annoyed at being wrenched from her thoughts.

"I said, are you okay?"

"Oh, *da*. Much has happened. It is not good waiting." *I hate it here.*

"I hear ya. I'm pretty antsy myself."

Minya stopped walking and raised her head to examine the temple. The
six stage pyramid was more than seventy-feet high and was amazingly well
preserved. On the stones, small fragments of colored paint remained—a sign of
the importance of this temple many years ago.

Stepping around the base, Kelly examined the central stairway.
Protruding from the facing blocks was a series of massive, serpent-like heads
armed with fangs, each on an elongated neck ringed with a large plume of
feathers.

"Quetzalcoatl," Minya said.

Despite the evil appearance of the sculptures, all Kelly could see was
K'in—innocent and curious and always in his way or under his feet. He glanced
over at Minya and studied her for a moment before prying again. "I noticed
you have a tattoo on your shoulder. It's quite a specific—"

"*Da*? So?" she snapped.

"Hey, I'm just saying that …" He stopped and sighed. "Look, you seem uncomfortable."

You have no idea.

"I understand you. I really do."

She stood there silently, for what felt like an eternity, before simply saying, "We should walk back."

They trudged back through the citadel and toward the camp. Yet, to Kelly's astonishment, Minya strolled right on past and made her way to the large stone stairs at the north ridge. He paused for a moment and glanced at Freya and Teller, who were watching him. Kelly shrugged before jogging after Minya.

"Hey, where are you off to?"

Irritating man. I need to send message. "Just for a walk."

"I'll join you."

"Fine." She lit a cigarette, hung it from her lips, and climbed the huge stone bricks.

Kelly scrambled after her.

As they crested the embankment, Minya turned north and led him along the street. Kelly glanced around, studying the enormous mounds on both sides, and the regular high partition walls with well-constructed sluices at their base.

Minya sensed questions beginning to rise in the American's throat, so she decided to preempt him. "You know, it is unclear who built this place."

Happy she had spoken, Kelly didn't interrupt. Flowing conversation was key if he was to get any information from her.

"The Aztecs gave the pyramids names when they arrived here. But it is unclear why they chose them. This is very ancient place. Even name, *Street of the Dead*, was given by visitors—the conquistadors. They thought the mounds were graves." She waved the hand holding the cigarette at either side of the street.

"And what are these big partitions for?"

Minya craned her neck to see them. "As with much, there is no clear answer."

"Oh."

"But ..."

"But?"

"But one of your countrymen, Dr. Schlemmer, had a theory. He believed this was not street at all but row of linked reflecting pools. Water would have flowed from a loch at Pyramid of the Moon down to citadel."

"Do you believe that?"

"This place is known to have a series of canals and waterways that extend to Lake Texcoco. So it is not so crazy to consider."

"That's more than ten miles away."

"*Da.*"

Kelly stopped walking and looked around, taking in his surroundings. He closed his eyes and conjured the image of the great pool system. The starlight reflecting off the water's surface, glowing ripples sliding from one edge to another. It would have been the perfect place for K'in's people. Yes, this Dr. Schlemmer might have been on to something.

"Falling asleep there?" Freya had come to investigate.

Kelly pried his eyes open. "No, just thinking."

Minya huffed. *Great. Now two of them.*

"Just thought I'd come and see what was so interesting up here."

"Jealous much?"

"You wish," Freya snapped.

Minya groaned.

Kelly changed the subject. "You got any news on the whereabouts of Wak or Vicky?"

"No." Freya shook her head. "It's a little strange. I'm just not sure how they're going to make it across the mountains to here."

"Perhaps they do not go over," Minya said aloud.

"What's that?" Freya asked.

Kelly span around, searching the street for clues.

"Waterways. You said the old waterways went back as far as Lake Texcoco, right?"

"*Da,* exactly."

"What are you talking about, Kelly?"

"This place used to have a mess of canals and waterways. I'll bet some of them went underground. We're sitting here like dumbasses on the surface. Is there a way down?" He stared hopefully at Minya.

She swayed on the spot, unsure if she should answer.

"Answer him," Freya said.

"*Da,* possibly. The Pyramid of the Sun," she began. "It was built over man-made tunnel, a passage that leads to cave almost twenty feet below, beneath the center of structure. Originally, it was believed to be lava tube. Natural."

"But?" Kelly raised his eyebrows.

"More recent excavations have led some to believe it was made by men. Perhaps a royal tomb. But some have said it may be the place of Chicomoztoc—the place of human origin, according to Nahua legends."

"This chamber," Kelly interrupted. "Is it a dead end? Are there others?"

"There have been investigations. But no more tunnels were found."

"But that doesn't preclude them from existing, does it?" he pressed.

"No."

Freya glowered. "Strange you didn't mention this before."

"I was not asked."

"You know, it strikes me as funny, Minya, that—"

"Now, now, ladies. No need to fight."

Neither laughed, instead giving him equally scathing glances.

"Let's just go back. I don't like us being so far from the camp. It's not safe." Freya turned on her heel and marched off toward the camp.

Kelly and Minya trudged after her, their heads hung low like those of reprimanded school children.

CHAPTER FORTY-TWO

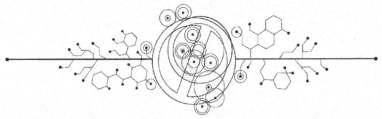

Location: Russian transport plane, somewhere over the Atlantic

T he turbulence shook the virtually empty, modified 747. Occasionally, the aircraft plummeted twenty or thirty feet and then slowly climbed again. Normally, this kind of journey would result in numerous vomit bags being opened, followed by the sound of heaving, but not today. The few passengers on board were used to it. They were trained to deal with such circumstances.

Sasha and fifteen of his best soldiers sat silently and calmly in their seats, spread throughout the plane to allow an even distribution of weight. Their bear-like statures combined with heavy combat gear made the men appear like Thracian Gigantes. While not of Mediterranean decent, these Russian warriors were just as fearless.

The Polkovnik stared at the message on the screen of his cell phone for the fifth time.

Urgent. Situation changed. Do you have what we need?

The situation had changed—again. Nothing had been the same for more than a year since the covert war had overflowed into Russia. It grated on him. Not only had he been dragged into a battle that was not his, but he was now forced to align with a nation he disliked with every fiber of his being. It didn't matter which side his government chose, he would be displeased regardless. Sasha preferred isolation. There was no need to make friends with foreign nations, only to understand to what degree they were an enemy. But his personal feelings were not of concern.

It wasn't the first time this had been asked of him. He had been trained from a young age to slip into American society unnoticed like another slack-jawed idiot who knew nothing of the world's geography beyond the local bar. He'd been located in Virginia during the early eighties. Although he had a menial job working as an accountant, it had afforded him opportunities to launder money and siphon funds to his KGB comrades in the U.S.—plus, it was within close proximity to the CIA headquarters in Langley.

During his time in that backwater state, he'd been ordered to investigate something the CIA had become interested in—a religious faction that was touting a new doctrine called the Nine Veils. This strange concept had been gaining traction, mainly because it went beyond simple faith and claimed to underpin the world's powers and economy.

Unlike the CIA, Sasha, or George as he'd been known then, was able to penetrate this group through the church. The group was tight-lipped and, being so close to Langley, very good at spotting CIA agents but Russians, not so much.

Sasha had become particularly friendly with a strange, nervous, little man named Bob Jefferson. Bob was passionate about his faith and more than a little paranoid, though it was some years before he would start wearing a tin hat to prevent his brainwaves from being read. Still, Sasha had followed orders—no matter how crazy they seemed to him at the time. He'd attended their secret meetings and partook in their strange rituals. He had spoken to every member and gathered their perspective on the Nine Veils. For some, he discovered, it represented the true path to God, while for others, it provided the route to enlightenment. Simply stated, the doctrine outlined specific barriers, or *veils*, that blocked human understanding of the world. An individual's ability to penetrate the veil depended on a number of factors, including education and the ability to see beyond the physical world.

The first three veils, according to the theory, had been penetrated by a large proportion of western society. The common person understood and accepted that people could vote and have some influence on their lives at a minimal level, but really, the resources of the world were controlled by extremely wealthy and powerful families. These families utilized their old world assets to underpin the world's economy.

From this point, the proportion of people penetrating each successive veil dwindled. Those who got through the fourth and fifth veils discovered secret organizations, such as the Illuminati, Freemasons, and the Green and Red societies. These societies were believed to transfer arcane knowledge down through generations and use it to keep the plebs in political, economic, and spiritual bondage.

Bob, in particular, believed the more outlandish parts of the doctrine— these societies were so far advanced technologically that time travel and interstellar communication were possible. This was where Sasha had become most skeptical. The concept of interstellar and time travel, discussed in the fifth veil, seemed implausible. The sixth veil was even crazier, purporting that the dragons and aliens from our childhood stories were real. According to the theory, a species of non-humans, lizard-like creatures, once or even currently sat above the secret societies, controlling them. Bob had been convinced something sat in Area 51, and the U.S. Government had one of the lizards in captivity.

Beyond the sixth veil, a select few people on Earth passed through the seventh, eighth, and ninth veils and acquired the ability to see the universe as a series of complex numerical codes. They were able to comprehend the very fabric of time, space, and parallel universes until it eventually led them to God.

Of course, Sasha had reported that the investigation was pointless, and he should be reassigned. Eventually, he had been, and when the Cold War had ended, he had been pulled from active duty in the U.S. and sent back to Mother Russia.

Yet, hindsight is a powerful thing. If he had delved a little deeper, he would have discovered Bob was quite correct; the Americans did have something in Area 51, and Russia could have avoided being in the middle of someone else's war, aligning with one side through necessity. But regret was something he could not afford.

A crack of thunder and a flash of lightning snapped him from his thoughts. He clasped the satellite phone in his hand and keyed in a reply.

Yes. Contact has requested assistance due to change in circumstance. Permission to comply.

A moment later, the phone pinged to life—one new message. He opened it.

Granted.

Sasha exhaled. This was it.

Location: Teotihuacan, Mexico

Bubbles percolated to the surface and popped as they broke the meniscus. The water was just below boiling temperature—perfect. Kelly lifted the dented, metallic kettle from the flame and poured the hot, colorless liquid into the pot containing his tea concoction. He plonked himself cross-legged on his sleeping bag and waited for the beverage to steep.

The tea was supposed to be an escape, but it never really worked. Just a ritual to take his mind from Chris, Izel and Carmen. But recently, his mind had been occupied with something else. *Someone* else. Freya. He couldn't really explain why in words. It was just a feeling in his chest, in his insides. He needed her. He wanted her. Even while he had hidden away in the jungle for months, he'd thought of her, thought of that look she gave him—the one that said, *you can't hide, Kelly Graham. I know you. And it's okay to be you.*

But, of course, he would always ruin it and make some sort of stupid comment. Kelly shook his head. *Why can't I just be serious for once?* Not that it mattered. Freya was with Wonder Boy now anyway. He had missed his chance. And that was that.

He huffed loudly, angry for wasting time on pointless *what ifs*. Things were as they were. He had to focus. Vicky needed him now, and he should be concentrating on her.

Kelly poured some of the tea into a cup, took a sip, and held it in his mouth. Ugh. It was disgusting. But if he could have another vision, he might understand where Vicky was. He swallowed and gave an open-mouthed tongue shake to rid himself of the taste.

He placed the cup on the floor next to his feet and picked up the battered guitar laid to his left. He'd found it on the train during their trans-Siberian jaunt last year, a kind of memento. He strummed the open strings and began to sing, if not poorly.

> *"And I— wish*
> *that I could let go, And I— wish*
> *that I could go home, And I— wish*
> *that I could tell you, But I— know*
> *that I'll die alone."*

"How did you manage to bring that thing along with you?" Freya stood just outside the tent, peering through the open flap.

Her eyes sparkled in the firelight. *Damn, she's beautiful.* "Don't you knock?"

"Knock on what?" Freya asked with a laugh, stepping inside.

"Oh, please, come in." *Shut up, Kelly!*

"Just thought I'd check on you. I could smell your tea from my tent, and I know you only drink it when you're feeling down."

"I'm okay."

"Sure you are," Freya replied, taking a seat next to him.

Would any other woman in the world be this pigheaded? Probably not. But glad she's here. "So, what can I do ya for?"

"Well, besides seeing if you're alright, I wanted to ask you about Minya. Does she seem off to you?"

"Off? If you mean the whole ice queen thing, sure, she's off. But by that count, so am I. I can understand her position, I think. We're pretty similar people."

Freya scowled.

He laughed. "Jealous?"

Yes. "Don't be absurd. She just seems a bit shifty. You pick up on these things, Kelly. I think she's hiding something, and I don't trust her."

"Well, she's got prison ink, but—"

"She has?"

"Yep, on her shoulder. I saw it earlier."

"She's done time? An archaeological researcher? That is, of course, if she's a scientist at all. We did a background check. It was pretty patchy to say the least." Freya pursed her lips and mused on that thought.

"Just because someone's been inside, doesn't make them a bad person." He gave her a knowing look.

"Indeed."

"What about Captain Kirk out there? He's been a bit shifty. Practically attached to that phone of his, making calls and texts. Where is he anyway?"

"Asleep. His shift is in a couple of hours, so he's resting. And he's NSA, Kelly. Of course he's secretive. He's good at his job. He's a good man. He's—"

"Sure, of course. That's why you're in here rather than in his tent, right?"

Freya shuffled uncomfortably on the spot. "He's a good man. In many ways, he reminds me of Benjamin. He's so smart. He's just career-focused."

Kelly knew this trap. If he continued down this road, it would bite him in the ass. *Hold your tongue, Kelly.*

"I guess sometimes I just wish he was a little more heart and a little less brains. You know? Like you and Izel. Maybe that's it. I'd just like to feel as loved as that."

Kelly cleared his throat. "Loving someone that much is dangerous. Trust me."

"But isn't it amazing? To feel that way."

He stared at her for a moment. "It's scary as hell. You always know one way or another they'll be taken from you—old age, murder, an accident. Nothing is forever."

"And you really don't believe in anything beyond?"

"Nothing I've ever seen shows that to be true. Believing in the beyond is just humans dealing with the need to not be afraid or believing we are more important than we are in the universe. We're not."

"That's a very bleak way to see the world."

"I just don't live a lie." Kelly looked down, and when he spoke again, it was seemingly to himself. "It scares me there is nothing after, and when I die, that's it. But then, sometimes, I don't see the point of carrying on. I miss them so much it hurts. My whole family, my best friend—they're gone. What do I have to live for, really? I always come out of these things unscathed, but everyone else dies. It's like I'm being punished. Ever wish you would just go to sleep and not wake up?" Kelly raised his head to see Freya staring at him, a worried look in her eyes. He shook off the moment of vulnerability. "He's not me. I'm sure he loves you in his way—probably a healthy way, not all-consuming and soul-destroying."

"Are you?" she pressed. "Sure about him, I mean."

"Sure."

She paused for a second. "Does that bother you?"

"What?"

"Well, you've been acting a bit strange since you found out."

Kelly leapt up from his seat, spilling his tea, and threw the guitar on the sleeping bag. "What do you want, Freya? Huh? What do you want me to say? That he's not right for you? That you don't love with your head? That a laundry list of character traits is not a reason to be with someone? You love with your heart for fuck's sake. You can't box it, or file it, or understand it.

You just do it." He stormed about the tent, shaking his head and gesticulating wildly.

Freya clambered to her feet and grabbed his arms, holding them so he had to focus on her. She stared into his eyes for as long as she could without blinking. "I want you to tell me."

"Tell you what?"

"Tell me," Freya repeated.

Kelly didn't respond.

"God damn you, Kelly Graham, you are a stubborn ass."

"Hey, name-callin' ain't gonna make me suddenly start—"

Freya grasped the back of his head and kissed him hard and fast.

He froze.

She pulled away and searched his eyes. "I'm not Izel," she whispered, now holding his face. "And I'm not trying to replace her. But it's okay to live. It's okay to be happy."

Kelly stood unmoving, his eyes glassed over, a stone in his throat. "I'm not sure I remember how to be happy. I don't wanna hurt anymore, but I can't let it go—let them go. They were all I had. And they accepted me, warts an' all, for the asshole I am. No one else would."

Freya locked her stare onto his and, without losing eye contact, moved closer before kissing him as softly as she could.

CHAPTER FORTY-THREE

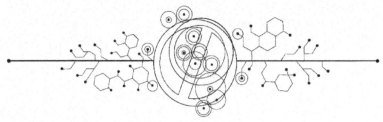

Location: Teotihuacan, Mexico, South America

One by one, the soldiers shouted their names out.

"Chandler!"

"Grisome!"

"Radley!"

Sixteen more names followed.

"Green, we're missing Green!" Tom yelled.

"Dammit! What hit us?"

"I don't know!"

Freya bolted awake, sitting upright and blinking away the sleep from her eyes. She searched the tent. For a moment, she was confused. It wasn't hers. The familiar groan from the body next to her brought it all rushing back. She was still in Kelly's tent. A small smile broke across her face as she clutched at the sleeping bag and pulled it around her naked torso.

Another clap of gunfire broke her dream-like state and snapped her into programmed military action. Far from thinking of her embarrassment, Freya leapt naked from the bag and grabbed her Beretta. For a few minutes, she crouched on the floor, waiting. Gunshots echoed through the night. Men shouted. But they were at the other end of the camp.

Satisfied no one was close, she pushed Kelly's shoulder and whispered as loud as she dared. "Hey, wake up."

Kelly groaned and rolled onto his side. He saw Freya's big, green eyes, sparkling and wild, staring back, inches from his face. "It's still dark. You woke me up for round two?"

"Shut up and listen."

Silence.

"What am I listening for?"

An explosion tore into the atmosphere, followed by machine-gun fire.

"That."

Kelly scrambled out of his warm cocoon and into the crumpled pile of clothes that had been hastily dumped there just hours earlier. By the time he'd found his boots and put them on, Freya was already geared up and crouched by the tent entrance, ready to pounce.

She peeked through the gap in the tent to survey the situation. "Shit, I can't see anything."

"Wak? Vicky?"

"I don't know. C'mon." She beckoned him to follow and darted out of the tent.

Kelly opened his mouth to voice his protest and to say the one thing he wanted to in case he wouldn't get to later. But she was gone. He huffed away the thought and sprinted after her.

Freya crashed into the midst of her comrades and skidded to a halt. She unholstered her other Beretta and handed it to the panting Kelly, who had careened in behind her.

"Oh, so I get one this time?" he wheezed.

"You saw what that thing did to the last crew. You need some form of protection."

"I don't think it's Wak," Kelly replied.

"What?" Teller yelled over his shoulder.

Kelly stepped toward him until he was close enough that his hushed voice could be heard. "I don't think it's Wak. You said it yourself—it only ever attacks when provoked, and it usually hits everyone at the same time. This feels ... off."

Teller narrowed his eyes. "We can't see. They're using the shadows."

"Fuck this." Kelly pelted away from Teller and burst through the protective circle, barging past two of the soldiers and bolted for the Chinook. He slammed into the side of the cockpit and flung open the door. Before he could climb inside, a boot met him squarely in the jaw, sending him flying backward and into the dirt. The headlamps of the chopper burst into life, flooding the camp in bright yellow light.

Freya stared past the crumbling walls and low-level shrubbery at the now visible army of Chinese men, each wielding a pistol, blade, or hatchet.

"Sha⁻!" screamed the voice over the chopper's loudspeaker. The one-hundred-strong army cried out and ran at the Americans. Kelly jumped to his feet and ran back to the relative safety of his group, protected behind Teller's wall of soldiers.

"Motherfuckers stole my idea." Kelly struggled for breath.

The clash of metal on metal was deafening. Gunfire exploded in random directions as the Chinese killers deftly dodged and slid around the Americans.

"Fall back!" commanded Teller. "Regroup! Everyone with me!"

The soldiers regained their composure and formed a loose huddle, backs to each other, with Freya, Minya, and Kelly at the center.

"Stop!" yelled the voice from the helicopter.

The Triads ceased their onslaught and waited some twenty feet from the group. A slender figure sauntered down the stairs of the Chinook and stepped out onto the dirt track, brandishing a large meat cleaver. He confidently walked the fifty yards from the helicopter and stood, facing the Americans, between two of his minions.

"Who the fuck is this guy?" Kelly asked.

"I'm the man who will take the ultimate weapon from you and then kill you. Or, perhaps, I'll kill you and then take the weapon. I haven't decided yet."

"Okay, you're a politician. Never actually answering my question."

"Sagane," Teller said through gritted teeth.

"Very good. Now, where is the creature?" the Shan Chu hissed.

Freya leaned into Teller and whispered, "We're too open here. We'll never survive this. We have to fall back. We need to get to higher ground. We can fall back to the pyramid just east of the road. It'll give us the advantage."

He nodded. "How far away is it?"

"About one mile, but there's a pretty steep incline first."

"Where is it?" demanded the Triad leader again.

"You know, I've had it up to here with assholes wanting to get their hands on this goddamn thing," yelled Kelly through the wall of soldiers. "Have you even seen it? It's nuts. What am I saying? Look at you."

"Shut up!" Teller yelled. "Boys, delta-bravo-delta, one mile! Move it!"

The soldiers moved as one, opening fire on the first row of Chinese attackers.

Freya grabbed Kelly by the scruff of his neck and wrenched him. "Run!"

351

she screamed.

They raced across the grounds of the citadel, protected by the moving wall of gunfire spraying into the night behind them. Reaching the top of the stairs, they fell over the crest before sprinting for the Pyramid of the Sun. Their feet kicked at the rocky ground, breaking their gait and slowing their escape.

A deafening explosion ripped into the night and pieces of metal pinged and clanged in the distance. Everyone—Americans and Chinese alike—threw themselves into the dirt and covered their heads.

Teller pulled his arms from his head and glanced backward. The Chinook had been blown to smithereens. *Fuck. That was our ride out of here.* "Move it!" he ordered. "Move your fucking asses!"

The soldiers scrambled to their feet and pelted forward, taking refuge behind one of the large walls of brick that were evenly spaced along the Street of the Dead.

"Reload and regroup!" Teller ordered.

The soldiers complied, clicking new magazines into their weapons.

Kelly rested the back of his head against the wall, his eyes screwed closed and heart pounding. "Jesus, we gotta get the fuck outta here."

"I know, we gotta—"

Teller's reply was interrupted by a white flash streaking across their path.

"What is it?" Freya asked, looking over her shoulder at the Chinese assailants who had regained their footing.

"Wak," Teller whispered.

"Shit," Freya replied, whipping her head around to see.

"Where?"

"I don't know. It was just there—"

From beneath a crooked, gnarled tree, a low-slung form slinked across the dusty road. Not quite on all fours, the naked creature moved on two bent hind legs, using its forearms for support. A shock of greasy, limp blonde hair hung from its head and covered its face. It hovered there in the middle of the street, swaying from side to side and stared at the Americans.

"Jesus, that's Vicky," Freya whispered, horrified.

Victoria cocked her head to one side and then the other but did not speak. It was as if somewhere in the recesses of her mind she knew the hairless, two-legged animal was trying to communicate, but she could not understand.

From the shadows behind Victoria, the large, muscular form of Wak appeared. Matching her stance, it sidled up to her, its eyes narrowed and focused, watching—waiting.

"Damn, look at that thing," Teller said.

Kelly opened his eyes to see what his military comrades were bleating on about. He stepped away from the wall and peered between the shoulders of Teller and Freya. "Vicky?" Kelly asked the question but expected no answer. It was her. He just didn't want it to be. He stretched out a hand. "Vicky, come with me. It's okay."

The woman backed away.

Teller glanced behind. "Shit. We don't have time for this. They're almost here."

Kelly watched his friend closely. She wasn't herself anymore. He didn't know what she was. She had devolved to a state of animal instinct to survive. It was all because of that creature and their bond—intertwined with its twisted mind. She wasn't strong enough. He had to break it. If he could just hang on to the goddamn thing, maybe it would sense Kelly had been bonded to one of its kind before. It would let her go.

"Fuck it." Kelly sprang forward, his arms outstretched to envelop Wak and tackle it to the ground.

As he flew through the air, Victoria launched herself at him, driving her head into his solar plexus. A sickening crunch filled his ears as she pummeled him into the earth as if he were a child's toy. She squatted on him, her bare and bloodied feet flat on his chest and her rough webbed hands gripping his t-shirt.

Kelly yelped in pain and screwed up his eyes.

Victoria craned her neck and pulled him close, sniffing at his skin. Her blood-red eyes stared out from sunken sockets.

"Vicky," wheezed Kelly.

Wak tore across the path again, grabbed up Victoria, and swiftly disappeared down a small, dark tunnel in the stonework beneath the great pyramid.

Once again, Kelly howled as the pressure on his ribcage was relinquished and the bones protecting his heart and lungs flexed back into position.

"Kelly!" Freya screamed, flying to his side.

"Jonathan, we need to get him up."

Teller took quick and powerful strides over to Kelly and in one motion bent down and grabbed him by the armpits.

Kelly groaned.

"C'mon!" ordered Teller.

A lone bullet screamed past Minya's right ear. She instinctively fell to the ground and covered her head. "*Yebat!*"

"They're too close!" yelled Freya. She pulled her Beretta, pointed it in the direction of the Chinese, and released several controlled shots while stepping slowly backward.

"Hold your fire! Save your ammo!" commanded Teller, dragging Kelly by his armpits.

The soldiers complied but still held their defensive line, guns drawn and aimed high. A horde of Chinese warriors trudged forward, maneuvering between the dead bodies of their fallen brothers. Their chests were heaving, sweat pouring from their brows.

"Wait," called their commanding voice again. The Shan Chu skulked out from the dark and came to the fore, presenting himself to the Americans as if he were bulletproof.

Freya didn't wait for him to open his mouth and fired off a round directly at his chest. As if he had anticipated her move, the Shan Chu had already sidestepped and thrown a shuriken that sliced through the air and clanged against the barrel of Freya's Beretta, knocking it from her hand.

"I will not ask you again, stupid Americans," he hissed. "Where is the creature?"

"Fuck you!" Freya spat. "Come and get it, asshole."

"Thanks for that, honey," Teller said under his breath.

"You bore me." The Shan Chu snarled, pulling his cleaver from its holster.

Teller sighed, accepting that this was probably where he was about to die. But if that was to be the case, he wasn't going to go down without taking a few of those bastards with him. Just when he had resolved to dump the limp Kelly to the floor and launch directly at the arrogant Chinese leader, a loud *whump* sound snapped him back to the real world.

A second whump reverberated off the old brickwork as one of the Triads slammed into the ground, his head exploding and splattering brain matter across the dirt. The Shan Chu instantly turned tail, slipping into the night like a ghost.

Freya, her eyes wild, scanned her surroundings for the weapon. "What the hell is that?"

"Help," Teller replied, almost laughing.

"What?" yelled Freya. The constant deafeningly loud screams were difficult to be heard over as massive shells tore through men's bodies.

"Kobayashi Maru. I don't believe in no-win situations, remember? Quick, down here." Teller hoisted Kelly back into a comfortable position and dragged him down the hole through which Wak had disappeared.

Freya grabbed up her gun and fired off several shots into the throng of wailing Triads before grabbing Minya by one arm and heaving her up. "Move!" she screamed in the Russian woman's face. "Now!"

Minya didn't protest and quickly dove through the wide crevice in the ground.

"Tom, move your ass!" Freya called over her shoulder.

The soldier obeyed and scrambled after Freya, followed by the few remaining members of his unit.

CHAPTER FORTY-FOUR

Location: Under Teotihuacan, Mexico, South America

They slumped to the ground, breathless and sweating. They had run down the length of the tunnel until they'd reached an opening into a wider section, a small cave no more than fifteen or twenty feet across. It was roughly circular in shape with one exit behind them and one in front of them. The atmosphere was remarkably cool and incredibly damp. The musty air filled the nostrils of the beaten soldiers. Despite the dankness, it seemed to be a good place to stop—especially since the light from outside was no longer bright enough to light their way.

Freya unclipped a small flashlight from her belt and held it in her fist, wielding it like a knife. The bulb pointing out from under her pinky finger, she clicked it on with her thumb and swung the beam of yellow light methodically, turning a full 360-degree circle. The slim finger of illumination seemed pathetic in the all-consuming dark that dwelt within the cavern. Occasionally, a rock or a jagged crack came into view, but the walls were smooth as if man-made and gave no information as to their exact location. It unnerved her—so much so she had an uncontrollable need to call out into the void simply to hear a voice, even if it were her own. "Sound off."

"I'm here." Teller panted.

"Tom," the soldier replied.

Three more men called out.

"I am here," Minya replied.

"I didn't hear Kelly. Kelly?" Freya yelled. "Kelly!"

There was a faint groan from somewhere in the cave.

The soldiers clicked on their flashlights. Their collective beams illuminated the grotto and the broken body of Kelly, huddled against a wall.

"Kelly!" Freya leapt to his side and pulled his head back to look at his face. "Are you alright?"

He grunted and opened his eyes, though they remained squinted,

356

reflecting his pain. "Yeah. Gotta say, though, I've felt better. My insides are killin' me."

"C'mon now, beaten up by a girl?" She forced a laugh. "Get your ass up." Freya swung one of Kelly's arms over her shoulder and attempted to lift him, but his dead weight collapsed on her, driving them both to their knees.

"Whoa there." Teller jogged over and pulled Kelly directly upward into the exact position Freya had been attempting. "I gotcha. C'mon."

Kelly groaned again. He didn't want to be rescued by this guy.

Freya clambered to her feet and scanned the cave. A couple of the soldiers were pulling gear from their packs, halogen lights with foldable rigs to illuminate their surroundings. Tom and the last soldier were scanning with their flashlights, weapons readied. Minya was shuffling nervously on her own, the glowing end of a newly lit cigarette illuminating her worried face.

Freya stormed over to the Russian woman, grabbed her by the scruff of her neck, and slammed her into the wall. Minya's cigarette fell from her lips.

"You!" Freya shouted. "I've seen you with your pager or whatever the hell that thing is." She released one hand and patted the woman down, eventually forcing her hand into a pocket and yanking out a small, electronic object.

She waved it in Minya's face and threw it away. "You've sold us out to the Chinese. Don't think I've forgotten your dig in Siberia was funded by them. You let that one slip on our last meeting." Freya shoved the woman in frustration.

"Minya Yermalova," droned Sasha as he stepped out of the gloom from the tunnel that exited to the outside world. He was followed by several of his personal strike force.

Freya stepped away from Minya and pulled out her Beretta. "Freeze, motherfucker. I swear to God I will blow your fucking head off. Identify yourself."

"Help," Teller said. "Let him past, boys."

The American soldiers parted, allowing the Russian contingent through. Freya glared at Kelly. "What?"

"I am Polkovnik Sasha Vetrov, FSB."

"What the hell are the FSB doing here, Jonathan?"

"They're working with me," Teller replied.

"He's here for her," Freya deduced. "To take this treacherous bitch away."

The Russian officer eyed Minya but stood his ground near the entrance to the tunnel. "Minya Yermalova. Former resident of a Siberian prison. Drug running for your uncle, if I'm not mistaken?"

"*Petookh opooscheny,*" Minya said under her breath.

"Oh, *da*. Prison slang, Minya?"

Silence.

"She's spent time in a Siberian prison? Then how did she get to be a professor of anything?" Freya asked.

"It wasn't a normal prison. It was a sharashka, a secret research laboratory," Sasha explained. "A remnant of the—"

"I know what a sharashka is," Freya snapped. "A Gulag labor camp. And I know the scientists at a sharashka were usually picked from various prisons and assigned to work on technological problems for the state. But these were all shut down decades ago. She's what, mid-thirties, forty max? That would have meant the prisons were still around in the eighties."

"They still exist now," Sasha replied.

"And how would she escape? How—"

"She was sponsored," Sasha interrupted.

Freya frowned. "Sponsored?"

"Yes. Her language skills were put to good use in the sharashka. She could communicate between the scientists. She learned a lot. Eventually, someone paid to take her from the prison and continue her education." Sasha spoke to the group, but his gaze was fixed on Minya.

"That crazy bastard outside. He sprang you." Freya slammed Minya into the wall, again.

"Actually, no," Teller replied.

Freya spun around and stared at him, bewildered. "What?"

Teller slowly lowered Kelly back to the floor and propped him against the wall. "Minya's sponsor was a little closer to home."

"Stop being cryptic, Jonathan."

Teller held his palms outward in a calming motion. "Alejandro. It was Alejandro." He eyed Freya carefully. She had become a wolverine, angry and defensive, and all because Kelly was injured.

"Kelly's Alejandro?" Freya pressed, incredulous.

"Yes." He nodded slowly. "He found her while working up there. He paid the Gulag guards for cheap labor on his digs and expeditions. It seems he took a shine to her."

Freya turned back to the Russian woman. "That's how you knew him?"

Minya stared into Freya's eyes. "*Da*. He helped me. Gave me education and money for school."

"Why? Why you?"

The Russian woman jerked free of Freya's grasp, her eyes flaring. "I was pregnant when he came to the prison. A gift from one of the security guards. The old man took pity on me. He paid much money to take me away."

"I don't get it. If he was your friend, why betray us?"

"Oh, she didn't," Sasha replied.

"Tell. Me. What. The. Fuck. Is. Going. On," Freya seethed through clenched teeth, her firearm now pointed directly at the Polkovnik's head.

"Okay, okay, calm down," Teller said, his tone as calm and comforting as possible.

"Minya hasn't been communicating with the Chinese. She's been texting her son back in Saint Petersburg," added Sasha. "Nikolaj."

Freya scowled at Minya, who only nodded to confirm Teller's story.

"Then how did that crazy bastard find us? How did he know we were here?"

"Because you do have a traitor in your midst, don't you, Mr. Radley?" Before anyone could move, Sasha had pulled his MP-443 Grach and pointed it at the soldier's head.

"Tom …" Teller sighed. "Goddammit."

The soldier froze, his eyes cold.

Even Minya frowned in confusion.

Freya raised her Beretta, arms locked, and pointed it at Tom's left eye. "I'll paste your fucking brains all over the walls, you bastard."

Teller walked slowly across to Freya and placed his hand on top of hers, gently coercing her to lower her weapon, while never taking his eyes off Tom. "You sneaky bastard. You know, I was looking at my own team. For a while there, I even suspected pretty boy back there." He motioned to Kelly.

Tom shuffled on the spot.

"But you were right under our noses, sitting in Dulce Base the whole time—up close and personal with the clone. Sasha, how long have you known?"

"Not long. Actually, I did not know until I arrived. I recognized his face. At first, I couldn't place it, but then, it came to me. He was a sleeper agent living in the U.S."

"A sleeper agent?" Freya asked.

"Yes. A good one. Or, at least, he was. One of a team of us that were sent to live in California. Until he went AWOL."

"You were a sleeper agent, too?" Freya asked. "And you want to trust this guy, Jonathan?"

"Ms. Nilsson," Sasha said. "I have saved you and your fellow Americans from being destroyed first."

"What the hell are you talking about?"

"You retrieved it," Teller said, rolling his eyes at his own stupidity for not having seen it sooner.

"Yes," Sasha replied.

"Retrieved what?"

"The uranium. My men and I tracked the Triads to Chechnya and found the facility. They were heavily armed, but we prevailed."

"That didn't quite come through in the report I received from Washington," Teller said. "We were told a whole lot of uranium had gone missing, and the scene was littered with a bunch of dead Chechen Mafia."

"Communicating we had taken their weapon could have been intercepted. Your instructions were to come and assist. So I knew I could tell you here."

"Come and assist?" Freya echoed. "Why did you ask him to do that, Jonathan?"

"Because the Triads were keeping tabs on American forces. The last thing they were expecting was Russian help. Always thinking six moves ahead, sweetie."

Freya wrinkled her nose.

Teller ignored her. "So, did you find out what he was going to do with it? Was he going to set it off in America? How would he ever get it into the country?"

"No, he wasn't trying to smuggle it in," Sasha replied.

"Long-distance?"

"What difference does it make?" interrupted Freya. "I don't wanna be the heartless one here, but one warhead? He'd take out, what, half a city? What would be the point?"

"He wasn't aiming for a city," Sasha replied. "He was aiming for the upper atmosphere above America."

"What would be the point in that?" Freya asked.

"Project Teak and Orange," Sasha replied.

"Ah, crap."

"Jonathan?"

Teller drew a deep breath. "A stupid project from the Cold War. Somewhere, someone wanted to know what would happen if the Russians exploded a nuclear device in the atmosphere above the U.S. So they thought they'd try it themselves."

"What?"

"Yes," Sasha confirmed. "The American Government thought it a good idea to detonate two 3.8-megaton nuclear devices twenty-eight miles above the Johnston Atoll."

"Didn't know you guys knew that," Teller said.

"Mr. Teller, the fireballs they produced burned the retinas of every living thing within a 225-mile radius. You almost blew a hole in the ozone layer."

Freya choked on the realization. "Oh, God, he was going to fry us. He was going to blast a hole in the ozone."

"Yes, fry the Americans and drown everyone else. The result would have been the rapid melting of the icecaps. The entire Atlantic seaboard would vanish, along with Florida and the gulf coast. Anything low-lying in the rest of the world would disappear."

Freya furrowed her brow in disbelief. "He was trying to recreate the great flood, the one that brought the ancients."

"It seems so," Sasha replied.

"And now your government has the weapon?"

"We have confiscated the uranium."

Freya narrowed her eyes.

"Does he know you have his toy?" Teller asked.

"We don't think so."

"That means he's still coming for Wak. He wants to use the creature after the flood somehow."

"Yes, and I bet this fuckin' weasel knows how." Freya pressed her gun harder against Tom's temple, forcing him to bend away.

The soldier grimaced against the force of the Beretta being drilled into the side of his head. "They replicated an orb," he spluttered.

"What?" Teller and Freya asked in unison. Freya released the pressure slightly.

"They cloned it. The clean-up team in Siberia left behind some residue from the orb that got destroyed when the original creature died. They collected it."

"Shit," Teller whispered.

"And you've been leading this lunatic right to us?"

Tom didn't respond.

"Hey …" Kelly groaned from behind them. "What's going on?"

"Hey," Freya replied softly. "You're awake." She turned her attention from Tom, walked away, and hunkered down next to Kelly.

"Guess so. Who's the new guy?" Kelly rolled his eyes in the direction of the Russian officer.

"That's Sasha Vetrov," Teller replied. "He's a friend."

"Another Russkie? Hey, Minya, you gotta friend."

"Hardly," she muttered.

"He just rooted out our mole, who's been feeding the Chinese information," Teller added.

Kelly raised his eyebrows.

"It was Tom. Turns out he's an ex-KGB sleeper agent. Bought by the Chinese."

"Oh, Tom. You dumbass," Kelly wheezed before breaking into a coughing fit.

Freya put her hand on his arm. "How do you feel?"

"Like shit. You got any painkillers?" Freya shook her head. "No."

"How about that tea?" Teller suggested.

"I guess that might work. Kelly, where is it?"

"There's a baggie in my side pocket."

"Keep an eye on Tom there, boys." Teller stepped forward to retrieve the tea and paused. "Freya, perhaps you should fish it out."

Kelly coughed a laugh. "Missing an opportunity there, Teller."

Freya searched Kelly's pocket. Her fingers grasped the plastic bag, but it was wedged inside, so she tugged harder. It broke free, dragging his passport along with it.

Teller picked up the passport and opened it to the main page. "Kelly Angelo Graham. Wow, your parents didn't like you much, huh?"

Freya stifled a giggle. "I think it's cute."

"Just make the tea, jesters."

Teller and Sasha organized a defensive perimeter while Freya set up a small portable stove. After quickly boiling a little water, she poured it into a tin cup containing the last of Kelly's tea. She blew on it several times, much like a mother would for her child, and brought the cup to Kelly's lips. He closed his fingers around hers and tipped the cup, allowing the foul-smelling liquid to trickle into his mouth. He didn't even notice how hot it was, gulping it down quickly.

"Whoa, slow down there." Teller laughed.

Kelly swallowed, out of breath. "You ever drink this stuff?"

"No."

"Then don't tell me to drink it slowly. It tastes like feet."

Teller and Freya laughed. Even Sasha had to smirk.

"Get some rest, Kelly. We'll set up camp in here," Freya said. "Jonathan, do we have any idea where Wak or Victoria are?"

"No." He shook his head. "The boys are on the perimeter, keeping alert, but we are in no position to go tracking them. There aren't enough of us. I've radioed for a new chopper. We have to wait. And, in the meantime, decide whether or not to execute this bastard." Teller motioned to Tom, who had been forcibly knelt on the ground, fingers interlocked atop his head.

Kelly nodded, wrapped his arms around his midriff, and closed his eyes before falling into a restless sleep.

CHAPTER FORTY-FIVE

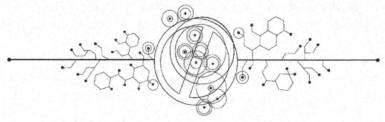

Location: Under Teotihuacan, Mexico, South America

Kelly awoke with a jerk, his shirt wet with sweat. In the dim of the halogen lights, he surveyed the interior of the cave. A few soldiers, American and FSB, paced the perimeter of the underground camp. Teller slept soundly on an uncomfortable-looking rock, as did Minya. Kelly narrowed his eyes, searching for the Russian guy, Sasha. He couldn't find him. Still, he could have been one of the amorphous masses lying about the ground. Finally, he met the worried face of Freya. She was sitting cross-legged, holding her knees with the insides of her elbows, her hands locked together.

"Bad dreams?" she whispered.

He nodded.

Careful not to make too much noise, she eased herself into a crawling position and crept to where he lay. "What was it about?"

"Huh?" He rubbed his eyes.

"Your dream. You said it was a bad one. What was it about?"

"Oh. Well, it was kinda weird. Did I ever tell you that back when I was bonded to K'in, I had a dream in which I was looking through his eyes? Actually, I had a couple. They were strange."

"No, you didn't mention them." Freya drew her knees to her chest and wrapped her arms around her shins.

"Well, I did. It's a very weird thing to experience a dream without language, just pure emotion. Anyway, I just had another one."

"You saw through K'in's eyes?" She asked, confused.

"No." He shook his head. "Not through K'in. Through one of his kind. It sounds weird, but I think I was seeing a past event. There was a comet or a meteor, and it slammed into the earth. There were others of his kind. All were scared—no, terrified. I remember seeing a young one. It was looking at me as if it wanted help. Then a shockwave ripped through the ground, and

364

everything went black. It got bright again, and I met a little tribal girl. She looked South American—maybe Mayan or Quechua. She touched me ... the creature."

"Perhaps the meteor you saw caused the great flood? Remember, the one that Professor Alexander told us about? K'in's people were meant to have come after it happened. It drove them from their homes."

He nodded. "You know," he began before stopping abruptly and wincing, clutching his ribcage.

Freya shot out her arms, ready to catch him should he reel back. "You okay?"

"Sure," he replied, forcing a grin, before propping himself up. "As I was saying, after we left Russia, I did a bit of research before I left for the jungle. I guess I wanted to try and understand a bit more. Maybe make myself feel better."

"And what did you find out?"

"Not too much. To be honest, I got a bit bored." He chuckled. "But there was an article in the news. They talked about how some scientists had found evidence to suggest a massive meteor crash around twelve or thirteen thousand years ago. Something to do with a layer of platinum in the Greenland ice. They reckon this layer could have only been laid down by a massive meteor impact."

"So, more evidence for the great flood. The timing is right."

"Yeah, I guess so."

"You know, it coincides with something Alejandro told me," Freya said. "Oh?"

"Yeah, about earth crust displacement."

"Ah, Hapgood's theory."

"You researched that, too?"

"No, but the old goat loved that idea about the whole Earth's crust slipping over the core. He went on about it."

"Well, all the timing adds up. Meteor strike, massive climate change, Hapgood's theory, K'in's people."

Kelly heaved a sigh.

"What's wrong?"

"Nothing. Just Chris would have loved this like his old man did. Izel too, to be honest. The whole family were intellectuals. Too good for me."

"Too good for you?"

"Yeah, come on. We both know I'm no brainiac. I live by experience. I believe in what I can see, feel, and smell, ya know? I ain't got much time for highbrow theories."

"That's bullshit."

"Excuse me?" He raised both his eyebrows, surprised at her blunt response.

"You heard me. Bull. Shit," she repeated. "You play dumb. I have no idea why. But you're not as stupid as you make out. It's just easier not to actually have a conversation with someone, right? Keep it flippant and people get bored and go away?"

Kelly paused, unsure how to respond.

"Well, I'm still here," she said.

"For how long?"

"What?"

"Look, if you haven't noticed, everyone who gets close to me bites the dust. Izel, Carmen, Chris. Now Alejandro. Shit, you even lost Tremaine."

"Oh, shut up. You can't believe only in what's around you, in real experience, and then use fate and greater powers to suggest you're bad luck."

Kelly's nostrils flared. "That's my experience. I don't need fate to make it so."

"So you're afraid something will happen to me? Is that why you didn't stay when I asked?"

For a second time, he didn't have an immediate retort. Mainly because she was at least in part correct. "Like it matters. You're dating Wonder Boy over there." He nodded at the sleeping Teller.

"Only because you left." As the words escaped her lips, she realized her mistake.

Neither of them spoke for several minutes.

"Kelly, I … what we did in your tent. I mean …"

"Forget it. I gotta get up—my ass is killing me." He grunted and placed both palms on the rocky ground before attempting to shove himself upward. The white-hot pain ripped through his insides as something ruptured deep within him. He yelped and immediately passed out, slumping back to the ground and smashing the back of his skull into a nearby boulder.

Freya fell to the ground next him and shook his shoulders. "Kelly? Kelly?" She turned and yelled. "Jonathan! Wake up!"

Teller jolted up, firearm drawn. "What? What is it?"

"It's Kelly. Something's wrong."

Jonathan holstered his weapon and raised his palms to his soldiers, who were now fully alert. "It's okay, boys. Stand down." He stepped over to Freya and dropped down to his knees. "What's going on?"

"I don't know. He tried to get up and then screamed and passed out. I think he may be bleeding internally."

Teller studied her. The fear at the thought of losing this idiot was burning through her wide eyes. He huffed and pursed his lips. "Okay, let me look." He placed his right hand flat on Kelly's stomach and pressed lightly. The tissue beneath felt hard against his fingers. Teller paused and thought for a moment. He lifted Kelly's t-shirt.

Freya watched Teller's expression darken. "What is it?"

"Cullen's sign."

"Shit, are you sure?"

He nodded and pulled Kelly's shirt higher for Freya to see.

"Bruising around the umbilicus. He's bleeding out internally pretty bad."

"We have to move him."

"There's nowhere to move him to, Freya. We're waiting for a new chopper. Besides, if you move him, you'll make it worse."

Freya fell silent. She knew he was right.

Teller took off his jacket, rolled it, and placed it under Kelly's head. "I'm sorry, Freya. I really am."

"Are you? Really?"

"What's that supposed to mean?"

"You're a tactical genius, a strategist who calculates risks to win. You must have seen this coming—you and the Russian—plotting to stop the Triads."

"I did what I needed to do to save as many lives as possible."

"As many lives as possible? Are you kidding me?"

"It's my job, Freya. It's your job, too."

"What about our lives, Jonathan?" She hushed her voice again. "It's why you let us go on this trip, isn't it? You were drawing the Triads out, giving them the opportunity to try and grab Wak. You knew they'd never get into Dulce Base. So you agreed to Kelly's idea, because it presented the chance you needed."

Teller weighed his response in his head. "Kelly provided an opportunity, yes. It was a calculated risk. The needs of the—"

"Don't you dare quote that sci-fi crap at me! You were happy to put me at risk?"

"No, no, of course not. I was always there to protect you. I promised the General I would end this, but I'd make sure you were okay."

"Benjamin? He knew you were going to use us as bait?"

"It was one scenario we'd considered. I didn't see how it would arise. But it did. Look, I'm sorry. I am. But we're almost done."

"You lost at least twenty men, and Kelly's dying. Just, just leave me alone."

"Seems to me Kelly is the only one you actually care about."

Freya hesitated just a fraction too long.

"See, I don't even need you to say anything to know I'm right. Just like I don't need to ask where you were when we got hit by the Triads."

Again, Freya didn't respond. She fought to maintain her anger, her stern expression. But the guilt seeped through her gaze.

Teller studied her. She was the strongest, most stubborn, and, quite frankly, sexiest woman he'd ever met. She could hold her own and was lethal with a Beretta. But perhaps he had only been allowed to see what she wanted him to see—her business face. When all was said and done, the man currently dying in her arms had an effect on her like no other. Around him, she became almost maternal, protective, and irrational.

"I'm sorry," Freya managed, her voice barely audible.

"Me too," he replied, bobbing his head. "Me too."

Teller left Freya cradling Kelly. He made his way back to the spot where he'd been lying before to try to settle down again. But he didn't sleep.

CHAPTER FORTY-SIX

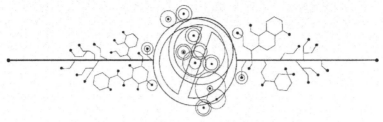

Location: Under Teotihuacan, Mexico, South America

Kelly lay there in the dim light. Only a single halogen rig provided any kind of illumination. Its strange glow amplified the sickly pallor of his clammy skin. As he clung to a rock on the ground, his anchor to the living world, Kelly's breathing slowed.

Freya was the first to notice. She'd been up all night, keeping watch. Every time she nodded off, she'd jolt back awake and force another cup of disgustingly cold coffee down her throat. There was no way she was going to let sleep be the reason he died.

She flung her sleeping bag open and quickly crawled along the rough cave floor to position herself behind Kelly so she could elevate his torso somewhat and rest his head, facing away from her, on her chest. "C'mon, you. You're not giving up on us that easily. I've seen you shot, nearly drowned, hooked up to electrodes, and bonded with a salamander. You're telling me a girl beating you up is the thing that finishes you off?" She forced a weak laugh.

He didn't reply. Instead, he squirmed and screwed his eyelids tighter together.

She put her chin on top of his head and held one hand to his sweaty forehead. He was so hot, a fever burning through his skin. Freya rocked him ever-so-slightly from side to side.

From the other side of the halogen rig, and completely unnoticed, Teller watched Freya intently. It was difficult to be angry with her. You don't choose who you fall for. He caught her eye and spoke through his gaze. *Is everything okay?*

Freya stiffened her lips and gave a micro shake of her head. *No.*

Kelly coughed awake, his eyes darting from side to side. Forgetting his injury, he lurched forward to stand, but immediately crumpled back into Freya's arms.

"Whoa there. Don't try and move, okay? You have to rest," Freya said, her voice a soothing tone.

He forced his chin to the sky so he could look up at her. To him, she was upside down. He blinked slowly, his breathing labored. "You know ..." he wheezed. "I can see right up your nose"

She smiled at him and shook her head. "For God's sake, Kelly Graham. Are you ever serious?"

He huffed a laugh from his lungs but couldn't sustain it.

"How you holding up there, big guy?"

Kelly dropped his chin again to see Teller sitting on his haunches in front of him. Just the way Chris used to sit. "Big ... guy?"

"Hey, it felt like a 'big guy' moment." Teller winked at him and quickly glanced at Freya.

Her vacant stare belied the torrent of thoughts racing through her mind.

Teller turned back to Kelly. "So, this is how you steal a guy's girl. Gotta say, it's ingenious. A little extreme but ingenious. Kirk would be proud."

His attempt at humor was sucked into the cold atmosphere—perhaps because it wasn't funny, or it was too close to the truth, or simply because Kelly was too out of it to comprehend.

"Anyway, you gotta—" Teller began.

"Shhh!" Freya hissed. "Did you hear that?"

Everyone froze, their heads cocked to listen in the dark.

"Hear what?" Teller asked, his hand already poised over the handgrip of his sidearm.

"That," Freya replied, listening to the faint scratching sound.

"Where's it coming from?" Teller had now drawn his weapon and was pointing it into the cave where the light could not penetrate.

From within the gloom, the hulking pallid form of Wak skulked into the orangey glow of the halogen rigs. Its eyes were burning a deep red, and even though no pupil could be seen, it was clear the animal was scanning each and every one of the humans before it.

"Nobody move," Teller whispered. "Sasha, keep an eye on our Mr. Radley there."

"Jonathan, it's just staring. Where's Victoria?"

"I don't know, Freya."

The animal swayed slightly from side to side and then suddenly jerked its neck in a spasm, screwing its eyes together before relaxing again.

"That thing has issues." Kelly's voice came out weak. Even in his crippled state, he couldn't help but be sarcastic. Unfortunately, that made his presence known to the animal.

Wak turned its gaze to Kelly, boring a stare into him.

"What's up, gorgeous?" he asked. "You wanna kiss?"

The animal curled its lips as if it were annoyed. Before Kelly could make yet another irritating quip, his attention was drawn to the slender figure sidling up to Wak—Victoria.

"Now what?" Freya mumbled.

No one answered.

A horrible gurgle spluttered from behind Sasha. The Russian had diverted his concentration for a split second, and as he turned back to Tom, he caught sight of the man's open throat, blood surging from the precision wound. The soldier slumped lifelessly forward.

A dull thud of pain entered through Sasha's jaw, knocking him to the ground. He was quickly followed by the rest of his unit.

The Shan Chu deftly snaked his way through the American soldiers, delivering bone-crunching strikes to their faces and heads as he sprang from wall to wall. In his left arm, he held the glowing, blue, gelatinous orb, which cast sinister shadows on the roof of the cave. His lightning-fast serpentine movement took Teller and Freya so completely by surprise they were only able to watch helplessly.

Within seconds, the Triad leader was upon Wak. He stood inches from the animal, his shoulders heaving with his breathing. Wak stared at the Triad leader—studying him and calculating. Victoria mimicked the animal's motions, syncing to its movements.

Freya raised her Beretta but had no clear shot.

Wak grabbed the orb and tugged on it, but the Shan Chu kept hold.

A blinding light exploded from the orb, filling the cave. The Shan Chu spasmed and writhed. He screamed as the full consciousness of Wak flowed into his brain, burning its emotions and memories into his neurons. Crashing to the floor, he clutched at his own head with one hand while the other still firmly gripped the orb. He stayed there on his knees for a long moment, his eyes screwed up and his jaw clenched.

Wak slumped to the floor, completely sprawled out, as if the ordeal had drained it of all energy. Victoria followed suit, collapsing onto the rocky ground, her breathing shallow.

Freya kept her sights on the Triad leader.

"It's done," hissed the Shan Chu. "I can feel it. Feel the power, the knowledge within me. The strength." He threw the orb to one side. It rolled across the ground and came to rest a few feet from Kelly.

The Shan Chu beat his hands on his chest. "I feel it growing."

"You got shit, you fucker," Freya yelled.

"Stupid woman. Soon I will destroy the world with a great flood. And once again, the supreme race will lead the way from darkness. My race."

"There's gonna be no flood, asshole. We got your nuke. You got nothing." Her voice strained with fury.

"Then I kill you first. The rest will follow."

Sasha climbed to his feet and joined Teller's side.

"I've had enough of this asshole," growled Teller.

The Russian nodded.

"Shall we?" Teller asked, waving his arm forward.

"*Da.*"

The two men launched themselves at the Shan Chu. He responded in kind, ducking, spinning, and slicing his way through the air, dodging the onslaught of punches and kicks the soldiers rained down upon him. His Wing Chun-style martial arts allowed him to intercept the men's fists and deliver crushing strikes. Yet, compared with his usual lithe skill, the Shan Chu was frustratingly slow.

"Get out of the goddamn way so I can shoot this bastard!" Freya screamed.

Sasha and Teller weren't listening. Any distraction could mean the end of their lives. Teller took a roundhouse kick to the jaw, which sent him sprawling onto the cave floor. Sasha, taking advantage of the Shan Chu's concentration on the American, thrust an elbow into the back of the Triad's head. But it only served to anger him more.

"Goddammit," Freya said through gritted teeth. "Just let me—"

She was suddenly distracted by movement on the floor. Kelly was convulsing.

"What's wrong?" Teller shouted over his shoulder, never taking his eyes from the Shan Chu as they fought.

"I don't know, it's Kelly. He's got the orb."

"Get him out of here."

Freya dropped to the floor and crawled across to Kelly. She pulled his head back. Two blazing cobalt-blue eyes stared back at her, flashes of white and green dancing within. "Kelly?"

He smiled, though he wasn't looking at Freya. He reached up, letting his fingers wave gently in the air, feeling an imaginary object. "*Jumalaykuw kutiniskix.*" The words came from his mouth but were carried by a strange voice.

"What is it?" Teller yelled before taking yet another strike to his ribs.

"I don't know. There's something wrong with him."

"*Jumalaykuw kutiniskix*," Kelly repeated.

"What language is that? Is it Quechua?" Freya murmured.

"*Nyet.*" Minya had circled the room and crouched beside Freya.

"You say something?" Freya asked.

Minya huffed. "He speaks Aymara."

"Aymara? What's that?"

"It is perhaps oldest language in world. Spoken only in Bolivia and Peru. The designed language."

"*Jumalaykuw kutiniskix.*" Kelly was still smiling, his mind clearly somewhere else.

"Designed language?" Freya pressed, one eye on Teller and Sasha mid-combat.

"Yes," Minya replied. "Using a special algorithm, you can translate English into French, Spanish into German, Spanish into French, and English into German. The syntax of the language is specific and so organized it's like it was designed for this very purpose."

"I get it. The ancient species used it to communicate on every continent, but what the fuck is he saying?" yelled Freya in frustration.

"*Ju-ma-lay-ku-wa ku-ti-ni-ska-i-xa,*" Minya replied slowly, enunciating each syllable. "It means 'she is returning for you.'"

Freya's eyes widened. "Don't you fucking dare, Kelly Graham. Don't you dare." She grabbed him, trying to break him from his trance.

"Who? Who is returning?" Minya asked.

"Izel. His dead wife, Izel."

The Shan Chu suddenly stopped and clasped his head. Pain drove itself like an icepick into his brain. He shrieked and dropped to one knee.

"Now," Teller shouted.

Sasha pulled a knife from its sheath and thrust it at the Triad leader, but it was intercepted. The Shan Chu hammered the blade away, climbed back to his feet, and grabbed Sasha by the throat.

"Now I kill you, Russian."

Teller leapt onto the Triad's back and yanked hard, pulling him from Sasha. They both crashed to the ground. The Shan Chu clambered back to his knees but couldn't stand. Instead, he clutched at his head again, growling in pain.

"Something's wrong with him, too!" Teller ceased his attack and watched the exhausted man struggle with what seemed like immense pressure inside his skull.

"What's going on?" Freya yelled.

"I don't know. It's like there are too many minds linked to the orb. They're all messed up."

Struggling to his feet, the Triad leader shouted and shook his head. "It's in me. The power. It needs to escape. Our souls are one. We are the ultimate being. I must release it!"

Teller and Sasha backed away from the Shan Chu, confused.

"He's lost it," yelled Teller.

The Shan Chu pulled his cleaver from its holster and chopped into his own torso. Each dull thud wedged the blade into his flesh. He screamed wildly, yanked it out, and hacked at himself again. Chunks of blood-covered muscle and fat were flung across the cave.

"Fuck me, he's gone berserk."

"Look at the rest of them," called out Sasha.

Teller glanced backward. Indeed, Kelly, Victoria, and Wak were all convulsing on the floor, their bodies contorted and awkward.

Freya was forcibly pinning Kelly to the ground with all her might. She looked up to see the others writhing in agony. Finally, she steeled her resolve, leapt to her feet, pulled out her Beretta, and aimed at the Shan Chu's head.

He momentarily stopped his self-flagellation, arms spread wide, the cleaver firmly gripped in one hand. He twitched only slightly, giving away his intention to attack.

Her hesitation was less than a microsecond. The force of the bullet from Freya's Beretta caused the back of the Triad leader's skull to explode onto Sasha's combat pants. "Fuck you."

His body hung in mid-air momentarily, blood streaming from the perfectly round hole in his forehead before he fell to his knees and finally onto his face. His blade clanged about on the rocky ground.

Freya walked over to the spasming creature, Wak. It struggled to lift its massive head up to see her. From the look in its eyes, she knew the animal would not fight her. It needed peace.

The creature lowered its head in acceptance. Freya didn't waste any time putting three bullets in its brain. The animal instantly stopped breathing. Without a second glance, Freya stomped back to Kelly, purposely squashing the orb with the heel of her boot as she did so. The fluorescent liquid burst through the gelatinous skin and leaked across the ground. Teller and Sasha stared in bewilderment.

"Now they're free," Freya said. She dropped to Kelly's side, her fierce façade fading and her emotions rushing to the surface. "Kelly, please. Please come back," she begged, fighting the lump in her throat and the well of tears in her eyes. "Please."

Kelly suddenly inhaled, his chest expanding beyond its limits, forcing his spine to arch. The serene expression of his face melted away as he exhaled. A fine blue mist, crackling like a dying fire's embers, slipped past his lips and dissipated into the cold air. Kelly slumped back into Freya's arms.

"Kelly, talk to us."

With a squirm, Kelly blinked open his weary eyes. For a few seconds, he remained quiet as he surveyed the now-darkened cave. He fixed his gaze on Freya and spoke through a husky, weak voice. "Wak. Wak is free. I saw it. And K'in. K'in was there. They were there, too. Chris and Izel ... and Carmen."

"I know, Kelly, I know." Freya stroked his head.

"I was wrong, Freya." Kelly held her hand, stopping her from stroking him, making her pay attention to the seriousness of his voice. "I was wrong."

"Kelly?"

He smiled weakly and turned his head to see Victoria lying naked on the floor just a few feet from him. Her eyes were slightly open, exhausted, but not red anymore. The blue of her irises shined back at him. "Vicky?"

She blinked slowly.

"Vicky, is it you?"

She nodded weakly, her eyes barely able to stay open. Teller quickly grabbed a backpack, pulled out a sleeping bag, and covered Victoria with it.

Kelly exhaled in relief. "She's … she's okay. We did it."

"We did, Kelly. We did. Now you just have to hold on." Freya sniffed hard.

Kelly didn't respond.

"Kelly?" She called to him, but in her heart, she already knew there would be no answer.

In a final exhale, Kelly's last breath of life left him.

Freya gurgled a breathless sob, hot tears cutting a path down her dirty face. She clasped his head to her bosom, and managed a gasp of air that allowed her to finally voice the anguish coursing through her very being.

Kelly was gone.

CHAPTER FORTY-SEVEN

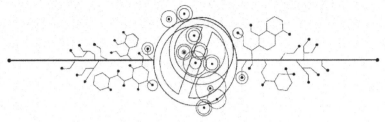

Location: Under Teotihuacan, Mexico, South America

For a moment, it was eerily silent. Teller, Sasha, and even Minya hung their heads in respect at Kelly's passing. The faint hum of the spotlights provided an almost comforting ambient noise. Victoria lay under the sleeping bag, unconscious.

Without warning, Freya opened her eyes and jerked into action. "You think you get out of it that quickly? Huh?" she screamed at him, the blood vessels in her neck straining against her porcelain skin. "Well, you don't." She slapped him in the face. His head lolled to the side, and she slapped him again—harder.

"Fuck you, Kelly Graham! You don't get to opt out. The rest of us have to go on. Why should you get to leave?" She thumped his chest with balled fists and slapped him again—over and over. The onslaught accelerated with more slapping, punching, thumping, and grabbing in desperation. "Come back, you fucking asshole. Come back!"

Teller grabbed Freya's wrists, ending her assault on Kelly's lifeless body. "Hey, hey, hey …" His voice was soft and empathetic. "You gotta stop. He's gone."

Freya ceased her barrage and glanced up at Teller, her face wet with tears and eyes red with salt. "It's not fair."

"I know," he said softly, pulling her close. "I know. It never is."

Freya sobbed uncontrollably into Teller's shirt.

From the corner of his eye, Sasha noticed a faint blue haze. It was a single spot on a far rock-hewn wall that seemed to emanate from the buried crystalline structures as if the material itself were alive. He frowned, staring at it. Another spot appeared a few feet away from the first, and again, it was a strange, blue haze with a definite light at its center. Then another formed—and another.

"What do you suppose that is?" Sasha asked, never taking his eyes from the pinpricks of light appearing in the dark.

Still clinging to Freya, Teller lifted his head to investigate. "It's scheelite. It's a crystal that glows blue when exposed to UV light. It's probably just reacting to our halogen rigs." He dismissed it and returned to tending to the woman in his arms.

"No, this is different. Look." Minya gazed about the cave in wonder.

Millions upon millions of tiny crystalline pyramids lined the walls. Each one emanated a low-level, perfectly clear, sky-blue light.

"How did we not see these before?" Teller asked, his attention now fully removed from his patient. "It looks like scheelite, but this is unbelievable. Freya, look." He nudged her shoulder, prompting her from her fetal position.

She blinked away the sting of tears and focused on the tiny blue specks that were beginning to fill the black backdrop of the cavern like stars emerging after dusk. "What's going on?"

"I honestly don't know," Teller replied.

The soldiers raised their rifles in readiness but remained in awe of the sparkling display before them.

"Look," Sasha said. "There." He pointed to a much larger, pyramid-shaped crystal that was fluorescing so intensely a small blade of azure light stretched out from within it and into the room.

"And there," Teller said, pointing at a similar crystal not far from the first.

Within a few seconds, more than twenty oversized crystals were projecting their stream of photons into the center of the cave.

As Freya stared at the center of this light show, the billions of elementary particles coalesced. Slowly, a shape formed. Freya recognized it—it was K'in.

The serene face of the animal, transparent and glowing blue, stared at her, its head cocked to one side. The ghostlike emanation waddled with a familiar gait to the woman and stopped in front of her and Kelly.

Freya pried herself from Teller's arms.

K'in blinked his translucent eyelids and studied Kelly's lifeless body. Freya reached out to touch the animal's snout but felt nothing. Yet K'in ruffled his gills and shook his head as if acknowledging the gesture.

The animal lowered its pointed face near to Kelly's and hovered there—motionless. Sasha, Teller and Minya watched the strange ghost in silent awe. Freya didn't speak. Her heart was full of hope she dared not voice. *Please.*

The phantom animal backed away from Kelly and glanced at Freya. It padded toward her, fixed its warm gaze on her, and lowered its head, nuzzling her midriff. A tingling warmth spread up through Freya's body. Her eyes were fixed wide open and wet with tears as the realization hit home. *Is it possible?*

The light of the crystals faded and with it the form of K'in. For a brief moment, Freya thought she caught the tiniest smile on the creature's thin lips. Then he was gone.

It was dark again, except for the spotlights, now seemingly dull and pathetic, dotted around. For a long while, everyone remained silent in the dim glow. Deep in their hearts, they had hoped K'in would bring Kelly back to them. Even Teller was saddened it hadn't happened. But it was the way of the world. Despite all they had seen, escaping death wasn't part of the greater plan.

Teller stared at Freya, who was frozen to her spot, her gaze somewhere off in the distance, her mind unable or unwilling to comprehend what had just happened. He took a step over to her and put his hand gently on her shoulder. She slowly turned to him, her face full of anguish and apathy—as if the meaning of her own life had been ripped away.

"I'm sorry, Freya. Come on. Let's get you out of here. The chopper should be here any minute. Time to go." Teller nodded toward the exit.

Freya stared blankly at him for several seconds before clearing her throat and sniffing back the tears. "Just give me a minute, okay?"

"Sure. C'mon, boys. Let's get the hell outta here. Someone get Victoria and help me with Kelly."

The soldiers complied. One scooped up Victoria in his arms while two others helped lift Kelly and carry him out. Sasha nodded once in sympathy to Freya and followed the Americans.

Freya fixed her gaze on Kelly's form for as long as she could until the soldiers had carried him so far into the darkness of the tunnel he was no longer visible. "Bye, Kelly," she whispered. Though she tried to regain composure, tears streamed down her face. She couldn't help but think of her discussion with Kelly just a few nights earlier. She and Teller had asked him what his thoughts were about everything he'd been shown while being joined with K'in.

"What have I learned? I learned that humans are never

379

really complete," he'd said. "We search for something or someone—our Huaca, our special place. The person, place, or thing we believe will make us whole. To fill the void. But perhaps we'll never find it. Because the ones who can show us are extinct. We killed them all a long time ago. K'in and his species. Some of us, if we're lucky, find something close to it. Someone we feel is our other half. And if we're really lucky, the other person feels the same way."

She let out a heavy sigh. But what if you find your other half and they are taken away? Didn't she deserve a chance? She'd lost her parents when she was young, too young to understand. And then Benjamin, her godfather. And now Kelly. Yes, he was an ass, but the overwhelming ache in her chest from losing him crushed her heart, making it apparent all too late that she loved him—and had never got to say it. This must have been what Kelly felt every single day after losing Izel and Carmen. How did he live with it? Deal with it? But then she remembered he didn't deal with it.

A light scuffle of boots on gravel broke Freya's train of thought and brought her attention to Minya, who had sidled up to her. The woman looked decidedly uncomfortable and never made eye contact. Minya paused for a long moment, her lips parted as if she wanted to speak but didn't know how to find the words. Freya stared at her, waiting.

"Sometimes," began Minya slowly, "something happens we never thought possible. Someone comes into our life who we feel connected to … in way we cannot describe. They make us whole."

Freya nodded solemnly. "But now he's gone."

Minya fixed her gaze on Freya's and held it for a few moments before speaking in the most empathetic tone she could muster. "I do not talk about Kelly." She pulled from her pocket a crumpled picture of a small boy with dark tresses and bright eyes and showed it to Freya.

Freya stared at the picture.

"Nikolaj," Minya whispered. "It matters not how he happened. He makes life worth living." She gave a knowing nod and a weak smile to Freya's belly before wandering slowly out of the cave.

Freya stood alone in the dark, stunned, and unconsciously rubbing her abdomen. It was so warm. A light smile broke across her face. K'in had known. In his way, he'd told her. Perhaps the animal and his species hadn't enlightened humanity in one fell swoop but one human at a time, showing them what it meant to be bonded with another and be whole—to really love, to understand there was something beyond the physical, beyond even death.

Kelly wasn't really gone; he was free. Free from his pain and anger. He was where he belonged. And he'd left behind a piece of himself within her. She was closer to Kelly now than he would ever have been able to let her be in life.

Freya sniffed hard, wiped the tears from her face, and marched out of the cave toward the bright-white light of day that shone at the end of the tunnel passage—toward a new beginning and a new life.

EPILOGUE

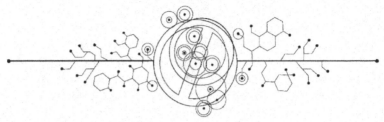

Location: Three years later, Connecticut, USA

Even after living in the big white house for the last few years, it was difficult to get used to. Not because she was in a small town on the coast of Connecticut, instead of gallivanting around the globe. Not even because she had given up her life in the military to concentrate on being a mother and the inside of this place had become her universe-cum-prison. No, this was strange because it was her Godfather's house. The place that she had called home growing up, at least when not moving from base to base. This was Benjamin Lloyd's home. And while he languished in prison, he had offered it to her.

The smells were the same. The walls were the same. Even the way the fifth stair creaked was the same. Sometimes, walking from the drawing room to the kitchen, she'd see a little ghosted-version of herself running past, calling out to Benjamin to come see the pond she'd made in the garden. And then of course, closely following her memory, a three-year-old little boy scurried behind, clutching his latest artwork. Today was no different.

"Mommy! Mommy, I made you another picture."

"Come show me, sweetheart." Freya dropped to floor, resting on the balls of her feet, to meet her son. Her hair was pulled back in an efficient pony tail as always, but she'd swapped military gear and corporate, tight-fitting, skirts for a pair of comfortable jeans and oversized wool pullover that hung off one shoulder.

"Do you like it?" he asked, a smile fixed from ear to ear, his bright blue eyes shining from behind a mop a wavy chestnut hair.

"Do I like it?" she asked with mock indignation. "Kelly Junior Nilsson, since when have I never liked one of your pictures?"

The young boy giggled.

"But I must confess, I don't know what this one is." Freya took the picture and examined it, cocking her head and rotating the paper this way and that. A black crayon had been used to haphazardly cover almost the entire surface.

"It's a hole!" he said, beaming with pride.

"Of course it is! And what a lovely hole it is, too."

"Can we go and see it one day, mommy?"

"The hole?" she asked, confused.

"Yes."

"Sure we can. Where is it, honey?"

He shrugged. "I don't know. Far away. In another place. It would take a long time if we walked there. Shall I draw you a map, mommy?"

"That's a great idea, my little Mr. Man. Go draw me a map."

Kelly Junior giggled and ran off to his room.

Freya got to her feet, groaning as she did so. She held up the picture, crinkled her nose, and studied it. He never drew normal things. Trees. Other children. Cats or dogs. They were always abstract. The sky. The bottom of the ocean. A hole. But of course, little KJ wasn't normal. She'd known that from the moment he was born. From the moment he'd opened his eyes to reveal a sparkling, iridescent blue that she'd seen only once before. In his father's eyes when he was bonded to K'in. Whatever had happened to Kelly then had changed him on a genetic level, and he'd passed it on to his son.

Sure, KJ in many ways was just like any other three-year old. He ran and jumped and played. Cried when he couldn't get his own way. He was also a little carbon copy of his father. Cheeky and charming, and well on his way to becoming a womanizer, despite Freya's best efforts. Already a local celebrity in the small town, almost every shop keeper knew him and every female patron fawned over him whenever they crossed paths. KJ would even make noise, bat his eyelids and smile as wide as he could at a specific pretty woman or girl he'd scoped out nearby—just to get attention. And of course it was only the pretty ones.

But there were subtle differences. Small things that perhaps only a mother would notice about her son. His tendency to sink into his own thoughts to the point that no amount of calling his name could draw him from his trance. The fact that he would sit for hours at a time in the garden playing circus with a host of local wildlife, birds, rabbits, voles, that seemed to follow his instruction to crawl and jump over the obstacle course he had made. Any other mother might think that cute. For Freya, it screamed of K'in's and Wak's ability to bond. To control. All she could do was observe.

Sit and wait to see how these little nuances would manifest as he grew.

Freya sighed, then pinned the picture to the refrigerator with the twenty-six other drawings he'd made that week. It was a rolling board of artwork. *Time to make his lunch.* She flicked on the kitchen TV, but kept the volume low. It wasn't that she wanted to watch anything, only that the deep, soft voice of a man narrating some documentary was comforting.

Cutting the crusts of yet another piece of wholemeal bread on autopilot, Freya prepared her son's favorite: peanut and jelly sandwiches. But even this reminded her of him. Of Kelly. She didn't really know why, but sandwiches always did. Whenever she made them, all she could see was his face, mouth full of sandwich, pointing the rest at her as he explained the next hare-brained part of his ill-thought out plan. Flicking the hair out of her eyes for the fifteenth time, she thought, *damn I miss him.*

A shrill squeal broke her train of thought. Coiled and ready to sprint to her son's room, she was cut short as he came careening around the corner, his arms held high, tears streaming down his face.

"Ow!" he cried.

Freya dropped down to the balls of her feet and held out her arms for a cuddle, which was gratefully received. "What happened, Mr. Man? Did you hurt yourself?"

KJ sniffed, and held out his right hand revealing a clean one-inch cut across his index finger. "The paper cut, cut me," he stammered between sniffs and sighs.

"Okay, okay. Remember what to do?"

"Yes," he whimpered.

"Here we go."

KJ held up his finger to Freya's lips. She lightly blew across the fresh wound as he counted to ten.

"One, two, free, four …"

By five, the wound was already closing, zipping up from one end to next.

"Eight, nine …"

And by ten it was sealed. Only a faint pink line remained which itself would eventually disappear. Another gift he'd from K'in. But one she definitely had to keep secret from everyone else. KJ had the ability to heal, like an axolotl. Perhaps to even regrow limbs, like Victoria had done. This would scare the children. Hell, it would scare the other mothers. So instead,

Freya pretended that she was magic and that a kiss or other gesture could make things all better. KJ bought it, for now.

His face still wet with tears, but now smiling, KJ threw his arms around her neck and laid his head on her shoulder. He silently requested to be picked up. Freya hoisted him up and twisted her body from side to side, rocking her little man. Then it caught her eye. The giant black space in the middle of a snow-covered land projecting from the TV. She picked up the remote control with one hand and turned the volume up.

> *"... global warming has over the last few years begun to defrost many parts of Antarctica and Siberia, revealing enormous sink holes and even underground lakes and cavernous systems. Many of these holes are several miles deep and the caverns many hundreds of miles long. Scientists are still investigating what secrets to our past these natural time capsules may hold."*

Siberia. The original corpse. K'in. Freya's mind raced.

KJ turned his head to see the TV. "Look, mommy. My picture. The hole."

Freya locked her gaze with her son's, his bright eyes shining back at her. Cobalt flames danced within. "Your picture? Is that what you drew?"

He nodded enthusiastically. "Uh-huh. Can we go?"

She held him closer to her chest and pressed his head to her shoulder, adrenaline coursing through her veins. She didn't want to think why he wanted to go. Or what they would find there. But she knew it was inevitable. Necessary even. To protect him, she had to understand him. And maybe the answer was in a sinkhole thousands of miles away in Siberia, where it all began.

"Maybe, sweetheart, when you're a big boy," she whispered. "When you're a big boy."

CHILDREN
OF THE
FIFTH SUN
ECHELON

SHE THOUGHT THERE WAS
NOTHING STRONGER THAN A MOTHER'S BOND.
SHE WAS WRONG.

AWARD-WINNING AUTHOR
GARETH WORTHINGTON

CHILDREN
OF THE
FIFTH SUN
E C H E L O N

She thought there was nothing stronger than a mother's bond.
She was wrong.

FIFTEEN THOUSAND YEARS AGO, the knowledge bringers—an amphibious, non-humanoid species known as the Huahuqui—came after a great global flood,
gifting humans with math, science, and civility.
We killed them all.

Seventy years ago, we found one of their corpses preserved in ice and eventually created a clone named K'in. Our governments fought over the creature and we killed it, too. Now, a sinkhole in Siberia has opened, revealing new secrets.

FREYA NILSSON spent the last five years trying to forget her role in the Huahuqui cloning program. She hid her son, KJ, from the regimes and agencies she believed would exploit him for the powers he acquired through his father's bond with K'in.

An innocent trip to help KJ understand his abilities results in the conspiracy she fought to bury exploding back to life. Chased by new foes and hounded to put the world first, all Freya can think of is protecting KJ—at all costs.

CHILDREN
OF THE
FIFTH SUN
RUBICON
THE AGE OF MAN IS OVER
AWARD-WINNING AUTHOR
GARETH WORTHINGTON

CHILDREN
OF THE
FIFTH SUN
RUBICON

IT HAS BEEN SEVENTEEN YEARS since the Nine Veils abducted half of the Nenets children and their bonded Huahuqui from Antarctica. Despite years of searching by Jonathan Teller and the NSA, no one has heard from the clandestine organization, or the abductees.

KJ Nilsson, the remaining children, and their Huahuqui—collectively known as *the Stratum*—have grown up in relative safety at Alpha Base in Antarctica. Thanks to the work of Lucy Taylor, now President of the United States, the Stratum are to be recognized as a unique, symbiotic, race and legal citizens of several great nations.

But, things do not go as planned when the Nine Veils come out of hiding— with their own army of Huahuqui—determined to become the most elite power on the planet.
Now, KJ and the Stratum must prove they deserve their new status by defending the citizens of Earth—against their own kind.

Whoever wins, the age of man is over.